Rachel's Destiny
as Written in the Stars

Volume One
of
THE NEFILIM SERIES

To Michele,
Many Blessings
Julie Brescini

Rachel's Destiny
as Written in the Stars

AN EPIC JOURNEY IN JUDEO-CHRISTIAN KARMIC RELEASE

JULIE BRESCIANI Ph.D.

Volume One
in the Nefilim Series

ASTRAEA CIARA PUBLISHING CO.

FIRST EDITION

Library of Congress TXu 664-745 12/9/1994

ISBN 0-9657958-0-2

Cover painting by Gonzalo Medina

All illustrations throughout the book are by Cindy Klinger.
Illustrations on Part One, Two, Four, Five, Six and Seven are of Sumerian seals
dating from 3,000 B.C. from the author's personal collection.

Composition by Sans Serif Inc., Saline, Michigan

To Jonathan
in appreciation of your
help in finding a new way

To the Family of Light

To Universal Brotherhood and Sisterhood
and the Fulfillment of the Aquarian Promise

Contents

Acknowledgements

First and foremost I would like to thank my husband, Jonathan Saturen, my partner in the Higher Marriage, for his unfailing encouragement and belief in me, as well as for his excellent editorial assistance.

My heartfelt thanks to my Peruvian spiritual brother, Gonzalo Medina, for seeing with the Ancient Spirit Eyes and lending his enormous talent to creating the cover of this book; and to Viviana Martinez for helping us get beyond the language barrier, and the Peruvian postal system.

I would also like to thank my mother for having encouraged me to write about what was bothering me, and for her support of my work which has meant so much to me.

I am also grateful to my very talented friend, Cindy Klinger, for her generous assistance with the cover design, and all the illustrations throughout the book.

Thanks to Miriam and Oscar Lubow for giving my manuscript such a careful and thoughtful reading and always providing helpful feedback at just the right time; and to Yak Saturen for his assistance with reference material.

I also want to thank my brother Nicholas Bresciani for his comments on my manuscript, and for being the kind of brother who would stand with me in the light of truth.

My grateful thanks to Dr. Scott Storrie for helping to keep me in my body throughout the long years of labor giving birth to this book; and to Martin Edmunds for his assistance with my manuscript in its earliest stages; and to Vivian Bradbury of Sans Serif for the crash course in publishing.

I would also like to thank Zecharia Sitchin for his amazing series

ix

THE EARTH CHRONICLES. His brilliant work, based on many years of scholarly research, was a great source of comfort and inspiration to me, as it backed up so much of the information on Earth's ancient past I had received through my meditation, dreams, and research into the ancient myths.

Last but not least special thanks to my son, Alex, who though young in body, is very old and wise in spirit and has always been an inspiration to me.

Prologue

I was first introduced to the Biblical story of Rachel, Leah and Jacob at age eleven, in my fifth grade Catechism class at Notre Dame School, a private convent school in New York City, dedicated to Our Lady. From my first reading, this story offended me, arousing a wide spectrum of emotion ranging from sympathy, pity, abject disappointment, all the way to rage. This plethora of emotion set me on a unique journey to understand why the Spiritual Mothers of all Judeo-Christian culture were treated like chattel.

I was eighteen years old when I began researching the ancient Sumerian culture (3800 B.C.–2000 B.C.), the civilization from which the Bible sprang. It was disillusioning to discover that women once had freedom and the right to their own destiny, and lost it.

When I was twenty one, I became fascinated with the ancient science of Astrology and discovered its relationship to archetypal mythology. I had just graduated from college in Art History, (my passion being Ancient Art), and I was working at the Metropolitan Museum of Art in N.Y.C. Roaming around the museum's incredible maze of library stacks during my lunch hour, I happened on THE ARCHETYPAL WORLD OF HENRY MOORE by Erich Neumann, a Jungian Analyst from Israel. A whole new world opened up to me, the world of the archetypes. I had always been interested in iconograpy, the study of symbolic imagery in a work of art. Here was a book which took this further than I had ever dreamed.

Around the same time, my wanderings in the library stacks led me to ancient tomes of Egyptian papyri in which astrological symbols appeared. I decided to study Astrology as an ancient symbol system. I was amazed to find out that Astrology was more than a symbol system. It really worked. I was on fire. Finding Astrology felt like I had come home. Continuing my study of Erich Neumann's works led me to C.G. Jung. I was delighted to learn that Jung had understood the merits of Astrology and used it in his practice; and that he had a daughter, Frau Gret Jung Baumann, who was a practicing astrologer in Switzerland.

At age twenty-two I made a pilgrimage to Switzerland to have Frau Baumann read my Star Chart. Frau Baumann told me I was a healer, but that I had other work to do as well. She said I came from a great spiritual lineage, and it was my task to bring it back. When she asked about my religious background, I told her I had Cardinals on my father's side. She explained that what she saw in my Star Chart went much further back. I left puzzled. It took me many years to realize that what Frau Baumann meant was my ancient roots in the Naditu Sisterhood. My Nefilim series is about the Naditu Sisterhood. Their counterpart, the Great White Brotherhood, will appear in subsequent books in my Nefilim Series.

My acquaintance with the Nefilim, the Starry Ones from heaven, comes from my study of the ancient Egyptian Star Wisdom, and from my dreams. These dreams began in the late 70's, and really accelerated as I got working on this book.

My first day attending the C.G. Jung Institute in the fall of 1976, I was assigned the early part of Genesis in Dr. Edward Edinger's class on the Old Testament, and asked to select a Biblical character and show their continuing influence as an archetypal figure in the human psyche today. I chose Rachel.

The Bible is a profound part of our patriarchal mythology and legacy. According to Jung, myths show the unconscious processes of whole tribes of people and embody the typical psychological themes— the archetypes—which are common to all humanity and form the substrata of the human psyche. Archetypes are essentially dynamic predispositions of energy and reaction which structure our experience and are ready to produce over and over again the same or similar, mythical ideas, feelings and experiences. What dreams are to individuals, myths are to an entire culture. They display the hidden aims, motives, and values which are at work on a grand scale in a culture, unconsciously determining the psyche and behavior of an entire people.

As I explored the archetypes of Rachel, Jacob, and Leah, my interest was further stimulated by their relevance to the issues my female and male analysands brought into my office. In the late 70's I wrote my doctoral dissertation on these archetypal figures, entitled THE NARCISSISTIC INJURY TO PATRIARCHAL WOMEN'S EGO FROM THE LOSS OF THE GODDESS. In the early 80's I wrote a shorter version as my graduation thesis for the Jung Institute in N.Y.C.

Rachel and Leah are the Matriarchs of the twelve tribes of Israel, the founding mothers of all Judeo-Christian culture. They are an essential part of the matrix of patriarchal men and women's psyche. Both Rachel and Leah help support and develop the birth of the heroic masculine ego in their husband Jacob, and their many sons, while they themselves remain ego-less. Their story poignantly underscores the debilitating adaptation of the Feminine to Patriarchal consciousness.

My background in Astrology helped me see the tale of Rachel as a story of the transition from the Matriarchal Age of Taurus (ca. 4500 B.C.) into the Patriarchal Age of Aries (ca. 2250 B.C.). We stand now at the threshold of another great transition, the transition from the Age of Pisces (ca.100 B.C.) into the Age of Aquarius (ca. 2100 A.D.). Pisces is the great Age of the Fishes. Its symbol is two fish bound together in the middle, with one fish swimming up to heaven and the other swimming down to hell. True to its symbolic representation, the Age of Pisces has been an age of great duality and the polarization between spirit and matter, masculine and feminine, good and evil, to name a few.

We are awakening from the collective dream of Pisces. The unknown history of Earth and our solar system is beginning to be revealed to us. The September 1996 issue of Popular Science announced the presence of life on Mars in ancient times from deposits found on a meteorite which landed here. Important research by John Anthony West, a great American scholar of ancient Egypt, and Dr. Robert Schoch, a professor of Geology at Boston University, has shown that the Sphinx was weathered by water. This important find implies the Sphinx was built before 10,000 B.C., after which time Egypt's climate became more desert-like. There is an Akkadian cylinder seal dating from the third millennium B.C. at the State Museum in East Berlin that depicts the solar system as it was known to the ancient Sumerians. It has twelve planets in it, all arranged in their proper size and order around the sun, despite the fact that Uranus, Neptune and Pluto were only discovered by our scientists in 1781, 1846, and 1930. (See THE TWELFTH PLANET, Book One of the

Earth Chronicles, by Zecharia Sitchin, Avon Books, N.Y.C. 1976 for more information on this important find.) Earth's ancient past is in the process of being rewritten.

This is the dawning of the Age of Aquarius. Great secrets are going to be revealed to us. No longer can we be bound by limited truths and polarized against each other. Aquarius is to be an Age of Unity, Liberation, Equality, and universal Brotherhood and Sisterhood. But for us to move forward into the promise of Aquarius we must understand and heal our past.

Jung had Aquarius rising in his star chart, which is why his theory is so important for our time. Jung's theory encourages the confrontation with our own Shadow as a moral necessity, so we do not project our own inner darkness and evil outside ourselves on our Brothers and Sisters. His theory asserts that just as each of us have male and female chromosomes, we have unconscious male and female characteristics as well. Jung calls the unconscious feminine side of men the anima, and the unconscious masculine side of women the animus. To foster development and achieve wholeness a man must integrate his unconscious feminine soul, the anima, and a woman must integrate her unconscious masculine spirit, the animus.

It is time for the female voice to be heard. We must bring the Masculine and Feminine perspectives together to reach wholeness. I wrote this book to help unlock the secrets of Earth's ancient past, and to heal the warring Brothers and Sisters archetypes at the root source of the Patriarchal psyche.

RACHEL'S DESTINY AS WRITTEN IN THE STARS is Volume One of my Nefilim Series, a series of psycho-historical novels designed to usher in the New Millennium. Volume Two, presently in preparation, will explore the archetype of Kingship in the life of Hatshepsut, the only female Pharaoh during Egypt's 18th Dynasty. Others will follow.

Come with me back in time through the deep inner layers of your psyche on an epic journey of Judeo-Christian karmic release.

"When men had begun to be plentiful on the earth, and daughters had been born to them, the sons of God, looking at the daughters of men, saw they were pleasing, so they married as many as they chose. Yahweh said, 'My spirit must not forever be disgraced in man, for he is but flesh; his life shall last no more than a hundred and twenty years'. The Nefilim were on the earth at that time (and even afterwards) when the sons of God resorted to the daughters of men, and had children by them. These are the heroes of days gone by, the famous men." {Genesis 6}

Nefilim translates, those who came down from heaven

PART ONE

Life with Father

1

THE RITES OF SPRING

THE CRIES OF MY MANY CHILDREN ARE FULL OF PAIN AND HOPE AND call to me so powerfully I am moved to tell my story, in my own voice, not as the patriarchal fathers have told it. The Great Ages are shifting, opening a window in time that I may reveal myself to you. I am your patriarchal mother source. I live in you and through you. You are the daughters and sons I yearned for, but could not have as the tide of the world's clock was turning from the Mother's rule to the Father's rule. I was but one in a vast line of ancient priestesses swept away in the advancing wave of the patriarchy.

I speak now, and speak I must, for once again the world clock changes. This time it moves toward Aquarius, sign of the Waterbearer, the great Angel of Heaven who guides the Earth during its sojourn through the cosmic light of the Photon Belt. The Waterbearers shoulder this starry light of heaven pouring it forth to birth a new Golden Age of freedom, and true Brother and Sisterhood upon Earth A great change in human consciousness is about to occur. The Waterbearer's cosmic light will reveal Earth's ancient history divulging humankind's ancestry from the stars, and the founding of all the ancient civilizations upon this planet by the Nefilim, the Starry Ones who from heaven came.

I also speak now, because my daughters have awakened from their slumbers. Their yearning is a never-ceasing cry that rises like a great column of incense to the Goddess. The pathos of their vigil pierces my heart and mind, and beckons me to return to my duties as Priestess calling forth those of my ancient lineage to resume the sacred work.

You live between two great Ages, the Age of Pisces and the Age of Aquarius. Great changes are in store for you. But for you, children of Aquarius, to move forward you must understand your past. My story is the tale of the transition from the lunar age of Taurus into the solar age of Aries. There is always great difficulty during times of transition. So I share my experience with you in the hope that you can benefit from my mistakes.

Your great book speaks of me as one of Jacob's many wives, but I was a Naditu Priestess of the Eye Goddess Ninhursag before he arrived. I was chosen to be one of the ancient Sisterhood of Seers long before I ever heard of Yahweh, God of the patriarchal fathers, Abraham and Isaac. A Naditu Priestess of She Who Watches was I. My lineage flowed from the great Eye temple at Brak in the Khabur valley of northern Mesopotamia, where Noah's descendants flourished after the Great Flood. I was one of the noble Sisterhood as was my mother Anna, in the same tradition as Rebekah, Jacob's mother, and Sarah, Abraham's wife before her. It was because Rebekah and Sarah were Naditu Priestesses, that they were worthy to be the mothers of Yahweh's chosen.

A consecrated priest must have a Naditu Priestess for a wife. Only a Naditu woman can endure the fire of the gods, and serve as partner in the sacred work of expanding consciousness. Only a Naditu woman can bring the highest spirit down to birth in the flesh, when the God and Goddess so ordain. Thus, Rebekah sent her favorite son Jacob to Haran for me to wed. It was preordained, and I was waiting. But my story must begin at its true beginning, my first overshadowment by She Who Watches, when I was a child of eleven years.

My childhood was a time of vast and sweeping changes throughout the ancient land of Sumer. Great Ages were colliding, changing from Taurus into Aries. The rambunctious Ram and Ewe were replacing the stolid Bull and Cow. The Anunnaki, the Ancient Ones from Nibiru, the hidden twelfth planet in our solar system, had ceased to live amongst us. The noble Golden Age when the Star People walked the Earth had devolved into the Silver Age of the demigods, then into the Bronze Age of the righteous human rulers chosen by the Ancient Ones of Heaven.

We were approaching the Age of Iron, and in our troubled times kingship no longer came down from heaven. No king of the ancient blue blood seeded by the Star People could be found to sit upon the throne and rule the land in wisdom, strength, and justice. The Brotherhood of the Black Hand had all those who controlled our state wrapped around their fingers. Pure gold and silver were no longer the means of our exchange. The debasement of the precious metals in our coinage was paralleled by the dissolution of the ancient blue blood seeded from on high, and heralded the erosion of all the standards and values which once upheld mighty Sumer.

No longer did the God and Goddess rule together from the seat of joy, presiding over the temples and their massive storehouses. The worship of the Mother Goddess was fast receding. No longer were the temples the heart and soul of each city state. The corrupt lugals no longer protected their people, or ruled with honor according to the dictates of the Starry Ones of Heaven. Instead they ate their people live, feeding upon them through the incessant wars they fabricated to fill their coffers. Even constant war was not enough to satisfy the greedy lugals, who had fallen from the grace of heaven. They taxed the people until their backs were bent beneath the heavy yoke of their tyranny.

The lugals were the puppets of the Brotherhood of the Black Hand, the unseen hand behind all events. Without the people even taking note, they introduced the Babylonian debt system which brought proud Sumer to its knees, turning a whole nation and its people into debtors. Great numbers were forced to sell their children into slavery just to pay their creditors. The degenerate lugals brought these woes upon their subjects, while their palaces grew so lavish, they came to rival the majesty of the ancient temples.

Yet into the darkness of these times there shone a glimmer of hope. A blessing, as in the days of old, came down from She Who Watches at our annual springtime celebration at the well in Haran. The well needed no stone to cover it in those days preceding the great three hundred year drought which fell upon the land of Sumer like a shroud. So long as we women still revered the Goddess and performed Her ancient rites, the forces of nature were held in balance. There was no fear of drought, or the well drying up. The people of Haran understood the well to be an ancient power center emanating from deep underground springs sacred to Enki, Lord of the Sweet Waters which flow beneath the earth. So long as Enki and the Earth Mother Ninhursag were happy in their spring bed, nature rejoiced and water was plentiful.

On the morning of spring's arrival, a gentle rain fell to nurture the winter wheat and barley crop. The people's hearts were glad to know the God and Goddess were rolling about in heaven making thunder. By afternoon the rain stopped and all the women of Haran assembled at the well bedecked in their myriad scents and colors, like one enormous bouquet of spring wildflowers in honor of the Goddess. Women were still known then as the Keepers of the Circle of Life. For centuries the women of our region had gathered at the well on the first day of spring to strengthen the web of life being reborn. Young and old, they came together to glorify the Ever-Virgin aspect of the Goddess and regenerate themselves in Her.

First came the ritual bath which enabled the mature women to renew their virginity along with the Earth Mother in Her season of rebirth. I can still see the women dancing barefoot on the earth, and hear the ancient chants as they fixed their baths. Some poured exotic scented oils into the large terracotta cisterns reserved for these rites. Others placed herbs, special rocks or shells, and other treasures in the sweet regenerating water.

After mother blessed each tub, one by one the women all disrobed and plunged in. How proud I was to watch mother officiate at these holy rites. So contagious was the women's laughter, so intoxicating the scents. No matter each woman's age, their shape, or size, all of Nature seemed to smile upon their glistening flesh. After the women had bathed and dressed, they asked the Goddess for aid with their special favors. No favor was too large or too small to lay in the lap of She Who Watches.

The spring circle honored the youthful Ever-Virgin aspect of the Goddess. We young virgins were awarded fragrant floral wreaths and invited to join in the festivities. This was the first year I was to participate in the holy rites. I had come of age the previous winter when my wise

blood began to flow, and I had been initiated at the Temple of She Who
Watches in Brak. This was the day I would be brought before the wise
women to see if Ninhursag had blessed me with Her ancient Spirit Eyes,
the gift of sight.

When mother stepped forward a hush came over the entire assembly. Her face was radiant as she said, "Come! Let's all join hands and welcome our new members! Young and old we are all Sisters in the Goddess.
We have a special rite for the young women here today. In keeping with
the pulse of spring that quickens all desire, you are to gaze into the well
and ask the Goddess for a sign of who you are to marry."

My heart swelled as I took my place within the circle, so pleased was
I to be included among the grown women. Today I would be put to the
test on this sacred proving ground before all the wise women of our village. I prayed this rite would declare me a Naditu woman, thus privileged to follow in mother's footsteps!

I sat at mother's left and squeezed her hand as each virgin took their
turn gazing into the well. Leah, my elder sister was called. She rose with
a smug look on her face, pleased to have been chosen before me, then
sauntered toward the well. A shadow crossed my heart casting my spirits
downward. Why did it have to be like this . . . always a competition?
Didn't Leah understand? She had her own destiny and I had mine.

Leah stood before the well shifting her fulsome weight back and
forth between her solid feet. After taking more than her fair share of
time peering into the well, she still had no vision. Leah's eyes were weak.
My heart went out to my sister. This was the third spring she had gazed
into the well with no result. Once again she had shown the wise women
that she did not possess the Spirit Eyes.

Mother rose and stood beside Leah inside the murmuring circle of
women. The hum of their whispers ceased as mother lifted up her arms
and gazed into the well. Watching mother at her work was always inspiration to my soul. A soft starry light descended upon her until she fairly
glowed from the unearthly light.

Mother looked up to speak to Leah, as she had to each of the girls
who'd gone before. "This is your third season at the well Leah, and still
Ninhursag has not granted you Her vision. Never fear! The gift of sight
is a heavy burden, and not for everyone, my dear. The Goddess has
many gifts to grant. And She Who Watches has not forgotten you."

"Ninhursag has spoken! She tells me She has fashioned you a Sugutu woman! Your power will reside in your hips! You shall be a fertile birth mother. Those strong hips of yours will bear many sons. But you must use your Goddess given power wisely, Leah! And I am told to warn you not to covet what is not yours, or your power as a birth mother may work against you, and all our people."

The silence in the women's circle was deafening. No one dared to move as mother gazed into Leah's glaring eyes.

Finally Leah shook her head back proudly, and retorted, "I don't have to listen to your warnings, mother! I take my instructions from father, and he's already told me that I am to be the mother of many sons."

Mother looked away in troubled silence, as Leah sat down heavily beside me usurping her place. My heart stopped. That was no way for Leah to behave. I waited for my heart to stop pounding, then I put my hand on my sister's shoulder and whispered, "You shouldn't have spoken to mother that way!"

Tears welled in Leah's dull cow eyes. My anger began to melt. Leah always knew how to play upon my sympathy.

"Don't cry, Leah!" I said more gently. "You'll use your power wisely. A great destiny lies before you. You shall be one of the most fertile Sugutu women. She Who Watches will bless you with many sons."

Leah dried her eyes and looked at me with contempt. "I don't need your's or mother's pity, Rachel! And I certainly don't want your advice! What do you know? You're just a child!"

I breathed in deeply bracing myself against the bitterness of her reproach.

My sister was impossible for me to fathom. She was a fire breathing dragon and a vulnerable little girl all rolled into one. Never did she miss the opportunity of lording it over me that she was the elder sister. She was so temperamental and moody, I never knew what to expect. Her feelings vacillated so wildly, it made me dizzy. One moment she loved me all the way up to heaven. I was the only one she could turn to in her moments of need. The next moment she'd be seething at me with hate. Leah was like a viper that could strike out at me at any time. I was exhausted merely holding my own and trying to keep my balance.

I'd have to prepare myself for the aftermath of this event. Knowing Leah, she'd make it a difficult night for me. Already I was dreading the scenes which might ensue. She was still fuming when my name was called.

I rose warily, struggling to put my sister out of my mind. This was the first time I was to stand alone before the ancient well. I prayed to be overshadowed by the Eye Goddess, though I feared any success would only incite my sister further.

A curious warmth entered me as I began to pray, and the water of the well rose mysteriously to my gaze like a shimmering magic mirror. I saw myself in the full bloom of young adulthood alone beside this well surrounded by a flock of sheep. My hair was lush and dark and cascaded down my back. My lips and cheeks were blushed with a rosy hue, but a strange sadness played around my eyes and mouth.

A dark handsome stranger approached from the south. His hair was parted in the middle and reached down to his broad shoulders. His eyes were the eyes of a prophet and a dreamer. They penetrated my soul caressing me alluringly. His nose was straight, his forehead broad and strong. The mysterious stranger looked weary from the road, but when our eyes met renewed life entered him.

He addressed me as I continued staring into the glistening water. "Hail beautiful angel! What is this heavenly oasis I have come to? I'm on my way to Haran."

"This is Haran." I said looking him in the eye.

"Thanks be to God, that He brings me here to you." he said beaming. "Do you know Laban? I'm his nephew Jacob, son of his sister, Rebekah."

I shook my head and responded smiling. "Laban is my father! I am his younger daughter, Rachel."

Jacob gazed at me in wonderment. "Are you real, or is this a dream, the answer to my most fervent prayers?"

Then he kissed me searchingly, as if trying to find out if I were real. The vision melted back into the far reaches of the well.

I continued gazing at the water hoping for further signs. But the well was still once more. My spirit was ignited. The scene etched forever on my soul. After saying a prayer of thanks, I turned to face the eager group of women.

Mother smiled at my jubilant face, and inquired, "Did She Who Watches grant you a vision, Rachel?"

The joy rising inside me, I burst out, "Do I have a cousin Jacob, mother?"

Mother looked startled for a moment, then responded. "Yes! Jacob is Laban's nephew, your aunt Rebekah's son. She had twin boys in her later years named Esau and Jacob. Tell us what you saw."

The excited faces of the women lent me courage. Flushed and ready to respond, I inadvertently gazed at Leah. I turned away quickly, but it was too late. The poison in her eyes was already boring into me, draining my joy away.

Why did I have to look at my sister? When had Leah ever been glad for me? I struggled to regain my composure. Finally when I could answer. "I saw myself some years hence at this very well, mother. Only an enormous stone was covering it. I was here to water a flock of sheep, when a handsome stranger appeared from the south. He told me he was my cousin Jacob. Then he kissed me."

The women's whispers crackled with excitement. The young girls giggled, sighing breathlessly with images of romance. When things quieted down mother declared, "The Eye of Heaven is upon you! She Who Watches overshadows you, Rachel. You ARE a Naditu woman. Your senses are attuned to spirit. You have the Ancient Eyes that see by the light of the Eye Star, Kak.Si.Di. I must prepare you for initiation at the Eye Temple in Brak."

Leah glared at me with hatred, as I sat down.

Moving away, she declared in a sullen voice, "You think you're the only one with a special connection to the Goddess!"

I was shaking my head in bewilderment when mother called Zanni's name. Zanni rose to take her turn peering into the wise depths of the well.

Leah's unhappiness must have been evident. I could hear mother speaking to her off to the side. "Have faith! You will not be forgotten. The Goddess favors you in a different way."

When I turned around Leah was in mother's embrace. I couldn't help feeling resentful. Why was Leah being comforted after the way she'd spoken to mother? But that didn't matter. Mother always forgave Leah.

I couldn't let Leah spoil this day for me. I turned and looked back at Zanni, my closest friend. I hoped her experience would be special too.

When I arrived home later that evening mother called me into her sanctuary. It always felt so special to be called into that sacred space, which housed mother's terafim. Mother's face was glowing when she opened the door. She took my hand inviting me in.

Once I'd come through the purifying veil of incense at the threshold, we stood together before the altar. The pungent sage and mugwort incense heightened all my senses. There was always great comfort and inspiration for me in this ritual. It was mother's way of preparing me for her speaking from her Higher Self.

She closed her eyes and said the silent formula that linked her with her starry light body, the wise ones from Magan called the Ka. Then we sat down together on pillows before the altar of the Goddess. When mother picked up the terafim I felt light-headed. The terafim, her precious oracles, were two small figures, one a lioness, the other a coiled serpent, both wound round with precious stones and metals. She used the terafim to communicate with the Starry Ones of heaven.

Mother spoke, terafim in hand, as Priestess of Ninhursag from the depths of her stellar being. "Today was a wondrous day for you, my daughter. It marks your spiritual coming of age. She Who Watches overshadows you. She has chosen you for the Naditu Sisterhood. Your starry destiny unfolds."

I sat motionless, riveted by mother's every word. She continued in a voice resonant with authority, "Jacob is Rebekah's younger son. Rebekah was a Naditu Priestess from the Temple of She Who Watches. She is an opener of the way for you. Rebekah met Eleazar, Isaac's messenger, at that same well. There she was chosen to be Isaac's wife. These are potent omens!"

All the joy, which fled with Leah's withering look, came flooding back.

"That's not all, my daughter. I have conferred with the En Priestess. Much has been revealed to me concerning the future. Great changes are in store."

I was suddenly confused. How could mother have conferred with the En Priestess? The En Priestess was leagues away in Brak at the Eye temple in the foothills of the Taurus mountains. There was no time for questions, however. Mother's voice had taken on a note of urgency that alarmed me. I sat up straining to listen to her every word, and look deep into her heart.

Mother spoke to me from trance, her fingers stroking the terafim like a lyre. Mother often held the terafim when she spoke as Priestess. She consulted them on all important matters. But tonight there was something different in her use of them. They appeared to be an anchor connecting her to Earth.

"I only have a little time left." she began. "You must remember all I have to say to you, Rachel. There may soon come a day when the Goddess is no longer worshipped, and mothers and daughters will not be privileged to speak as we do tonight. These are grave and turbulent times. The rivalries of the Anunnaki have spelled doom for ancient Sumer. Ninhursag was powerless to stop them. The Anunnaki unleashed a mighty blast. Its evil wind destroyed their spaceport and turned Sumer's once proud cities into dust. We have only been saved because we are nestled here in the foothills of the Taurus mountains close to the Eye temple, and Mt. Ararrat, the World Mountain sacred to the Nefilim, the Starry Ones of Heaven.

"We live between two great ages, Rachel, the Age of the Bull, and the Age of the Ram. There is always great difficulty at times of transition. The Precession of the Equinoxes has moved the Zodiacal Wheel from Taurus, which represents the great propagating powers of the Moon, into the warring solar Ram of Aries. Yahweh, the Great Ram of Heaven, seeks to take over power from the Anunnaki of Nibiru. Great have been the excesses of these reptilian overlords of Earth. It is time for a change. But in seeking to sow a new consciousness, Yahweh claims all power for Himself and denounces ALL the Olden Gods of Heaven. This means that He and Nanna/Sin will now both be determined to crush the power of the Goddess. Heaven help us! Great stress shall be placed upon all those who live in the ravaged birth throes of this new era."

"From the star chart of your birth I know that you have a significant role to play in these times, Rachel. You have the constellation Libra rising with Shamash, the sun, in Aries in the seventh house of marriage. Athtar/Venus, the Star of Love, is never far from the sun, but at your birth it was setting along with it. Athtar shines upon you always, ruling your ascendant in close conjunction with your sun. You are blessed to have Athtar rule your chart, Rachel. Athtar is a liberated planet, its inhabitants highly evolved light beings. Their path to spiritual evolution was through the development of the heart. It was their enormous love and compassion that caused them to transfer life to Earth in ancient of times. That is why emotions are the key to spiritual evolution here."

"I named you Rachel after the stellar Ewe. It is your destiny to be partner in the Higher Marriage to the Solar Ram. You must hold love in your heart to balance the warring combative tendencies of Aries. Your love is to forge a new integration of Male and Female working together in harmony to enable humankind's reconnection with their higher spiritual nature. It may be our only hope for moving the Naditu order into the future, as the Black Hand has vowed to eradicate the Sisterhood. The worship of the Goddess has been humankind's greatest tool in the evolution of the heart. Without the Goddess I fear power will be valued over love, and violence will overtake the Earth."

My blood ran cold at mother's words, but I continued listening carefully.

"Your name means she who is to move forward, or be overshadowed. I named you Rachel knowing you had the potential of being overshadowed by the Eye Goddess Ninhursag. She and Enki are highly evolved Star Beings from Kak.Si.Di. They came to Earth to assist humankind in their evolution, not to exploit the riches of this planet as did the Anunnaki. Enki and Ninhursag have remained true to the star wisdom of Kak.Si.Di., the Eye-Star, the sun behind our sun, which will one day be called Sirius."

"The Anunnaki are from Nibiru, the twelfth planet in this solar system. They are part human and part reptile with little access to feelings or emotion. They live for thousands of years and can travel between dimensions because they possess incredible ships which roam the skies. They are very aggressive and possess vast stores of weapons with which they control Earth. They came to Earth to mine gold. But seeing what difficult work it was, they created humans to be their slaves. Enlil, their leader here on Earth, fashioned the first humanoid creatures. But they were not capable of reproducing, so they called upon Enki and Ninhursag for assistance."

Mother breathed in deeply, looking at me with sorrow in her eyes before continuing, "There is much I could tell you of Earth's ancient past, my daughter, but there is no time. Suffice it for me to explain your role. You are a Naditu woman. Your destiny is not the propagation of the species. A Naditu Priestess is an unsown field, one who lets her womb live in the wisdom of the stars. In olden times Naditu Priestesses lived cloistered lives within the Temple, but in these grave times we are called to active service in the world."

My back stiffened and my heart began to ache. What did mother mean there was no time?

"Your mission is to find a way of moving forward by creating a Higher Spiritual Marriage, a marriage in which both partners' spiritual purposes are aligned. If you are successful it will forge harmony and balance between the sexes for all time. The potential for the Higher Marriage is mapped out in the heavens, even as it is in your own star chart! It's depicted through the constellation of Libra, the Scale of Balance, which complements and pacifies the warring sign of Aries on the ascendant for the New Age. The diplomacy and peace of Libra is Aries highest fulfillment. The Higher Marriage will ensure the equality of the sexes. It will be humankind's Scale of Balance, their greatest tool in stemming the tide of disequilibrium, violence, and war which will threaten to consume the Earth during the Age of Iron."

"The Eye of Heaven is upon you. She Who Watches will be testing you. Be guided by your spirit vision and your dreams. This is how the Star Beings from Kak.Si.Di. will instruct you. Your destiny is not the propagation of the species. That has already been accomplished in the Age of Taurus through the fertilizing powers of the stellar Cow and Bull. Do not allow the instinctual urgings of the Cow to get ahold of you. During the Age of Taurus humankind still labored under the necessity of repopulating the Earth after the Great Flood. That rampant breeding must now transform giving way to a new and higher union between the sexes."

"But that is not all! What happened in Ur can also happen here. The downfall of mighty Sumer came about through the Brotherhood of the Black Hand, a secret group of men in league with the Anunnaki. Their plotting destroyed Ur. Now listen well! The Black Hand has control of the Ehulhul temple here in Haran. The Ehulhul is the exact replica of the Egishnugal temple to Sin in Ur, Rachel. It was fashioned by the Black Hand in the event that Ur would fall."

"Beware of the Black Hand, my daughter! They cloak themselves in a secrecy as dark as the gloves they wear. Their goal is to occupy all positions of power and gain control of Earth. They hate Ninhursag and the Sisterhood, and have sworn to stamp out the Goddess and Her worship."

Mother breathed in deeply before continuing. "There is something more. You must be on constant guard with Laban, Rachel. He is one of them."

I gasped out loud. "Father??"

Mother continued on as if under great pressure. "Today Ninhursag overshadowed you for the first time. This is the sign I have been waiting for. You shall inherit my terafim and eye bead necklace. They will attune you to the Nefilim, the great Angels of Heaven from Kak.Si.Di. Be wary of the Anunnaki from Nibiru. The Anunnaki are very clever. They have taught the people of Sumer much. But though they have great knowledge and power and have fashioned themselves human-like bodies, remember their hearts are cold. They do not love humankind, and they have little mercy or compassion. Many wars have they fought in heaven and here below for control of Earth. I fear more are still to be fought, as they control the Black Hand."

"The Brotherhood are masters of deceit, who control through fear. They engender envy and jealousy to fragment people. Listen with your heart and ponder all things with your Ancient Eyes. Or else, I fear even your heart will become a battleground in the wake of the Age of Iron. The Anunnaki want it that way. First they incite, then they feed on all the discord on the Earth."

Mother's eyes turned away from me. "Soon I must say farewell. My work here is near completion."

Mother's words were bittersweet. Great joy as well as sorrow overcame me as we sat together in silence feeling the Goddess's starry presence. I repeated every word mother said over and over again in my mind, hoping to imprint them there forever. But my heart was heavy and I felt confused.

At long last I had to ask, "What do you mean you have only a little time left?"

My words penetrated mother's trance, and she was recalled back to me in an instant. Her eyes were somber, as she said, "I am a Naditu Priestess, my child. It is not for one of the Sisterhood to question the Will of Heaven. Never fear! You are in the Goddess's care. All shall be revealed to you in time. The Goddess reveals Her will to us, but slowly. Our Wise Mother only lets us know what is necessary at the time."

Mother continued, "It is a wonderful gift to possess the Ancient Eyes of the Goddess. But it is also an enormous burden and responsibility. You have to be strong to bear all you see, my darling. Now leave me. It's been a long day. I'll see you in the morning."

A heavy weight settled on my shoulders. I felt like I had aged years. Not wanting to chance meeting Leah, I went directly to my room. There was much for me to ponder that night, and for many nights to follow. To mark the importance of that day, I took out the clay tablet with my star chart and hung it on my wall. I would begin studying it on my own.

Still I could not understand what mother meant when she said her work was near completion. What would her next work be? Her words were so unsettling. They left me with a dread that sliced its way even through my joy that the Eye of Heaven was upon me.

2

THE LOSS OF THE GODDESS

THE GODDESS'S WILL WAS SOON REVEALED TO ME. MOTHER BECAME very ill and withered away mysteriously before my eyes. I tried to remember her words on the evening of my overshadowment. I sought to trust her faith in the Goddess. But mother's failing health was dreadful to behold. The sudden nature of her illness was also very puzzling. It had all the uncanny markings of an arratu curse. Only, **who** would willfully plot against mother?

Mother had always been such a model of strength, love, and understanding, not only for our family, but for the entire region. She was from a long line of Naditu Priestesses. The blue blood of the Star People ran in her veins. Mother's ancestors were descendants of Noah's son Shem. Her family tree could be traced back to the time when the Great Flood subsided and the ark was deposited near Mt. Ararat. Such a renowned and highly respected Naditu Priestess, who would dare to cross her? Who would risk the consequences? So long as mother was Priestess the ancient rites were fulfilled, and peace, and fertility blessed our land.

Mother's death occurred during a total eclipse of the sun. That entire day the distant Taurus mountains, hallowed abode of the Gods, were obscured by a veil of black fog. Given these baleful omens, everyone feared that with her passing, chaos and confusion would envelop the land. Only father seemed strangely unconcerned about the unusual circumstances of her death. His behavior vexed me. All the more so, as he was a high ranking priest of the Anunnaki Moon God Nanna/Sin and officiated at the Ehulhul, Sin's temple in Haran. A wizened moon priest, his strange lack of concern with the omens was most perplexing. And I was forced to remember mother's warning to keep a watchful eye upon Laban.

There had always been a peculiar lack of sympathy between father and I. At times, it mounted almost to an antipathy which only mother could hold in check. I never could understand why mother married Laban. Their's appeared such a loveless match. No glow of happiness radiated about them. Mother always seemed relieved that he spent so much time with his many concubines.

My parents were so unlike each other, they even worshipped different gods. This was most unusual in a Sumerian family that traced its lineage back to the ancient Gods of Heaven. We, Sumerians, were proud to be seeded by the Nefilim. Each of us had our own personal God and Goddess who insured our health and general welfare. Tracing our lineage from the Nefilim made intermarriage essential, and most Sumerian families shared the same personal gods. Mother's lineage was from the star Kak.Si.Di. Laban's ancestors were from the Anunnaki and the fallen Sin temple at Ur.

Only when I grew older did I come to understand that mother's marriage had been arranged by the Eye Temple to help maintain the tenuous balance in our region between the Goddess temple at Brak, and the Ehulhul temple in Haran. The Ehulhul was governed by the priests of Nanna/Sin, and Sin's mysterious Brotherhood, the Black Hand.

In light of the strange omens and mother's warning, I took it upon myself to do a thorough investigation. The Ehulhul **was** an exact replica of the original temple to Sin in Ur. It was established after Nanna/Sin had stolen the Tablets of Destiny from his father Enlil. Supreme of all the Gods of Nibiru, Enlil was ruler of Nippur, the spiritual center of ancient Sumer. The Dur.An.Ki., the sacred bond between Heaven and Earth, was maintained by Enlil at Nippur. Sin's absconding with the

THE LOSS OF THE GODDESS

Tablets of Destiny posed a serious threat to the Dur.An.Ki. and violated the divine 'me' which kept everything on its rightful course.

Ninurta, Enlil's son by Ninhursag, was able to finally recapture them and bring Sin to justice. Thus began Sin's vengeance against Ninhursag and the Naditu Sisterhood. Sin's treachery caused the Anunnaki to flee Earth. Sin was forced to remain behind exiled in Haran with his retinue of degenerate priests. Eventually he retreated to the underworld, leaving his infamous Black Hand in charge.

The Brotherhood of the Black Hand was the strong arm of Nanna/Sin. It was a male secret society bent on world domination and keeping all power in the hands of men. Sin had stolen rulership of the moon from the Goddess. Now he and his Brotherhood sought dominion over Mother Earth as well. The Black Hand had attempted to build the infamous Tower of Babel. Their treachery was one of the reasons the Great Flood had been sent to cleanse the Earth. They were also involved in the unleashing of the poison wind, the Anunnaki's greatest weapon, which levelled all the ancient city states of Sumer, and turned the Dead Sea into salt.

The Black Hand offered human sacrifices upon Sin's altar. Nanna/Sin had come to love the scent of burning human flesh so well, the Brotherhood had increased their sacrifices in hopes of drawing him back. It was rumored Nanna/Sin had encampments on the dark side of the Moon, and that he and his reptilian horde dwelt in deep underground caverns inside the Earth. It was impossible to learn any more. The meetings of the Black Hand were convened with secret rites and held in places hidden from the light of day. A vow of secrecy bound the Brotherhood together. No woman, or outsider, was to learn their secrets under pain of death.

Reports of the Brotherhood chilled my blood. Their plan to suppress the Goddess, and take all power away from women, would cause such gross imbalance, I feared for the Earth. I too, became afraid that with mother's passing deep ruptures and chaos might ensue within our land.

Mother's high status as a Naditu Priestess entitled her to burial in the Ashera grove at the Eye Temple of She Who Watches in Brak. Mother had trained there in childhood, and it had always been her cherished haven. Burial in the sacred grove was the highest honor. Though it saddened me her remains wouldn't rest at home with us upon our land, I accepted mother's wishes. They were the will of the Goddess.

Only father had the audacity to rail against the arrangements. Thus began Laban's vindictive feud against Ninhursag and the Eye Temple.

I had been up all night crying. Weak and ravaged by grief, I was stealing a quiet moment alone at mother's altar, when the En Priestess arrived. The En Priestess embodied the Goddess on Earth. She was High Priestess of She Who Watches, the famed Oracle Priestess, who alone could approach the Stone that Whispers at the base of the holy shrine. Only the En Priestess could hear Ninhursag's hallowed words and communicate them to the people.

The En Priestess entered mother's sanctuary silent and graceful as a cat. Even with my back to her, the hair on my arms bristled from the exaltation of her presence. I turned to face her awesome holiness. Never had I the honor of being alone with her before. I felt suddenly shy and awkward.

"I heard your call." said the En Priestess coming toward me with a knowing smile.

Startled, I asked shyly. "How did you learn of mother's passing?"

The En Priestess opened wide her arms to me whispering in my ear. "Your mother communicated with me through the terafim."

My childish reticence vanished and for one long moment in that endless day the En Priestess's grace enveloped me. Swaddled in her boundless love, I was taken out of time, enfolded in the warmth of her luxurious robes like protective wings. In that moment she became the primordial Mother Vulture, All-compassionate Succorer of the Dead, who alone could turn death back into life.

Gathering strength in the En's loving embrace, I listened carefully as she instructed me in what needed to be done. Her voice was thin as a whisper, yet deep and still as a purifying flame surrounded by the echoes of the ages. "I charge you to carry the terafim! Only you may take up your mother's precious oracle! Bring them with you to the procession. Don't allow them to leave your person for a moment. Hold the terafim in great respect, my dear. The serpent oracle was your mother's link to the Nefilim. The cat oracle was her link to Kak.Si.Di., the Eye Star of She Who Watches. Your mother bequeathed the terafim to you, but I want you to bring them to the Goddess's grove for safekeeping. Hang them on the Ashera tree beside your mother's grave to keep them safe from

Laban. They will await you there until you complete your training. You are also to have your mother's eye bead necklace and her silver divination cup. The eye bead necklace will strengthen your inner sight, and give you the fortitude to get through these next few days. Your mother wanted you to have these special tools of our order. It is also the Will of Heaven! You may still be a child Rachel, but you have been chosen to serve the Gods."

The din of the arriving mourners broke through the timelessness of our embrace. Determination seized me as the En Priestess placed mother's beads around my neck. "The Eye of Heaven is upon you, Rachel. Receive this necklace in solemn purpose. Walk in truth and light upon the Earth. Treat every woman as your Sister in the Goddess."

Then the En Priestess smiled and left the room.

For the first time since mother's death light penetrated my grieving heart. She Who Watches had chosen me. Rejoicing, I picked up the terafim for the first time and held them to my heart. Then I gazed down at their intricate coiled tails of precious metals, gold, silver, copper and electrum. The innermost coil of their eyes and tails were crafted of a rare heavy metal from KaK.Si.Di. Their eyes were inlaid with precious stones.

The terafim were all I had of mother's cherished wisdom. I had expected the terafim to comfort me. But as soon as I touched the oracle an unusual rosy light flooded the room, and the ground beneath me began to tremble. A voice issued from the Earth, saying, "BEWARE OF TREACHERY FROM THOSE YOU HOLD AS DEAR."

Hands trembling, I wrapped the terafim in their black silk cloth. Then I placed them beside my crescent sickle inside my basket for the long trek to the Eye temple.

All the wise women of our region, numerous relatives and friends, a retinue of Naditu Priestesses from the Eye Temple, and a small group of father's cronies from the Brotherhood, came to walk with us in solemn procession to mother's burial mound. It was a hot sweltering summer day. Not a single breeze blew for encouragement as we set out upon our lengthy journey to Brak. Each of us was dressed in black and carried a flickering oil lamp. We made a ghostly spectacle, walking like shadows in the noonday sun. The scent of oil mingled in the air, hanging limp and lifeless adding to the deathly pall.

The ground trembled again, when I took my place beside father and Leah at the front of the procession line behind mother's coffin. I clutched my basket grabbing father's arm for support. These maneuvers were in vain, however. The earth movement was only exacerbated. I was about to ask Leah if she could also feel the shaking, when the En Priestess appeared.

Her arrival was the sign the mourners had all been waiting for. Ancient death chants rang out as the procession started forth. The En Priestess's presence had a calming effect, and the trembling stopped beneath my feet. Soon I too could enter into the heartfelt songs of lamentation. I found comfort in the moaning tones of the death chants. They were the right beacon to accompany us along the serpentine path across the dusty plains to the Eye Temple.

The grim journey seemed endless. I slept little, and the days flowed together in one long endless stream. Still we trudged on with no sight of the Eye Temple or its verdant Ashera grove. After three and a half days I was relieved to spy the Kabur river gleaming like a band of gold in the distance. My eyes thrilled to follow its sinuous course, and see the flocks of brightly colored birds crowding its lush banks.

It was already well into afternoon. The sun, which had beat down on us mercilessly all day, now glared painfully in our eyes as we arrived in sight of the Temple. At last the heavy wooden door creaked open and we were ushered inside and taken to the visitor's lake. I'd been fasting the entire journey, and was grateful when the Priestesses passed cups of lemon water around for us to drink.

I hadn't been to the Eye Temple since my overshadowment. Now to my surprise my senses opened as I drank the refreshing water. I gazed around me in wonder at the holy shrine, thinking of the ancient crypt beneath its central vault. Then I removed my necklace and bathed it in the lake. When I finished my ablutions I placed it back on my neck. It felt cool and pulsed gently against my skin, quickening my breath.

The brief stay at the lake revived us. Our chanting was reinvigorated as we pressed on through the heat toward mother's burial mound. After the sweltering days out on the treeless plains, the Goddess's grove looked most inviting. A wind came up as we entered the sacred grove of Ashera. Ancient terebinths, oaks, and pines swayed in the breeze, welcoming us with the enchanting music of the charms tinkling in their branches.

My spirit was revived in the cool depths of the Ashera grove. My eyes followed a shaft of light filtering down through the trees to a great heap of river rock. A stalwart terebinth stood beside it. Next to it was a gaping hole. A gust of wind rose up along with the wails of the mourners as the En Priestess ushered us over to the spot. The charms and offerings in the trees played their sweet compelling music, reminding me of the duty I'd been given. I was holding the basket to my breast contemplating my task, and watching the En Priestess direct the men in the placement of mother's bier, when father's voice boomed up behind me competing with the doleful sounds of the dirge. My heart sank. He was complaining to Leah again.

"Who does the En Priestess think she is, not allowing me to direct my Brothers in the placement of your mother's bier? . . . Why?. . . . I'm not only the bereaved husband. . . . I'm the most powerful moon priest around! She'd best not forget it, or, I just might have to remind her."

I held my breath and looked around furtively. Father's words had been so loud. They'd obviously not been meant for Leah's ears alone. Since mother's death Leah and I had been forced to listen to his endless litany of complaints about the En Priestess and the Goddess Ninhursag. Fear took me over. Did father now crave a larger audience for his invectives?

The En Priestess ushered first our family, then mother's closest friends and relatives over to the bier. Father seized the opportunity to be the first to mother's grave. Not having shed a single tear until then, he became the grieving husband and grand master of ceremonies with all his Brothers flocking round. Crying and tearing his garments in full ritual display, he exhorted the weary onlookers to follow suit. The more who followed, the louder grew the wail of his lament. Throwing himself over mother's bier, he shouted loudly so all could hear, "Anna! Oh Anna! How could you have left me in my prime? No sons to help me! Only daughters! Why did you have to leave so young? And why be buried here and not at home with me? The Goddess! Always the Goddess Ninhursag! Never did you think of me! . . . Is your untimely death the Goddess's reward for all your faithful service? Is this how She Who Watches treats

Her favorites? Nanna/Sin would not be so heartless. There's small comfort here compared to what I could offer you!"

I thought we had put this behind us. I was so ashamed of father's words. The instructions for her burial were mother's parting wish. Her last breath had been spent confiding them to me. Father had railed against me concerning mother's burial. It had taken all my strength to make him finally comply. I prayed he wouldn't ruin mother's funeral and desecrate this holy place.

The En Priestess came up behind him steering him away from the open coffin. In another deft movement, she offered him the chalice of consolation and bade him drink. Caught off guard, even Laban could not insult the En Priestess's thoughtful gesture. Obliged to stand at a polite distance, he drank the fragrant herbal draught.

With father so occupied, his men disbanded, and mother's closest friends and relatives filed by rending their garments and beating their chests. I watched tearfully as the older women bared their breasts and pierced their tender skin. My heart was wrenching when it came my turn. This would be the last time I'd gaze upon mother's face.

I opened my basket and removed the ram-jaw sickle I'd prepared with mother's help in the dark hours of the previous winter. It was to have been my ritual sickle. Never had I suspected I'd first use it here. I breathed in deeply to steady myself, then made a shallow cut above my heart. After I finished I put the sickle to my hair and began to hack away. Mother had shed her blood that I might live. It wasn't enough merely to rend my clothing. Mother was gone, and with her went my childhood. I had to mark this passage for all time.

A hush swept over the crowd as my hair fell to the ground. Someone grabbed my arm from behind with a whimpering cry. I turned to see Leah's horrified face. She was afraid that she too would have to cut her hair. I didn't want her interfering. This was my choice. My first ritual gesture without mother's guidance.

Looking at her sternly, I said, "Let me be, Leah! This has nothing to do with you. It's my choice."

My hair had never been cut before. The sickle was dull. I hadn't realized how much it was going to hurt. Now my tears were from physical pain, as well as grief. Cutting my hair was difficult and slow going, but I would manage. This was my rite of passage, an acknowledgement of the child in me who died with mother's passing.

The sweat of my brow mingled with my tears. I was weak and near exhaustion by the time my work was done. There upon the ground was a great pile of dark shining hair. I gathered it in my arms and cradled it like a baby. It wasn't much, but it was all I had. I placed it beside mother, then bent down to kiss her. There was no solace in that kiss. Mother's cheek was as cold as ice. I had not kissed my mother, I had embraced death.

When I looked up my vision had altered. It was as though a veil had fallen from my eyes. Father was standing amidst his black gloved cronies. They were a sinister lot. I had the uncanny sense they were planning something. Father was staring at me coldly, scrutinizing me as though I was a stranger. When his eyes met mine they narrowed in like a predator's upon his prey. Leah stood beside father inside the circle of men basking in their presence. She glowered at me and gripped father's hand, then looked away stroking her hair nervously.

That one look told me more than I could bear. I had not just lost my mother. I no longer had a family. And in my bones I knew the Black Hand was to be a powerful presence in my life. The security of my childhood was broken, and along with it went the feeling I was loved. How could I live with father and Leah? There'd be no end to their ridicule and scorn when we returned home.

I felt suddenly light-headed and dizzy looking down into the grave. Clasping my basket, I moved away from the gaping hole in the earth. The En Priestess must have sensed my distress. When I looked up she was offering me the cup of consolation. I thanked her, and braced myself for what I imagined to be a bitter brew. But the potion was as sweet and calming, as the En Priestess's gaze.

I looked into her inscrutable cat eyes. The En Priestess was older than mother, and seemed to possess an even greater strength and wisdom. I knew I could trust her.

I heard father through the baleful moans of the mourners, speaking in his most reassuring tone to Leah. "You don't have to do as your sister does, my dear! Why make a spectacle of yourself? Rachel just wants attention. Keep your lovely locks! You're more attractive that way. When the time comes you'll command a higher bride price."

Those two had always been close, but since mother's death they were inseparable. What was to become of me? I prayed with all my heart that I could stay here and be trained at the Temple.

A drum beat signalled the continuance of the ritual. Gripping my basket to my heart, I struggled to put father and Leah out of my mind as I took a place further back in the procession. After circumambulating the grove several times, an extraordinary shaft of light pierced through the canopy of trees shining down upon mother. The En Priestess returned us to the illumination of the gravesite. It took time for my eyes to adjust to the brilliance of the light streaming down on her. What was this amazing light? It was more than sunlight. Was mother being translated to the starry vault of heaven? Outside this miraculous stream of light, we all looked pale and ghostly in comparison to her.

The drum sounded again as all the Priestesses came together in a circle. In the last precious moments of that glorious light, the En Priestess sung mother's soul through the seven gates of the underworld. Hidden from our gaze she wrapped mother in the gossamer shroud of the dead. When she was finished the circle of Priestesses opened, and mother was revealed lying on her bier swaddled in a red cocoonlike wrapping. The death shroud was blood red, like the placenta of birth, to remind us of the cyclical nature of life and death.

The light from above disappeared suddenly. Shrill cries resounded from the mourners as mother's bier was placed inside its earthen womb. When the coffin was completely covered the Priestesses sprinkled poppy seeds on the newly piled ground to speed mother's soul to rest.

As the En Priestess sprinkled the seeds with water from the Eye pool, she prayed. "GREAT MOTHER NINHURSAG, SHE WHO WATCHES US HERE BELOW, WE THANK YOU FOR SENDING DOWN YOUR STARRY LIGHT TO GIVE US FAITH IN THIS TIME OF DARKNESS. GRANT US YOUR WISDOM AND SOLACE. GIVE US FAITH TO UNDERSTAND THAT THE CIRCLE OF LIFE CAN NOT BE BROKEN, NOT FOR ANNA, NOR FOR THOSE SHE LEAVES BEHIND.

The En Priestess's words were still resounding in my heart when I heard her call my name. "Come Rachel! It's time for you to build your mother's altar."

A wave of surprise swept through the entire assembly. It was the task of a Naditu Priestess's successor to consecrate her altar and lay her soul to rest. To be called so young was a rare challenge. Every rock had to be placed just right. Mother's transfer to the starry reaches depended on it. The days since mother's death had been full of challenges, and I felt sorely pressed to this new task.

I stood overwhelmed before the great pile of rock. Never had I built an altar to the Goddess, though I'd watched mother do it several times. I listened to my heart. If I had faith all would be revealed. I placed my basket on top of my head and closed my eyes, starting the rhythmic breathing mother had shown me. Could it be? Yes! The terafim were pulsing inside the basket. My faith swelled thinking of the terafim. As I lifted my arms above my head in the traditional stance of the Goddess, a tingling sensation started in the tips of my fingers, spreading through my hands and arms. I gathered up the energy, and sent it through my entire body. Then I opened my eyes and put the basket down beside me.

My sight deepened as I gazed at the rocks. Every stone had its own unique quality. I only had to feel them and I knew their rightful place and function. My hands moved with a knowledge all their own. In no time the altar was fashioned in the familiar pillar of the Goddess.

Five Priestesses positioned themselves in a crescent formation in front of the pillar, as the En Priestess held up an urn with a star and the spiral of the Goddess etched on it. Smiling down upon my altar, she offered me the urn. It was filled with a thick fragrant oil. When it coated my fingers, I drew a star and a spiral on the center of the pillar to signify Kak.Si.Di., and the galaxies of stars I hoped would be mother's new home. Then pouring the remaining oil on the pillar I prayed for mother's soul.

All the Priestesses opened baskets in unison letting loose scores of colorful butterflies. I delighted in their soaring movement, feeling profound relief to see them winging high into the sky. Deep peace settled over the assembly as we watched the graceful creatures glide away.

The beauty of the moment was shattered by father pushing his way noisily through the crowd. Brushing by, his elbow struck me sharply in the side. I was catching my breath, when he grabbed some wine and made a second libation over the pillar I had just consecrated. Then bowing low he invited all the guests to follow.

No one moved. The mourners were frozen in anxious suspense. No one had ever seen such a mockery. Only with father's insistent urging, did Leah finally step forward.

The En Priestess positioned herself in front of Leah eclipsing her from view of the crowd. Preparing the cup of consolation for the entire assembly, she chanted, "I AM STIRRING THE WATERS OF THE GREAT WOMB OF REBIRTH."

Drawn into the soothing chant, the assembly soon relaxed and calm was restored. As the communal cup was passed around Leah slinked away positioning herself beside father.

All that remained was the bequeathing of mother's treasures. I slipped my arm through the basket and started walking toward the Ashera tree holding the terafim close to my heart. I moved surreptitiously, suddenly fearful father might claim them for himself. A breeze began blowing from behind urging me onward. I was glad for the encouragement. I could already feel the fabled power of father's evil eye hot upon my back.

When I reached the Ashera tree I was moved to hug it. My senses were immediately heightened, and the tree began to whisper. It told me to circle it three times touching its gnarly branches. When finished I was moved to climb to a place high up where several branches came together, creating the perfect hollow for the terafim.

Father's booming voice rang out as I removed the terafim from its basket. I continued, pretending not to hear him.

"Show me what you have there, Rachel! Stop pretending you can't hear me!" he shouted angrily.

I kept about my task though father's voice was getting closer. Now he was at the foot of the Ashera gazing up at me, and shouting, "I can see what you have there, Rachel. Give them to me! They're mine! Bring them here! The terafim belong to me now that your mother's gone!"

Would father dare shake the tree and dislodge me, the terafim, and all the sacred objects in its branches? I prayed for strength imaging Ninhursag holding aloft her mirror of truth. Clasping the terafim to my heart, I declared, "The terafim don't belong to you, father! I'm placing them here as the En Priestess has directed!"

Father's eyes flashed with fury and his Brothers crowded round. It didn't take much to enrage father, but I'd never seen him like this before. The entire assembly cringed to see his countenance, as he turned to face the En Priestess with his wrath. Only the Naditu Priestesses were undaunted. They positioned themselves in a circle with the En Priestess at its center. I marvelled at these Naditu women. They were as strong and brave, as they were wise and beautiful.

The En Priestess locked father with her eyes. Still furious, he stepped back in an effort to release himself. His fury slackened. Even father could see he was dealing with a different order of women here. Though he was with several of his Brothers, they were on unfamiliar ground and greatly outnumbered.

The Priestesses took out the copper knives that hung inside their robes. Mother had worn such a knife, but I'd always thought of it as strictly ceremonial. Plainly they were not. The Priestesses knives shone with frightening intensity. They were poised to throw.

Father was transformed before us. No longer the raging bull, he shifted his weight nervously back and forth between his feet, careful not to move a step forward. Finally he cried out plaintively, "Isn't it enough you have my wife? Must you also steal the terafim, and turn my daughter against me as well? "

The En Priestess kept father rivetted with her stare. When it suited her she responded, "The terafim don't belong to you, Laban. They belonged to Anna. She received them from this temple. They are now being recalled for Anna's successor. We'll keep them here for Rachel until she's ready to receive them. You have no say in this matter, Laban! Don't interfere, or you'll risk the Goddess's extreme disfavor.'

Father put on his most unctuous smile. Bowing low, he began retreating. Sighs of relief issued from all the mourners, though I didn't dare take my eyes off father. Never had I seen him give up on anything so easily before. Father was bowing low and smiling, but he was moving closer to me and the Ashera.

Before I could think of what to do, he shook the Ashera violently. I fell in a heap at his feet clutching the precious terafim. Peels of scornful laughter rang out from his Brothers. A cacophony of sound issued from the charms raining down upon us from the holy tree. I lay stunned on the ground. Father grabbed the terafim and jerked me to my feet. The ground groaned beneath us, then suddenly began to heave. Using me as a human shield he ran off through the mazelike paths of the grove, holding the terafim high in the air. His exultant Brotherhood followed up the rear.

The quakes intensified as father dragged me through the narrow pathways. Leah followed close behind the triumphant Brotherhood. I could hear her panting and constant pleas to slow down. Father didn't listen. He raced on hour after hour though the earth shook with vengeance at his every step, dislodging rocks and felling trees around us.

The Earth Mother was enraged. Would we be cursed forever? Would the ground swallow us up in retribution? Father had his host of worries too. He kept turning around checking behind us, tightening his grip on me.

My body ached with every step. I prayed the En Priestess would not forget me. I prayed she'd come to save me from Laban, and the Brotherhood of the Black Hand.

3

RACHEL'S CONFINEMENT

EVERYWHERE WE WENT THE RUMBLING OF THE EARTH PURSUED US. THE ground was still writhing beneath our feet when we finally reached Haran and parted company with father's men.

"Farewell Laban!" exclaimed swarthy Eli. "We really pulled one over on them, didn't we? Zaltan will be pleased to hear of the chaos we created at the Eye Temple."

Another one of his cohorts chimed in, "You did well, Laban! You really made fools out of those self-righteous women. They're finished now that we have the terafim."

Laban was still chuckling as we started down the deserted sunbaked streets. Anyone who could be spared from work was still at mother's funeral. I looked with yearning down the narrow lanes, remembering all the times I walked them with mother when she'd been called to assist friends and neighbors.

I was mortified. How could I ever face these people again? It was sweltering hot, but my body was cold and trembling as father dragged me through the streets. My mind was whirling. How could father be so brazen? Hadn't he understood the seriousness of what he'd done?

His behavior at the Eye Temple was a breach of Taboo, the gravest of offenses against the Gods. The Laws of Taboo were as ancient as man himself. They had been given by the Gods to safeguard all that was sacred. After such a disgraceful breach of a Taboo I knew father was beyond redemption. There would be no way to reason with him now. Did he and his Brotherhood think they were above the law? In their ravenous craving for power had they put themselves above the Olden Gods of Heaven. The Law was the Law. The quaking of the ground beneath our feet was but small token of the Goddess's outrage. I dreaded the penalties yet to come.

The majority of the townspeople were decent folk who still obeyed the Law. Would they shun us in fear of dread contagion? Shame seized me with a grip as strangulating as father's, and threatened to envelop me like the trembling earth beneath my feet. I was wondering how much more I could stand of this being dragged and bullied, when I caught sight of our farm with its old familiar gate post and the ancient oak, our family's guardian tree. But today even these friendly landmarks brought no relief.

As we approached the entrance to the farm the earth sounded one last great rumbling groan that stopped us in our tracks. It split open a deep crevice bringing down the mighty oak. The stalwart guardian fell to the ground with a mighty thud, blocking the entrance like an angry sentinel denying our admission. The crevice snaked through mother's herb and rock garden. I stared in wonder. Mother's garden was gone, swallowed up as if it never had existed. Father's crazed flight had come to this end.

Cursing loudly, father finally halted to take stock of our situation. Seeing this as my chance to free myself, I began squirming in his grip. But he just grabbed me even tighter.

Leah came up behind us, crying, "Our journey has come to this? What are we to do, father? A chasm has been placed between us and the outside world. Are we cursed? . . . Is this the Goddess's retribution? . . . It's plain for all to see!"

"Daughters!" father bellowed, giving vent to his fury. "What good are you? You, Leah, crying and whimpering like a frightened child! And your sister Rachel, here, she's even worse! She brought this on us! Just look at her! The black sheep is shorn and has no place to go. Yet all she can think about is trying to get away."

Leah glared at me. "Father's right! It IS all your fault! You brought this on us, Rachel! How could you? We're your family . . . your own blood!"

Father interjected before I could reply. "Not another word out of either of you, or I'll get the switch! I'll find a way across this abyss! Damn that Ninhursag! This is my land! Nothing is going to bar me from it!"

Not able to tolerate father's profanities, I blurted out, "You mustn't speak that way about the Goddess, father! . . . It's disrespectful. . . . She'll smite you for it."

Father turned on me savagely, twisting my arm behind my back as he spoke. "One visit to the Eye Temple and listen to you. Enough of this haughty behavior, Rachel! Who do you think you are speaking to me this way?"

Spying the eye bead necklace around my throat, he grasped hold of it shouting, "So they gave you this as well! No rewards for you, you brazen child! The attention from the En Priestess has gone to your head. You brought this trouble on us! I could crush you with one fist, if I wanted to. One more word out of you, and maybe I will! You'd make a fine sacrifice on Sin's altar."

Father stuffed the necklace in his pocket. Dragging me along he went to assess the full extent of damage. He was holding me so tight, I could hardly breathe. I was feeling faint, when he finally relaxed his grip. "Great Sin is watching out for us! Look! The chasm ends here! It's not impassable. We can get across if we clear this brush away."

I was bruised and near exhaustion by the time we reached the house. But father wasn't finished with me yet. He dragged me to his room, and threw me on the floor. "Not another word out of you, or I'll get my skull oracle! From hereon you'll obey my every command! Or I'll pour your blood out on the altar, like I do with all those other little wretches. I could make another oracle with your skull. The only thing that's stopping me is the fine bride price I'll get out of you one day."

I shook my head feebly through my tears. Without another word father picked up his gruesome skull oracle and dragged me to my room. Throwing me inside he shouted, holding his oracle up in front of me. "I'll

33

see you in the morning, Rachel. Don't try to escape! Or I swear by Sin, I'll find you, take you to the Ehulhul temple and sacrifice you on the altar. Nanna/Sin particularly enjoys young virgins."

"Besides, you have no place to go. I've seen to it that you're no longer welcome at the Eye temple. You're going to have to stay here with me, and obey my every rule. That small twist of your arm was only a small taste of what I could do to you."

I heard father alright! Holding his oracle, every word he said sent tremors through my entire body. His skull oracle had mysterious powers. He made it from the head of his firstborn son by Suzannah, one of his concubines. He'd sacrificed the tiny infant to gain his own dark power. I slept very little that night, and for many nights to come. Whenever I closed my eyes I saw the glowing eyes of that fearsome idol, and father's words echoed in my mind. Would he sacrifice me, as well? I couldn't take the chance.

I was sleeping fitfully later that night when I heard a commotion in the front room. I rose hoping someone had come to set me free. But it was only Leah. She was with father, and he'd been into the cups again. He was always at his worst when he drank too much. Concerned for Leah's safety, I kept peering through the narrow crack.

Father stumbled grabbing hold of Leah. I couldn't hear everything they said, but father was pouring himself some wine and handing a cup to Leah. He was smiling and turning on the charm. Leah looked up at him adoringly, nuzzling closer to him. My mind was in turmoil. I could hardly believe it at first. But father seemed to be sweet talking Leah. For a moment I was relieved. At least he wasn't getting violent with her. But then I saw something even more upsetting. Father put his arms around Leah and began stroking her breasts, fondling her. Leah glowed from the attention and pressed her body close to his. Father grinned lasciviously. Then without another word he dragged her to his room.

My knees went weak. Father was breaking another Taboo. Where would it end? I sat down to steady myself. My stomach churned until I was afraid I'd start retching. What was happening to us? I didn't want to believe what I had seen with my own eyes. Mother had only been put in the ground. Father had many concubines. What was he doing taking Leah to bed? I shuddered as an even more horrifying thought came to me. What if he made advances to me as well? The thought was so loathsome I started trembling. I got down on my knees and prayed, and kept on praying that someone, anyone, would come to free me. I had to get away from father, and Leah. I had to make a move, if not tonight, then in the morning.

My thoughts turned to the funeral repast, the traditional breaking-fast meal shared with all the mourners at the home of the deceased. It was a simple meal consisting of honey cakes to appease the hungry souls of the dead, and wine to brace the spirit. The first rays of dawn were beginning to appear. Soon fathers concubines were moving about getting ready for the day. The soft hum of their gossip was coming out of the fire hut. I could smell the honey cakes baking in the mud brick oven.

Our relatives would be returning from their pilgrimage. I prayed they'd soon arrive to break bread with us. Someone would ask after me. Or better still, perhaps the En Priestess would come to take me back to the Eye Temple. I waited inside my room all morning in suspense, but no one came. With father's disgraceful behavior at the Eye Temple and the Goddess's mark of fury at our gate, no one dared come near our house that morning, or the whole long day I waited like a prisoner inside my room.

It took one full year to fill in the gaping chasm at the entrance to our farm. With that mark of the Goddess's outrage at our gate no one could forget father's sacrilegious behavior. No upright soul dared to cross our threshold for fear they'd incur the Goddess's wrath. That gaping hole kept everyone from entering, everyone, except for the Brotherhood of the Black Hand. They came more frequently now, as father rose in their ranks, a touted hero for having defiled Ninhursag's grove and absconding with the terafim.

It was late afternoon before anyone other than the concubines could be heard in the front room. I sprang up quickly and peered through the crack in the door. Leah was walking about. I called out, "Leah! Leah! Let me out! Please let me out!"

Leah disappeared into father's room without a word. When she reappeared, it was obvious she was enjoying her new felt power. She tarried about the front room, washing her face and combing her hair, ignoring my frantic pleas.

When Leah got around to opening the door, she sounded just like father. "I hope you get what you deserve, Rachel! What gall you had taking the terafim without father's consent. Who do you think you are . . . the En Priestess? Not a soul has showed up here all day. Father's so upset he can't get out of bed. You're to blame for this."

I was about to respond, when Leah hurled me across the room. Thrusting me in front of mother's copper mirror, she continued, "Just look at yourself! You had to be such a showoff . . . the center of attention! You look awful! I hope you're pleased with yourself now."

Leah left for father's room, careful to leave the door open so I'd hear them chatting in their new familiar way. In all the pain and confusion I'd forgotten about my hair. Looking into the mirror I hardly recognized myself. Leah was right. I did look awful. My hair was ragged and chopped off to my chin. My eyes were red and swollen. I looked ancient and haggard. The child in me had died.

I brushed the tears from my eyes and went back to my room to get something for my head. I'd feel better once my hair was covered. Returning to the main room, I took another look in the mirror. I couldn't allow my vanity to get the better of me. My hair would grow back. I couldn't be so vain and foolish as to worry about my hair. There were more important things to contend with.

I went over to the basin to wash. The water felt cool against the anguish of my tears. I held a cloth to my eyes. When I began to feel better, I turned and stared blankly around the room. It was another hot sweltering day, but I felt chilled and goose bumps were raising up on my arms and legs. Our house had an eerie feeling. It looked strange and unfamiliar. Nothing had visibly altered in the room, but all the love was gone.

The honey cakes were on the table where father's concubines had left them. They were untouched and had begun attracting flies. I stood motionless, staring down at them for a time, all my worst fears crowding in on me. No one had come to share the breaking fast meal with us. Would anyone ever come again?

"Get in here Rachel!" cried father from the other room. "I want to speak to you!"

I was afraid to even think of what he might want. How could I look at him? Whenever I closed my eyes I saw his hideous skull with its glowing eyes, and his words echoed in my mind. The little sleep I'd gotten had been interrupted with frightening dreams that replayed the scene between us over and over again.

Not about to be put off, father called out again from the other room. "Get in here Rachel! Or do you prefer being locked in your room again?"

I had to go in to him. I couldn't bear being imprisoned in my room. I knocked on his door though it had been left ajar.

"Get over here so I can see you!" he answered gruffly.

My skin crawled as he leered at me. "Things are going to be different around here now that your mother's gone. There are new rules. You'll obey them, or there will be serious consequences. I'm going to dismantle your mother's altar tonight. Sin will take it over, just like he will the Eye Temple one day. Henceforth, there shall be no mention of Ninhursag, or the Eye Temple in this house. Do you understand?"

A grim weight fell upon my shoulders, and my heart sank. I nodded sadly. I had lost mother. Now father was going to take the Goddess away from me as well. I'd be completely motherless. I breathed in deeply, trying not to show my grief.

Father went on, his eyes boring into me in an effort to control me. "You and Leah are confined to the house for the next forty days in observance of your mother's passing. If you behave yourselves, after that time you'll be allowed to go outside again. But you are never, and I mean never to go to Haran without my permission. You're also forbidden to return to the Women's Circles in town. My Brotherhood and I are going to see to it that those antiquated Goddess rites are abolished."

"Most important of all, you are never to go near the En Priestess or the Eye Temple. And don't you get any fancy ideas about your being a Naditu woman, Rachel. You're my daughter! And you'll be Sin's daughter, too! I'm in control here now. Or must I take out my skull oracle again to convince you?"

My face went white at the thought of that fiendish oracle. "No, father! Please don't! I understand!"

How could I live without my spiritual freedom? Oh father was clever! He knew exactly what he was doing cutting me off from my strength and my only solace. I felt all alone and hopeless. I wanted to run away, and never look at him again. But there was no escape. I was powerless to resist him. He had the vast network of his Brotherhood. They would see to it that I didn't get very far. Just as he had somehow seen to it that mother would waste away and die precisely on the eclipse.

I'd had my suspicions about mother's death. But after these last few days, and my limited acquaintance with his skull idol, I was sure he'd poisoned her.

Breathing in against the suffocating weight on my chest, I responded, "I understand, father! I have no choice but to obey."

"That's right!" he said, regarding me shrewdly. "You have no choice! Now go!"

I couldn't wait to leave them. I just couldn't understand how Leah could sit there gloating like a fat contented cow. I was repulsed. Maybe Leah had gotten what she deserved last night. I only prayed father would leave me alone. I didn't want him to ever touch me again.

Time went by so slowly. We were completely alone now. No female relatives came to help us with the purification of the house, or to receive mother's belongings, as was the custom. No one came to visit our family that first day, or for any of the other forty evenings following mother's burial. True to his word, father didn't allow me outside. I couldn't even feed mother's doves with the honey cakes that had been left uneaten.

I chafed under the enforced seclusion. How I missed the Goddess's sacred birds, and the feeling of the good earth beneath my feet! By the time the forty days were over the doves had all departed. It was the rainy season, but the rains never came. The great drought had begun. Though father didn't seem to notice. He didn't care that the garden had gone to rack and ruin, or that all our fields were parched and burned. His heart was poisoned, and for one full year he didn't speak to anyone except his Brothers from the Black Hand.

I couldn't bear the presence of those horrid men. While mother was alive father never dared to bring those rascals round. But now he set up a private meeting room in mother's sanctuary, and placed his skull upon her altar table. The Brotherhood wandered through the house all times of day and night wearing their dark aprons, and carrying bags of the potent extract of the flower of the dreamers in their black gloved hands. Traders arrived with long lines of poor slave children destined for sacrifice at the Ehulhul temple. Their pathetic moans were lost in the heavy clank of gold and silver changing hands, and the pungent smell of opium and dragon's blood incense that father used to seal his nefarious deals.

When the forty days were over I moved out of the house and set up my own quarters in a tent away from his grim transactions. Even father's concubines were loathe to enter the house now. They only came when father threatened. Leah and I took over the household chores and did everything we could to bring things back to normal. But it was to no avail. Father was filled with rancor, and became more miserly and greedy with every day.

He refused to speak of the events of the funeral. He blamed Ninhursag for everything, even mother's untimely death. The more blasphemous father became toward the Goddess, the more our fortune seemed to turn. I tried pointing this out to him, but it fell on deaf ears. I was treated like a traitor whenever I inquired about the terafim. But with them in his possession there was little I could do except watch as our livestock got sick and died, and our entire farm fell into disrepair.

One day in utter desperation, I begged father to let me take care of the sheep. She Who Watches must have been smiling on me, as he reluctantly consented. I was grateful for the work. It gave me an excuse to be out away from father and Leah's watchful eyes. Instead of being privy to father's sordid transactions, I could wander the hillsides with my flock pondering nature's wonders. I meditated with the changing of the seasons and the rhythms of the moon. My inner vision quickened out in nature and my spirit had room to soar. She Who Watches drew closer to me when I was out in the fields with my flocks. Goddess of the Foothills, I could feel Her awesome presence as I roamed the hillsides with my herd. She spoke to me through the doves, her sacred birds, the opening of flowers in springtime, and the breathtaking wonder of the night sky.

My work was my only refuge against the black moods which poisoned father. His sullen unhappiness infected everything at home. His favorite pastime was pitting Leah against me for sport. I was always happiest in the spring my busiest time. With the spring shearing and lambing I could be out on my own for days at a time, only coming home for supplies.

I returned home late one evening after dinner was over. Many of the younger ewes were expecting. A cold north wind was blowing and the weather so capricious, I'd brought them to the shelter of the barn. Father and Leah were sitting together by the fire. His look was dazed and sullen when I opened the door. He'd been into the cups again. Leah was curled adoringly at his feet.

I braced myself, as he inquired, "What are you doing coming back so soon? How's the lambing going?"

"All's well, father. But the weather's taken a turn for the worst. So I brought the pregnant ewes in to shelter."

Father looked up with a glazed stare. Pushing Leah aside, he said, "Wise decision! Come have a seat by me! You've been working hard. Your taking over the sheep is working out better than I expected. Sit with me here beside the fire."

Leah skulked away like a wounded animal, as I tried to desist. "No need to disrupt Leah, father. I'm tired, and need to go to sleep. I just came in to report to you, and see if there was any dinner left. I haven't had a hot meal in days."

Father was insistent. "Sit down beside me, Rachel! Leah, go tell those lazy concubines to bring a hot meal for Rachel!"

"Since when do I have to do Rachel's bidding!" asked Leah sulkily.

"You're not doing Rachel's bidding." bellowed father. "You're doing mine! Now get going this instant! Rachel's the only one around here who does any work. You're getting as fat and lazy as those concubines!"

Leah was irate as she started for the door. When she got to the door she turned and glared at me hatefully for being so displaced. Afraid to be left alone with father, I quickly said, "Don't trouble yourself for me, Leah! I have to go wash up anyway. I'll stop by the firehut and see what I can find."

Father and Leah were arguing as I stole out the door. As much as Leah irked me, it was sad to see my sister sink so low. But without the Goddess, and the Women's Circles, what else was there to fill the void since mother's death? Poor Leah! She welcomed even the slightest attention from father, living for his approval and favoritism.

It was a relief to get away from them. There was never any peace for me at home. Father's tricks were deplorable, his temper even worse. He looked for any excuse to use the switch. The only peace and freedom I knew was out in nature with my flocks. I made an altar to Ninhursag, Lady of the Foothills, on a high place in the hills that had a large flat boulder beside an ancient oak and babbling stream. It was a holy spot well watered by the gods and distinguished by a profusion of foliage.

I consecrated my altar with fires of cedar and acacia branches, and renewed it each month with the wise blood of my moon change, marking the holy days with pungent copal and frankincense. Sleeping beside my altar with the flocks I loved listening to the babbling stream. My flocks liked it too. Many a time a pregnant ewe would wander there to give birth. And so the power of my shrine grew, as I also grew in the strength of the old ways.

My solitude was my solace beside the altar or roaming the hillsides with my flocks. It opened me to the wisdom of nature and I taught myself about the stars. At home it was another matter. There my solitude bored into my soul. Leah and I grew more estranged as time went by. How could it be otherwise? Her entire world revolved around father's influence and power. She waited upon him and his fiendish Brothers day and night, receiving many a fine token for her solicitude and favors.

My sister was such a disappointment to me. Any rapport we'd once had was obscured by her endless competition for mother's place. Leah seemed to have lost all connection to the Goddess, and with it went any self-direction she once possessed. She consulted father about everything now, hanging on his every word. She was indoors with him so much the color left her cheeks. Everyday she seemed to grow more sour and matronly in appearance. Was the Goddess punishing her for her neglect?

Leah continued in her intimacies with father, which sickened me. But what was I to do? One day as I was gathering up my things on my way out the door, I encountered her leaving father's room.

Pleased with herself, she announced to me smugly, "Father called me in to him again last night."

"Do you really think sleeping with father is something to be proud of ?" I burst out, unable to contain myself. "What are you doing, trying to take mother's place?"

"You're only jealous father hasn't chosen you!" said Leah shrugging her shoulders contemptuously.

My mouth dropped wide open in disbelief. This was my sister, my own flesh and blood. I continued in desperation trying to save her. "I'm not jealous, Leah! He's an old man and your father! It's Taboo to share your body with your own father. What would people think of you if they knew?"

Looking into the mirror, she replied testily, "Why should I be concerned about antiquated Taboos, or what anyone thinks? Father's a distinguished Moon priest! He and I have something special. We're not bound by the same conventions as everyone else. We're above the law! Father told me so. You're just jealous!"

I breathed in deeply, trying not to get baited. I wanted to help Leah, and I didn't want this to turn into just another venomous spat. "Please, Leah! Let's not fight! You're my sister. I'm only trying to help you see what you're doing to yourself."

"There you go again preaching to me! You're always so perfect! So good! So pure! You say you care about me! I don't believe a word of it! You just want to spoil things for me. You want me to feel bad about the only thing that makes me feel special. Oh, it's easy for you. You're beautiful! You were always the center of attention in the Women's Circle when mother was alive. Now I'm the one who's chosen! And I won't let you spoil it! So go off with your stinky old sheep! I hope you never return!"

"Father has banned the Goddess, Leah, but must we lose the code of Sisterhood as well?" I asked pleading with her.

Father ventured into the room just then. "What's this talk of the Goddess, Rachel? I warned you to never bring Her up!"

Turning toward Leah he continued, "What are you two arguing about now? Must there always be a problem between you two?"

Leah looked at father, saying indignantly, "Don't blame me, father! It's Rachel's fault! She started it. She's always the one who starts it. This time she was scolding me for being with you last night."

Father's eyes narrowed in on me. Then he turned on me with a vengeance. "Oh!! You object to that, do you? I'm merely exercising my rights as a moon priest! Besides, every daughter's in her father's bed! How do you think you got here? But I don't owe you any explanation for my behavior! Who do you think you are objecting to my actions? Get me the switch, Leah! Hurry! I'll teach Rachel to mind her own affairs. I can't wait to instruct her tender flesh."

Leah returned with a thorny sapling, and a huge smile on her face. The reward for her trouble was to watch as I was beaten. This wasn't the first time father had taken the switch to me. I'd had to endure many a brutal thrashing since mother's death. I'd get through this one, as well. It wasn't the prospect of the whipping which frightened me. It was the look in Leah's eyes. There was no Sisterhood in them. I was her rival nothing more. My being punished was a victory for her.

What happened to our family? What had become of women's Sisterhood in the Goddess? But I couldn't think about these things now. I had to pray father wouldn't beat me so hard I couldn't go off with the flocks. I would need to get away. As father positioned me and took up the switch, I began planning my day. I'd go to my shrine in the foothills. The Goddess's presence was most powerful there. I'd bathe my wounds in the stream. Water always soothed me.

The rod stung. The thorns tore my flesh, but I didn't cry. I didn't want them to see how much it hurt. I couldn't straighten up when the thrashing was over. But that wasn't my deepest injury. There was a more intolerable pain than father's switch. My cuts went deep. I was bruised all over, but my body would heal. Only how would I recover from the look of hatred in Leah's eyes, and the obvious pleasure she'd received from seeing me in pain?

PART TWO

The Courtship

4

THE GIFT FROM HEAVEN

I WAS RESTLESS AND COULDN'T SLEEP, CAUGHT UP IN THE QUICKENING bursts of spring. Even with the longer daylight hours there was not enough time to finish all my chores. So I was up before dawn heading out to the far pastures to gather my herd. I was glad to trade the wide open spaces for the confines of my tent. A pregnant stillness bathed the landscape as I set off in the darkness. The only sounds were the stirrings of my heart, as my eyes adjusted catlike to the moonlight. Leah was afraid of the dark, but I wasn't afraid alone out in the darkness. I felt protected beneath the stars. The starry vault of heaven was a soothing blanket for my soul. The full moon and Athtar, the morning star, were my unfailing lamps. The zodiacal circle of animals were the friends that guided me.

How I loved this fertile land, and the Earth Mother Ninhursag, Lady of the Foothills! This was Goddess country. She Who Watches breathed through every tree. I knew every facet of this rolling terrain. Every rock was precious and alive to me. The wind blew warm and dry out of the south announcing the end of winter. The earth was moist and fragrant ready for the surging growth of spring. This was my season, the verdant time of my solar return. My youthful vigor rose and soared along with the aromatic sap in the trees and the cooing of the doves mating in the branches. Even in the darkness I could feel the tides of nature rising to the first full moon of spring.

I travelled at a brisk pace anxious to meet my flocks. Only the first rays of dawn peeking up over the horizon stopped me in my tracks. I gazed in awe from atop a high hillock. As the light increased I could see my flocks out in the distance by the river. Nathan, our foreman, was with them, and so was Zack, my trusty sheep dog. I always looked forward to being with the flock. But today there was something strange and power-ful in the air. The hair on my arms and legs stood upright up like a cat's. Goosebumps were rising on my skin as they did just before a lightning storm. Powerful currents were weaving themselves around me. Skies were clear. The wind was calm. But something was going to happen. I could feel it in my bones, as I approached the herd.

A ball of fire was hurling silently across the heavens coming in this direction. It splashed down in the Balikh just beyond my slumbering herd. What a miraculous sight! Never had I witnessed anything like it before. Nathan was still asleep, but Zack and my flocks took note rousing with a start. I ran towards the Balikh, looking for any trace of the amazing fireball.

The great Balikh, a tributary of the vast Euphrates River, was a mani-festation of Ba'al, Lord of this land, as was the rain and all the moving water on the surface of the Earth. Water was revered in these parts, but the Balikh was especially dear to me. Mother had often brought me here to listen to the great Speaker of the River when she came to bless the waters in spring. If only mother could have been here to see this miracle. How she would have gloried in the Balikh being favored with a flaming fireball from heaven. Mother would have known the meaning of such a portent. I could only guess. Had I witnessed a sacred mating between Heaven and Earth? I fell to my knees putting my forehead to the ground in thanksgiving for having witnessed this blessed event.

Then unable to contain myself a moment longer, I ran to immerse myself in the consecrated water. My laughter travelled along with me, ringing out over the undulating pasture land high above our village. It filled me with glee to realize I had father to thank for witnessing this incredible event. Afterall, it was he who insisted I be out tending the flocks before dawn. If he only knew what I had chanced to see.

It always pleased me to see my flocks come bounding forth, sheep dogs nipping at their heels, when they caught sight of me. But today they were bubbling over with excitement. They too had witnessed this rare event and their excitement sped them across the pasture toward me. When we met up I surrendered happily to their nuzzling advances. I took a moment to pet Zack. Then I signalled the dogs and was off again for the river, herd following behind.

As soon as Nathan left I took off my clothes and ventured out into the surging river with my water skin. The water was cold and took my breath away. Undaunted I waded out into the fast moving current, headed for my favorite bathing spot. Zack and a few of the more daring sheep joined me in the river. The rest remained on the banks watching with curiosity. By the time I reached my favorite area between the boulders, I'd grown accustomed to the water. I sank down to immerse myself and took a drink.

The water was steeped in power. A veil lifted from my eyes and all my senses were enlivened. I could see and feel beneath the surface of things with extraordinary depth and clarity. Was She Who Watches overshadowing me? I began breathing slowly and evenly putting myself in the Goddess's hands. The sun was gaining strength. A deep peace came over me, as it spread its light out glistening like flickering stars upon the water. The sadness I'd been carrying since mother's death began to lift. I settled back content until I heard a low gurgling sound. It started out faintly, then grew into an insistent roar. The Speaker of the River had awakened. It spoke in its mysterious babbling tongue. FIRE, AIR, WATER AND EARTH HAVE ALL MET HERE UNDER HEAVEN'S LOVING SMILE. YOU WERE PRIVILEGED TO WITNESS THIS MIRACULOUS EVENT SO YOU COULD BE INSPIRED TO MEET YOUR DESTINY. NOW QUICK! SEARCH THE RIVERBED FOR THE GODDESS'S PRIZE! SHE SENT IT DOWN FOR YOU."

A gift from on high for me? What should I look for? Not having a clue, I sat up bewildered for a moment. Then I took another drink, filled my water skin, and stood up. The spirit of the river had spoken. There was no time to waste. I perused the lengthy riverbed and started walking toward the bend in the river where I spied a curious steaming cloud. As I drew near a shape formulated in the mist. An image of Ninhursag appeared in the mysterious vapor. Her hair fell gracefully to Her shoulders above Her voluptuous breasts. She was holding a sheaf of wheat in one hand, as I'd often seen Her pictured. Beneath Her image was a curious whirlpool in the water.

I fell to my knees in wonder. The river surged over me, removing my hesitation. This had to be the place the fireball came down. The water was curiously warm and churning. I mustered my courage and put my hand into the whirling vortex. My reward was a mysterious cone shaped object. It's surface was marked with tiny holes that resembled the molten rocks the Earth Mother belched out of Her mountain craters when She was angry. Only this material was heavier than lava rock, and possessed an unusual gripping potency. I was captivated by the intriguing stone.

The rock was strange, but somehow familiar. Finally it came to me. I had seen a rock like this before. It was on my first trip to the Eye Temple when I had come of age. There was so much I'd been exposed to on that first visit, I'd been unable to take it all in. But the longer I thought about it, the surer I was. There had been a rock like the one in my hand in the Holy of Holies, the underground crypt beneath the Temple. It was also cone shaped, only much larger.

The image of the Goddess vanished in the mist. I took another drink from the river. Contemplating the stone from heaven my vision opened. The Eye Temple appeared before me in the chatoyant surface of the river. I could see everything that had happened on my first visit to the temple.

Mother was walking toward me carrying the red robe of initiation into the Blood Mysteries. "Today's a special day for you, my darling! Today you are a woman! Come! We leave for the Eye Temple where you will be instructed in the ancient ways. Wear your best white robe! And bring the linen with your first blood with you. You must offer it to the Goddess and hang it on Her holy tree."

It was curious being a spectator to my own story. I watched myself as if in a dream. Only this was no dream. This had actually happened. Mother and I were inside the great mud brick wall of the Eye temple. Its blue enamel tiles sparkled in the sunlight, as she escorted me to the Eye pool. The Goddess's oracular fish swam playfully about as mother instructed me in the temple rites of purification. Then she took me to the Ashera grove, where I tied the linen with my first blood on the Goddess's Tree of Life and pledged to do my part to maintain the circle of life.

The sun was going down as mother led me to the temple's moon lodge with its sacred fire, which burned with a blue flame. Its curious glow danced upon the walls of the ancient hut, revealing a multitude of mysterious symbols. I looked at the incredible place where I had been sequestered. The hut was strangely warm and comforting, like being inside a womb. Before mother left she instructed me in the maintenance of the holy fire, and explained the dread consequences of its going out. I was to stay there in ritual seclusion for two nights. If I was lucky the Goddess would send me a dream.

Mother's face was apprehensive as she left me at the door. My ears suddenly opened, and I could hear her say, "You've never been on your own before Rachel, but never fear. You won't be lonely. In the light of the Goddess's fire you'll be united with all the generations of women who came before you. The Eye of Heaven is powerful here. She Who Watches will send you an initiation dream."

"I'll be back in two days to take you to the Holy of Holies beneath the Temple. There you'll meet the En Priestess and consecrate your wise blood on the altar. After that you can don your new red robe, and join the circle of women in the spring. You've come of age, my darling. "

The scene ended abruptly. I was grieved for it to be over. It was wonderful seeing mother again, and being back in the comforting womb of the Goddess. I clutched the rock from heaven and breathed deeply, hoping to recapture the scene, but it was to no avail. I took another drink of water and continued looking until the vision was restored. Mother was escorting me down an ancient spiral stairway hewn from rock to a cave carved deep in the belly of Mother Earth. In its center was a great stone altar. On the altar was a large coneshaped baetyl rock, beside it was a huge lioness with golden fur and emerald eyes. I remembered how my heart had raced at the sight of her. Though she started purring loudly when I walked in.

I saw myself kneeling before the wondrous baetyl stone too awestruck to look up. Mother nodded at the great cat, then patted me on the head and left. The En Priestess appeared. The lioness rose and approached her for a caress, rubbing against her like an affectionate house cat. After the En Priestess scratched her head she knelt before the altar forehead to the ground. Then she came and stood before me. When she gazed in my eyes, I knew she could see into the depths of my heart.

"Welcome to the House of Life, Rachel! Has the Goddess blessed you with a dream?"

Still kneeling, I responded, "Yes, oh Wise One! I dreamt of a huge ziggurat, so high, it seemed to touch the sky. Magnificent beings of light were climbing up and down it. Some went alone, others held hands and climbed together. A radiant being, his face shining like the sun, waited for me at the base of the ziggurat holding out his hand. We were about to ascend together, when a cow and a ewe entered walking in solemn procession."

The En Priestess listened intently, her eyes never leaving me.

"The ewe was supposed to walk at the head of the procession, which had previously been led by the cow. But the cow got in front of the ewe, and took the procession down the wrong path. A voice in the dream said, 'Only the blood of the ewe can atone for this.'"

The En Priestess's expression was grave, as she went to the altar to consult the Stone that Whispers. When she returned she commanded me to remove my robe. "Wet your right hand with the wise blood of your moon change, Rachel. Then paint with it on the altar before the Stone that Whispers drawing any symbol that you choose."

I stood naked before the En Priestess and the Goddess, stepping up to the ancient rock altar covered with symbols from the countless women who had stood there before me. I closed my eyes and allowed my hand to be guided.

After I finished drawing the mark of an X, the En Priestess came and stood beside me. Looking down at the symbol I had drawn, she said, "You drew the cross of the virgin, Rachel. It's the mark of the Naditu Sisterhood. Did your mother discuss that symbol with you?'

I shook my head no, saying, "It was in my dream the second night, oh Wise One."

The En Priestess looked me in the eyes for a long moment, then said, "You show great promise, Rachel, but there is much you must overcome."

After ushering me away from the altar, her voice rang out. "Today you are a woman, and come before the Eye Goddess, your true mother. Welcome to the circle of all women!"

"Your moon blood marks you as a daughter of the Goddess, Rachel, and attunes you to the cycles of heaven. Be proud of your wise blood which assures the continuance of life on Earth! When the moon goes into hiding, women bleed and nature is renewed. When the moon is a proud circle in the sky shining forth the rays of the sun, a woman's moon egg is ripe for fertilizing. This great law of heaven shall prevail so long as women remember they are Daughters of the Goddess, and live in harmony with the rhythms of Heaven and Earth. The pineal gland at the back of the neck is sensitive to the light of the moon and causes women to bleed at the same time. This shall be so, as long as women do not replace the light of heaven with the artificial light of man."

"There is great power in women's blood, Rachel. It can be life giving or life destroying. Honor your bleeding time! She Who Watches draws close to us then and whispers words of wisdom in our ears. Always take time apart then so the Goddess may speak to you."

The En Priestess handed me my new red robe, saying, "The power of the womb is sacred, Rachel! Be proud to be a woman!"

When I stood before the En Priestess in the red robe of womanhood, she continued, "Those were important dreams, Rachel. Do not forget them! You have been chosen by the Gods for a special purpose. You are named after the Ewe Goddess. Your name means the ewe and she who is to move forward, or be overshadowed. Beware of your sister! The name Leah means wild cow. Stay true to the Goddess, and all shall be well. You will be overshadowed by She Who Watches and not your sister's competition and envy."

"As one of the ancient Sumerian line you have your own personal Gods. I have consulted the Stone that Whispers and received their names. Your guardians will intercede for you before the Assembly of All the Gods. They are the Eye Goddess Ninhursag, and Enki the God of Wisdom. Together they fashioned humankind. Your totem animals are the dove, and of course, the ewe."

My mouth dropped open with surprise, and I stammered forth. "But . . . but . . . ! Don't I have father's god, Nanna/Sin?"

The En Priestess looked me sharply in the eye, "Never question the Will of the Heaven, Rachel! Sin is the son of Enlil greatest of all the

Anunnaki from Nibiru. But Sin has fallen from the grace of heaven and been exiled. Now he resides in the abyss, the deep underground caverns beneath the earth, with the ancient serpent race. Enki and Ninhursag are your protectors. You will need them and all their star wisdom to stand against the Brotherhood of the Black Hand. They are Sin's tool. More shall be revealed to you in time. Now step forward and I will initiate you with the blood of a sheep and the feathers of a white dove."

As I stepped forward the vision faded. I tried to get it back, but it was to no avail. I looked down at the wondrous rock in my hand, shaped like the cone shaped baetyl rock in the Goddess's Holy of Holies. I was saying a prayer of thanks for the incredible gift when Zack paddled over reminding me I had work to do.

As I stood up the stone began to whisper. GO TO TOWN TODAY, RACHEL! BE SURE TO TAKE YOUR FLOCKS AND WATER THEM AT THE WELL. A SURPRISE AWAITS YOU THERE.

Only the En Priestess could approach the Stone that Whispers. Only she could hear the words of She Who Watches and communicate them to the people. Was She Who Watches speaking to me through this wondrous stone? Was this the day? I would take no chances. It was a good two hour walk to town with my flock. But I would visit the well today. I could be there by noon if I washed my hair quickly, and dressed. The stone from heaven would give me strength to meet my fate.

The flock was so stirred up by the morning's events, I'd need all our sheep dogs and my sturdy crook to get them to the well. But they had to be there. They were in my vision. Besides, watering them there was a good excuse in case father heard of my visit from one of his cronies.

The sun was high in the sky when I reached town with my rambunctious herd. My skin was glowing from my morning bath, and my hair shining in the sunlight. For the first time since mother's death my spirits soared. I needed to fortify myself, however. There was no telling how the townspeople would greet me. I took another drink of the miraculous water. Then I lined up my feisty flock to usher them down the narrow streets.

All was quiet. Only a few little children crossed my path. They were full of fun and smiled as I passed by. I breathed a sigh of relief. I had almost forgotten what it was like to be smiled at. These children were too young to be infected with the townspeople's dread of spiritual contagion from the sight of me or my family. After three years I was still unnerved, when old friends and neighbors ran and barred their doors against me, as if I were a demon.

The first hurdle was getting through town. I had to reach the well before noonday. The shepherds always congregated there in the late afternoon and I wanted to avoid them. I couldn't bear their shunning, the boisterous jokes, or their endless sneers behind my back.

After their last trip to market father's concubines reported the water of the well had receded further down this year. The rainy season, what little there was of it, had just ended. And already there was little water in the well. This was the third year the water was down. The situation was so grave the townspeople had placed an enormous stone upon the well, their first step in rationing.

The water being down again this year posed a serious threat to us all. From reports I'd heard the wise women could no longer see into the well. They claimed the drought and the water's silence were tokens of the Goddess's outrage. Rumors blamed the condition of the water on father's behavior at mother's funeral, and the bitter strife which had ensued between the Naditu Sisterhood and the Black Hand.

Clearly something had to be done. It was only the beginning of spring and the water was low. What would it be like in the scorching heat of summer? I'd searched everywhere for the terafim, and failed to locate them. I had to return them to the Ashera grove for safekeeping. Only their return could restore balance to our region.

I held the rock from heaven walking down the narrow streets of town. It seemed to possess extraordinary powers. Had it been given to me for a special purpose? I'd bless the well with it and pour in some of the miraculous water from the Balikh. Maybe that would help, I had to try.

I was still pondering these matters when I reached the well with my flock. All was peaceful. I was the first to arrive. Still my heart was sad. Today was the first day of spring and it appeared the Women's Circle would not be meeting. There wasn't a single tub in sight, and no flowers draped the ancient well. A few people were milling around in the shade of the old oak tree nearby. They were from the Black Hand. I could recognize them even in the shadows with their telltale gloves. What were they up to? Were they here to make sure the women's rites not take place?

The townspeople grimaced at the sight of me. The women clutched their breasts to counteract their dread fear of contagion. Jeers and whispers started up among the men. Beads of sweat broke out on my forehead as the women began their thrilling cries intended to drive demons away. I struggled to hold back my tears. What had I done to become everyone's dread malefactor? The townspeople shunned me because I was father's daughter. They saw me as his accomplice at the Eye temple. While father claimed he was innocent and I the cause of his misfortunes. It was so long since anyone took my side, I'd become confused. They couldn't all be wrong! Perhaps I was the evil culprit? Shame crept up my back. Nausea gripped my insides.

The blackest sheep in the fold began bleating miserably. It was Jesse, my favorite ewe. We'd bonded when I saw her through a difficult lambing the previous year. Animals had heart. Was she sympathizing with my misery? Hearing her piteous cries I couldn't help but remember the yearly Scapegoat Ritual of Atonement. The one in which the townspeople gathered to put their darkest sins upon an innocent lamb or goat. Then drove the poor frenzied creature out of town to rid themselves of their own wickedness.

The jeers of the townspeople were battering my spirit. I wanted to run away like the poor scapegoated beast in the ritual. I wanted to hide in the mountains far away from everyone. But there was no escape. I couldn't run away. My flocks would not allow it. They gathered around me in a protective circle making it impossible to move. Calmer now, Jesse stood beside me nuzzling me affectionately. The sweet expression on her face touched me, like that of the children on my way here.

Kindness still existed, if only I had the courage and will to seek it. The morning's events came flooding back on me, too real and powerful to forget. I groped in my pocket for the potent rock from heaven. Just clasping hold of it my shame began to lose its choking grip. I closed my eyes, comforting myself with the fact that I'd been graced to find this wondrous stone. She Who Watches had forgiven me. Perhaps the townspeople would one day as well.

I was here to meet my destiny and had to stand my ground. I chose a spot for my herd and planted my feet. I had a right to exist. The sun came out from behind a cloud just then hitting me in the eyes, melting my shame away. I gave thanks to the Sun God, Shamash, Lord of Justice. Thanks to him, I didn't have to see the anger and cruelty in the people's eyes.

THE GIFT FROM HEAVEN

My herd received no such solace from the glaring sun. Soon they grew agitated. Even with the miraculous rock in hand, I dared not move them to the shade of the old oak. I was considered unclean. There were stringent codes of Taboo that had to be observed. Copious laws outlined correct behavior for the treatment of tabooed parties. I might chafe under the burden of those strictures, but thanks to them no one would dare speak to me directly.

The women started backing away from me in unison. I couldn't see their faces in the intense sunlight, but I knew their eyes never left me. I could feel their burning stares, and watch as their hands clutched for the safety of their breasts. The home of the heart and source of mother's milk, women's breasts had strong enough power to counteract my dreaded state. I didn't look at the women too closely. Their united power was awesome. Even with the sun blocking their stares, I could still feel the intensity of their gaze.

The men remained stalwart and unmoved. Huddled together in the shade of the tree they watched me intently, murmuring between themselves. I drew my flock back cautiously. Were they organizing something? With all the anxiety from the well water being low, there was no telling what they might do.

Seconds seemed like hours. I was alone with five good sized men, not counting the trio from the Brotherhood. My heart was beating with dark foreboding. Three of the largest men started coming in my direction. My legs began to tremble. I closed my eyes and began praying for courage, touching my breast with the potent rock from heaven. I knew what these men were capable of in their so called righteousness. I'd already had more than my fair share of father's self-righteous beatings.

When I opened my eyes, I could see the men had no intention of coming after me. They'd made directly for the well, and were straining to lift the mighty stone to seal it off from me. From the frantic quality of their gestures it was obvious they were too frightened to even look at me at this close range. When they finished, they exchanged self-satisfied looks and retreated to the shade.

I was safe for now. My water skin was full of miraculous water from the Balikh, and my flocks well watered from this morning's adventure. But slowly the awful truth, the full precariousness of the situation hit me. I didn't need their water today. But what would we do in the heat of summer when there was no snow from the mountains to feed the Balikh? And what would the townspeople be driven to do if the well ran dry? Clearly something had to be done. I had to bless the well and pour in the miraculous water from the Balikh.

I was mulling this over in my mind when I saw him coming up over the crest of the hill. I could hardly believe my eyes, but it was no mistake. My cousin might have been a stranger to me, but in the depths of my soul I knew him. I recognized the determination of his step and the rhythmic cadence of his walk. I had replayed the vision of our meeting over and over again in my mind until I knew every detail. Jacob was here. He'd come when I needed him most. It was as though I'd conjured him up with my prayers.

Jacob was on foot. He appeared tired and dusty from the road, but there was something special about this man. The distance between us gave me time to take him in with my inner eye. He bore the mark of a man set apart. Beneath the youthful buoyancy of his step was a strong presence, and an air of authority which belied his years. His charisma shone even through the dust of the road. This was a consecrated priest. The blessing of his God was all about him, and powerful energies emanated from deep within his being.

When he arrived at the well he came directly over to me. Taking in my situation he bowed gallantly. "Salom, alecheim, beautiful angel of this well! Allow me to remove the stone so you and your flocks may drink."

His voice had the ring of magical power. His eyes were those of a seer. They were dark and penetrating and lingered on me, drinking in my every feature. Unlike other men, he looked me in the eyes the entire time he spoke. My heart began to flutter. When our eyes met, I could walk right into his very soul. He was unafraid and welcomed me. He too had the gift of vision. My heart started pounding so loudly I could barely hear him speak. But there was no cause for words. Jacob had read my need completely, and was already struggling against the mighty stone.

Watching him strain against the ponderous weight, I insisted, "Please kind stranger! You're hot and weary from the road. Stop and have a drink from my water skin. Rest against this pillar and gather your strength."

Only with reluctance did Jacob stop straining to the task. "Very well, fair maiden! I haven't had a drink all day." he said smiling at me with the open warmth of a child, as he rested against the pillar of the Goddess to receive my waterbag.

Joy exploded inside me. Time stood still. We were alone together in a timeless realm where perfect understanding flowed between us. I could see he felt as I did. His eyes were beaming and lingered lovingly upon me, drinking me in along with the enchanted water.

His smile was so contagious it seemed to illuminate the atmosphere around us. The air between us suddenly began to sparkle. Though it was broad daylight I could feel the presence of the stars above. My heart expanded along with the uncontrollable smile on my face. I felt reborn basking in the warmth of his smile. It was hard to believe I'd ever been unhappy. Father, the Brotherhood, the men at the well, Leah, all the suffering in my life receded.

After he had drank his fill, Jacob bounded up with renewed determination. I watched captivated as he poured the miraculous water around the edge of the stone where it met the lip of the well. Returning the water skin to me, he said, "Thank you, kind angel! Never before have I felt so refreshed! Allow me to return your gift by opening this well so your flocks may drink."

Then he wedged himself against the pillar of the Goddess, and with the combined strength of his arms and legs pushed the mighty stone from the well. It was an incredible feat. It had just taken three strong men straining with all their might to do what Jacob seemed to do so effortlessly. I smiled and reached for the wooden bucket to gather water for my flock. But Jacob would not allow me even this small task. He took the bucket from me and filled the trough for my sheep to drink, his every movement deft and sure.

Only as he finished did I recall the true reason I wanted the well opened. With the wondrous stone in hand I leaned over the edge of the well, and poured in a some of the miraculous water from the Balikh, praying.

"GREAT MOTHER NINHURSAG, SHE WHO WATCHES, PLEASE HEAR MY HUMBLE PRAYER! DO NOT FORSAKE US, YOUR CHILDREN HERE BELOW. HOLD US IN YOUR GRACE AND SPEAK TO US ONCE MORE. REMEMBER THE GOOD PEOPLE OF HARAN. BRING LOVE INTO THEIR HEARTS AND MINDS THAT THEY MAY LIVE IN YOUR HOLY TRUTH. FORGIVE THEM

AS YOU HAVE FORGIVEN ME THIS DAY. POUR FORTH YOUR MERCY AND ALLOW THE PRECIOUS LIVING WATER TO RISE AGAIN."

When I looked up Jacob was beside me intent upon my every movement. When our eyes met my spirit soared.

Jacob was the first to speak. "What heavenly oasis is this I have been blessed to come to? Surely you are its angel!"

My cheeks colored as I replied, "Welcome to Haran, kind stranger."

Our hearts were already twinned. His joy was palpable to me. His feelings communicated themselves to me without the use of words.

I looked at my flocks drinking from the trough, and continued with gratitude, "Such helpfulness from a stranger, and such strength! Who are you that I must thank for this amazing feat?"

Jacob responded with a flourish, bowing low. "I am Jacob, son of Isaac from Beersheba. Far have I travelled to arrive here this day. Pray tell, do you know Laban, son of Nahor? He is my uncle. I'm on my way to visit him."

For the first time in my life I was pleased to claim my relationship to father. My heart beating in my throat, I replied, "Laban is my father. I'm his younger daughter, Rachel."

"You ARE my angel!" said Jacob with a starstruck look in his eyes. "Is this a dream, or is this real? "

Not waiting for my reply, he took me in his arms and kissed me fervently.

This was my first kiss. I had waited long for it. Jacob was here. He had finally come. His warm embrace, the honeyed sweetness of his words all made the wait worthwhile. I surrendered to the rapture of his presence, glorying in his strong arms that enveloped me. We were one in love and desire. My mouth hungered after his. Waves of bliss rippled through me taking my breath away. The blessing of the Goddess was shining down on us.

Even after our embrace Jacob would still not let go of me. He gazed searchingly in my eyes, as if trying to make sure that I was real. At this close range I could feel the presence of his God. I breathed in deeply taking in the powerful surge and looked up to heaven, sure the Gods were watching. A snow white dove flew in from the east, hovering above us floating on the breeze.

THE GIFT FROM HEAVEN

The Eye of Heaven was upon us. I let out a joyous squeal of delight. It was answered by the cooing of the dove as it alighted on the Goddess's pillar. My heart softened, then warmed and opened like a flower. Jacob was here. My vision had been confirmed. I had met my match. A new strength and balance took hold of me. I felt calm and steady, confident in the Goddess's truth.

Jacob spun me round, tears of joy in his eyes, to view the heavenly bird. As we turned the waters of the well rose miraculously spilling over the rim. The well was speaking again. Its water reflected our visage united in a golden glow against the backdrop of the starry heavens. The bonds of the Higher Marriage were being forged. The Gods were pleased!

The first shepherds had begun arriving from the east just in time for this miraculous event. Their arrival brought me back to reality. I dropped Jacob's hand and began gathering my flock. I didn't want to be here when the shepherds arrived. And already the sound of the water overflowing the well was attracting the men in the shade of the oak. They started moving toward us cautiously.

I turned in haste, making my excuses to Jacob. His eyes lingered lovingly upon me, endearing him to me further.

"Please forgive me, cousin. But I must run on ahead with word of your arrival. Father will want to prepare for your visit. Take your time. I'll take the shortcut with my flocks to get home quickly. Follow the old road out of town until you're in the high country. Take the first left at the fork and follow the sheep path up over the northernmost hill. Our farm is nestled at the far end of the valley. I'll wait for you there. Walk in peace until I see you again."

The men were already crowding round Jacob as I gathered up my flock. I could hear their furtive whispers. "Who is this stranger that causes the waters to rise? . . . Who is it that has wrought such a miracle? . . . Could he be the Shepherd of the People we have all been praying for? . . . A man of God as in the days of old . . . an answer for our troubled times."

Heading out I could see the Brotherhood crowding around Jacob. They confronted him haughtily. "Who are you stranger? What magic have you that causes the waters to rise? And by what right do you take such liberties with a daughter of Laban?"

5

The Arrival

I FLEW HOME OVER THE VERDANT HILLSIDES WITH MY FLOCK, NEVER stopping once until we reached the entrance to our farm. Leaning against the familiar gatepost to catch my breath, I looked around me with new eyes. For the first time since mother's funeral I didn't stop to mourn the loss of the ancient oak, or mother's herb garden. A smile fluttered across my lips, like one of the gentle spring breezes as my sheep gathered round. Such a day of wonder and rapid changes! It possessed all the hallmarks of the first day of spring.

There was no time to take my flock to pasture. So I brought them into the yard. Given the exuberance of their mood it took my sturdy crook and fullest concentration to get them through the narrow gate. Even then their passage seemed interminable. Coming through the gate with the last of the flock I noticed Abdul Shahor's donkey hitched to the post in the front yard. Beside Shahor's donkey was another miserable looking group of children he'd rounded up for the slave market. Tied like beasts, the poor children waited crowded in a narrow patch of shade.

They looked tired, undernourished, and pushed to the limits of their endurance.

Since mother's funeral only the Black Hand, or the utter dregs of society such as Shahor, ventured through our gate. Only the most corrupt merchants of Babylon, and those whose greed was stronger than their fear of the Gods, dared break the taboo and consult with father. I couldn't fathom why father would stoop so low. Mother would never have allowed such people to enter our house, never mind aiding them in their nefarious deeds.

I had once gotten up the courage to confront father. I felt there was no choice. I had to live in the truth of She Who Watches and not be an unwitting party to his nefarious dealings. Of course, I was thrashed for speaking up. But what appalled me most was finding out what father actually did with these children. He wasn't selling them into slavery. He was purchasing them for the Brotherhood to sacrifice on the Ehulhul temple's altar in hopes of luring back the evil Sin.

I'll never forget the demonic gleam in his eyes when he asked, "Do you want to know what I do with those filthy little brats? I perform a noble service for society. I take those useless eaters and give their lives a noble turn by sacrificing them to Sin."

The depravity in his eyes told me he was possessed by the Evil One. Then I could understand why he thought he was above the law, and why he drew such despicable people to him. Father was a stranger to truth. As far as he was concerned each person had their own truth, and the end always justified the means. He took no responsibility for his own behavior, and blamed everything on me. It was my fault that no one but the most loathsome traders consulted him. My fault for taking the terafim, and forcing him to steal them back.

Father was so clever with words. I never knew what to say when he got into his convoluted diatribes. He could be so cold blooded and calculating, he seemed to possess the wiles of a serpent. His agile tongue and unflinching stare could chill my blood and lock me in. Over and over again he'd come back to the same point, my stealing the terafim, until I went limp and couldn't think. All I could do was flee to escape his stifling gaze. After one of these discussions I'd be confused for days, not knowing what to believe. Maybe it was all my fault? Leah thought so too. It would take me days to find my own ground again.

I was still brooding over these matters when I arrived at the door. I knocked and waited, but alas there was no answer. Was father already working in his study? I pushed open the heavy wooden door. The front room was empty. My heart sank. There'd be hell to pay for interrupting father at his work, but I had no choice. I walked up to the door of what had once been mother's sanctuary, and knocked loudly. There was no answer. With no time to lose, I opened the door.

A shaft of sunlight flooded in behind me, a sword of light breaking up the foul specter in the center of the room. My skin crawled. The sickening odor of the flowers of the dreamers was heavy in the air. I could hardly see father and Shahor through the cloud of incense and poppy smoke. Once the ghastly specter dispersed, Shamash's light was everywhere illuminating the room and causing the men to wince.

Bowing low I begged forgiveness. "Please excuse me for interrupting, father. But I have important news that cannot wait."

The silence which followed was heavy as the dead. Father was seated beside his skull oracle wearing his black gloves. His pet snake was curled up in his lap. It raised its head at the sight of me, and poised itself to strike. I froze, hardly daring to breath. My nostrils burned from the cloying odor of the poppies and the pungent dragon's blood incense father always used to seal his deals. Through the smoke I could see the smouldering eyes of father's oracle skull. They were mesmerizing like those of the cobra on father's lap and seemed to pull me in.

From the quality of father's inward gaze I knew he'd been divining and was still in trance. I wanted to turn and go, but time was running out. My eyes fixed on father's snake, I grasped the stone inside my pocket to help me stand my ground.

A cough came from the corner of the room. Through the billowing smoke, I could see it was Leah rubbing her eyes in response to the sunlight streaming in behind me. If Leah was still there with the coffee urn, Shahor's consultation was far from over. I glanced down at the cups on the table beside the men. It appeared she had just finished serving the first cup. I sighed heavily not knowing what to do. Father's sessions often entailed elaborate divinations, sometimes even sacrifices. They could go on for hours with course upon course of coffee being drunk.

I looked back again at father. Slowly he began to move. As he regained awareness, the cobra slithered from his lap retreating to the far corner of the room. I began again, bowing low. "Please excuse me father! Forgive my interruption! I would never have disturbed you, but I have important news."

Father's face was a sickening white, like the moon on a frigid winter night. But as soon as he recognized me it reddened in agitation, and he began drumming his fingers on the table. Slowly and with unmasked loathing, "How many times have I told you never to disturb me at my work? Didn't your mother, or any of those foolish women, ever teach you the seriousness of breaking into someone's trance? I should set my skull upon you for such a grave infraction!"

Trembling and bowing low as father liked to see me do, I replied, "Please accept my apology, father! I meant no harm! But my news cannot wait."

Father broke in, his face marked with grim impatience. "Nothing's important enough to warrant interrupting my work! And didn't I tell you not to come home until all the sheep were shorn! Wait outside until I'm finished! I'll be out with the strap!"

Abdul Shahor's sly reptilian face, expressionless up until then, contorted into a wide grin at mention of the strap. The mere thought made his right hand twitch in jerky whiplike movements.

I was revolted and glad to shut the door behind me. It was a relief to be out of that heinous room. Out in the fresh air and sunlight I had to wonder how Leah could stay cooped up in that dreadful room with the two of them? And, how could she serve that repulsive Shahor?

Still trying to compose myself, I looked over at the unfortunate children. They were frail and sickly. Several were moaning as they tried to sleep. They looked as if they hadn't tasted food in days. I went quickly to the fire hut, hoping to find something for them to eat before Shahor showed up. I had just finished handing out a loaf of bread and some goat cheese, when Leah appeared with the coffee urn. Seeing what I was up to, she hurried across the yard.

"Why do you bother with these filthy wretches? They're full of lice and bugs! Don't you have any sense? Leave them alone, or I'll tell father." she remarked testily.

"You're a fine one to talk!" I replied in annoyance. "All I'm doing is trying to help these poor innocent children. While you've been inside fraternizing with demons, and waiting on that repulsive Shahor. I'd rather serve a mangy dog than Shahor."

"There you go again acting so superior! You think you're better than everyone else. You always have something so smart to say until father mentions the strap. Well, things have changed around here thanks to you! Or haven't you noticed? You may not like Shahor, but he's a very wealthy man. He can help father . . . and . . . he always remembers me. He brought me this silver necklace from the east today." she said showing it off proudly.

"Look at things around here!" she continued, glancing around in disgust. "All the crops are dying in the drought. Our animals are barren. Only your stupid sheep reproduce at all anymore. We need help! Or, do you like things the way they are? Stop being so naive! No reputable person is ever going to help us. Thanks to you, no respectable person will ever set foot here again!"

"That's what I was trying to tell father. Someone has come! Help is here!" I said interrupting.

Leah looked at me with her dumb cow eyes, then started up again. "I don't believe a word you've said! You're nothing but a dreamer! The right kind of help will never set foot here!"

I broke in, smarting with irritation, "Please listen to me, Leah! Help is coming! Cousin Jacob will be here any moment."

Never had I dared speak of Jacob before to Leah. The mere mention of his name took the wind out of her. Her face reddened, and her whole demeanor changed. Smoldering with irritation, she replied, "Cousin Jacob! Cousin Jacob was just another one of your insubstantial visions! You can't eat visions, Rachel! What good did mother's sight do her? It didn't save her in the end. She died an early death."

"Cousin Jacob IS here! It's no vision!" I said trying to make Leah understand. "I met him at the well in town this morning. Why do you think I'm home so early? I came to tell father that Jacob's on his way! He'll be here any minute! I swear it!"

Leah continued looking dubious, as I pleaded. "Please Leah! Father will listen to you! Tell him Jacob's on his way. He'll praise you for the news. Help me sister! Remember the Women's Circle! We have to stand together, or we don't have a chance."

Leah looked at me contemptuously. "Help you! Remember the

Women's Circle! What good did the women's circle ever do me? Where are all the women now? If they don't care about us, why should I remember them and their ways? Why should I even believe you now? You're nothing but a trouble maker and a dreamer!"

Before I could reply Leah was off in a huff making for the fire hut.

One of the youngest children, no more than three years old, started crying for his mother. His pathetic cries grew louder and louder, bringing me back to the children's sorry plight. When Leah was out of sight I went to fill an old water skin at the rain barrel. After bringing the children a drink, I stopped to comfort the small boy.

I had just finished with the little one, when I heard father ring for Leah to bring refreshments. This was my chance. Father was no longer in trance, and Leah would not have had time to prepare things yet. With father expecting to be interrupted, I could slip in and relate my news. I steadied myself with a prayer walking toward the door. Only the Goddess could give me the courage to face father and his dreadful oracle again.

I opened the door to father's study. Sunlight flooded in behind me once again illuminating the noxious scene. This time I didn't wait. Bowing low I began speaking. "Cousin Jacob, your sister Rebekah's son, is on his way here. I met him at the well in town this morning, father. Please forgive my interruption, but I thought you'd want to know. He'll be here any minute."

"Not another word out of you! Get outside!" replied father in a chilling voice.

I turned on my heels and left, satisfied to have delivered my news. Closing the door behind me, I was just in time to see Leah hastening with another steaming urn of coffee and some cakes. She was obviously peeved to see me coming from the house. From the look on her face, I could tell she'd had time to take Jacob's arrival seriously. She brushed by me deliberately burning my arm, as she hurried past me on her way to father. Then with a self-satisfied look on her face, she turned and closed the door behind her.

After the door closed, I did my best to put Leah, Shahor, and father from my mind. I'd done what I could. The rest was up to them. I took a deep breath rubbing my arm, and looked toward the horizon to console myself. Jacob would soon be here. Sitting down on the steps, I relived the incredible events of the morning. She Who Watches had not forgotten me as father wished me to believe. The Goddess had heard my prayer. The water of the well had risen in Her name. I put my hand on the precious rock inside my pocket and prayed Jacob's arrival would be a new beginning for me.

Things began happening shortly after my prayer. Leah opened the door bowing low, as father escorted Abdul Shahor briskly out the door.

From the look on Shahor's face I could see he was none too pleased with the way his consultation was ending so abruptly.

"There's a lot at stake here, Laban." said Shahor in bewilderment. "Are you certain the next new moon is the right time for my caravan's departure? The mountain passes can still be treacherous this time of year. Are you sure the snows have ended?"

"Have no fear, my good man!" said father with a reassuring look. "You're in excellent hands. Have I ever steered you wrong before? I consulted my skull oracle. The oracle is never wrong!"

Even Shahor grew uneasy at the mention of the skull oracle. Clearing his throat nervously, he replied in his high pitched nasal voice. "I assure you, Laban! I meant neither you, nor your oracle any disrespect! It's just that my audience with you has come to such an abrupt end."

Father was growing impatient. His back stiffened and he proclaimed in his most authoritative voice, "The oracle of Sin has spoken! If you are wise, you will follow the dictates of the oracle. If you are not wise enough to follow the oracle, there's nothing more I have to say. Now take those children to the Ehulhul Temple! Get them out of my yard! I don't want to have to look at the accursed things."

In the midst of a long litany of apologies Shahor slinked over to his donkey and removed a package from the saddlebag. Handing it to father with his most unctuous smile, he said, "Thank you for your advice Laban! I will follow it to the last detail as always! Along with my thanks please accept my payment. Everything's there as you requested. The finest frankincense and myrrh from the east, coffee beans from the south, the blessed poppies, and of course, the usual bag of silver for your services."

Shahor watched father inspect the silver making sure it was the purest grade. "Go ahead test the coins, if you like! But I assure you, Laban, I use only the purest silver in all my dealings with you and the Black Hand."

When father looked up satisfied, Shahor continued, "Just more thing. Do you have any word for me on my admittance to the Brotherhood? We discussed it at our last meeting."

Father glanced nervously at the horizon in the direction of town. "These things take time, Shahor. You must prove yourself absolutely indispensable to the Brotherhood. Then of course, you have to be tested. We must be absolutely sure you can be trusted. Then of course, you have to survive the initiation. You're well aware those who can't keep a secret are permanently silenced!"

Shahor nodded, then turned away not wanting father to see his dejection. Laban walked Shahor to his donkey, slapping him on the back. "Don't take it so hard! I'll put in a good word for you with Zaltan! Now take these brats to the Ehulhul temple, and ask for Ham. He's the one you need to contact. These little wretches will come in handy. He'll let you know what else you can do to make yourself indispensable. Tell him I sent you!"

Shahor's face brightened. Glancing over his shoulder he caught Leah's expectant gaze. He walked toward her with an expansive stride, proffering forth another smaller satchel. "Never fear! I wouldn't forget you, my young lovely. Please accept this fragrant oil along with the beads. My thanks for all your hospitality."

Leah smiled coquettishly and offered him her hand to kiss. How could she sink so low? I turned my back on them like a cat, and looked longingly toward the horizon waiting for Jacob to appear.

Shahor was just out of earshot. The cloud of dust heralding his departure still billowing in the yard, when father began hurling questions at me.

I braced myself against the barrage, not having the slightest clue as to how to answer. I hadn't noticed whether Jacob was traveling alone, or as part of a caravan. I didn't know if he was equipped with servants. They weren't with him when we spoke, but perhaps they followed up his rear. It hadn't occurred to me to question him. I didn't know if he was travelling with animals, or laden down with gifts and provisions.

I stared at father blankly, not knowing what to say. Why was it always like this between us? It was as though we spoke completely different languages. When I had something to say to him, he didn't want to listen. When he asked something of me, I didn't know the answer. I was always at a loss with father. We were like oil and water, and couldn't mix. I always felt awkward and stupid around him. I couldn't do anything right in his presence.

Irritated by my silence, father scrutinized me carefully. Trading on my discomfort, he glanced at Leah saying with a smirk. "What are we going to do with your sister, Leah? One moment she can't wait to tell me Jacob's coming. She even dares disturb me at my work. Then when I'm all ears she has nothing to say."

Glancing back at me, he continued, "You have eyes don't you, you stupid girl! Why don't you use them?"

Remembering suddenly, it fairly tumbled out of my mouth. "Something important did happen in town today. A miracle occurred! The waters of the well have risen. They rose while Jacob and I were standing there getting acquainted. It was a real miracle father! Some of the townspeople witnessed it. Maybe they'll forgive us now."

Father was incensed. "Enough out of you, Rachel! In another moment you'll be telling me that you performed the miracle! That you caused the waters to rise! You think entirely too much of yourself, interrupting me at my work, and telling such stories."

Looking around he commanded. "I'll have to temper that pride of yours. Don't be idle, you vain girl! Go inside! There's much to do before your cousin arrives. Quick! Tidy things up! But I warn you, if this was one of your daydreams and Jacob doesn't come you're in big trouble!"

I glanced at Leah as I went inside. She wasn't going to lift a finger to help. She was too busy opening the package Shahor had given her. In another moment wafts of fragrant musk filled the air and followed me into the house. I sighed loudly as I went to work. Why was it that Leah was always treated like a princess, and I was harnessed like a maidservant to the labor? Indoors or out, I was always the one called upon to do the onerous chores. The cooking and indoor cleaning were supposed to be Leah's chores. But even these few things she managed to escape by getting either Billah, or Zilpah, father's daughters by his concubines, to do them. It was small wonder Bilhah and Zilpah preferred to work in the fields, rather than stay at home under Leah's tyranny.

After a while father and Leah came inside to wait for Jacob. They were both uncharacteristically silent as I hurried about trying to put things in order. Of course, Leah never moved to help. But I could catch glimpses of father out of the corner of my eye as I scurried about the room. Looking around anxiously, he began to frown. It was as though he was waking from a deep sleep, and seeing for the first time the terrible disrepair that had come over things since mother's death. Father was a proud man. He didn't want his sister to receive word of his decline.

Leah was unperturbed. She was too busy anointing her neck and wrists with her new oil. When she finished she went to mother's copper mirror to arrange her hair. Leah always spent a great deal of time before the mirror. It was a source of wonder to me what she did there. She didn't use mother's mirror to know herself better, or to bring out the truth of her own beauty. Instead she seemed to use the mirror to change herself. For some reason she tried to resemble me. She worked on her face with kohl and amber, even using a raven henna on her hair to darken it like mine. Perhaps that was why her eyes were often red. In any case Leah's time before the mirror was very important to her. It had become a fervent ritual taking the place of her devotion to the Goddess.

When she finished at the mirror, Leah looked me up and down critically. She must have been comparing herself to me, because I suddenly felt awkward and self-conscious. Her self-satisfied grin told me she had managed to regain her composure. Father's making me into a household servant always pleased Leah. It seemed to lend her greater stature.

Leah was ready. She would take over now. Positioning herself at the front door, she began reporting the moment Jacob came up over the hill. "Jacob's travelling alone, father. He's on foot and doesn't have a single bag with him. No animals are to be seen. I thought you said Isaac and your sister Rebekah were well to do."

Then she started reporting on every feature of Jacob's being from head to toe in exact detail, answering all of father's previous questions. Leah didn't have the eyes to see what I had seen in Jacob. She mentioned nothing about the nobility of his presence, or his spiritual demeanor. Though she didn't fail to notice he'd known hard times. She said he appeared poor and threadbare, tired, and run down.

Father seemed heartened by Leah's report. He grew more relaxed with every word of her account, appearing to accrue power from the information she provided. Father and Leah were two of a kind! She could always pique father's interest. He was a mystery to me! How he could gain comfort from someone else's hardship, I couldn't understand.

As father stepped outside and made his way through the flocks, the distance between us gaped wider and wider. The Goddess had given me the privilege of greeting Jacob first, but now I was back under father's watchful eyes. Could my extraordinary luck hold out under his controlling grip? Father was not the only one I had to contend with. Leah had positioned herself in front of me to block my view.

My sister's domineering temperament made it such I had to strain to make a place for myself. Over the years since mother's death, she'd taken it upon herself to become father's watchdog. She felt it her place to intrude on everything I did. This occasion was no different. She planted herself inside the door frame like a sentinel, making sure Jacob couldn't see me and trapping me inside. I had to stand on tiptoes and peek over her shoulder just to catch a glimpse of what was going on.

Father was shrewd, but never had I seen him in such rare form. His sudden change of mood was most intriguing. It was hard to believe the man sauntering over to Jacob, flashing his most beguiling smile, was the same one who'd just been inside with us. He interrogated Jacob with aplomb, disarming him with seductive warmth and candor, all the while boring into the secrets of his soul.

"Greetings, weary traveler! You must be Jacob. Welcome, son! This may be the first time we meet, my dear boy, but I feel like I already know you. I'm your uncle Laban, your mother's brother, son of your grandfather Bethuel. Come! Sit with me here in the shade out of the sun. Let's get comfortable so we can get acquainted. You look tired from your long journey."

Jacob seemed different too, less confident, less self-assured. He smiled diffidently, though obviously delighted by father's warm welcome. He stepped forward bowing low. Father wouldn't allow Jacob leave to bow. He drew him up, and embraced him heartily. Then putting his arm around Jacob's shoulder, walked him over to the tree in our front yard. Looking about gesturing expansively as they went, he said, "Forgive my farm's appearance, nephew. I've known hard times since my wife passed away. It's a great trial to be left with no sons to help me in my declining years. But enough of my sorry fate! What luck brings you here?"

Obviously flustered by father's warmth and directness, Jacob replied, "My mother and father sent me to you, uncle. I've been travelling for weeks. I pressed on despite great hardships and difficulties, determined to arrive with the advent of spring. My journey from Beer-Sheba has been long and arduous. But the Lord my God has been with me on my pilgrimage following in the footsteps of my grandfather Abraham. And I'm proud to say I've had the pleasure of viewing the magnificent land the Lord has promised me and my people."

"Two times, uncle, was I beset by thieves. Once in broad daylight at the noonday hour as I walked through the town of Shechem. I couldn't even discern my assailant's shadow, so bright was the glare of the sun, when he stole the scroll of prayers given me by my father. And once in the dead of night when the moon was down, and I lay fitfully trying to sleep, a man jumped me stealing the golden prayer bowl and ruby passed on to me from my grandfather Abraham. Neither time did I see my assailant's face, though they stole all my worldly goods, even the gifts mother and father gave me for you. I stand before you today as empty handed as the day I was born. It's only thanks to Yahweh I escaped with my life."

Noticing the disappointment on father's face, Jacob continued, "Don't be mistaken, uncle! My hands may be empty, but I am no poor man! I have Yahweh's blessing. It has come down to me from my grandfather Abraham. I have wondrous prospects. The Lord, my God, came to me in a dream while I rested at Bethel with only a stone for a pillow. He showed me the ladder the Nefilim use to ascend and descend from heaven. The Lord spoke to me himself, saying, `I am Yahweh, the God of Abraham, and Isaac, your father. I made my covenant with Abraham, and I make it again with you. I give you and your descendants the land on which you are lying for as far as you can see. Your descendants shall be as numerous as the specks of dust upon the ground. They shall spread east, and west, and north and south. All the tribes of Earth shall bless themselves by you for I am with you always. I will keep you safe wherever you go, and bring you back to your father land. Worship me alone, and I will not desert you before I have done all that I have promised.'"

Father smiled slyly listening carefully to Jacob's dream. "The Gods speak to you! You were allowed to see the Nefilim's ascension ramp! Your dream is a wondrous portent, Jacob. May it come to pass! I've been expecting you. My God Nanna/Sin speaks to me through my oracle. He sent me word of your coming."

Jacob looked flabbergasted. Stepping back, he inquired, "You had word of my coming through your oracle?"

Glad for this chance to brag about himself, father responded, "Yes! The Gods speak to me as well! I am a senior moon priest at the Ehulhul Temple to Sin in Haran. The Great God Sin speaks to me through my skull oracle. He tells me a great many things!"

Jacob stepped back, a frown on his face at the mere mention of the Ehulhul temple. "Father told me about the Egeshnugal temple to Sin in Ur, uncle. My grandfather Abraham left Ur to escape that place and its degenerate priests."

Father smiled slyly. "Yes! But Abraham and Nahor came here to escape them, didn't they? Haran is a far cry from Ur."

Jacob relaxed as father continued, "Does your determination always lead you with such certainty to your goal? Today is the first day of spring. The tides of the moon are full. It's a most auspicious time for you to have arrived. I will, of course, consult my oracle later. But tell me, what caused your mother to send you to me without prior notice?"

Jacob's face paled. It must have been a good minute or two before he spoke. Then he chose his words carefully, "It was not my intention to burden you with my life story so soon, uncle. But since you are so kind and generous as to be interested in me, I will speak plainly. Mother sent me here to safeguard my life."

Father's interest was piqued. "To safeguard your life! Who would possibly wish to harm you?"

Pain etched across his face, Jacob continued with a sigh. "It's a long story uncle. But I had to protect my life from my brother, Esau."

Gripped with fascination, father's words leapt out. "Your brother? Your twin brother, Esau? But why? "

Jacob continued, "It was over our father's blessing. You see, uncle, Esau is the elder twin. By all rights father should have bestowed the blessing on him, as is the custom. But before our birth the Lord confided in mother while we were struggling in her womb. The Lord told her. 'The elder should serve the younger'. And so it came to pass, when it was time for our father Isaac to bestow the blessing, his eyes were weak. Mother seized this opportunity to disguise me in my brother's clothes. She put the skins of a kid on me, as my arms are smooth and my brother's arms are rough and hairy. Then she prepared a savory meal so father would sup with me and be deceived into thinking I was Esau. My father gave me the blessing thinking I was Esau. We ate and drank together, and it was sealed forever."

"Since that time my brother lays in wait to kill me. Esau's wrath is known to all. He's a fierce hunter, a rough and ready man of quick impulse and ready temper. He merely waits upon father's death to do the deed. Given father's failing health, mother in her wisdom sent me here to you."

Father replied with a knowing smile, delighting in Jacob's story. "Yes indeed! It was a wise decision for her to send you here. And you, my boy, did well by showing such great cunning. We have much in common. You truly are my flesh and bone!"

Father's words echoed in my mind sending a wave of discomfort throughout my entire body. Was Jacob really so akin to father? If they had so much in common would father be able to lead Jacob away from me, the way he had done with Leah?

My thoughts were interrupted by Leah. She had repositioned herself and was now obstructing my entire view. I breathed in deeply struggling to gain control of myself, and squatted down so I could see. Putting any unpleasant thoughts out of my mind, I consoled myself with the fact that Jacob was here. He was welcome. I would be alone no longer.

Though I watched from a distance, I felt no distance from Jacob. I felt even closer to him hearing about his problem with his brother. Jacob was my other half. I knew him with an uncanny intimacy. He would understand my plight, as I could understand the pain of his relationship with his brother. I could also identify with his being overlooked by his father. We were two of a kind, even as father and Leah were two of a kind. Listening from inside the doorway, I was coupled with Jacob. At one with him in his anguish and suffering, as I had been in the streams of joy we had both felt at our meeting at the well.

Father began walking Jacob through the flock and over toward the house. Jacob examined the sheep thoughtfully as he moved through them. Before reaching the steps he took something from a pocket inside his robe. His face shining, he declared, "I don't come totally empty handed, uncle. I've been a shepherd since my youth. I have a natural touch with livestock. I'm a good worker and can make anything grow."

Thrusting his hand out, he presented father with something, saying,

"Do you recognize these seeds, uncle? They're just what your flock need! I found them in the hill country of Bethel near the place I had my dream."

Father looked quizzically at Jacob's outstretched hand, "No! What are they?"

"They're seeds of the blessed thistle, uncle. Something compelled me to gather them. Now that I see your livestock, I realize why. Your flock is in sore need of them. Tomorrow I'll plant these seeds in the high pastures where your sheep graze. They'll grow with the power of the full moon. Wait and see the difference they'll make to your herd. Your flocks will become fertile and produce lots of milk. They'll be built up in droves. Even the barren will become fruitful. Never fear, uncle! I may not be laden down with gifts and belongings, but I have Yahweh's blessing. Wait and see how well things will go for you now that I am here."

Father gazed at Jacob's smiling face. Grabbing the knife which hung from his belt, he seized the ewe nearest him and in one swift movement slit her throat. Her warm blood fell on the awakening ground, as father said, "Welcome, son! May this blood seal the ancient bond of blood kinship between us."

Father moved forward sprinkling the ewe's blood ceremoniously on the steps and across the front door. Then he called Leah to bring the sacrificial bowl to gather the remaining blood. Adroit at anticipating father's every wish, Leah was already waiting for the summons. This was my chance to catch Jacob's eye, and see which of the ewes had been chosen for sacrifice. I gasped, clutching the door frame for support. My favorite black ewe, Jesse, the one who'd stood by me in the village bleating her piteous cry, had been chosen. Seeing her dead on the ground in all her youthful innocence, my heart stopped.

Oblivious to the blow he'd struck me, father was stooping down to examine the creature's entrails. When he finished he rose with a pleased expression on his face, and quite by accident got blood on my robe. Anxiety gripped me. Was this an omen?

When I regained my balance I looked up, but it wasn't Jacob's eye I caught. It was father's staring at the blood stain on my robe. He stood before me, a dark malevolent figure blocking the sun and eclipsing my view of Jacob. The sheer weight of his stare was staggering. I closed my eyes, and put my hand on the rock inside my pocket. Even with the

Goddess's gift it took all my strength to rise from beneath the weight of his oppressive stare.

Leah approached with the bowl sliding in between father and me. As Jacob ascended the steps, she wedged herself in front of me adroitly blocking me from view. Giving Jacob her most winning smile, she handed father the bowl.

Father tore the heart and liver out of Jesse in full ritual form. After examining them, he caught the remaining blood in the bowl. His booming voice called out, "The signs are propitious! The heart is well shaped and strong. It's still beating. You come with a full and open heart today, Jacob. The entrails are clear and unobstructed. You bring with you no guile. The sacrifice speaks further. You are here to seek a wife, and have much to give."

Jacob's face reddened as father pushed Leah at him. After a moment of awkward silence father went down the steps. Pouring the remaining blood on the earth, he declared, "From this day forward we shall be one blood. My friends are your friends. Your enemies are my enemies. Tonight we feast on the slaughtered beast."

Smiling knavishly, he glanced down at the scattered entrails about his feet, and continued chuckling. "And if you have the stomach for it, let us also grow to be of one heart and mind as well. Now come and meet my daughters! This is Leah, my elder daughter. She's a jewel and would be a credit to any man. She's an excellent cook, and a fine homemaker. She weaves and sews. You can see for yourself her hips are right for childbearing. I'm very pleased with her."

Jacob looked uneasy as he smiled politely down on Leah. Then glancing around anxiously, he interrupted father's praises for his eldest. "Uncle, please! I mean no disrespect. But where is your daughter, Rachel? She is my angel! I met her at the well in town today. The same well where my father's servant, Eleazar, met my mother many years ago. I can't see Rachel, but I know she she's here. I feel her presence, and her sheep are all around."

Confusion consumed father's face. He hated being interrupted in mid sentence, and was used to things going his way. The introduction to Leah stuck in his throat. At the same time he wanted to please Jacob and make a good impression. Taking a moment to clear this throat, he looked around for me as if it were his own idea.

Leah's body went rigid in front of me. Embarrassed she'd be caught in the act of hiding me, she stepped aside. Leah had actually made room for me! I beamed up at Jacob, my deliverer.

Jacob reached out his hand. I stepped forward into the light of Jacob's love, all memory of the blood on my skirt forgotten. Jacob's love would erase the stains of blood, and stave off all my fears. Our smiles were a bridge our hearts leapt across. When I looked into Jacob's eyes they told me everything I needed to know. The fire of love lit with our first kiss was blazing now.

6

THE SHEARING OF THE SHEEP

JACOB'S ARRIVAL BROUGHT FAR-REACHING CHANGES TO OUR LIVES. BE-
fore coming out to the farm he had spoken with the men at the well and
introduced himself. Word travels fast in Haran, and this was no ordinary
day. Jubilation resulted from the water rising in the well. A holiday was
called. Before the shepherds had all watered their flocks at the well Jacob
was renown. In the eyes of the townspeople Jacob was a hero as in the
days of old. He had single handedly removed the stone and caused the
waters of the well to rise. Was Jacob the answer to their prayers? Could
he remove other obstacles as well? Did he have the blessing like Abraham his forbear? They called him Shepherd of the People sent to lead us
back into the grace of heaven.

Jacob was our guest, and one of our family. I too was present when
the water in the well had risen. It didn't take long for the wise women of
Haran to remember my vision at the well on the day of my overshadowment. From that first night friends and relatives began visiting us again.
Women came seeking my help with their problems, as they once had

sought out mother. Conversation and laughter had a place within our home again. What grace had caused these changes? Was it Jacob's blessing? Was it the Goddess's prize from heaven? Was it the power of our love? I didn't know for sure, but at last the dreadful shunning ended. We were forgiven.

With Jacob so obviously delighting in me, father's attitude toward me soon changed. Overnight, I went from being his troublesome burden, to his prize bait to hold Jacob and his blessing fast. Father's most fervent wish had been granted. Jacob was the son he had always longed for. The mother's brother was the true and rightful father according to lunar matriarchal law. With Jacob as part of his household father was convinced his power would increase. He even dared hope Jacob's arrival would further the influence of the Black Hand

Only Leah was not elated by Jacob's arrival. Now that he was here she was no longer allowed to sleep in the main house with father. Her room was turned over to Jacob. I had to share my tent with her to my chagrin. It rankled me deeply, as I was used to being on my own. Leah also chafed under the imposition, though she was too proud to voice her discontent.

I hardly slept the night of Jacob's arrival from all the excitement. My heart raced with joy. My cheeks were hot and flushed as I lay there tossing on my pillow. Leah's presence only increased my turmoil. Her silence was like an oppressive rain cloud swollen with envy and threatening to burst at any moment. I lay awake for hours agitated by the tension of her presence.

Finally, not knowing what else to do, I got up and dressed hurriedly, hoping not to wake Leah. I put the stone from heaven in my pocket, grabbed my satchel with the shearing implements, my water skin, and escaped into the fresh morning air. It felt good to be outside again, away from Leah. I was at home beneath the starry canopy of heaven.

The full moon was so bright, it outshone the stars. Only Athtar, the star of love, was not diminished. It twinkled down on me, setting my course to the rain barrel. My flocks were asleep in the front meadow, but they roused as I approached. The water was a cool welcome refreshment after the sweltering night. I was drying myself off when I heard the front door open behind me.

I turned around my heart in my throat, praying it wasn't father. To my delight, it was Jacob. He came bounding towards me, the moonlight hiding none of his pleasure at finding me alone. By the time he reached me, he was brimming over with love and smiles. Even the sheep seemed to sense the excitement of our meeting. An exuberant host, they crowded round nudging and pressing us together. We surrendered gladly, collapsing with laughter in each other's arms.

Sparks of joy seemed to leap from my heart. My entire body warmed to Jacob, purring like a cat. Never had I experienced such bliss. We stood delighting in each other's arms neither of us speaking, afraid to break the spell.

At long last Jacob said, "I prayed you'd be up early with the flocks this morning, Rachel. The night was so long. It seemed interminable, and every moment endless."

I thrilled as he continued.

"I see you have your shearing implements with you. Allow me to help, my angel! We'll be alone together."

Inner recesses of my soul were awakened looking into Jacob's eyes. Who was this man with the courage to speak his heart so plainly? Most men kept their feelings to themselves, thus seeming boring as a result. Or else they hid behind their power like father, and were slaves to their possessions, so full of themselves they could only give orders, or reprimands.

Thrilled I answered, "It would be a pleasure to have your help, Jacob. The sheep are always so rambunctious during shearing. And last night the moon was full. Are you ready? We should leave before everyone gets up. Father might have other plans for you."

A smile blazed across Jacob's face warming the cool morning air. "I've been ready and waiting for you all my life, my angel!"

My heart bursting with joy, I said, "Just one moment. Let me get a few things so we don't have to come back to eat. I'll get us some cheese and bread and be right back."

When I returned, Jacob was already lining up the sheep and guiding them through the narrow gate. His ability as a shepherd was most apparent. I couldn't help but smile, remembering the time I'd had filing them through the day before. My body tingled with strange new sensations as I drew close to Jacob. How much everything had changed in one short day!

Our love so united us the work we shared seemed effortless and joyful. In no time at all we were on our way up to the far pastures. The frisky sheep were as relieved as we to be out of the confines of the farm. The young lambs leapt for joy running along beside their mothers. I wanted to return to the Balikh, the site of the Goddess's apparition the previous day. It called me with a gripping urgency. I couldn't wait to share my favorite spot with Jacob and offer our love there to the Goddess. Our love would be my offering for the healing of this land so disrupted since mother's death. It would also be the perfect place to shear the sheep and plant Jacob's seeds. I could take the first wool to my shrine later.

The spring breezes were pushing at our back hurrying us along, until we stopped to admire the dawn. Jacob took my hand and pulled me close to him, as we gazed out across the valley, a vast undulating sea of grass. Each hill rose before us like a cresting wave enveloping us in expansive peace.

Looking out in the direction of the rising sun, there was so much to be thankful for, my heart was full to brimming. The sky ablaze in florid color announcing our new love, I prayed.

"HAIL SHAMASH, KING OF HEAVEN AND EARTH! JUDGE OF ALL THE LIVING AND THE DEAD! THANK YOU FOR BRINGING YOUR LIGHT INTO OUR DARKNESS. HELP US TO ALWAYS WALK IN YOUR LIGHT. THANK YOU FOR BRINGING MY COUSIN JACOB TO US. MAY HE BE HAPPY HERE AND PROSPER.

My prayer over, I was wrapped in ecstasy inspired by the morning light until I began to feel a peculiar hollowness around me. Jacob dropped my hand. When I turned to him he averted my gaze, seeming uncomfortable and restless against the golden backdrop of the sky. What had changed his mood so abruptly? I looked at him more closely, and inquired, "What is it? You seem out of sorts, dear cousin."

He looked at me guardedly, before replying, "I was just thinking of my homeland, the hill country around Beer-sheba. It's God's country! I miss it so!"

"Someday it will all be mine, Rachel!" he continued swelling with pride. "The Lord promised it to me and my descendants."

Gazing into his eyes I could see there was something more. So I continued looking at him intently.

He began squirming, then continued in a more serious tone. "There is something else, Rachel. It wasn't Shamash who brought me here. It was the one true God the Lord, my God, Yahweh. The old gods have all departed. A new dispensation was given to my grandfather Abraham. The blessing has been passed on to me. You mustn't pray to those antiquated gods, Rachel. Their time is past! Yahweh is the Master of Heaven and Earth, the one true God. All other gods are false."

I stared at my cousin in amazement. He continued less sternly to break the tension building between us. "You mustn't concern yourself with such matters, Rachel! Spiritual matters should be left to us men!"

I was burning with anger, but tried not to show it, as I inquired, "But what of the Mother Goddess, Jacob, and the sacredness of Mother Earth? Even the great Yahweh can not be both father and mother to his people. . . . Won't he be lonely without a mate, even if He is Master of the Universe?"

Jacob looked at me as though I were a querulous child. "Yahweh is both father and mother to his people." he said disapprovingly. "He is omniscient, omnipresent and almighty. He lacks for nothing, and requires no mate! The Earth is his creation. I am his chosen one. My descendants will be his chosen people. Yahweh has given us dominion over Earth."

Perhaps my cousin and I were not as close as I had thought. The differences between us were becoming painfully clear. Jacob didn't believe in the Goddess, or have proper respect for the Mother Earth. He thought the Earth belonged to his God. Did he actually believe Yahweh could hand over the body of the Earth Mother to him and his descendants? From the time I was little mother had taught me that we were all the children of the Earth Mother Goddess Ninhursag. She had created the first adam along with the wise God Enki. The Earth was sacred. She was our primal Mother who sustained us. We should be grateful to the Earth and serve as righteous stewards of its creatures and all its resources.

Fear clutched my heart pondering Jacob's words. Yahweh was not an evil God like Nanna/Sin, but mother had been right. They would both be against the Goddess. I began to feel afraid. If Yahweh gave dominion over the Earth to Jacob and his descendants would the Earth Mother be forgotten?

I looked at Jacob with new eyes, as I quieried, "Surely you must have respect for women's spirituality, Jacob? After all your mother was a Naditu Priestess. She was trained here in Haran. I too am a Naditu woman. I was born to be a priestess, like your mother, and mine before me."

Jacob was regarding me suspiciously, when he replied, "That may once have been true of my mother, Rachel. But much changed after she came to live in Canaan. Mother had to give up her false gods when she married. My father was the spiritual head of our family, as it is meant to be. My father Isaac is a wise man. He helped mother see the error of her ways."

Then sensing my discomfort, Jacob took me in his arms smiling down at me. "Don't fret, my angel! You will share in the greatness of my future. We are of one heart. We will grow to be of one mind as well. You'll see the truth in time. I'm convinced of it."

I had been father's demon and neglected for so long. To have Jacob take me in his arms and speak his honeyed words, I could forgive him anything. All I wanted was to be within the charmed circle of his embrace.

I closed my eyes, telling myself that I would show Jacob. Why start an argument that would only lead to an impasse? I'd teach Jacob to revere the Earth in simple ways, as mother had taught me when I was a child. Yet there were many things along our walk that day I wanted to share with Jacob, and didn't. I told myself I was being diplomatic. There would be plenty of time to get to know each other better. I remained silent to bask in the sunshine of Jacob's smile. His smile made the world a happy place for me again.

Living with father, I was used to keeping my beliefs and practices to myself. I told myself I could be open to Jacob's God and continue to love the Goddess in my heart. Things would be different for us than they were for Jacob's parents. In the fullness of time I would be able to introduce Jacob to my beliefs and customs. He didn't need to believe as I did, so long as he was tolerant and respectful of my belief in the Goddess.

The sun was shining brightly by the time we reached the river. The Balikh had risen dramatically over night. It was now swollen and overran the banks in several places. The water was sparkling clear and inviting. Jacob was as enchanted with this place as I. Though he wore a waterskin tied about his waist, he ran to the Balikh and began drinking its enchanting water.

We lay down on the lush grass along the riverbank and looked up at the sky as the sheep watered. I soon felt the heightened effects of the miraculous draught. My body was enlivened, my senses more acute. We lay together in charmed silence, until Jacob said, "This is an enchanting place you've brought me to, my angel! Only once before have I felt so refreshed from simple water. That was yesterday at the well when you offered me a drink from your waterskin. Did that water come from here?"

Being in this hallowed place made me bold, so I replied boldly. "Yes! But how can you be so sure this is simple water? Yesterday the moon was full. The moon effects all the tides in nature. This is the great Balikh, that nourishes our entire region. It's named after Ba'al, the husband of the Goddess. This is his haunt."

More relaxed and open after his refreshing drink, Jacob replied contentedly. "Wherever I go with you is enchanting, angel! Let's relax here a little while, then take a swim before we begin shearing."

I nodded happily. It had always been my custom to take moon baths at the new moon and the full. I closed my eyes and gave my body up to the earth warming beneath me. Jacob possessed vision. He was a man of the living spirit. Something within him had responded to the magic of this place. His entire demeanor had changed since drinking the vivifying water. Surely he had inherited the Ancient Eyes of the Goddess from his mother. I would have no trouble initiating him in the old ways. I prayed that She Who Watches would continue working Her subtle magic, and open Jacob's spirit in tolerance.

It was wonderful lying in Jacob's arms. But the frolicsome flock soon brought us back to reality. One of the newborn lambs had fallen into the river's surging course. Its mother was bleating loudly, and struggling toward it through the fast moving current. By the time I sat up, Jacob was beside it in the swift current. In the next moment the lamb was safe in his arms.

Jacob was my hero once again. Even the sheep seemed to cheer the fact. The anxious mother returned to the riverbank, and waited with the other sheep bleating loudly. Back on solid ground Jacob checked the lamb to see if it was sound. Then he returned it to its mother. The mother sheep nuzzled the little one and began licking its head, while looking up at Jacob in admiration.

I walked toward Jacob with gratitude in my heart. "Thank you, Jacob! You certainly are the hero! You've made a friend of that mother sheep for life. It's a good thing, too. I call her, Bossie, because she's one of the most ornery."

Jacob smiled broadly, then dragged me into the river playfully. I came along laughing merrily. After a few cold plunges I caught my breath and guided him over to my favorite spot between the boulders. "This is where I come to listen to the river at moontide. Be attentive! The river may speak to us today."

"Come now, angel! Rivers cannot speak!" said Jacob petulantly.

"How can you be so sure, Jacob." I said laughing. "You're a stranger to our parts. Different rules and customs apply here. Come! Sit down and be still. You may learn why they call this river the Balikh."

We sat together content to listen to the rippling current of the river, until our silence was broken by a roaring sound like the wind rustling through the trees before a storm. Jacob looked at me in alarm, shouting above the roar. "What's that noise, Rachel?"

The great roar of the river diminished, as I whispered, "The jinn spirit of the river is announcing he's about to speak."

No sooner was I quiet than it began, TODAY YOU ARE CHILDREN AGAIN, BORN ANEW THROUGH THE POWER OF YOUR LOVE. GUARD YOUR LOVE CAREFULLY! IT IS ONE OF LIFE'S GREATEST TREASURES. THERE ARE THOSE WHOSE HEARTS ARE A STRANGER TO LOVE. THEY KNOW ONLY POWER, GREED, AND COVETOUSNESS. BEWARE! THEY MAY SEEK TO COME BETWEEN YOU!

After another great whirling sound, the jinn spirit of the river departed.

Jacob turned toward me, his eyes wide with astonishment. "I heard something, Rachel! I swear I heard something! Did you hear it, too?"

"Yes, Jacob! I replied laughing.

"Whose voice was that, my angel?"

"That was the spirit of the living water, the Ba'al of this great river, Jacob. It speaks to me here from time to time, like your great Lord speaks to you in your dreams."

Jacob's face tensed. "You can't compare some inconsequential nature spirit to Yahweh! Yahweh is the one true God, Rachel! All wisdom, knowledge, and power flows through Him, and Him alone."

THE SHEARING OF THE SHEEP

"I meant your God no disrespect, Jacob!" I replied not wanting to get into an argument.

After a few minutes of heavy silence, I grabbed his hand saying, "Come! We've had our bath. It's time to get to work. Just look at those pesky sheep! Let's put them in the corral over there. We're going to have to keep our eye on them today."

Then to avoid an argument, I pulled Jacob to his feet and dragged him merrily across the river toward the flock. After getting them all inside the pen, I grabbed a ewe by its hind legs and pulled her over to the knoll beside my satchel. Taking up the copper shears incised with the Goddess's sign, I handed the other pair to Jacob.

No one had ever helped me with the shearing before, and I felt nervous as we began. Jacob was such an accomplished shepherd. I'd had to teach myself everything by trial and error. Yet in only a few minutes we had found a rhythm all our own. Working together was like a dance, each of us building upon the work of the other. It was hard to believe the onerous chore of shearing could go so smoothly. Even the sheep were better behaved having both of our attentions.

As we worked I gathered a clipping of first wool from each sheep and put it in my satchel. We continued straight through to lunchtime without stopping. It was wonderful having Jacob help me. The work went fast, and we never ran out of things to say. By lunchtime we had sheared nearly half the flock, and my satchel was almost full.

Before we sat down to lunch I took the whitest wool of a ewe and a ram and twined them together with a prayer. Then I threw it into the Balikh as an offering to Ninhursag and Enki. A shady spot beneath an old willow by the river looked inviting, so I spread a cloth out there. Then I laid out the olives, bread, cheese and wine, and burned some sweet grass to grace our simple meal. Jacob and I sat close together in the shade. Both of us were starving after the morning's toil.

When we finished we admired the huge heaps of wool we'd collected from the morning's shearing, and sorted them out according to color and quality. Then Jacob rose to peruse the area. "This is a beautiful spot! I'll plant my seeds here beside the river and pray to Yahweh to make your sheep fertile. You'll see the awesome power of my God. Their numbers shall increase rapidly and you will prosper."

After years of loneliness the feelings Jacob awoke in me took my breath away. When I looked into his eyes we melted together in a time-less realm. I could see into his heart, and feel all the idealism and nobility of his spirit. Every part of me responded to him with love. I was not alone anymore.

A brilliant dove, as white as the fleece I'd just offered, came gliding in. My heart opened to see its graceful flight. My offering had been re-ceived.

"Is this the same dove that graced our meeting at the well yesterday and led me to your home? Or do these heavenly birds follow you every-where you go, my angel?" inquired Jacob beaming.

My cheeks flushed the brilliant red of the poppies sprinkling the hill-sides. There was no need to answer as the graceful dove perched on my shoulder and began to sing. We both laughed out loud heartily. It re-mained on my shoulder as I put away our simple meal, and Jacob went to build sleds for the wool and find a stick.

When I finished packing away our things he returned with a sturdy branch in hand. The heavenly bird flew from my shoulder leading him toward the perfect place to plant. Jacob pressed his stick into the soil and dropped the seeds inside. I followed behind tucking them into their earthen beds. After we finished we watered them with the water from the Balikh.

Then it was back to shearing again. There was still much to be done, but neither of us tired. It hardly seemed like work, as we exchanged life stories and delighted in each other's company. It was almost sunset by the time we finished. We quickly wrapped and bundled the huge mounds of wool, then fixed them to the sleds Jacob had made for pulling them back home.

It was amazing how much we'd accomplished in one short day. But my work was far from over. I still had to take the first wool to my little shrine to offer to the Goddess. I explained my plan to Jacob, careful to leave out the part about my offering to the Goddess. Even so, Jacob was reluctant to part with me.

"Let me come with you." he insisted. "You'll be all alone, and it will be dark. The sheep may go astray."

"I won't have a problem, cousin." I assured him. "The sheep are tired and ready to move on to their evening pasture. They're always subdued after shearing, though by tomorrow they'll be friskier than ever relieved of their winter coats. Besides, I need you to send Nathan up to them, so we can be together later. Tell him I'm in the back pasture beside the stream, and ask him to bring Zack. He'll lead him straight to me."

The sun was a brilliant orange ball upon the horizon as we set off in the twilight. I breathed in contentedly enjoying the multicolored tableau of the sky. I wanted to savor each last moment alone with Jacob. There was no telling what the morrow might bring. Knowing father he'd probably have plans for Jacob.

The moon was already rising in the east when Jacob and I had to part. We held each other tight, both of us reluctant to leave. Then I pointed Jacob in the direction of the farm, and we kissed goodbye.

"Are you certain you don't need my help? You're carrying such a load for one so slight." asked Jacob plaintively as I prepared to leave.

"You forget dear cousin, that before you arrived yesterday I had to do all this by myself." I replied laughing.

"It's been wonderful being with you today, my angel! I wish the day would never end." said Jacob fervently.

We stood clinging to each other, Jacob a seemingly immovable object against the vast expanse of sky. After a few long moments I realized I was going to have to be the one to pull away. Gathering all my resolve, I clutched the precious rock inside my pocket for ballast, and made a running start heading east into the rising moon.

My heart felt as though it were being torn from my body as I pushed on toward my little shrine. When I reached the next hillock I turned around to see if I could spy Jacob. He was still standing where I left him. Afraid to be drawn back to him, I said a prayer to She Who Watches and started off again at a fast clip.

It was dark by the time I reached my altar with the sheep. They took a drink at the brook and started settling in for the night. It had been a long day for all of us and I was glad to put my bulging satchel down. I took out the first wool and held it proudly up to heaven, offering the fruits of our labor to Ninhursag. Then I placed it in a great mound upon the altar and went in search of some dry twigs. My firesticks were where I always left them beneath the altar.

Rubbing them together, I closed my eyes in prayer. "GREAT GODDESS NINHURSAG, MISTRESS OF HEAVEN AND EARTH! ACCEPT THIS OFFERING OF FIRST WOOL FROM MY FLOCK. RE-

CEIVE IT WITH MY GRATITUDE FOR YOUR RENEWED PRES-
ENCE IN MY LIFE.

GRANT ME THE COURAGE TO WALK IN THE LIGHT OF
YOUR HOLY TRUTH THOUGH JACOB MIGHT NOT APPROVE.
HELP ME TO OPEN HIS HEART IN TOLERANCE SO OUR LOVE
MAY KEEP ALIVE YOUR ANCIENT MYSTERIES AND FOSTER
BALANCE, PEACE, AND UNDERSTANDING ON EARTH.

When I opened my eyes the altar was ablaze in one consuming
flame, it's sparks shooting up like stars eager to join in the dance of
heaven.

7

THE PROPOSAL

JACOB'S PRESENCE WAS A BEAM OF LIGHT COUNTERACTING FATHER'S sullen ways, and gracing everything. The power of his blessing was apparent from the start. Rain fell from heaven. It was a glorious spring after bitter years of drought. Lush grasses and wildflowers carpeted the hillsides with their fragrant blush of color. The Balikh overflowed its banks filling the irrigation ditches to full capacity again. All of nature cooperated with the fertile earth. The hamsin winds from the southern desert alternated in a harmonious dance with the cool winds from the northern mountains and the moist air from the coast. All the fruit trees blossomed and were quickly pollinated. Cool wet winds arrived from the west in time to bless the ripening kernels of the spring wheat and barley crop. Jacob was the harbinger of this blessed season. Everything he touched became fruitful. The God and Goddess were smiling on our newfound love.

Father had never been a skillful husbandman. His talents lay more in the manipulation of people and events. He didn't have the stamina for

hard work or the ongoing nurturing required to run a farm. He was relieved to hand over the supervision of our estate to Jacob. With Jacob
managing the farm, and our neighbors and relatives visiting us again, father's dour temperament improved. He even moved his consultations to
the Ehulhul temple to shield Jacob from his nefarious affairs.

Only Leah soured with Jacob's arrival. Though she was too proud to
voice her resentment, I could read her moods as easily as the sediment in
mother's silver divination cup. Leah couldn't bear to see my happiness.
Displeasure marred her face and spoiled her manner with jealous irri-
tability. With father away from home all day, there was little to occupy
her anymore. Only her competitive spirit drove her onward. Always a
fine cook, Leah now spent all her time preparing extravagant meals to
curry Jacob's favor. For the first time in her life she even ventured out of
doors seeking Jacob out each day at noontime to serve him her delicious
fare. Leah hovered about Jacob each day like a bee around a flower.
When it became obvious she couldn't seduce him through his stomach,
she vented her discontent on me. Day and night she fussed and fumed
hoping to dampen my happiness.

On the next full moon I was off with the ewes at my little shrine beside the stream. Jacob was down below marking out a system of irrigation ditches for the new fields he'd planted. He would be busy with the
servants for the next few weeks. I was also fully occupied. After the
miraculous rising of the well the women in town had begun seeking me
out to interpret their dreams and star charts. Day after day they came
asking for advice on their decisions.

I'd had to turn a woman away today. It was the height of the birthing
season and two of my best ewes were ripe for lambing. The one I called
Rosey, because of her pink nose and rather thorny disposition had had a
terrible bout with parasites over the winter months. She was still weak
and feeling poorly, and I had to attend to her. I was feeding her an herbal
mixture Jacob had prepared to facilitate her birthing, when the other
ewe appeared to be going into labor.

It was her first lambing, and yearlings often needed help. So I left
Rosey and went to her side. She was lying in the shade of the oak tree
beside my altar breathing heavily. She calmed down as I approached.
She'd eaten the mixture of raspberry leaves and linseed oil that I'd left

her. I sat down to wait. These births could be quick, or stretch out for hours if there were complications.

The full moon was pulling with us, and we were in luck. The ewe's waters broke, and soon after a bundle of life was delivered on the grass beside me. I breathed a sigh of relief pleased all had gone so well. Then I sat back and watched this first time mother harken to nature's call, tearing open her young's birth sack and licking it clean to welcome it into life.

Though often privileged to experience the lambing process, the miracle of life still struck me with awe-filled silence. I was saying a prayer of thanks to the Goddess that all had gone so well, when I noticed the ewe growing restless again. Soon another bundle was deposited on the grass not far from the first. The yearling had given birth to a second healthy female. There had been so few double births since mother's passing, it seemed like an abundance of new life. I rose and examined the ewe's belly to see if there were any more surprises in store. Observing the ewe so content with her two newborn, I decided to call her Raspberry.

After I had seen the placenta was intact I returned to Rosey. She was the worse for my being gone. Her nose was hot and dry and she hadn't taken any of the raspberry leaf mixture I'd left her. Feverish and agitated, she lay with her belly to the ground as if trying to draw power from the earth. Even so she couldn't remain still very long. She thrashed around in pain while I mixed some Fever Few with water from the Balikh and forced it down her throat. Once that was accomplished there was nothing I could do but wait. When I saw she kept the mixture down, I drenched some raspberry leaf and linseed with honey and coaxed it into her mouth. Even in her anguished condition Rosey couldn't resist the sweet taste.

I sat beside Rosey the entire morning and well into the turgid heat of the afternoon, ministering her with herbs to keep her fever down. The other sheep kept a respectful distance and were unusually docile sensing her distress. The fertile tidings lent the day an eternal quality. It was a privilege to sit on the lap of Mother Earth in the thick of the Blood Mysteries. Before me was the sacrament of maternal love, protection, nourishment, and stimulation, the foundation of all life and development.

The heat of afternoon mixed with the fragrance of the pungent earth as Rosey's contractions intensified. Delirious with pain, her womb would still not open. I took out my trusty herb pouch grateful Mother Earth had provided us with a remedy for every ailment. I'd try the aromatic pennyroyal to unlock Rosey's womb. After massaging one of her tits for milk, I blended it with the pennyroyal.

Mixing the pennyroyal with Rosey's milk that was hot with fever, I implored Ninti, She Who Opens the Womb, to grant Rosey a speedy delivery. When the concoction was ready, I eased it down her throat. Then I sat back stroking her fevered head. Finally her body began to heave. Wrenching herself out of my lap she thrashed around bleating piteously. But when Rosey's waters gushed forth, they weren't clear like Raspberry's. There was blood and fecal matter mixed in as well, which was a bad sign.

Two small hooves came forth. I was relieved for a moment, but then nothing happened. The hooves were stuck with indecision at the door to life. Even in her delirious state Rosey was pushing valiantly for her young, but to no avail. I thrust my hand inside her and pulled out a little lamb. It lay still as death on the soft grass beside its mother. Rosey had no time for the lifeless bundle. She was frantic, and pushing again.

I picked up the lifeless bundle, tore open its birth sack and rubbed it gently to coax it into life. Rosey let out a deep moan, and another lamb fell to the ground. The ewe's anguished body finally quieted. She looked at her young through glazed and haunted eyes. Then still delirious, her tongue parched and stiff, she began welcoming it into life. I wanted to offer Rosey water from the Balikh. But critical bonding was taking place, and I didn't dare break into the circle of life being drawn between the mother ewe and her baby. Tears welled in my eyes as I observed the tender scene, and continued to massage the lifeless bundle in my hands. Though I feared it was hopeless, I wouldn't give up on the lamb without a fight.

I reached into my apron pocket and took out the wondrous stone from heaven. Gathering the power of the Goddess, I brought the motionless bundle to my face and breathed on it as I prayed aloud. Tears mingled with my breath falling on the little lamb. I was just about to give up when I felt it begin to stir. The way across the abyss had been crossed. I gave thanks to Ninti, Lady Life.

In no time at all the little one was breathing deeply. I cuddled the tiny creature in my arms. It was a dark hued female with the sweetest countenance. Ministering to her a name came to me. I'd call her Night Sky, because of her black coat and her two sparkling eyes. Had the Goddess sent me Night Sky to make up for the loss of Jesse, my favorite ewe the day of Jacob's arrival?

I looked over at Rosey. She was still weak and feverish. I searched around for the afterbirth, but all I could find were small bits and pieces. Retention of the afterbirth was serious. I started massaging her belly to bring the placenta down. But it was too late. Rosey slipped away. Her death was all the more poignant as the lamb she had ministered to tried to suckle her swollen udder to no avail. The little one was undaunted. As if following instructions from Rosey, she sniffed around until she found her way to Raspberry.

I looked on in silence not daring to move. It was unusual for a ewe to take another's young. But the little one nestled in right beside Raspberry's two and started sucking. Raspberry looked over at Rosey's lifeless form, then rearranged herself so all three could fit comfortably. In no time all three lambs were suckling contentedly in the peaceful shade of the altar rock. Raspberry had been generous accepting one of Rosey's lambs. It was too much to ask she also take the one on my lap. I lifted Night Sky up and held her to my heart. I knew how she felt. We were both motherless, I would care for her myself.

The day was winding down. The sun was setting, sending feathered washes of scarlet and gold across the heavens. I stood transfixed between the earth and sky, poised between the eternity of heaven and the great round of birth and death, which was the way of earth. The full moon was rising in the east as I glanced back and forth between Raspberry and Rosey pondering their fates. On my left was Rosey who'd poured out her life for her young. To my right was Raspberry. She too had given much of herself today, and was surrendering still more to the urgent need of the little ones who consumed her.

How could Jacob deny a place to the Great Mother Goddess? Life and death were the light and dark sides of the Goddess, who was the heart of the mystery of life. Mother's love brought life into the world, and sustained it. Rosey was a sacrifice to the Great Mother Goddess, her death making possible the life of her young. She had been their door, and with their entrance it was time for her to depart. I dragged Rosey's lifeless body over to the altar rock and placed her on it, giving thanks to the Great Mother Goddess for the gift of maternal love.

It was late so I went to check on my other pregnant ewes. It would be another few days for most of them. I'd leave them with Zack, and send Nathan up to them tonight. It was a somber walk home with the little bundle in my arms. I was still rehearsing the news of Rosey's loss to father, when I approached our weathered gate that creaked out its familiar welcome. I went to the fire hut and put some sheep milk in a skin. Then I took Night Sky to a manger in one of the sheds. When she was fed I made her a soft bed of hay, and laid her down for the night.

Approaching the house I sensed something in the air. I gazed up at the magic mirror of the sky in time to see a shooting star streaking across the heavens. With this wondrous omen I headed for the front door. I halted at the threshold and peered in unnoticed. The front room was softly lit with oil lamps giving off a warm glow. It was a peaceful scene within though I noticed father had rearranged the chairs. Jacob and he were both seated in the middle of the room. I could see both their faces well. From the fragrance in the air I knew they were having some of father's favorite date wine.

I was about to knock, when father began to speak. As he hated being interrupted, I waited outside for the close of their conversation. Father looked beseechingly at Jacob. "I'll be frank with you, son! I like having you here. It's a relief to have another man around the place. And you're not just any man. You have many talents. I see myself in you, as I was many years ago. You've gotten an amazing amount done in the short time you've been with us. You're good with the servants, and have a remarkable gift with animals. I swear you could make anything grow. It's a big relief having you manage the farm. I can't understand how your own father overlooked you."

Jacob's face tensed at father's last remark, and he looked away.

Noticing this, father continued in a more conciliatory fashion. "I just mean to say that I won't overlook you, son. You can't go home on account of your brother's wrath. But don't you mind! Your home is here with me now! I have great plans for us! We'll make a great team! There's much I can do for you. I have friends in high places. But it's not right you work for me without payment. So speak up, Jacob, and tell me what you want for wages!"

THE PROPOSAL

Jacob answered without a moment's hesitation. "I'll work for you seven years, if you promise to give me Rachel's hand in marriage. Then I have to go. Nothing could hold me. I must return to my homeland. An important destiny awaits me there. And I need to reconcile with my brother Esau. Only he and father know the words on the scroll that was stolen from me. That wisdom must not be lost."

Father sat back in his chair staring at Jacob without a word, then crossed his arms over his chest pensively. Why was father taking so long to answer Jacob? What was the old fox up to?

"This is an important matter." he responded finally. "I have to consult my oracle to see if you are worthy of my daughter."

Jacob sat in stunned silence, as father rose. Noting Jacob's expression, he said, "It's nothing against you, my boy. It's just that we, of the Brotherhood, never make any important decision without consulting the oracle first."

Jacob began speaking nervously, when father returned with his skull and divination bones. "You'll never find anyone more worthy of Rachel, uncle. My forebears are from the long line of Sumerian priests that issued from Nippur. Yahweh chose my grandfather Abraham to carry the Sumerian lineage onward. Abraham raised the ancient teachings to a new and higher level claiming Yahweh, as the one true God."

Father looked unimpressed, so Jacob continued. "Abraham was a great hero as well as a religious leader. Did you know that he and his cavalrymen took up arms for Yahweh? He defended the skyport of the Nefilim in the Sinai. He was one of the few mortals ever allowed entrance there. Your daughter will be safe with me. When the Anunnaki sent forth that furious blast destroying Sodom, Gomorrah, and most of Sumer, Abraham and our family had Yahweh's protection and were saved."

"Yahweh speaks to me. He came to me at Bethel and showed me the Nefilim's ascension ramp to the stars. On my journey here, He promised Canaan to me and my descendants. I am the bearer of Abraham's blessing. You heard how the water in the well rose at my arrival. Yahweh is with me in all I do. I have great prospects."

Laban beckoned Jacob to be silent as he placed his skull oracle on the table and began casting his divination bones. Gazing down at them, he exclaimed, "The oracle decrees a positive fate. A prosperous future lies before us. You will bring me great riches, and power. Seven years you say?"

Jacob nodded his assent.

"You'll do anything I say?" inquired Laban, narrowing his eyes.

"Anything that is not against the will of my God!" said Jacob regarding father suspiciously.

Father poured himself another glass of wine. "Very well!" he exclaimed, refilling Jacob's glass. "It's better to give her to you than to a stranger. Stay with me! I'll treat you like my own son. But what about that prayer bowl you lost on your way here? You can't go home empty handed. You're going to have to replace it. You'll need gold, and what did you say . . . a ruby to go with it."

Jacob's face reddened in embarrassment.

"Never fear, son! I know all the best craftsmen and traders in the area. I can get you whatever you need. You'll have no trouble earning the gold. My Brothers may need your help from time to time."

"I work for you, not the Black Hand, Laban!!" stated Jacob firmly.

"Of course!" said Laban grinning widely. "But we are a Brotherhood and sworn to help each other in times of need. So I may have to send you to their aid from time to time. You mustn't be recalcitrant, my boy! It's good politics and you'll be well rewarded!"

"So long as you understand I'll never step foot inside the Ehulhul Temple, or serve any God but Yahweh!" declared Jacob adamantly.

"Of course! Of course!" said Laban. "But you can help them with their flocks from time to time. Your talent with animals is amazing!"

"Why is the Brotherhood called the Black Hand, uncle? Does it have anything to do with Black Magic? I'll have no part in evil doings." said Jacob with resolve.

"Oh no!" said father cunningly. "It merely refers to the fact that we prefer our dealings to go on behind the scenes. The Brotherhood of the Black Hand is comprised of wise men. We see in the dark where others cannot. We've taken over the state and are in the process of closing down all the lesser temples in the region. I can say no more, as we are sworn to secrecy."

I was so overjoyed that Jacob wanted my hand in marriage, my bliss crowned out father's last remark. I was completely flooded with joy until I caught sight of Leah in the far corner of the room. She was out of

Jacob's sight, crouching beneath mother's copper mirror, half undressed and in a state of disarray.

So that was why father had rearranged the chairs!! Jacob must have come home at a most inopportune moment. Suspicion took over my brimming heart, spoiling my delight. Why did Leah and talk of the Black Hand have to be included in this transaction? Leah! Always Leah! There never could be anything private in this house! Her nose was into everything! Why did she have to be privy to Jacob's asking for my hand in marriage? There'd be no end to her jealousy now!

Anger flared in me like a burning torch. Why did Leah always have to intrude on what was mine? She was a parasite. Would I never have anything to myself? I wanted to scream out and reveal her as the culprit she was. But she was my sister, even if she'd renounced the Goddess Mysteries. I was a Naditu woman sworn to uphold the solidarity of Sisterhood. And father was a vengeful man. I would be unmasking him as well. He might put a curse on me. He'd been known to curse women with barrenness and worse.

I went to the rain barrel to soothe the angry tears boiling up inside me. My brow was feverish. What a day it had been . . . life and death . . . sorrow . . . ecstasy . . . and rage. I was exhausted from the gamut of my emotions. I sighed looking up at the moon. The full moon always had such a way of intensifying my feelings.

I heard footsteps and turned around. It had to be Jacob. Father wouldn't leave him alone with Leah crouching in the corner half undressed. Jacob quickly spotted me, and ran across the yard to embrace me warmly. Being with Jacob always made things better. I felt strong with him beside me. Together we could face anything. He wasn't only my beloved. He was my best friend as well. I was bursting to tell him about my day, but quieted myself to wait upon his news.

The splendor of his Lord shone in Jacob's eyes. Streams of joy radiated from him, as he said, "Your father made me very happy tonight, Rachel. Now it remains for you to make me the happiest man in the world. Will you marry me, my angel?"

Revelling in the warmth of his love, I answered, "Yes, Jacob! You speak the words of my own heart."

Jacob took me in his arms and held me close. When we parted from our embrace he walked me over to mother's herb garden. It hadn't been cultivated since mother's death, but Jacob had been drawn to it recognizing some of his mother's favorite herbs. He'd fashioned a small bench for us there so we could sit out alone together in the evenings.

The star jasmine was particularly fragrant on this night. Its small white flowers shone in the moonlight, like tiny stars. We sat together in blissful silence until Jacob opened his heart to me. "I've been searching for you all my life, my angel. I was afraid no woman could ever match my hopes and dreams. There isn't a woman who can compare with your light. Only you can satisfy the deep longing in me."

"I was never like my brother. Esau was always falling in and out of love with a pretty face or a trim figure. I watched his impulsiveness. I saw how quickly he tired of the pleasures of the flesh. He had so many foreign wives, father and mother finally despaired of him."

"I didn't want to be like my brother, Rachel. I needed more than just the flesh to warm my heart. I wanted a true love. Someone I could ascend to heaven with. Mother kept my hopes alive. She told me about this fertile land and the Naditu Sisterhood. She spoke of a Higher Marriage, that was a mating of spirit as well as flesh. A marriage that enabled both partners to attain greater spiritual heights. She spoke of the Higher Marriage as a sacred mating in which the spirit and body would fuse, and the lovers ascend like twin flames to the stars."

"I've always wanted a Higher Marriage, Rachel. From the moment I laid eyes on you, I knew you were the one. You are the only woman for me. A wondrous light surrounds you. It radiates through your eyes, and draws me to you. How I've thirsted for your penchant for truth, my angel! In you my heart has found peace at last!"

"But there is one thing I must ask of you for my love to be complete. Are you still a virgin, Rachel? I've waited for you. It's important to me that we save ourselves for each other until after our marriage. That way the spirit will be exalted in our mating, not the flesh."

I had been enraptured by Jacob. My soul rising and taking on wings with his every word. Jacob was my heart's beloved, my promised one. We both wanted the same thing and had remained true to its ideal. Nonetheless, I was taken aback by Jacob's question. My virginity belonged to the Goddess. It wasn't for Jacob or any man to place strictures on me. Of course, I was still a virgin. There was no one for me but Jacob. But as a Naditu woman my body and my soul were in service to the

Goddess. My virginity belonged to the Goddess. It could not belong to any mortal man.

Jacob's question amazed me! Where did these patriarchal men get their preposterous ideas of proprietorship? How could Jacob think my virginity belonged to him? I tried to check the startled look upon my face, but it was too late.

"You haven't answered me, Rachel! Aren't you a virgin?" demanded Jacob with desperation in his voice.

Hating to see the troubled look on his face, I replied, "Of course, I'm a virgin! There's no reason to doubt me. But I am a Naditu woman. My virginity belongs to the God and Goddess. It can not belong to you, or any mortal man."

Jacob recoiled from me as if I were a snake about to strike.

"Why are you pulling away from me, Jacob? You just said you wanted a Higher Marriage with a Naditu Priestess for a wife. Well, I **am** a Naditu woman! Didn't your mother explain to you that we Naditu women belong to the Gods? We must do their bidding in all things."

Jacob was vexed and strangely silent.

"Your own mother was a priestess of the Eye Goddess. That's why your father married her . . . and why she was the fitting mother for the one to carry Yahweh's Blessing. It's also why Yahweh God confided in her that you were to have the Blessing, and not your brother."

Jacob's face reddened, and he began looking irritated now. "That's enough about my mother! You speak as if you know her!"

"But I do, Jacob! We Naditu women are all one large Sisterhood. We're sworn to stand by each other like blood sisters. I also see your mother in you, Jacob." I said looking in his eyes. "You have her vision."

"I don't know very much about the Naditu Sisterhood." said Jacob uncomfortably. "As I told you everything changed for mother once she married father. . . . What's important is that you're still a virgin. You're not just saying that to please me?"

"Don't you trust me?" I asked in exasperation. "I swear to you in the light of truth that I am a virgin. There's never been anyone else for me, but you."

"I believe you Rachel!" said Jacob in relief. "But let's not talk about the Sisterhood anymore. Their's and the Brotherhood's time is past.

They're antiquated orders, though I'm glad you're of the lineage. Mother always stressed how important it was to maintain the bloodline."

I looked at him with fire in my eyes. "Don't ever speak of the Naditu Sisterhood and the Brotherhood of the Black Hand in the same breath, Jacob! They couldn't be more opposing orders! The Naditu Sisterhood is under the guidance of the Eye Goddess Ninhursag from Kak.Si.Di., the brightest star in heaven, the sun behind our sun. The noblest of all the Nefilim are from Kak.Si.Di. They are the Watchers, the guardians of light and love, who work to safeguard and uplift this planet. The Nefilim from Kak.Si.Di. uphold freedom, truth, and light throughout the universe. The Brotherhood of the Black Hand is a secret society of men out for their own gain. They are controlled by Nanna/Sin. Sin is one of the Anunnaki, the ancient reptilian lords of Earth who came from Nibiru. Sin is a wicked god. He fell from grace with the Anunnaki and was exiled here. That's why the Brotherhood of the Black Hand has become so powerful. They think they're above the Laws of Heaven. I've seen in father's eyes that he can be possessed by the Evil One. All those in positions of power within the Brotherhood are possessed by Sin. The Naditu Sisterhood is sworn to uphold truth and justice. They've been counteracting the wicked deeds of the Black Hand for centuries, which is why the Black Hand hates them and has sworn to stamp them out."

"I don't know of what you speak." said Jacob gravely. "I only know what Yahweh reveals to me, and what has been passed on to me through my forbears. But the Great Ages have changed from Taurus into Aries. The time of the Goddess is no more! Yahweh is the Great Ram of Heaven, the One True God. I carry His blessing. The ancient Sumerian blood flows through my lineage. We are Yahweh's Chosen People. But for this I need you, my unspotted ewe."

I wasn't getting through to Jacob, but it was late and I was tired. "Let's not argue!" I said nestling in his arms. "We both share the same dreams. Nothing could make me happier than to be your wife in the Higher Marriage."

Jacob was the issue of a Naditu Priestess. He was a man of vision. He would have the eyes to see the despicable workings of the Black Hand. I would be by his side. Together we could be invincible.

Jacob settled back whispering in my ear. "My snowy ewe! My tender beauty with the untainted fleece!"

THE PROPOSAL

I could feel his heart beating and the heat racing through his loins as he kissed me over and over again. I wanted him to never stop. I wanted to pledge our love with our hearts, our minds, and bodies, right there under the canopy of heaven.

Tears came to his eyes when he spoke again. "You are my one true love, my angel! The only woman for me. Promise you'll wait with me the seven years I've pledged to work for your father. I want us both to be virgins on our wedding night and have a Higher Marriage of spirit as well as flesh. Only the highest union should engender Yahweh's chosen people!"

This waiting seemed strange to me. Afterall we were pledged to one another. Such restraint seemed forced and unnecessary. We were young and vibrant. Why split our bodies off from our heartfelt love, living for the future and not the present? But it was important to Jacob.

The dove still fluttering in my heart, I nodded my acquiescence. Only when I said yes, I, too, was crying.

8

THE EVE OF THE DAY OF OLIVES

A TIRED EXASPERATED VOICE CALLED TO ME ON SPRING BREEZES through the veils of my tent. Could it be Jacob? Was he home at last, or was this a dream? I roused myself from slumber and slipped noiselessly from the tent, praying Leah wouldn't wake. I hadn't seen Jacob for days, and I didn't want Leah intruding on his homecoming. It was difficult enough that father's greed was so incited by the prosperity Jacob brought him, that with each year he claimed more and more of his time.

Jacob collapsed into my arms, oblivious to the stars shining down on us. "I thank the Lord to have you in my arms again, my angel. Thoughts of you were all I had to get me through this endless week. I hope your father had the courtesy to tell you where he sent me."

I shook my head, no.

"After the sowing Laban had me supervise the lambing at the Ehulhul temple again." said Jacob in annoyance. "This is the third year in a row he sends me. How I despise that wretched place! Its gruesome sacrifices are an abomination! But once again I showed them who the one true God is. Yahweh's blessing produced twins for all their ewes. Some even had triplets. Your father was very proud. Even Zaltan the High Priest took note! He sent me off with an extra gold coin."

Jacob continued chuckling, "I may be able to win the Brotherhood over to Yahweh yet! Everyone knows the greed of Sin's priests is greater than their loyalty."

Beaming up at Jacob, I kissed him squarely on the lips.

The color returning to his face, he continued, "Enough of this talk! I'm weary of work. One kiss from you is worth more than all the gold anyone could give me. I feel better just to gaze on you. Come! Let's sit in the garden. I need to rest my weary body, and feast my eyes on you."

Ambling over to the garden, I had to struggle with my irritation. I could never get a word out of father concerning Jacob's whereabouts. I should have known he'd sent him to the Ehulhul again this year. Nearing our seat, I declared in exasperation, "Father takes advantage of your generous spirit, Jacob! It's wretched of him to work you so hard! You do everything around here! Then he has the audacity to send you over to Sin's temple to make himself look good!"

Even in his weary condition Jacob smiled wryly hoping to counter my disturbance. "Your father's a shrewd man. He's merely trying to get the most out of me while he can."

Jacob's words were no solace. I looked away uncomfortably as I sat down. How could Jacob be so wise, and yet be such an innocent when it came to father? I breathed in deeply trying to calm myself. But it was no use.

I blurted out. "Why do you always make excuses for father? I can't bear the thought of the Sin temple benefiting from your blessing. I hear they've begun a series of vicious persecutions against the Naditu Sisterhood. They're increasing their sacrifices. And they've instituted a program of racial cleansing for those they consider undesirable. How can you bear to work for them? They have taken over most of the land in these parts now, and their flocks are legion. They don't need your help!"

Jacob looked away wearily. "I don't work for that fiendish temple, Rachel!" he said sharply. "I work for your father, so that I can have you for my wife. I don't think this is any way for my future wife to greet me after all the hard work I've done!"

I felt guilty, as Jacob continued. "Let's not quarrel, Rachel! I haven't the strength for it. I only make excuses for Laban because he's your father. What else can I do? I made a bargain with him. I gave my word. I'm sworn to work for him in whatever way he sees fit. You know I'm no friend of the Ehulhul temple. I'd rather die than set foot inside that demon shrine."

I was chastened by Jacob's words, though a shiver of fear ran down my back. I couldn't bear our love being taken advantage of by the Black Hand. Everyone who came in contact with that foul Brotherhood was brought low. What was worse, I felt responsible. I was father's bait to snare Jacob into servitude. Though I wasn't all to blame. Little went unnoticed by the priests of Sin. The wonders on the day of Jacob's arrival had piqued their interest from the start. Of course, father had also known how to make the most out of his nephew's gifts. He displayed Jacob's talents before the Brotherhood every chance he could. With the Black Hand's eyes fixed on self-aggrandizement, it hadn't taken them long to recognize the unusual resource they had in Jacob.

Only three years under Jacob's supervision and the temple's flocks had more than tripled. With the terafim and now Jacob's talents at his disposal, father had become Zaltan's right hand man. Father gloried in his newfound seat of power! While I could only watch with a heavy heart as the Black Hand resurrected their ancient dream of world domination, which once had caused them to build the Tower of Babel.

What was there to do? Every day the Black Hand tightened their grip with new laws and taxes that strangled every aspect of our lives. They had control of the leaders across Mesopotamia, allowing them to manipulate all tariffs on trade. For years now they had been bankrupting our farmers by bringing them under the Babylonian debt system. People were starving and so indebted, they were forced to sell their land, and watch the Black Hand buy it for nothing. From recent reports the Black Hand had now taken over the northern trade routes which controlled the vast supply of silver in the Taurus mountains. In no time they would usurp Mt. Ararat. Would the Habur Valley and the Eye Temple be next?

This was not all I had to contend with. Although minor in comparison to the Black Hand's treachery, there were the interminably long nights I had to spend with Leah in the stifling confines of our tent. Although Leah often chose to ignore me, there were times she gloried in criticizing and mocking me in the privacy of our small tent. Her attacks came out of nowhere, flaring up as unpredictably as the spiraling dust-devils that rode the wind in the summer heat.

So it came to pass that toward the end of Jacob's fifth summer with us, I found myself alone with Leah in our tent. It was the eve of the Day of Olives. I lay awake in the darkness pondering all the events of the day. It had been another blistering summer day, but tonight the air was moist against my skin. Grateful for the dew in the air, I said a silent prayer of thanks and sank back on my mat smiling.

When I was a child, mother had told me this sudden change in moisture was the Goddess's kiss of promise. The Goddess's kiss of dew blessed the pomegranates, dates and figs and the grapes heavy on the vine. Each year at this time it stimulated the olives to fill with their precious liquid gold, which graced our meals and brought light to winter. The Goddess's kiss also brought forth the white squill flowers, which opened at midnight around Olive Day each year, shining for one brief day. I loved the brilliant squill, that resembled torches of light saluting the sun and bidding fond farewell to summer.

Yes! The Goddess's kiss of promise was in the air! Tomorrow would start the few brief golden days of summer respite, before the ingathering and plowing for the winter wheat and barley crop. Morning mists would gather. Clouds would muster in the sky. The sun would still be hot and bright, though diminishing in power. These pleasant musings brought with them a remembrance of days gone by when mother was alive, and we would don our white gowns and go dancing in the olive grove on the Eve of the Day of Olives. I could still recall the moonlight playing across the silvery leaves of the olive trees, illuminating the women's white gowns as they twirled with their partners in the dance.

Swept up in this maze of memory, I reached out to my sister in the darkness. "Are you still awake?"

A petulant sigh was my answer. Finally Leah deigned to say, "Yes! I'm awake! How can I sleep? I can hardly breathe in this stifling humidity."

"I was thinking about tomorrow being Olive Day. Do you remember how we used to celebrate when mother was alive?

"I remember." she said sighing peevishly.

"Do you remember the white dresses we wore in honor of the squill?

And how mother used to let us stay up late so we could watch the dancing in the groves, and hear of all the betrothals?"

"There you go again living in the past." replied Leah, obviously annoyed. "I remember those days. They were never much fun for me. No one asked me to dance."

"That's not true Leah!"

Leah raised her voice. "Why do you bother with such foolishness? Mother's dead and gone! Soon the Goddess celebrations will be too!"

"They're all but over now thanks to women like you, who choose to ignore the old Goddess ways!" I snapped. "You say I live in the past. Well, at least I can still think for myself! That's more than I can say for you. And just now I was thinking about you and your future."

"Stop thinking about **my** future." broke in Leah angrily. "Keep your nose out of things that don't concern you!"

"But you never go anywhere, or do anything with men your own age." I interrupted. "Wouldn't you like to go dance in the olive grove tonight?"

"How ridiculous! Enough of this folly!" exclaimed Leah.

"But all the unmarried men and women will be there. You should be too! That's where the matchmaking takes place. You should go. You'd have a good time."

"Who do you think you are telling me what I should do?" retorted Leah angrily. "I don't want your advice. You say you're thinking of me, but you just want to get me in trouble with father. He'd be furious if he found out I went dancing in honor of the Goddess."

"I don't want to get you in trouble, Leah." I said more gently. "Father's in bed. I'll cover for you. I promise! I just thought you might want to be with someone your own age for a change. Simeon might even be there."

"Simeon?" Leah retorted testily. "He's never shown the least interest in me."

"How can he? You never go anywhere without father. When was the last time you went dancing? I don't mind, because I'm already betrothed. But it isn't right for you to sit home all the time. You mustn't waste these precious years!"

This was the first time I had ever mentioned my betrothal to Leah. No sooner had the words left my lips, than I realized I'd made a big mistake. My words sounded hollow and trailed off in the empty darkness, leaving me with a feeling of disease. Time passed. I grew uneasy. It wasn't like Leah to allow me the last word.

Leah began sobbing. "Why did you have to go and bring that up? Isn't it enough I have to watch you two mooning all over each other? Do you have to lord it over me as well?"

She continued, her anger building. "From the moment you were born I was cast into the shadows. Rachel the beautiful! Rachel's gift of vision! Mother's favorite! Now Jacob's! How do you think it makes me feel to always have to take the back seat? I hate you! I wish you were never born you spoiled brat! You freak of nature!"

Then she sprang at me through the darkness like a ravenous wolf, growling and biting, and scratching me all over with her nails. Her thick fleshy body arched over me shaking with fury. Kneeling on my thighs she grabbed my arms and pinned them down above my head. Then she vented herself on me, her anger coming down like an avalanche.

I went limp beneath the force of her attack, too startled to even defend myself. I was consumed with a fear I had never known before. This was my sister?? I was trying to pull myself together to respond, when she ripped into my arms with her nails shrieking. "This will help you to remember not to meddle in my affairs!"

Then she flew out into the night screeching like a bat.

I lay trembling on my mat, unable to believe what happened. I wanted to deny it, but my face still burned from her assault. My arms ached and were bruised all over with scratches. When I was sure she wasn't going to return, I began sobbing. What had I done to warrant her brutal attack? All I wanted was for her to have a good time. I had to be so careful around Leah. There was hell to pay any time she caught me enjoying myself with Jacob. Her moods were so suffocating and controlling. All my life I'd had to play myself down around her. Tonight I could see just how broken and depleted I was from all the strain. How could I continue living in such close quarters with her raging envy and hatred? I tossed and turned in misery crying fitfully until my body finally grew heavy with sleep.

The next thing I knew the tent flap opened and Leah walked in. My body cringed at the sight of her moving about in the darkness. Slowly, still fighting back her raging hatred, she cried out, "I hope that teaches you not to interfere with me! I've just had a talk with father. He has great plans for me! He's glad I gave you a good whipping. Don't bring up Olive Day, or the Goddess, ever again, or father will take care of you himself! The Eye Goddess is a thing of the past! Your star is tied to a sinking ship, Rachel!"

I felt totally defeated by Leah's triumphant tone, and her clandestine pact with father. Why had I even bothered about her? She wasn't my Sister in the Goddess! She wasn't even a decent sister! She was father's adoring daughter, who'd sell me out for one of his smiles. But this time Leah had gone too far.

Unable to bear her haughty tone a moment longer, I said, "You sound very smug and full of yourself, Leah. You think you can get away with anything, because of father. But you're mistaken! She Who Watches sees everything! The Eye of Truth is watching you! Not a single word or deed of yours, or father's, escapes Her scrutiny."

Scornful laughter peeled out in the darkness of our tent.

My arms were still burning, when I rolled over trying to get back to sleep. But somewhere in the place between sleep and dreaming, I felt cold fear and revulsion. The atmosphere in the tent grew heavy. So heavy I could hardly breathe. Dragon's blood incense filled the air. Father's hideous skull idol loomed menacingly before my inner eye. I called upon the Goddess and struggled to force myself awake. I sat bolt upright. Everything was still. Only Leah was in the tent, and she was fast asleep. Yet this was no dream. The air was thick with the aroma of dragon's blood. I got up to look outside. Clouds of acrid smoke were billowing from father's private room in the main house. He was working one of his fiendish spells.

I closed down the tent, trying not to leave a single crack for the smoke to enter. Then I got back in bed. With the stone from heaven in hand I prayed for protection. There would be no sleep for me tonight.

At the first signs of dawn I went to join my sheep. It was a relief to escape into the morning mist. It was a cloak of invisibility that would hide me. The sun appeared mid morning peering through the haze. By noontime it was clear and bright.

Jacob came looking for me around sunset. I was still upset and trying to figure out how I could manage not going home for the night. It was the first time I'd seen Jacob in days. He approached me eagerly, arms brimming over with fragrant squill flowers. The summer breeze was as laden as his arms with the smell of their perfume. The wind caressed me seductively, playing havoc with my skirt as I rose to greet him. The joy of seeing him mixed with my youthful enthusiasm and the redolent breezes, and I was intoxicated. One with the squill robing the country-side, I too longed to be opened, and all my hurts and bruises healed in the passion of our love.

I revelled in the brilliance of Jacob's smile, his confident stride, and the strong sinews of his well tanned body. This was Olive Day. My body, senses tingling, bade me do the mating dance of nature's primal call. All I could think of was being in Jacob's arms and carried to fulfillment.

Out of the corner of my eye I saw a green garter snake rousing from its afternoon slumber. It began a sinuous journey, crossing right between us. I laughed out loud in gay abandon. Jacob didn't appreciate my humor. He recoiled as if a viper had struck his innards with a deadly poison. Making light of the snake, I tried coaxing him into the mood of Olive Day swinging my hips.

"What's gotten into you, Rachel?" he inquired suspiciously. "What are you doing carrying on so? Don't tell me you like snakes, and relish them coming between us!"

I laughed out loud again, trying to alleviate the petulance of his mood.

"I hope it's not a bad omen!" he continued sighing. "I don't like snakes, Rachel, and my Lord, Yahweh, doesn't like them either! Father told me a story about the Anunnaki, those clever reptiles, and our first parents Adam and Eve. Like yourself, Eve was far too familiar with a ser-pent. What's more, I don't appreciate coming upon you in the fields writhing about like one of those slimy creatures."

I laughed mischievously in reply.

"It isn't funny, Rachel! What's gotten into you? Stop this nonsense!"

Jacob's words hit me like a rude slap.

He continued, a strong wind building up around him. "The Anun-naki are very clever. Though reptilian they fashion themselves attractive human-like bodies. The serpent who beguiled Eve in the garden of Eden was one of them, Rachel! He seduced Eve and got her with offspring, bringing her down into the corruptible earth body. When Adam yielded to his wife's carnality he too was lowered. That Anunnaki serpent brought on the fall of humankind from the spiritual light body given them by the Creator, trapping them in the physical body. My father told me Cain was the serpent's seed. The unfortunate Abel was Adam's seed. Yahweh has given the land of Canaan to me and my descendants. It's our God given right to take it back from Cain's descendants."

Enraptured by the power of the word flowing through him, Jacob had forgotten the flowers in his arms. They were swept up in the searing wind and carried away, breaking his train of thought. After regaining his composure, he continued, "I'm sorry if I was harsh with you, Rachel. But the frustration of our carnal desires is necessary to ensure we have a Higher Marriage that will resurrect the spiritual light body."

I was dazed and confused. If Jacob took the promised land back from Cain's descendants, it would result in bloodshed. Bloodshed begot more bloodshed, bringing everybody down. War and violence wouldn't help humanity regain the spiritual light body, only love, mutual understanding, and tolerance could. But I didn't dare say a word. Jacob was allowing the living word to take him. I wanted to understand Jacob and his God. But as I continued listening the gentle breezes of summer died down, and the wind grew fierce around him.

The power of the word still flowing through him, Jacob gathered me in his arms. "Yahweh spoke to the serpent in the garden, Rachel. He said, 'I will put enmity between thee and the woman, between thy seed and her seed.' Stand with me, Rachel! Understand the seriousness of my insistence that we wait upon our union. Everything must be perfect for us! Our seed must prevail against the Evil One!"

The spirit of Yahweh was upon Jacob, I could feel it inside the circle of his embrace. My body coursed with power. Every hair on my arms and legs stood straight on end. It was a privilege to be with Jacob while he was being overshadowed by his God. But the wind was cold and fierce and pierced through me like a knife, chilling me to the bone. The wind was powerful and holy, but I was shivering. And suddenly I felt self-conscious and guilty for my desires.

PART THREE

Return to the Goddess

9

Laban's Wedding Gift

At long last Jacob's lengthy years of service were drawing to a close. I was at the threshold of my bliss, ecstatic in anticipation of our wedding. All of nature seemed to smile with me. The crocuses were blooming earlier this year, purple, blue, and yellow spots of color to brighten winter's somber landscape. The rainy season was over and the pistachio and almond trees were busy fashioning their own bridal veils of fragrant ivory blossoms. The power of the sun was building and the earth warmed at its caress, spreading a lush carpet of wildflowers over the hillsides. Everywhere the spirit of renewal beckoned. It was spring-time once again.

A week before the wedding date I had so carefully chosen according to the stars, father came riding on a donkey in search of me. I was in the far pastures with the flock. My blood ran cold at his approach. Though I had to smile at how ridiculous he looked on the poor overburdened donkey as he rode over the cresting waves of hillocks.

After catching his breath, father got right down to business. "I've been giving a lot of thought to your wedding gift, Rachel. I believe I've found the perfect one. Though it will mean you have to postpone your wedding one week."

Horror struck at father's words, I began to protest. "That's impossible! I won't postpone the date! You're a moon priest! You know why I chose that date. It's the first full moon of spring, the most propitious day to marry! We've waited so long! You can't make me change it!"

Father was unruffled. Ignoring my every word, he began looking over the sheep. Sauntering over to Night Sky he petted her pregnant belly admiringly, then remarked, "Well, if you don't want to go to the Eye temple."

"The Eye temple!" I exclaimed, hardly believing my ears.

Father continued examining the sheep, then went on without even looking up. "Yes! I've enrolled you at the Eye temple for the next two weeks. I thought you would want to make a full ritual purification in preparation for your marriage. It seemed a fitting wedding present in lieu of a dowry, since my estate has fallen on such hard times."

My heart was racing. I was speechless with delight. My prayers had finally been answered. Father hadn't mentioned the Eye temple without cursing it in years. Could he be repenting? Was he recognizing me at last? I hadn't dared ask him about going to the temple for the sacred rites. Perhaps he had remembered mother's wishes, and wasn't so heartless after all. My heart overflowed to think of returning to my spiritual home.

Father was speaking again, only more quickly this time. "If you don't want to go, I won't force you. But it would be a nuisance! What if they won't refund the silver I sent them to secure your place? Jacob will have to make it up to me."

My joy found words. "Of course, I want to go! Thank you, father!"

Yet while thanking him, a strange feeling crossed my heart. I looked at him again questioningly. How could father have had such a sudden change of heart? But he was busy with the sheep and didn't meet my gaze.

It was a miracle. My prayers were finally being answered. This had to be the work of the Goddess. She Who Watches had to be behind this incredible turn of events. Never would I have expected father to work the Goddess's will for me.

Looking about me, I grew concerned. "Who will watch the sheep while I 'm gone?"

Father smiled reassuringly. "Don't worry about the sheep. Bilhah will watch them for you. Didn't she help you with the lambing last year? And I'll keep Jacob here to supervise. Don't worry! I've seen to everything. Now go prepare! You have to leave early tomorrow morning."

"So soon?" I asked in surprise.

"Why not? I've seen to everything." said father casually. "There's only one thing. Jacob won't be home tonight. He's in town taking care of the temple's flocks. I'll say goodbye to him for you when he returns tomorrow. Of course, I won't tell him where you're going. You know how intolerant he is of other Gods. Let's not rile him. He may not appreciate our rites and customs."

Everything with father had to be a devious intrigue. But what could I do?

Still examining the sheep, he continued impatiently. "Don't just stand there with that silly look on your face! Get going! Trust me! I've seen to everything. There's no need to speak of this with anyone. I told Bilhah you're going to the shepherd's fair in Carcamesh with Eli to purchase a red ram. Now run along home! Don't worry about a thing! I promise the wedding will go on as planned without a hitch. I'll see to everything. It's not every day I get to marry off my daughter!"

I was thrilled to be returning to the Eye temple. Nonetheless, I was dismayed by father's scheming. I looked at the innocent sheep wistfully. It was lambing season and close to the full moon. The Goddess had been good to us again this year. Many of our choicest ewes were ripe for lambing. Night Sky was heavy with young. Never had I seen a ewe so full before. We were still so close. She followed me around everywhere, as though I were her mother. I hated to miss her lambing. But I couldn't fail the Goddess. I went over to Night Sky, and rubbed her belly fondly saying goodbye. Then I ran off over the rolling hillsides, relieved that father had chosen Bilhah to tend the flocks while I was gone.

Bilhah was my favorite of Laban's daughters by his concubines. She helped me with the sheep, and did the onerous chores around the farm that Leah was loathe to do. She was well practiced in caring for the flock, and unlike Leah, didn't feel it beneath her to be out among the sheep. Bilhah was a simple girl with an ease with all living things. The sheep would do well under her watchful eye. But why did father have to tell her I was going to the shepherd's fair to buy a ram? Laban was always lying and scheming! Just imagine, a red ram!

The sun rose proudly along with Athtar, the star of love, as I climbed aboard my donkey and started for the Eye temple. Athtar, so close to the sun, blushed a rosy hue. The Goddess was smiling upon my journey. The God and Goddess had come to meet and send me on my way back to the Eye temple. I was going home. I would be motherless no more. I appreciated this special sign. It helped ease the ache of my separation from Jacob. We'd never been apart for such a long time before.

I felt graced and protected beneath the Goddess's star. The whole world seemed glorious and new, bathed in its wondrous light. Dew sparkled like jewels on the wild grasses and flowers. My breathing deepened, as I settled upon my mount. Life felt good as it had been before I lost mother and the Goddess in one fateful blow.

Eli, mother's oldest and most trusted servant, rode beside me with my satchel. His reverent silence told me he too was glad to be returning to the Eye temple. He stayed beside me at a protective distance the entire journey. Feeling comfort in his presence, I meditated on the beauty of nature as we rode along. The early morning sun was cleansing, and I was grateful for this quiet time. Everything had happened so quickly, I was dazed. Now, with each step forward, the reality of my undertaking was sinking in.

I was thrilled to be on my way, yet as we neared the Eye Temple a host of worries assailed me. It had been years since I'd made this pilgrimage. How would I be received at the sacred shrine? I remembered my last visit all too well. Passing each landmark along the way, I could feel the strangling grip of father's hands, and remember the earth writhing beneath us like a snake. These painful memories filled my heart with shame. I had been part of father's sacrilege. The terafim had been stolen from my hand. Would I be as welcome by the wise women of the temple, as before? Had the En Priestess forgiven me? My guilt wasn't limited to the past. My disgrace was renewed by having to return to the sanctuary without the terafim. But there was nothing I could do! Father had secreted them away. For all I knew they could be at the Ehulhul temple. I feared the worst.

My feelings were so confused. I was exuberant with expectation, yet also filled with shame and doubt. My uncertainty was exacerbated as the sanctuary rose up on the horizon sparkling in the late afternoon sun. The brilliant blue tiles of the entrance made it seem Ninhursag's heavenly kingdom had been brought down to earth. A gust of wind rose up out of nowhere as I gazed at the awesome sight. The wind was fierce and seemed to attack us as we rode forward, searing through my cloak and finally into my very bones.

I prayed the wind would slacken. But with every step it strengthened until it formed a column of dust towering high in the air. I started to fear it would reach down and carry me away. Even Eli seemed to sense the threat. He rode in next to me. Grabbing hold of my reins he pulled me onto his donkey, then pressed me inside his cloak just in time to keep me from being whisked away. Once I was secure Eli braced himself. Then he rode into the wind muttering fervent prayers beneath his breath, as he guided his well-seasoned donkey toward the massive gate.

When we were near enough to glimpse Ninhursag's winged lion cherubim, the temple's threshold guardians, the tempestuous column of wind transformed into a giant rearing its ugly head. It stood before us, a towering goat headed demon, barring our entrance to the ancient shrine.

I shook with fear inside Eli's cloak. What was this looming monster? Was it the epitome of all my fears, or some gruesome seal the Black Hand had placed upon the temple?

The feline guardians at the gate stood on either side of the entrance behind the raging demon. Concentrating on their stern beauty, I remembered the cherubim from Kak.Si.Di. I closed my eyes and uttered a prayer to invoke their power. "GREAT GODDESS NINHURSAG, AUGUST LADY OF THE SKY CHAMBER, WHOSE POWER ENCOMPASSES HEAVEN AND EARTH, DO NOT FORSAKE US! OPEN WIDE YOUR GATES AND GIVE US SHELTER. SEND FORTH YOUR WINGED LION CHERUBIM! GRANT US THEIR PROTECTION!"

When I opened my eyes the whirling demon had disappeared. We stood alone before the gate. The ancient doors creaked open. We were ushered within.

Eli looked at me with careworn eyes. Tears welling in them, he declared, "Never in all my days have I seen such a monstrosity! Yet it dispersed with your simple prayer. The Mother must be watching over you, my lady."

The starry light of She Who Watches came down around me, as I said, "May the Goddess watch over you Eli, and return you safely home. The Sisters will see that you have a good night's rest. I'll see you after the full moon."

The wind was raging furiously outside, but all was calm inside the temple walls. The winged lion cherubim must still have been with me, for it was Nahmi who opened the gate. She had been one of mother's dearest friends. My heart warmed at the sight of her.

Nahmi smiled and opened wide her arms. "I thank the Goddess that you're safe, Rachel! That demon wind gave me quite a start. I've been waiting for you since noontime. All was quiet until I could make you out a tiny spot upon the horizon. Then that foul wind started up. I feared for your life, Rachel! I suspect that evil apparition was the work of the Black Hand. They've been busy of late with their evil seals and spells. I hoped the temple would be spared."

The temple had been targeted. My worst suspicions had been confirmed.

Nahmi looked at me intently, as she said, "I'm so pleased that you've returned to us at last! And bless you, you have your mother's courage! Just look at the beautiful young woman you've become! Come! You must be exhausted. I'll take you to the Eye Pool. You can wash off the dust from the road there, and make your ablutions."

It had been years since I'd felt such close female bonding. Tears of joy and relief came to my eyes. Though all I could manage was a grateful smile, as I was overcome by feelings of unworthiness.

Following along behind Nahmi grief assailed me at every turn, as my losses were brought up anew. My sorrow was only relieved by the sight of the heavenly temple doves. The dazzling birds came flying in out of nowhere to greet me, shining luminously against the azure sky. One hovered just above my head with wings outstretched like an angel. I felt forgiven when it settled on my shoulder and accompanied me to the Eye Pool.

Nahmi stopped in her tracks at the sight of us. "Such a positive omen! I've never seen a temple dove alight on anyone's shoulder except the En Priestess. She Who Watches is opening her arms to you in welcome, Rachel. I can't wait to tell the En Priestess."

The presence of the dove loosened my tongue. "I love doves, Nahmi. They and the sheep I tend were my only comfort until Jacob arrived. It was so awful when father wouldn't let me come back here. I thought my life was over."

Compassion was in Nahmi's eyes, as she responded, "We knew it must have been hard for you, Rachel. I thought of you so many times over these past years. I wanted to take you away from Laban. But the En Priestess said it wasn't right to interfere with the course of your destiny."

When Nahmi gazed in my eyes, love and understanding passed between us as easily as sunlight through a leaf. I reached out to her. She took me in her arms. Her hair smelled of amber, reminding me of mother. My heart began to thaw releasing a flood of tears. All the anguish from my estrangement with the sanctuary came tumbling out. Not wanting to burden Nahmi, I tried to stop my tears, but it was in vain.

"Forgive me, Nahmi!" I sobbed. "But I've been so lonely! I lost mother and the Sisterhood in one fateful blow. I was afraid I would never set foot here again."

"You were only a child when that happened, Rachel. It wasn't your fault! You weren't to blame! There was nothing you could have done to stop Laban. Nevertheless, it is your destiny to come to terms with him. Follow me! I'll take you to the Eye Pool. Your heart will be cleansed there."

Ninhursag's holy mountain was shining like a rainbow in the distance. The magnificent cruciform temple took my breath away. How I wished I could share this with Jacob! And oh how I wished we could be married there, instead of at home with father and Leah.

Passing by the temple, a shadow crossed my heart. Soon I would enter the abode of the Goddess for my conference with the En Priestess. Would the lioness that guarded the Holy of Holies devour me? Would the En Priestess be as understanding as Nahmi?

A pair of majestic rams greeted us at the Eye Pool. The white ram, the more inquisitive of the two, appeared to be their leader. He came over to scent me out, then began nuzzling me affectionately. The black ram followed suit. After coming through their inspection, they stood beside me, a stalwart pair of escorts, alert to my every move.

Nahmi laughed aloud, satisfied I had passed their inspection. Then she inquired, "Did you bring an offering for the Goddess?"

"Yes! I brought the finest of the first wool from this year's shearing. I'd been saving it for my marriage offering. I hope She Who Watches will find it acceptable."

Nahmi smiled approvingly and stepped back. The two great rams positioned themselves on either side of me, watching with full attention. I bent over shyly, unused to such scrutiny, and removed the milk white bundle from my satchel. The rams' nostrils flared menacingly as the scent of wool exploded in the air.

The white ram pawed the ground with his hooves. So I held the wooly bundle out to him for his perusal. With this he soon calmed down. Though he continued watching me intently as I removed the precious stone from heaven from my pocket and rubbed it over my offering praying. "GREAT GODDESS NINHURSAG, RECEIVE THIS HUMBLE OFFERING, AND ALLOW ME TO ENTER UPON YOUR HOLY MYSTERIES THIS DAY.

Then I threw the wooly bundle out into the lake waiting upon the Goddess's judgement. The wool appeared luminous in the late afternoon sun which played upon the oils on its surface. I stood entranced, forgetting for a moment that the Goddess only accepted offerings which sank into the pool. When the wool reached the center of the lake I began to worry. Just then it disappeared, all except for one small fragment which was snatched up by a golden perch.

The Goddess's oracular fish had accepted my offering. My spirits soared.

Nahmi smiled at me saying, "Another favorable omen! The Goddess must be pleased you're here to send one of the oracular fish to accept your offering. Now prepare yourself for the ordeal of truth! You may drink the pool's illuminating water."

It was a privilege to drink the Eye Pool's hallowed water, but it was also a solemn test. For those of impure heart it was like drinking poison. I had heard of those who had been killed or driven mad from even a small sip. I braced myself and took a drink.

A bolt of lightning went off inside me. I was filled with light and catapulted into the mysterious depths of the pool. Immersed beneath its surface, I opened my eyes in time to catch a glimpse of the golden perch before it slipped into the dark recesses of the pool. A curious joy and lightness gripped my soul as I followed it down. Mother's face appeared smiling before me. It changed into Nahmi, warmth and understanding shining in her eyes. She was speaking with the En Priestess. The En Priestess's face was timeless and serene, but serious. She and Nahmi seemed to be conferring about something of grave importance.

The scene changed, and now I saw father. He was in his study surrounded by his oracles crushing the flower of the dreamers into a fine powder. The scene changed abruptly. Now father was with Jacob and Leah. They were at home and it was a cozy scene. All appeared to be having a good time. While Jacob was absorbed in conversation with father, Leah mixed a powder in some wine and offered it to Jacob. She was seated beside him wearing my best red robe. She was flirting with Jacob and doing everything in her power to be enticing.

Father's abrupt change of heart had taken me so offguard, I hadn't thought about what might be going on at home without me. I was unnerved to see Jacob so comfortable and unguarded. A weight descended on my lungs ending my vision. I swam frantically to the surface gasping for air.

The cooing of my friend the dove welcomed me as I lay panting on the shore. Despite the bird's reassuring presence I was panicked by what I'd seen. Father could be turning over a new leaf, but was there a knife hidden somewhere beneath it? Seeing Jacob so intimate with Leah sent jealousy through me like wild fire. Should I return home at once?

My mind still racing, I realized it was no use. Jacob would only say what he always did when I brought up Leah's seductiveness. 'I was being insecure . . . or sick with jealousy. He was only being nice to Leah, because he felt sorry for her and didn't want to hurt her feelings.' But what would happen if he took that drink?

The white dove was the only ray of sunlight shining through the dark foreboding that had me in its grip. Gazing at the bird's innocent beauty, I recalled my first meeting with Jacob at the well. I told myself I had nothing to fear. Love was the most powerful force in the universe. Our love would keep us true to one another. Jacob was a man of spirit. He wanted a Higher Marriage. His God would protect him.

But even after I put on my novice robes and retired to the moon lodge to tend the sacred fire, a curious anxiety possessed me. The light of the Goddess was strong inside the sanctuary. It lit up every nook and cranny in my heart. I was forced to realize how enthralled I was with Jacob, and how far I'd grown away from the Goddess since his arrival. Even now inside the sanctuary in deepest meditation, thoughts of Jacob could take me over. Had Jacob succeeded in taking me away from the Goddess, where father had tried and failed?

She Who Watches sent me a dream later that night. Two men appeared in the darkness of the moon lodge. I couldn't see either of them directly, only their shadows. But they were tampering with the sacred fire. Before I could stop them the fire had gone out.

The fire was well fed. I had banked it securely before I closed my eyes. Nonetheless, I awoke in a sweat, terrified the fire had gone out. I was so unnerved, that even when I could see the flames with my own two eyes, a terrible fear possessed me. My skin crawled. I was so sensitive to every shadow that played upon the walls of my chamber, I couldn't take my eyes off the sacred flame.

When Nahmi knocked on the door, I jumped with a start.

"What's the matter, Rachel? Didn't you sleep well last night?" she inquired solicitously.

Her question only fanned my fears. "I had a disturbing dream. I'll feel better soon."

"Would you like to discuss it?"

"No!" I said shaking my head firmly.

Nahmi nodded. "As you choose. You'll be able to share your dream with the En Priestess soon enough. She wants to see you this afternoon."

In my present state I wasn't comforted by the news. Of course I wanted to see the En Priestess, but I was afraid she would bring up what happened at mother's funeral. Now to complicate matters further, there was my disturbing dream, and my vision in the Eye Pool. The En Priestess had inquired about my dreams on my first visit to the temple. Would she ask again?

Nahmi stared at me, puzzled by my silence.

"I didn't think the En Priestess would want to see me so soon." I said averting her gaze.

"The En Priestess has something very important to discuss with you. But we'll stop by the Ashera grove and visit your mother's grave first. You'll find comfort there."

"Thank you, Nahmi!" I said with relief. "I've thought about the grove so often. It's as though I left a part of myself there."

"Wait until you see how lovely the grove is in springtime!" said Nahmi smiling.

10

INVITATION TO THE HIGHER MARRIAGE

THE ASHERA GROVE WAS A WONDERLAND OF BLOSSOMS. I STOOD AND gazed at it in awe as Nahmi left me at the path leading to mother's grave. This was my first time to enter the grove alone. It felt eerie even with the sunlight pouring through the lacy canopy of trees, as memories of mother's funeral came flooding back to me. Mother's burial mound had grown substantially in beauty and was covered by a flaming carpet of scarlet and orange poppies. The stone pillar I erected was still intact, and had recently been anointed with oil. Brightly colored butterflies flew about the pillar, dancing with the breeze then alighting on it from time to time.

The Ashera tree was dressed in sultry yellow blossoms, its charms sounding a mesmerizing song. I reached into my pocket for the precious stone from heaven and placed it beneath the tree as an offering to replace the terafim. Then I took the last of the precious water I'd been saving from the day of Jacob's arrival and poured it over mother's pillar. The ground beneath me began to hum. I fell to my knees and looked up at the hollow I'd selected years ago for the terafim. A remarkable spotted leopard was seated there, staring at me with emerald eyes.

The spirit of the Ashera began to whisper. YOUR MOTHER IS IN THE STARRY REACHES WITH SHE WHO WATCHES. YOU ARE AT AN IMPORTANT CROSSROADS. REMEMBER WELL HER IN-STRUCTIONS! GREAT CHALLENGES ARE IN STORE FOR YOU. YOU WILL BE TESTED IN YOUR THINKING AND FEELING, AND IN YOUR ACTIONS TOO. AND REMEMBER TO BEWARE OF TREACHERY FROM THOSE YOU HOLD AS DEAR!

The leopard stood up, curled its tail looking me straight in the eyes, then disappeared. I felt incredible joy to realize that mother was one of the chosen. She was with the pure resurrected spirits who lived in heaven clothed in bodies of light, as stars. She wasn't eating dust with the miserable souls in Arallu. Yet my head was spinning at the warning from the wise spirit of the Ashera. I was to be tested?? My time of trial was over. I was here to prepare for my forthcoming marriage. Why was I being warned of treachery when all my fondest wishes were about to be fulfilled?

Father's hatred of the Eye Temple had softened. He'd allowed me to return for the sacred rites. I was to marry Jacob as soon as I returned home. Things could not have been going better for me. What could the oracle possibly be warning me about? Who should I beware of? Father? I would soon be married and out from under his control. There was nothing he could do. My marriage had been agreed upon. Father could ply Jacob with wine and try to charm him, but Jacob was a man of vision. He would not allow our love to be compromised. He would see through father's ploys.

But what of father's sudden change of heart? I was used to his many moods and manipulations, but the thoughtfulness of this gift threw me off balance. His generosity had so taken me by surprise, I turned all my doubt upon myself. Perhaps my dreams and visions were nothing but my own fears and insecurities . . . or punishment for my having neglected the Goddess? Or was I being driven mad from having tasted of the Eye Pool's potent waters? I was so beset with uncertainty I even questioned the Ashera's wisdom. So enthralled was I with Jacob, my thinking had been swayed. The spirit of the Ashera could be trying to lead me back to the temple. Or maybe I was as bad as father and Leah thought, and I had lost my inner sight as punishment?

I was so beset with anguished thoughts. Finally, out of respect for the tranquility of the grove, I paid my last respects to mother and departed, oblivious to the wonders all around me.

When Nahmi came to fetch me for my audience with the En Priestess, I was in the shade of the giant cedar tree where she'd left me. I'd never developed father and Leah's facility for disguising my feelings, but today I wished I had. I didn't want to burden Nahmi with my self-doubts.

I tried to force a smile, but Nahmi wasn't fooled. "The En Priestess will see you shortly, Rachel. Have you any questions before your audience?" she asked solicitously.

"No! Thank you, Nahmi. I'll prepare for my audience in silence as we walk."

"Very well!" she said with a smile of disbelief.

I followed at a slow pace my apprehension building with every step. The En Priestess would see through me, as mother always had. Did she expect me to have the terafim? Would she be angry with me when she learned I didn't?

We headed down the grand processional way to the Temple. The awesome cruciform temple maintained the sacred bond between Heaven and Earth. It was aligned with the rising and setting of Kak.Si.Di. an invitation to Goddess for the sacred rites. The Processional Way faced east in the direction of Mt. Ararat, the World Mountain. The great Angels of Heaven were known to still visit there from time to time. Three other processional walks soon converged with ours. At least here all roads still led to the Goddess.

Ninhursag was the Great Mother of the Sky Chamber. The Eye Temple which loomed before me, had once been a landing platform for Nefilim ships. Before the Great Flood She Who Watches had stayed here on visits to Earth. Everything was humbled in the shadow of the Goddess's shrine, which was as near to heaven as I had been. It took my breath away to see it shimmering like a rainbow in the afternoon sun.

She Who Watches was here. I could feel Her presence as I approached the sacred shrine. Power coursed through my body. My vision deepened. Gazing up at the Eye Temple I remembered Jacob's and my dream of a ladder reaching to the stars with angels ascending and descending. Jacob and I believed in different Gods, but we aspired for the same thing. We merely approached from different paths. Our heart was one. Surely with time our paths would meet as they did here. Everything converged in the truth in the end. But oh how I yearned for us to ascend the temple's ceremonial ramp together, and be wed in the Sacred Mating rite of the God and Goddess.

I trembled at the sight of the colossal statue of Ninhursag seated on her lion throne in the center of the square. Six more winged lion cherubim flanked the ascension ramps protecting the portals to the holy shrine. My knees went weak standing before the magnificent feline guardians reminiscent of the Sky Walkers from Kak.Si.Di. I stood there awestruck until Nahmi encouraged me to approach the statue of the Goddess. I knelt down and looked directly up into its all-seeing eyes. A ray of sunlight struck the statues's blue sapphire eyes. The star which dwelled within them came to life.

I heard the Goddess in my heart. TRUST YOURSELF, RACHEL! YOU HAVE THE ANCIENT EYES AND EARS OF THE NADITU SISTERHOOD. HAVE COURAGE! YOUR VISION IS YOUR STRENGTH. DON'T ALLOW YOUR FEARS AND SELF-DOUBTS TO UNDERMINE YOU. HAVE FAITH IN THE DIVINE PLAN. GATHER YOUR COURAGE AND DO NOT SHRINK FROM WHAT LIES BEFORE YOU. IT COULD BE YOUR DOWNFALL.

In the next moment everything was still once more. All I could hear was my heart pounding inside my breast. The Goddess's words struck deep chords in me. I put my forehead to the ground and surrendered to Her wisdom. I don't know how long I stayed in the peaceful umbrage of the Goddess, but Nahmi finally beckoned me. Her expression was grave as she led me to the Eye Temple.

I paused before the winged lions at the entrance, giving thanks for their timely rescue the previous day. Then I asked their permission to enter the holy shrine. I was filled with awe as I crossed the hallowed threshold. It was cool and dark inside. The sweet smell of amber incense lingered in the air. When my eyes adjusted I could see the main altar on the south wall. Nahmi led me back into the potent recesses of the shrine, and left me at the spiral stairway leading down into the Holy of Holies beneath the temple. I was to make the descent alone.

It was black as night gazing down the unfathomable reaches of the stairwell. The darkness was so thick, I couldn't distinguish the steps before me. Fear pawed at my back, and caught my breath. My novice robes suddenly felt strange against my skin. Each step had to be earned by my searching hands and feet as I went on down the seemingly endless spiral stairway. There was no sense of time in the inner recesses of the temple. But at last my feet touched ground with a heavy thud. I reached out in the dark like a frightened newborn at the portal of the holy cave.

What was I to do now? Finally, as I grew more comfortable with the impenetrable darkness, I remembered mother had stopped here at the threshold to pray and ask the Goddess's permission to enter Her holy womb. With hands upon the ancient door, I beseeched the Goddess. GREAT MOTHER NINHURSAG, PORTAL OF LIFE, PLEASE FIND ME WORTHY TO ENTER YOUR HOUSE OF LIFE. ALLOW ME TO BE REBORN IN YOUR FORGIVENESS. AND PREPARE ME FOR A HIGHER MARRIAGE WITH MY BELOVED.

The ancient door creaked opened, and I was blinded by the light of a single oil lamp. The next thing I knew I was face to face with the En Priestess. The golden lioness, the cave's guardian, stood beside her. It came straight to me and sniffed my hand. The En Priestess was radiant and serene, untouched by the years. The flame inside her eyes reached into my soul. I stood motionless before her gaze, hoping for a sign of welcome. I was about to lose my nerve when the great cat started purring and licked my hand. The En Priestess's lips parted in a knowing smile, and she ushered me within.

Power surged up my spine as I crossed the threshold, and I was reminded the entire temple had been fashioned around this sacred spot. Though it had been years since I'd been inside this primal womb, it felt like I was home. My gaze was drawn to the walls embedded with multitudes of glistening eye beads. The warm glow of the oil lamp illuminated hosts of signs and symbols drawn over the centuries in women's wise blood. On the altar was the Stone that Whispers. My heart fluttered at the sight of the enormous rock from heaven. Streamings of pleasure coursed through my body when the great cat crossed in front of me, and sat down peacefully beside the altar.

The En Priestess stood before me, intense yet subtle as a flame. Her monumental presence rooted like an ancient tree. My heart warmed as she took my hand and brought me to the altar. We stood together before a golden incense burner carved with two winged creatures with eagle heads and the strong sinuous bodies of lions, who were crushing two giant serpents beneath their feet. The magnificent relic was smoldering with hot coals. A tremor ran through my body at the sight of the magnificent creatures from Kak.Si.Di.

I breathed in deeply as the En Priestess fed the coals with fragrant chunks of copal and myrrh. I had the distinct impression my trials were about to begin. We watched together in silence as the smoke billowed in an ever widening column rising upward. I closed my eyes and stepped forward into the purifying veil of smoke.

As it filled my nostrils, I prayed. "OH GREAT MOTHER NINHUR-SAG, ACCEPT MY HEARTFELT LOVE. BRING ME SAFELY THROUGH MY TRIALS AND PREPARE ME FOR MY MARRIAGE WITH JACOB. BLESS US WITH A TRUE LOVE. SHOW US THE WAY TO A HIGHER MARRIAGE SO THAT YOUR GRACE MAY FLOW TO EARTH ONCE MORE."

"You've turned into a beautiful woman, Rachel! The Eye Goddess surrounds you with heavenly light. Come! Stand here before me!" said the En Priestess smiling.

I stepped out of the incense into the wisdom of her gaze. Looking into her eyes I felt a peace that went deeper than all my fears. The En Priestess's eyes were a warm brown tinged with gold. To stand within her gaze was like basking in the sun at noontime. There was no place to hide.

"I can see that it's been very difficult for you since your mother's death. There is great sadness and disappointment behind your eyes. Your light has been sequestered. It's buried deep inside you now. You're afraid to let it out. . . . You're still a virgin. . . . Tell me, how does it go with you and Laban?"

My breath halted. No longer accustomed to being seen, I looked away startled by the En Priestess's penetrating insight. "All you see is true, oh Wise One." I replied after a moment. "It has been difficult with father since mother's death. He changed greatly when he no longer had mother to balance his ravenous greed for power. He's risen in the ranks of the Brotherhood of the Black Hand. They're always around now."

I cast my eyes downward and continued with a heavy heart. "He forbade me to return here after mother's funeral. It broke my heart to think

I'd never see you again. I haven't been allowed to speak of the Goddess or attend any of the Women's Circles in our village. I don't even know if they have them anymore."

"I continue observances on my own, but father's ways are cunning and most convincing. He has a fiendish oracle that he fashioned on an eclipse of the moon with the skull of his firstborn son by Suzannah, his concubine. He summons up demons with that foul tool that haunt you while you sleep, and turn your mind upside down and inside out until you no longer know yourself. Then of course, father understands the persuasions of the rod very well. He takes it to me whenever I confront him with the truth, or differ with him in any way."

Relieved to have that out of the way I looked up at the En Priestess again. "Leah's denounced the Goddess. She sides with father in everything. I was miserable til Jacob arrived. Everything's improved since he came. Even father treats me better now that I'm his bait to keep Jacob working for him. Father's prosperity has returned thanks to Jacob's blessing. He's always on his best behavior when Jacob's around. He may actually be fond of Jacob . . . well . . . as fond as he can be of anyone. But I mustn't go on like this. Father and Leah hate it when I talk too much."

"I'm sorry it has been so difficult for you, Rachel! Why do you think Laban's allowed you to return to the Eye temple at this time?"

The En Priestess's question caught me so off guard, I replied haltingly, "He said it was a wedding present. I didn't dare question him. I was afraid he might change his mind."

The En Priestess looked serious. "I've long known of Laban's connection to the Black Hand. Your mother married him so he could be watched and tempered. Laban's a powerful moon priest. He's clever, but his heart is as black as the gloves he wears."

"The Black Hand is an unscrupulous secret society. Morals, values, and compassion have no place in their covert agenda to bring the world under their control. The Brotherhood worship riches and get their power from that ancient Dragon of Heaven, Nanna/Sin. Envy and lust for power are what fuel the Evil One. He fosters these vices in all those who worship him. Sin and his minions feed off human misery and violence. His purpose is to undermine humankind. The Brotherhood are masters at perverting love and wisdom. They're expert at creating social chaos to get people to hand over their liberty."

"Sin and his Brotherhood are decidedly anti-female. Sin made that clear when he seized the lunar power of the Goddess and claimed it for his own. To be against the Feminine is to be against the wellsprings of life. Imagine the audacity it took for a male God to seize the rulership of the moon which regulates the Blood Mysteries of the Feminine, and all the tides of birth and death upon the Earth!"

"Even rulership of the moon was not enough to satisfy Nanna/Sin's greed for power. He stole the Tablets of Destiny, which establish the sacred measures that uphold the universe, from his brother Enlil. When they were in Sin's hands the Anunnaki were forced to abandon their cities. Only Ninurta, Ninhursag's son, stayed behind to capture them. After he got them back the Anunnaki called a council and voted to cast Sin and his evil host out of heaven. They exiled Sin to Earth as punishment. Enlil sent a storm from heaven to destroy Ur, Nanna/Sin's city. The storm was more devastating than any other. It began with a huge explosion and a great mushroom shaped cloud that set off fires which couldn't be contained. It brought with it an evil wind whose poison gas fouled the earth, the water, and the air, destroying everything in its path. Dead bodies were mounded up in heaps that melted away before it like fat in a flame. Entire cities were levelled no more to be seen. With Sumer in ruins the Anunnaki fled."

"Since Sin and his minions have been exiled here, humankind has been degenerating. The Anunnaki had been tampering with humankind for untold centuries. In their effort to control, they cut humanity off from more than 85% of their brain capacity. Because of Sin and those reptilian Anunnaki, earthlings have been severed from their spirit vision and intuitive faculties, their direct link with the Creator, and confined to the dull world of the senses. Hence the need for the terafim to connect the worthy with the Nefilim."

A wry look came over the En Priestess's face, as she said, "Laban probably thought he was emulating Nanna/Sin when he stole the terafim at your mother's funeral. His possession of them has allowed him to rise high in the ranks of the Brotherhood. Do you know where he keeps the terafim, Rachel?"

My face paled at the mention of mother's oracles, and I responded full of shame. "Please forgive me, your holiness. I haven't seen the terafim since mother's funeral. I've no idea where father hides them. They're not with his other oracles."

"That's unfortunate!" declared the En Priestess. "The Black Hand despise Ninhursag because it was her son Ninurta, who vanquished Sin. They've vowed to wipe out the Goddess and the Naditu Sisterhood. They want the terafim to deprive us of our most powerful tool. The terafim are a bridge between heaven and earth, the world of spirit and the world of sense. If your heart is pure and you have the necessary knowledge and training, you can use the terafim to communicate with the Nefilim. If Laban figures out the secret of their power, there could be dire consequences. Promise me, you'll try to recapture them!"

"I promise to do my best!" I said fervently.

"Very well! At least we can be thankful Laban has sent you back to us. It was the answer to my prayers, Rachel. You've been on my mind very much of late. Your time has come to be of service. It's wonderful how the Goddess works."

The En Priestess's words filled me with hope, that lifted me above my shame.

"Spring is the season of rebirth, the time when the fates are decreed for the coming year." she continued. "The fate of all the crops are determined by the delicate balance in the opposing forces in nature at this time. That's why the Sacred Mating has always been consummated at this time of year. The earth's productivity, and all cycles of fertility depend upon the enactment of this holy rite. Do you know about the Sacred Mating ritual?"

"Mother spoke of it. She said it was an ancient rite enacted by the High Priest and Priestess. But she never explained its full meaning and purpose as you did just now."

The En Priestess drew near. Gazing deep into my eyes she inquired, 'Do you still want to become a Naditu Priestess, Rachel? . . . Do you want it with all your heart?"

Eyes welling with tears of joy, I said, "Yes, I do! I've always wanted it, your holiness. Is it possible without the terafim?"

"You could become a full-fledged Naditu Priestess, Rachel. But you must be willing to make the necessary sacrifices. And you would have to do exactly as I say."

The En Priestess paused for a moment. "You have been chosen by the Goddess, Rachel. Your mother was wise enough to see that in the stars at your birth. She named you Rachel, after the Ewe of Heaven. The Great Ages have shifted from Taurus into Aries, moving from the fertile lunar Bull into the warring solar Ram. A wondrous opportunity is being offered to you. You are being called to be of service as in the days of old. A window in time is being opened. It's in the scope of your highest destiny to be consort of the great Ram of Heaven. Are you willing to accept this invitation and bear the consequences?"

I regarded the En Priestess in puzzlement not understanding what she meant. "Consort of the Great Ram of Heaven? You must mean my cousin Jacob, your Holiness. I'm here to prepare for marriage with him. He is Yahweh's chosen. Is he the Great Ram of Heaven?"

The En Priestess shook her head solemnly. "No, my dear! I'm asking you to become the Nindingir, the Bride of Heaven. Lady of God, the chosen woman appointed to take the place of the Goddess on Earth in the Sacred Mating Rite. You would become the bride of one of the Nefilim as in the days of old when the Gods still walked the earth."

I stammered out, "But . . . but . . . how can that be? I'm not worthy! Father tells me all the time that I'm vain and foolish, and mustn't put on airs. Besides, I'm already promised to Jacob!"

The En Priestess looked me in the eyes. "Is that what your father tells you? You have the Ancient Eyes. The nature spirits speak to you. You are more than you know, Rachel! But I can't confide more in you until I know your answer."

I continued meekly. "I . . . I . . . don't know what to say, oh Wise One. I'm not even sure I know what you mean."

"You just told me you want to be a Naditu Priestess. Well this is your chance! To be chosen Nindingir is the greatest honor that can be granted. One of the Nefilim, the great Angels of Heaven, will come down. You would be the Bride of Heaven, Rachel. You would put on the bright pala robe and wear the horned headdress indicating that you have taken on the role of the Goddess on Earth."

"But . . . but I'm only a simple mortal girl." I stammered out.

"The horned headdress will enable you to access the ancient light body, and attune you to the stars. You shall wear the girdle of the Goddess, whose seven stones predict the fate of humankind. Your spirit will be expanded. You will await the God on the golden couch inside the

Goddess's chamber. The Stone that Whispers tells me one of the Nefilim will come down as in the days of old. You have only to acquiesce and he will appear at this next full moon."

"One of the Nefilim will come down to Earth?" I asked incredulously.

"The Gods are merciful. The omens are propitious. The full moon coincides with the first day of spring this year. The Stone that Whispers tells me it shall be an eclipse. These are desperate times that call for special measures. The evil wind has blown throughout the land between the two rivers destroying once proud Sumer. The Great Ram of Heaven has agreed to come down and enact the Marriage of Heaven and Earth as in the days of old. You have been selected for this great honor. The Sacred Mating is for the good of all the Earth, Rachel. It would be a healing. Heaven and Earth would be brought together in peace and love. You would conceive a star child. Kingship would flow from heaven again."

I felt lightheaded and had to steady myself. "But what about Jacob? I came here to prepare for our marriage. I'm promised to him. WE were to marry on that night."

The En Priestess narrowed her eyes. "Tell me about Jacob! Is he worthy of you? Does he understand our ways? Does he honor you as a Priestess of the Goddess and appreciate you for the special woman you are? Lastly, is he capable of being the priest of the Great Ram of Heaven?"

My time of testing was at hand. These were the most frightening questions the En Priestess could have asked. I took a deep breath before responding. "These are difficult questions, oh Wise One. Please try to understand! Jacob is Yahweh's chosen. He is a very special man. The blessing of his God is all about him. Everything he touches prospers. He's the only man I know with the courage and strength to resist the Black Hand."

"It is noble that Jacob resists the Brotherhood." said the En Priestess interrupting. "But these feelings you have for Jacob, is it true love, or mere infatuation? Does he honor you as a Naditu Priestess, and encourage you to take your power? Truth and love must be equally matched and the souls' purposes aligned for a Higher Marriage, Rachel. A true love recognizes us for who we are, and helps us to realize the fullness of our being."

I thought for a moment, then responded, "Jacob calls me his angel."

The En Priestess nodded. "Please go on!"

"Jacob is my true love. He loves me and respects me. He's still a virgin. He's been saving himself, because he wants a Higher Marriage. He was sent to me by his mother Rebekah. Do you remember Rebekah?"

The En Priestess nodded thoughtfully. "I remember Rebekah! She was one of us, though she was Laban's sister."

I nodded.

The En Priestess continued, "Jacob is blessed to have come from such a one. But tell me, what has become of Rebekah? I have received no word from her since she married Isaac."

"I don't know what has become of Rebekah, your Holiness." I answered meekly. "I only know that Jacob is her favorite son, and that she was taken into Yahweh's confidence. Yahweh told her the older twin would serve the younger. On account of their discourse Rebekah saw to it that Jacob received the blessing from his father even though he was the younger twin. Rebekah spoke to Jacob of the Naditu Sisterhood. She kindled in him the desire for a Higher Marriage. She shared these things with him in the hopes he wouldn't compromise himself, as his brother Esau did. Rebekah's words have been very important to Jacob. That's why he saved himself for me all these years."

The En Priestess remained silent, as I continued, "Jacob is an outstanding man. His Lord Yahweh speaks to him in his dreams. He's had visions of the Nefilim ascending and descending from heaven. It's just that Jacob is a bit intolerant. He doesn't believe in the Goddess, or understand our ways. He believes only in one God, the Father God Yahweh."

"He doesn't believe in the Goddess?" asked the En Priestess in astonishment.

"Not yet, Your Holiness, but I'm working to change that. I've had to keep my allegiance to the Goddess a secret."

The En Priestess stepped back. A look of sorrow, then indignation crossed her face. "Jacob receives his instructions and the blessing of his God through his mother Rebekah, a Naditu Priestess, yet he cannot accept the Goddess, or you as Her Priestess? How blind and ungrateful! No wonder your light is dimmed! Think what your life would be like with such a man!"

The stunning truth of her words cut through me like a knife, and I questioned defensively. "But what of my vision at the well? She Who Watches sent me a vision of Jacob on the day of my first overshadowment. I thought that vision meant Jacob was to be my husband!"

"I remember your vision! It was one of the last messages I received from Anna. Your vision told you that Jacob would be in your future. But he must be worthy and earn the privilege of being your husband. These are desperate times, Rachel. You must give this decision great thought. What kind of life would it be for you if Jacob doesn't recognize the Goddess? If he doesn't recognize the Goddess, he won't be able to recognize you as Her priestess, or respect you for the Naditu woman you are. Tell me, does he realize you may not be able to provide him with any offspring?"

I gasped aloud in surprise.

The En Priestess continued on unperturbed, "A Naditu Priestess is an unsown field, one who lets her womb live in the wisdom of the Stars. We, Naditu women, who possess the Ancient Eyes are under certain strictures when it comes to giving birth."

The En Priestess gave me a long hard look before continuing. "For every privilege there is a price, Rachel. We are dedicated instruments of the Goddess. Our power is on the spiritual plane, not the physical. The Goddess uses us in a different way. If we ever do give birth, it's to bring the highest souls down when the times require it. But these births are rare and according to the Goddess's purpose . . . not for our own gratification, or that of our partner's."

My heart sank at the En Priestess's words, and I turned my face hoping she wouldn't see the tears welling in my eyes. After a moment of tense silence I responded, "I didn't understand it in quite that way. Or at least, I didn't understand it as clearly as I do now after hearing it from you."

"There's more that I could tell you concerning these Mysteries, Rachel. But suffice it for me to say that as a Naditu woman your psychic and spiritual centers are highly developed. That is the mark the Goddess places upon Her own. A Naditu woman still has a connection to the ancient spirit body. As a result her reproductive centers remain in a somewhat dormant state, and are slowed down."

"A Naditu Priestess's procreativity is a divine prerogative. Of course, that is true for all women. It's the Goddess who blesses women with fertility. But only a Naditu woman is fit to carry the blood line from the Stars. For this honor she must sacrifice her will to procreate."

I was stunned and had to fight back tears as I listened.

"I've just offered you the privilege of becoming the Nindingir at this next full moon. As the Nindingir you would mate with one of the Nefilim. But She Who Watches does not bestow Her favors lightly, and this great honor would require much of you. You would be the Birth Mother of a star child, a Divine King, as in the days of old. You could take up residence here at the Temple, or return to your life at home. But you would have to stay in close contact with the Sisterhood through the terafim, or the temple doves. If you choose to return home, you may facilitate your place in society by marrying. Though your true husband would be the Nefilim, not your earthly husband. Jacob would be in service to the Nefilim, a guardian protector for you and your child. He would not have the same sexual privileges as a husband. Furthermore, he would have to agree to all of this before your marriage could take place."

"From what you have shared with me concerning Jacob, it seems unlikely he would consent to such an arrangement. Tell me, does he expect to have children by you?"

The En Priestess grew silent in response to the shattered look on my face. She closed her eyes drawing her power inward, praying for the Eye Goddess to overshadow her. My inner sight began to tingle and suddenly the whole room came alive with starry light. The Stone that Whispers began vibrating on the altar. The lioness came and stood beside her as the En Priestess pulled the mantle of the Goddess down around her. I forgot the confusion churning inside me, as I watched the miraculous transformation taking place.

When the En Priestess opened her eyes she had taken on the mien and power of the Goddess, and seemed to tower above me. Her voice rang out more formidable and inscrutable than ever, "YOU ARE A NADITU WOMAN, RACHEL, ONE OF THE SISTERHOOD. YOU HAVE THE CONNECTION TO THE SPIRITUAL LIGHT BODY. YOU MAY RUN FROM IT, BUT YOU CAN NEVER ALTER THAT FACT. I HAVE NEED OF YOUR SERVICE AT THIS TIME. IT IS FOR THIS REASON THAT YOU WERE BORN. YOUR DESTINY IS TO CLIMB THE LADDER TO THE STARS AND MATE WITH MY SON.

THERE HAVE BEEN GREAT ABUSES IN THE PAST. THE

ANUNNAKI WERE THE FOUNDERS OF THE SUMERIAN CUL-
TURE. THEY TAUGHT THE ANCIENT SUMERIANS ALL THE
ARTS OF CIVILIZATION. THEY TRAVEL BETWEEN DIFFERENT
DIMENSIONS AND CAN LIVE THOUSANDS OF YEARS. THEY
ARE VERY INTELLIGENT AND HAVE DEVELOPED VAST
WEAPONRY, BUT THEIR HEARTS ARE COLD. BEING PART
HUMAN AND PART REPTILE THEY HAVE LITTLE COMPASSION
FOR HUMANKIND. ENKI AND I ALLIED OURSELVES WITH
THEM TO BE A BENEFICIAL INFLUENCE, AND COUNTERACT
THEIR CALLOUS DISREGARD FOR HUMANS. BUT THEY ARE
DRUNK WITH POWER, AND SO CONSUMED IN THEIR OWN
JEALOUS RIVALRIES THAT THEY HAVE TURNED THEIR BACKS
ON THE STAR WISDOM FROM KAK.SI.DI. MANY OF THE
ANUNNAKI HAVE FALLEN INTO MATTER. SIN AND HIS EVIL
MINIONS HAVE JOINED FORCES WITH THE ANCIENT SERPENT
RACE. TOGETHER THEY CONTROL THE BROTHERHOOD OF
THE BLACK HAND.

ONLY A GOD KING SEEDED FROM ON HIGH CAN STAND
AGAINST THEIR UNITED FORCE. YOU MAY WEAR THE SACRED
GIRDLE OF THE STARS AND ENACT THE HIGHER MARRIAGE
WITH MY SON ON THE NEXT FULL MOON. IT WILL BE AN
ECLIPSE. A WINDOW IN TIME SHALL BE OPENED. CONSIDER
WELL YOUR CHOICE. THE FUTURE OF EARTH IS AT STAKE.

The Goddess's words resounded in my heart, like a deafening storm.
I was a simple mortal woman. How could I respond to the enormity of
the challenge? It seemed so distant and unreal after the simple life I had
been living. My heart belonged to Jacob. His warmth and love were real
and close at hand, something I could count on. While this invitation
placed a lonely burden on my shoulders. My mind was reeling. My heart
was stunned and silent.

I looked up at the En Priestess wanting to answer her. But I could
find no words. The conflict between my love for Jacob and the Goddess
was raging inside me. And with Jacob's influence, the Sacred Mating rite
now seemed like a strange alien rite.

The En Priestess studied my face carefully. When she spoke she was
no longer overshadowed by the Goddess, and there was disappointment
in her eyes. "The Sacred Mating is no strange alien rite!" she said sternly.

I drew back in shame and embarrassment. Could the En Priestess read my mind?

The Wise One continued on more evenly, "The Sacred Mating is the Marriage of Heaven and Earth. It was designed to uplift humanity and keep the wisdom and light of the Stars flowing to Earth. For untold centuries it has promoted spiritual harmony and balance. Great imbalances afflict the Earth as a result of the suppression of the Goddess and these holy rites. The situation will only become worse, if you do not enact the ritual. The drought . . . the Black Hand . . . the suppression of women and the Goddess, these and many other problems will only become more severe."

"The Great Mother Goddess is the instructor of the human heart, Rachel. If the Goddess is not revered the hearts of humankind will harden. In time women, and even life itself, will no longer be honored. Ponder these things carefully. Your enactment of the Sacred Mating would strengthen the Goddess's position here on Earth. It would result in an enormous influx of love to temper the rapacious greed and power striving rampant here. A positive fate would be decreed. Kingship would flow from Heaven again. The wisdom and justice of Kak.Si.Di. would preside once more. All the great stars of heaven would bow to your son. The Earth would rejoice and bring forth abundance, sharing her wealth and secrets with him. You would be the Spiritual Mother of a great people. Your sexuality an altar to heal the abuses of the past. The reptilian lords would be put in their rightful place. The whole world would be blessed through your service."

"Your suffering would end and you would be released from your thralldom to Jacob. The connection to your light body would be strengthened. Your Higher Self would be revealed in all its splendor through your communion with the Nefilim. You would be a blessed example to women and help prevent their degradation."

The En Priestess's words fell on deaf ears.

I was promised to Jacob, and missed him so. I had given him my word. I loved him with my whole heart, and longed to become one flesh with him. I was afraid Jacob wouldn't consider it a blessing, that I was chosen Nindingir. He might consider it an abomination. I could lose his love forever if I went through with the holy rite. Jacob wanted children, great numbers of children to inherit the land Yahweh promised him. He might reject me and take another wife, or hold it against me all our lives.

On the other hand I had always longed to be a Naditu Priestess, and this was a blessed opportunity. I should have been grateful for the chance to be of service and strengthen my relationship to the Starry Ones of heaven. And oh, how I dreaded disappointing the En Priestess again!

Why did my love for Jacob have to compromise my Priestesshood? Why was it so complex and difficult? Was it father's meddling? If I hadn't returned to the Eye Temple I would have married Jacob on this special moon. We would have offered our love to the God and Goddess in our own private rite. I would have gone on honoring the Goddess in my heart, as I did before. Why did it have to be a choice between my Priestesshood and my marriage? And if I failed to take part in this holy rite, was I placing my own happiness above my allegiance to the Goddess and the good of Earth? Was that admissible? Or would I be damned forever to walk the grim halls of Arallu?

My head was swimming with questions. All I could do was turn to the En Priestess, and inquire, "Oh Wise One! Why do I feel so torn apart? I don't want to compromise my loyalty to Jacob. I thought he was the Goddess's choice for me."

The En Priestess answered with sadness in her eyes. "This is an important time of reckoning, Rachel. We stand between two Great Ages at the end of a mighty civilization. Such momentous times are always fraught. The wars of gods and men have scorched the earth. Great Sumer is in ruins. The Goddess is being suppressed. The Tree of Life is being turned upside down. Women are forgetting the ancient ways, and are no longer honored as the source of life. Instead they are treated like chattel and given no self-determination. We have come through a period of great abuse of power, not only by men but by many of the olden gods. The ancient blue blood of the Nefilim has been corrupted and mixed with the red blood of mortal man."

"Since Sin has taken over the lunar power, the Blood Mysteries of the Feminine have been defiled. Women no longer listen to their wise blood, or give it to the earth in offering. The Black Hand fill women with shame concerning their Goddess given power. In time they shall rob them of all the ancient wisdom of the Goddess, and find ways to control the cycles of their bodies. Life itself is no longer sacred, when Sin and the Brotherhood pour the blood of innocent victims on the earth."

"You know the story of Nanna/Sin. His daughter, Inanna, is no better. She debased herself by falling in love with Sargon, a mere mortal with none of the ancient Sumerian blood of the Gods in his veins. Inanna has made a dreadful spectacle of herself. Using Sargon and his Assyrian empire as her tool, she went on a rampage against Sumer. Like her father, she attempted to usurp supreme power from the Olden Gods. Those Anunnaki reptiles are all alike in their greed for power and control. Inanna drove Sargon to conquer the four quarters, stopping at nothing, not even the downfall of Sumer to satisfy her lust for power. I fear that one day no one will have heard of Ninhursag. The only Goddess they will know is Inanna, the great Whore of Babylon."

"The Assyrian conquest has proved a disaster. Sumer has been toppled. Its arts and sciences have all been stolen. The human and the celestial have mixed, resulting in a great loss of purity and value for all. Even the Gods have been corrupted. As a result of her battle lust, Inanna too has come to hunger after human blood and the smell of burning flesh. She now exacts human sacrifice in her temples like her father. Only blood and more blood can appease their terrible cravings."

"These are the complex threads of destiny which topple the Goddess from Her throne. The Marriage of Heaven and Earth must be enacted in purity again to end all this. I fear it is our only hope. The Naditu Sisterhood must stem the tide of corruption which plagues this great planet. It's only thanks to Ninhursag and Enki that humanity has been saved, and a few of the Anunnaki have remained faithful to the instructions from Kak.Si.Di."

"The Age of Iron is fast approaching. It will be the Age of Yahweh. Yahweh is a mighty warrior. His wrath has been summoned up to sweep away the great abuses of the past. But Yahweh is a jealous God. And He too shall suppress the Goddess in his bid for power. He will use the transgressions of Inanna and Sin to dismiss ALL the Olden Ones of Heaven. He is determined to accrue absolute power to himself to correct the abuses of the past. Some of this is necessary, but even Yahweh goes too far when he disallows the Goddess. How can there be peace, justice, or balance upon the Earth when Yahweh seeks to eradicate the entire female pole of divinity? As above, so below! If the God and Goddess are not in accord in heaven, conflict and distrust will become rampant between the sexes. The very balance on Earth will be threatened.'"

"This is a crucial juncture, Rachel. You must decide whether you and I will stand together, or apart, in defining the future. Your decision is very important. It may well determine whether future women ever hear of the Naditu Sisterhood, or come to know of the Goddess Ninhursag. All they will hear of is Inanna. If the Sacred Mating ceases, communication with the Stars will diminish. Humankind will forget they were seeded by the Star People, and that there ever was a spiritual light body. The communion of the Masculine and Feminine will be shattered here on Earth."

The En Priestess's words fell upon me with a weight so heavy I was roused to defend myself. "Surely the entire future of the world cannot depend on me alone! I am too young and frail to carry such an enormous burden! I'm a simple mortal woman! How can I bear the enormous responsibility of this holy privilege? I'm only an insignificant person in comparison to the great forces of which you speak. How can my actions make such a difference to the world?"

The eyes of the En Priestess were blazing with a holy fire, when she said, "What is to become of us when even you forget your connection to the Star wisdom and the light body? I warn you, if you choose not to go through with this holy rite, you are putting Jacob in place of the Gods. That is idolatry!"

I was young, and unprepared. Such an enormous burden was too much for me to bear. Jacob was my life, the only happiness I had known. I had to save myself for him. How could I live without him? We would go ahead with the simple ritual I had planned. I would not forget the Goddess! Ninhursag was ever in my heart! I would be forgiven. Even the great Inanna had fallen in love and made mistakes. She Who Watches would understand, even if the En Priestess could not.

My marriage to Jacob would be a new beginning. We would forge a new way, a Higher Marriage that was all our own. Our love would move out of the temple and into life. We would weave the sacred into the very fabric of our lives. It would not be confined to the Goddess's temple once a year.

"Oh Noble One, please understand! I regret to disappoint you, but I must refuse! I will find my own way to honor the Goddess. May I have your leave to go?"

The lioness beside the En Priestess had been silent, but now it began to growl.

I stepped back in fear, edging toward the door.

The En Priestess's face was crestfallen. "You are young and head-strong, Rachel! Go if you like! But you have much to ponder. Think carefully! Your decision will have vast consequences that extend far beyond you, and even this age in which we live."

"Remain in ritual seclusion and finish out your time here. If you change your mind before the full moon, return to me at once. You have my permission to move freely about the sanctuary. I pray it will help you to see the truth."

When I closed the door behind me I was engulfed in a deluge of tears, as dark and impenetrable as the blackness around me. Was I lost? Had I abandoned the light of truth? I couldn't even find the stairs in front of me. With each faltering step I reeled under the enormous burden of the invitation to become the Nindingir.

11

VISIONS AT THE EYE POOL

AN EERIE SILENCE GREETED ME WHEN I OPENED THE DOOR OF THE moon lodge around sunset on the night of the full moon. Not a breeze was stirring. The moist air hung limp and lifeless. A baleful pall hovered over everything. I tried to ignore the strange atmosphere as I set off on my walk up to the Eye Pool, though none of the temple birds soared overhead, or sang their usual farewell address to the sun. By the time I reached the lookout knoll near the pool, the silence was deafening.

I turned and looked back in the direction of the Eye temple. All was dark inside the hallowed shrine. Guilt consumed me that there was nothing but darkness inside the temple on this sacred night of nights. This was New Year's Day! Why was no procession advancing down the Sacred Way? The Higher Marriage was to be celebrated, the fates decreed. What had become of the festivities? Why was no one else chosen for the Sacred Mating with the Nefilim? Had I brought an end to the holy rites? I had hoped the En Priestess was only threatening.

The sun was setting in the west. The round orb of the moon was beginning its majestic climb. The dance of the two great lights of heaven had begun. The celestial lovers were coming to meet. Soon the Earth would be bathed in their joyous light. I hastened to the Eye Pool, removed my robes, and stepped into the glistening water. The full moon hovered a golden ball upon the horizon. Mist rose up from the surface of the water as if answering a celestial command. The power of the Eye Goddess was weaving itself around me. Was I forgiven?

I cupped my hands to drink the pool's illuminating waters, then swam out to the center of the lake. Diving down into its primeval bottom, I beseeched the Goddess to forgive me. The silent depths of the pool was chilling, which reminded me of the eclipse. I rose shuddering to the surface and swam over to the pool's edge to begin my ablutions.

Gazing down into the water, I saw a vision in the moon's light. Flickering in the opalescent moonlight on the surface of the pool were father and Jacob. They were seated in the courtyard outside our house at a long banquet table dressed with myrtle. Boughs of myrtle? Whatever for? Myrtle was sacred to the Goddess of Love, and used primarily to dress wedding tables. Now what was this? There were other tables positioned around the courtyard also dressed in myrtle. Friends, relatives, neighbors, and members of the Brotherhood were seated at them feasting and drinking. There hadn't been such a large gathering at our house since mother's death.

My attention was drawn back to the banquet table with father and Jacob. Many of the higher ranks of the Brotherhood were there. Zaltan, the High Priest, was seated on father's left. Even Shahor was there at the far end of the table. They were all eating and drinking heavily. This couldn't be happening!

Eschol, father's personal servant, entered the scene leading a pregnant black ewe. He beckoned father to him. The ewe's belly was huge. She was so dark I knew it had to be Night Sky. Father rose swiftly pulling out a large knife. Brandishing it proudly, he walked over to the bleating ewe. The ewe's cries were piteous as father plunged the knife into her throat. No one dared move as father stooped to disembowel the poor creature. Its warm blood seeping into the ground, he raised the swollen liver proudly crying out a triumphant prayer to the moon above.

I gasped in horror. The moon was full, and that had to be Night Sky. She was the largest and blackest of all the pregnant ewes. There were her offspring. Three tiny lambs ripped savagely from her warm full belly. Now they lay motionless beside her. I cried out in revulsion, my entire body shaking.

Shahor came and stood beside father, smiling his unctuous smile and offering him a cloth to wipe his hands. An exultant father returned to the table amid applause from all the guests. Then he turned and shook Jacob's hand congratulating him. What did this mean?

Zilpah, another of father's daughters by his concubines, came and stood beside Eshcol. Painstakingly she began extracting milk from the ewe's lifeless body. Then she placed it in a large cooking vessel over the fire pit. Eshcol skinned the ewe, then skewering her through, placed her on a stick to roast. At father's command Zilpah lifted the lifeless lambs and placed them in the milk over the fire.

Father stood up beaming with pride. Elevating his wine cup he turned toward Jacob to make a toast. "Congratulations, son! That ewe had three fine lambs in her and all of them were male. My omens never lie! Mark my words! You will be blessed with many sons."

Another round of applause issued from the guests.

Still gloating, father turned toward the guests to begin another toast. 'I want to thank all of you, my illustrious Brothers, my relatives, and friends, for coming to share in our happiness tonight. Choice delicacies are being prepared for you. Wait until you taste the unborn lamb cooked in its mother's milk! It's a rare and special wedding treat."

A wedding? I gasped. This couldn't be! It was to have been my wedding night. Father sat down looking very smug and satisfied. He turned toward Zaltan, and they shook hands exchanging smiles. A chill ran through my body, to see father take the seal from around his neck and press it into the clay tablet between he and Jacob.

Cheers and music started up. Father put his arm around Jacob, and grinning from ear to ear, escorted him back to our wedding tent. Yes! It was our wedding tent before me in the vision. There was no mistaking it though the moon flickered strangely on the surface of the pool. I glanced up at the sky staring at its mysterious face. A harsh wind began to blow. The eclipse had started. Cold fear began escalating inside me. I modulated my breathing hoping to calm myself. I had to understand what was going on.

Struggling to put my fears aside I stared again at the shimmering surface of the pool. There was Jacob, my handsome bridegroom, looking as if he'd had a bit too much to drink. His chest heaved with pride. He was smiling a blissful smile. But what was this? He was standing beneath the same eclipsing moon as I. I rubbed my eyes to be sure, but it was true. Jacob's face was glowing with rapture. He wore the special look he always saved for me.

The entrance to our wedding tent opened and the canopy was fitted out. Jacob was being welcomed inside by a mysterious woman dressed in my wedding gown, and wearing my veil! Who could it be? That was my gown! . . . My veil! . . . And my groom! What infernal treachery was this? Who had father found to take my place? I gasped in horror. The breath piercing me like a knife, as I suddenly remembered the oracle's words. 'Beware of treachery from those you hold as dear!'

Father took the false bride's hand and placed it inside Jacob's. After exchanging a sly smile with the bride, he left the two alone. A shudder ran through me. Father was intimately acquainted with the woman inside my gown.

The moonlight dimmed as Jacob stepped inside the tent. I looked up. It was the same moon as above me. The life was going out of me as swiftly as the moon was losing light. I looked back at the surface of the pool. Jacob was now inside the tent. He was embracing the false bride in the privacy of our tent. How could this be? Who was it? Why was I not the enraptured bride?

So this was why father had sent me to the Eye Temple. Suddenly remembering the intimacy of father's look, I realized who the false bride was. It was Leah! It had to be Leah! I had seen them exchange that look so many times before. Yes! It was Leah wearing my wedding veil. The one I had so painstakingly embroidered stitch by stitch with love charms and talismans over the long winter months.

Gazing at the vision through my tears, I knew it had to be Leah. My cursed sister Leah receiving the thrust of Jacob's manhood I had waited on all these years. This abomination before me was what I had been waiting and saving myself for so patiently! Jealous rage and disappointment threatened to overpower me. What possessed Jacob? He had to be blind not to realize it wasn't me! Did he know me so little? Was his love so blind? Or had his penis simply eclipsed his heart and mind?

The flower of love within me died, and a bitter thorn took its place.

Jacob had degraded our priceless love to this blind groping in the dark. The pain of all I witnessed seeped into my body. My body never lied. Every fibre of my being told me the vision before me was true. Wracked with pain, I could watch no more. I slapped the water with my hand wishing it was Jacob and Leah's faces. Then flailing about in the shallow water like a dying fish, I wailed deep and low baying at the blackened moon, feeling as though my soul were being wrenched from my body.

In the midst of my pain my thoughts turned to Night Sky. Poor Night Sky, she too had been sacrificed at the threshold of fulfillment. But at least her pain was over. I was condemned to go on living, having lost everything, my beloved, my family, even my connection to the Eye Temple. I had nothing left.

Night Sky had been so special to me. Why did she have to be the one chosen to share my grief? Father had such a demonic way of knowing how to hurt me. What kind of man was he to use his own daughter as callously as he had used Night Sky? The gruesome scene of the slaughter was still haunting me when the wind picked up and hail started pelting down. Big robin's egg sized balls lashed out at me chilling me through and through. Limp with pain I dragged myself from the water, the wind fighting my every movement.

It was pitch black. The eclipsed moon held everything in its deadly spell. Even the surface of the lake was silent now. The vision had melted back into its unfathomable reaches. I gave myself over to the merciless beating of the hail. It was the punishment I deserved for making the decision which had destroyed my life. To move, even to dress, was an enormous effort. I breathed in deeply, praying for some reason to remain alive.

How could I have been so stupid and so blind? The Goddess had not abandoned me. It was I who had abandoned Her. She Who Watches had given me every chance. Now I was paying the price for my own folly. How foolish I had been to put my love for a mortal man before the will of heaven! I had failed the Nefilim, the Goddess, and myself declining the holy rite. It was only justice that in return I would have to live my life out with the memory of Jacob making love to my sister on this sacred night of nights. Disappointment and grief gnawed at my heart. I had betrayed the Goddess, the Eye Temple, and the Sisterhood, and in return I had been betrayed by all those closest to me. This was my just desserts!

My mind raced ahead of the enormous pain which threatened to strangle my heart and close it down forever. Jacob, my hero, had fallen from his pedestal. How could I bear the enormity of my disappointment? Jacob had said no woman could compare with my light! But he was blind and could not see in the darkness. That insensible coming together of bodies was my reward for the depths of love I had given him! How rash! How foolish! How blind! Jacob seemed to me now. How could I have been so undiscerning? Jacob was a trickster. He had tricked his own father and brother for Yahweh's blessing. I should have suspected a fatal weakness in the man. Son of a blind man, he too was blind and deceived out of the blessing of a Higher Marriage. Where was Yahweh now?

"Jacob's no man of vision! He **is** father's flesh and bone!" I cried, wailing out into the darkness. My body ached for all the passion I'd been holding back these seven years, to have what Jacob had called a marriage of spirit as well as flesh. Where were Jacob's high ideals now? The sharp sting of the hail was nothing to the hurt inside me. Jacob's words were sweet, but how could I ever trust him again?

There had been no change of heart in father. I should have known better. I was furious with myself for being taken in. Father couldn't change. He had no heart, and no conscience. He'd abandonned them long ago when he joined the Brotherhood and dedicated himself to the evil Sin. Tampering with people's lives was a cunning art for the old magician. Master of deceit, he'd played us all so skillfully. We were nothing to him but objects in his clever game of power and control.

His farewell echoed in my mind pushing me to the brink of desperation. 'I shall do everything in my power to see the wedding goes off without a hitch.' I knew now what he meant. How naive of me to think father was my protector! In his slyness, he'd used my love for the Goddess against me. How could I ever look at him again?

To what purpose destroy something so pure, so good? What was there to gain? Finally the ugly truth dawned on me. Father was Sin's stooge. It was his envy and hatred of women that had drawn him to the Evil One. All his spoiling interference in my life was a product of this envy. But there had to be something else to have lured Zaltan and so many leaders of the Brotherhood to this event.

Of course I knew father and the Black Hand were seeking to corrupt Jacob. Corruption was Sin's aim. I'd heard sexual perversion was rampant within the Black Hand. It was one of their primary means of breaking down their members' morals and character, so they could be manipulated. Father had certainly found an ingenious way to destroy Jacob's integrity. The Black Hand had also vowed to stamp out the Naditu Sisterhood. What better way to destroy the solidarity of the Sisterhood, than turning sister against sister making them rivals for life? But knowing father there had to be something in it for him.

Oh, yes! I understood. Jacob would have to work for father more years to have me as well. That way father and his Brothers would have Jacob's blessing working for them longer. It was perfect for father, who loved to control everyone. Of course, father would find some clever excuse to justify everything to Jacob. He had a special talent for making excuses for his behavior. There was never any problem with the Black Hand backing him. The Brotherhood was renown for their scores of petty laws and regulations that could be pulled out and enforced at any time to obstruct the freedom of the righteous. Yes! Father would hide his greed and cunning behind one of their petty laws.

Still wretched and grief stricken, my thoughts turned to Leah. She certainly was father's daughter! She knew how to play his power games to get what she wanted. First she whored herself to him. Then she served his Brotherhood for favors. She'd probably risen in the ranks herself now becoming father's deceitful accomplice. What could drive her to act like this? Was it mother's death? Was it the loss of the Goddess? Had she no pride, no scruples, no self-respect?

It was obvious why Leah had betrayed me. She hated me. I'd known it ever since her brutal attack on the Eve of the Day of Olives. Her deceitful betrayal was the bitter fruit of a lifetime's worth of envy. The Sisterhood had warned of envy's capacity to ruin the soul. They said it could become a consuming madness that ate away at all that was good. Leah had never had a nourishing spiritual life of her own. She was one of those women bereft of the Goddess, who spent all her time cozying up to men for power and favors.

Thinking back I couldn't remember a time when Leah hadn't festered with a devouring love and hatred for me. My sister was like a parasite sucking away at my life, always taking and never giving. She was always in my shadow like a clinging vine. Leah never took the time to make her own life. She preferred horning into mine. Now she'd get to share my husband too, tricking her way in with deceitful cunning. Why wasn't Leah content to live her own life? Whatever I had, whatever I did, possessed some mysterious attraction for her. She wanted it. The more I thought of it, the more I realized her most fervent wish had been granted in usurping my place. At long last she had gotten to be me.

But how could Leah do this to herself? What of her own happiness? Had envy so consumed her that spoiling my life was more important than finding her own? The tragic rift which loomed so large between us since mother's death had widened into an impassable gulf. The loss of the Goddess had sealed the rest. Was this to be the wave of the future with woman vying against woman for any scrap of attention they could get? What would become of us women, when female love and nurturance was lost in the motherless wasteland of the patriarchy?

I was spent and exhausted from Leah's envious rivalry. She was a blight upon my life sucking my joy away. I had always tried to rise above her scheming antics. I felt sorry for her and tried to forgive her. But this time Leah had gone too far. She had trespassed on my very soul. My life was in ruins. There was no escape. And what was worse, now I too was contaminated by her envy. Yes! I was in such agony, I was filled with rage, and couldn't help myself. At this very moment Leah was in Jacob's arms pretending she was me. There was no rising above the insidiousness of this intrusion. Jacob's arms had been my only haven. Now they too were spoiled by her envy. There was nothing I could do.

Rancor seeped into my very soul until I hated Leah. Though even as I opened to that foul hatred, I knew I was only hurting myself. Such feelings were a sacrilege against the Goddess and the Sisterhood of all women. Envy and hatred were like a wildfire in the soul consuming everything in their path. Their venom would devour the good in me as well. I struggled hard against these feelings, yet I couldn't free myself from the poison's hold. I was trapped in the bitter web of envy father and Leah had spun for me.

Leah was no longer my "sister". She was the instrument of the Black Hand. A mere pawn in their perverse game to divide and conquer women so they could be suppressed. Oh father and the Brotherhood were very clever. They knew how to defile the bonds of Sisterhood.

Masters of treachery, they'd used my love for Ninhursag to lure me into their trap to foul the bonds which held the Goddess Mysteries together. Would the hatred rising up inside me render me their tool as well? How would I find the strength to live the humiliating life they'd designed for me, not in the Higher Marriage I'd envisioned, but in this degrading patriarchal arrangement?

I fell to my knees and prayed to the Great Mother for forgiveness. I prayed my pain would stretch me to find compassion for my sister. But I had to pray and keep on praying because Leah's hatred had taken root and was growing inside me. I only had a few more days to prepare for the ongoing assault that was to be my married life.

Sometime in the wretched darkness of that fateful night, I remembered mother. I looked up at the sky and prayed for her guidance. Then I made my way slowly up to the grove. When I arrived I hurled myself down upon her grave, and made my bed there for the night. Praying for strength and healing, I repeated the ancient tenet of the Sisterhood. "All women are the Goddess, and the Goddess is all women" over and over again until I fell asleep.

It was strange waking up beside mother's grave. I felt like I was encased inside a dream. Everything had changed dramatically over night. The ground was cold and hard. Frost was everywhere, a thin gossamer veil sucking the life out of the fresh spring flowers. I felt as wilted as the flowers, so full of the promise the day before. I was stiff and cramped all over from the biting chill. My bones ached so, I felt like I was no longer inside the same body. As I rose and looked around I had to wonder, what would become of the spring wheat and barley crop? And what of the fruit trees? I prayed their blossoms hadn't frozen before they had a chance to pollinate. Had Bilhah brought the new lambs and their mothers into shelter for the night?

Looking over at the Ashera tree for inspiration, I saw that even it had been ravaged. I cried out in desperation. WISE ORACLE, YOUR TRUTH HAS BEEN REVEALED TO ME. PLEASE FORGIVE ME FOR DOUBTING YOU, AND SPEAK TO ME AGAIN. I NEED YOUR HELP NOW MORE THAN EVER."

I waited breathlessly. But not a leaf rustled, or a single charm tinkled, on its hallowed branches. The emerald eyed leopard was nowhere to be seen. Only a plaintive silence answered me. Finally in disappointment, I turned toward mother's grave to say one last goodbye. "I'm sorry mother! Please forgive me! I did my best. But I've been so alone without the women's circle and the Goddess worship. There's nothing to bond us women together anymore. Without the Goddess, we've lost our guiding light."

It was an eerie walk back to the Eye Pool. Frost had netted the entire grove in its icy spell. Not a single creature stirred. Only the muffled sound of my footsteps could be heard on the newly hardened ground. The same lethargy hung over everything outside the grove. As I approached the Eye Pool the temple bells peeled out, the only relief in the sullen stillness. Though today even they sounded discordant. I stumbled toward the lookout knoll before going on to the Eye Pool.

A long line of priestesses were walking in solemn procession heading for the Temple. The En Priestess waited for them there. She was praying before a huge bonfire in front of the colossal statue of the Goddess. When the Sisters arrived, the En Priestess turned to face them. I was too far away to hear what she said, but the assembly was grave. The priestesses were all dressed in black, which was most uncharacteristic for this joyous season. The En Priestess's face was strained and serious. Guilt rose in me to fever pitch, as moans of anguish issued forth in response to her pronouncement. The Priestesses cried out, striking their breasts and renting their garments.

Their anguished cries pierced my heart. I started for the Eye Pool, unable to watch another moment. Was the Eye Temple going to be abandoned? Was I to blame? I wanted to run and hide, but there was no way to escape my guilt. I could escape the horrific scene before the temple, but the gloom of the eclipse hung over the entire temple precinct like a shroud. Even at the Eye Pool there was no getting away from the deathlike atmosphere.

I wanted to see the proud ram kiribu of the lake, the very embodiment of stalwart stability. But the rams were nowhere to be found. The wildflowers which had decorated the pool's banks with bright colors the previous day had all greyed and wilted. Gazing at my reflection in the water, I too had changed. My face was pale and lifeless, etched with agony and disappointment. An unfamiliar frown crowned my brow. All the joy had left my face.

Aghast, I turned away and drank some water without thinking. In the magic mirror of the Eye Pool an irate Jacob was storming into father's room. Before father could even chase Suzannah from his bed, Jacob began shouting. "What infernal trick have you played on me, Laban? That wasn't Rachel you handed me in marriage! It was Leah! How could you do that to me? I've been fair with you. I paid you every moment of your bride price. Where's Rachel, my heart's beloved? What have you done with her?"

Father spoke in a baffled tone as Suzannah cowered beneath the covers. "Calm down my boy! What's all this fuss about? We're a civilized people with long standing laws and customs that have to be obeyed. It's against our code to marry the younger daughter before the elder. Would you have me break the law just to suit your fancy?"

"If it was one of your so called laws, why did you feel it necessary to trick me in the dark?" shouted Jacob in disbelief.

Father quickly changed the subject. "You needn't worry about Rachel! She's off preparing for your marriage. She'll be back at the end of the week. Marry her then, if you like . . . providing . . . of course . . . you agree to work for me another seven years."

"Another seven years!" shouted Jacob in dismay.

Father shrugged his shoulders innocently. "It's only fair! You made that agreement with me yourself. It's worth it. You'll have two fine healthy wives instead of one. I tell you what, I'll even throw in Billah and Zilpah, my daughters by my concubines. A man needs variety. When you're married for a time, you'll understand what I mean."

"Don't tell me what I should have!" exclaimed Jacob fuming. "All I want is Rachel! That was our agreement!"

"Now listen Jacob! I'm a law abiding man. I understand it's been rather a surprise. So I'll forgive you. But you have to think of Leah. She's your wife now. Your first wife at that!"

Then clearing his throat, he continued looking up at Jacob sheepishly. "How did it go between the two of you last night? You didn't come complaining to me then. I've taught Leah a few things."

Jacob looked at father in puzzlement.

"What I mean is . . . Leah certainly has her virtues, doesn't she?"

I had been watching the vision with bated breath. But father's last remark so disgusted me, I started to feel sick. I turned away from the vision fearing I would retch. It was abominable seeing father so full of treachery, yet feigning innocence.

Still I returned to the vision, hoping Jacob would redeem himself and triumph in my defense. Jacob was clenching his fists, as he said, "That's none of your business, Laban!"

Realizing he was only incensing Jacob, father continued in a different vein. "There's no reason to get riled up, son! I know you. We're two of a kind. And I assure you, I have only been thinking of you."

"Only been thinking of me!" cried Jacob furiously. "How can you expect me to believe that? Do you take me for a fool? You don't inform me of your laws. You stupefy me with powerful drink. Then you expect me to believe you were only thinking of me. Pulling out a large knife, Jacob continued in anger, "I should cut your tongue out right now, you liar!"

"It takes one to know one, my son! Perhaps we should ask your father and brother about your honesty." retorted father with a measured grin.

Jacob threw his knife against the wall in frustration.

A mischievous glint in his eye, father continued, "Enough threats and accusations! Trust me, Jacob! I did it for you. Haven't I always been good to you? I treated you like a son, when you came to me with nothing like a beggar."

Father dismissed Suzannah, and beckoned Jacob to sit down. Once she was gone, father continued in a more gentle tone. "I know you're angry, but please hear me out. There's something important I need to tell you. Then you'll understand I was only thinking of you. From the first day you arrived here with all your hopes and dreams, I've listened to you, Jacob. You remind me of myself when I was young. Oh, I know you love Rachel. But you're young, idealistic, and foolishly romantic. Marriage is a serious enterprise . . . a practical matter. And there's something you have to know about Rachel."

My blood began to boil.

"I'm a wizened moon priest. Believe me! I understand these matters. Rachel is a Naditu woman, as her mother was before her . . . and your own mother, Rebekah. These Naditu women are different from other women."

"Different! What do you mean?" asked Jacob in astonishment.

"Yes, different, and I'll tell you how." he continued, watching Jacob carefully, "Naditu women are not good breeders. Truth is they rarely give birth. They're just not suited for it. Look at your own mother! She was barren most of her life, and only gave birth to you in her later years. I'm telling you, Rebekah was lucky to have done it at all. Now my wife, Anna, was also a Naditu woman. All she ever gave me were daughters! . . . Two daughters in my old age! . . . These are the facts. . . . You must listen to me! . . . Naditu women are not good breeders!"

I was infuriated. Was father going to turn Jacob against me, or cause him to doubt me?

Father cocked his head scrutinizing Jacob as he said, "There's nothing to worry about! Our laws protect you. When you have a barren wife, you're allowed to take another. I've just been trying to make things easier for you, because I know you want a large family. Believe me! I have been watching out for you. I did you a favor! If you marry a Naditiu woman, you need a Sugutu woman like Leah as well. Sugutu women are the good breeders. They have many offspring. Think about it! You're going to need many sons, if you want to take over all the land Yahweh promised you."

Jacob calmed down. He began nodding his head, and sat back to ponder father's words.

My heart was in my throat. I wanted to scream. Father was only giving Jacob half the truth. He wasn't telling him that Naditiu women gave birth to the special souls. Jacob's mother was a Naditu woman. Isaac's mother, Sarah was a Naditu woman, and undoubtedly Abraham's mother before her.

Seeing he had Jacob's full attention, father went on obviously enjoying himself. "Of course, Naditu women have their charms. That's why we're so attracted to them. But it isn't easy living with a Naditu, son. They have their own authority and that troublesome Sisterhood to back them up all the time. They think for themselves. And if you ask me, they think entirely too much! You should have seen my wife Anna. And remember what your mother did to your father around the bestowal of the blessing."

Jacob looked at Laban quizzically about to interrupt. But father would have none of it. "Oh, you were lucky that time! Your mother's tricks were working in your favor. But think how it was for your father and brother! You can't always count on these Naditu women, and it's very difficult to control them. They're independent thinkers. Who wants to live with that?"

"You can't be foolishly romantic, my son! Marriage is more than just a romantic arrangement. If you want to be boss in your own household, you have to keep a Naditu in her place. And the best way . . . the easiest way . . . is to take other wives. That way you can play them off against each other. It makes them insecure, and you can always be in charge. It's really very simple. They have to vie for your attention, which keeps them busy trying to please you. And you can have as many children as you like!"

Jacob sat back. "Perhaps you have a point Laban." he said after giving it some thought.

A pleased smile crossed father's lips. He'd finally struck a sensitive chord in Jacob. I began to shudder. Father always knew how to play upon a person's weakness and find their secret craving for power.

"Of course, I do!" said father grinning. "Now go back to Leah. She has her charms. There's no reason to hurt her feelings. Have a pleasant week. Rachel will be back in no time. Then you'll have both of them Now run along! Enjoy yourself! What are you doing here gabbing with me during your wedding week?"

Jacob shrugged, smiling sheepishly, and left the room.

I got up from the Eye Pool more miserable and dejected than I was before. I should have listened to the En Priestess. There was no champion for me in Jacob. Last night Jacob failed me in the dark. But now he was failing me in the full light of day. Father, the black hearted magician, had slipped the noose around Jacob's spirit without his even realizing it. Where was my hero, the man I had sacrificed everything for? What had become of Jacob's desire for a Higher Marriage? Had his values been destroyed by the Black Hand like everyone else's? He didn't want the challenge and inspiration of having a priestess for a mate. All he wanted was a breed cow. I gasped out loud, suddenly remembering the dream I'd had on my first visit to the sanctuary. The one in which the cow had been put ahead of the ewe in the procession.

I raised my hand to strike the water that had revealed such a vision to me. But I refrained when I saw the Goddess's golden perch floating dead on the shimmering surface of the pool.

PART FOUR

Patriarchal Marriage

12

THE MYRTLE'S GIFT

WHEN NAHMI BID ME FAREWELL MY LAST MORNING AT THE EYE TEMPLE, her face was grave. "The grip of the Black Hand has tightened since the eclipse, Rachel. The Temple will be closing in the autumn. The Naditu Sisterhood is moving down to Magan, home of the great sphinx on the river Nile. It's the last bastion of the star wisdom from Kak.Si.Di., and there the Goddess is still revered. I'm sorry this will be the last time I see you. You always showed such promise."

Nahmi's words resounded with the weight of a searing judgment on my heart. My worst suspicions were proving true. When the Naditu Sisterhood departed who would remember the ancient star wisdom? There would be no one to do the Will of Heaven. I had to struggle to hold back tears as we proceeded.

Just before we reached the ancient gate where Eli waited, Nahmi turned to face me. "The En Priestess gave me one last message for you." she said staring me in the eyes.

My mouth was trembling, and I swallowed hard.

"She said that in making the decision not to enact the Sacred Mating, you are destined to have to carry the pain of patriarchal women's abandonment of their own Mysteries."

I staggered under the weight of her grim pronouncement, as Nahmi continued toward the massive gate. My limbs felt so heavy, I could hardly move. But my mortification was not over yet. The blow of Nahmi's words was still to be punctuated by the closing of the gate behind me.

I felt as though I had been cast out of heaven. Even the winged lion cherubim seemed to glare at me. My heart sank. It seemed like I was encased in a slow moving dream, when Eli drew the donkeys up beside me taking the satchel from my hand. This sense of being in a dream was reinforced, as I observed the ravaged landscape on our long trek home. The Goddess had shielded the temple from the worst of the icy blast the night of the eclipse, but now everywhere I looked was devastation. The blossoms on the fruit trees, and grapevines had withered and blown away. Was I to blame for refusing to enact the sacred rite and bring the Goddess's love to Earth? Tears flooded down my cheeks as we rode along.

Only the fields of wheat and barley had been spared. Their kernels were still plump and growing full of starch. When we came to a long stretch of cropland, I beckoned Eli. I wanted to say a prayer of thanks and light some incense to strengthen the guardians of the field.

Eli looked at me with wizened eyes. "Stop as long as you wish, mistress Rachel! You look like you could use a rest."

At least I didn't have to explain myself to him.

To my right was a small thicket of myrtle trees undaunted by the devastating blast. No wonder the stalwart myrtle was called the plant of immortality. Its sturdy branches remained fresh even long after cutting. Would that I possessed the myrtle's capacity to withstand abuse! I stepped through some leafy branches into a clearing deep within. Even inside the myrtle's sturdy branches there was no peace for me, as I recalled the decorations on the tables at Jacob and Leah's wedding. I smiled grimly. The noble myrtle was braided into wreaths for brides and placed beneath the marriage canopy to assure the couple's love through life's adversities. It was already all too clear my married life was to be one filled with adversity.

Offering my sorrow as penance to She Who Watches, I prayed for forgiveness. GREAT MOTHER NINHURSAG DO NOT PUT ME FROM YOUR HEART. PLEASE HEAR MY PRAYERS AND ACCEPT MY APOLOGY. DON'T PUNISH THE EARTH FOR MY MISTAKE. PROTECT THE WHEAT AND BARLEY CROP. NURTURE THEM WITH YOUR BOUNDLESS LOVE.

After pouring some water from the Eye Pool on the myrtle's roots, I lit some sweet grass incense, and prayed to gather strength for my dreaded homecoming. GREAT GODDESS NINHURSAG, GIVE ME STRENGTH TO FACE THE FUTURE UNAFRAID. PROTECT ME FROM FATHER'S MEDDLING CONTROL AND LEAH'S ENVY. HELP ME TO ACCEPT MY FATE AND NOT ALLOW THE DISAP-POINTMENT OF MY MARRIAGE TO CLOSE ME DOWN FOR-EVER.

Tears of anguish were flowing from my eyes as I finished my prayer. I put my forehead to the ground drawing in the healing power of the earth. Rising to go, a lush bough of shiny myrtle fell in my path. I picked up the sturdy branch with relief and gratitude. This was the first encour-agement I'd received since the night of the eclipse. I thanked the guardian of the myrtle and took up the branch as my protective shield.

When I arrived home, I was in shock as I glanced around me. Rem-nants of the wedding festivities were strewn about. Nothing had been put away to spare my feelings. Leah sat ensconced securely between father and Jacob. She gloated openly at me claiming full entitlement as Jacob's wife. Jacob blushed, then averted his eyes in shame, saying nothing.

"Welcome home, Rachel!" declared Laban jumping in to fill the awk-ward silence. "What are you gaping at? The guests have all departed, but have some cake. You're just in time for the end of Leah and Jacob's wed-ding party. Don't just stand there! Come here! Congratulate the newly-weds!"

His cavalier announcement stung my ears. Thank the Goddess I'd been forewarned, or I fear I might have lost my mind. Clutching my bough of myrtle I stepped forward, determined not to lose my pride. It was all I had left.

"I want you to know this comes as no surprise to me father." I said, looking him squarely in the eyes. "I saw your deceitful plot in a vision."

"So that's why you brought the myrtle!" said father smirking. "How thoughtful of you. Well! What are you waiting for? Try some lamb! Congratulate Leah and Jacob! Especially Leah! Afterall she's gone to the trouble of breaking Jacob in for you."

My skin crawled at father's remarks.

"That's enough Laban!" snapped Jacob. "Wasn't Rachel informed of our marriage before she left?"

Father glanced over at Jacob, replying casually, "I didn't have to tell her. I expected she knew the eldest would have to be married first. It's the custom in our region."

"It's common knowledge! Isn't it, Rachel?" he continued flashing me his most demonic smile.

I wanted to scream out and claw father's face, but that would not restore Jacob to me. Father had seen to everything. I was beaten by simply being there. A wave of passive resignation seized me, and I looked down afraid to glance at father. He might lock me in his withering stare and try to dominate my will. I didn't want to look at Jacob either. I was afraid of what I might see.

I heard father speaking to Jacob as if from a vast distance. "There! You can see by her silence. Rachel understands."

My blood ran cold and the ground seemed to give way beneath me. What could I do? They had all betrayed me, all three of them, as I had betrayed the Goddess. Yes! I had made my choice. Now I would have to live with it, and be overshadowed not by the heavenly light of She Who Watches, but by father's greed, and Jacob's blind lust and ambition that would assure him sufficient progeny to take over Canaan. And Leah? My sister's envy would be the wrath of the Goddess turned against me for abandoning Her sacred rites.

Father, always the grand master of deceit, was rambling on. He disgusted me! I wanted to flee this repugnant scene, when I noticed flies buzzing around a blood stained patch of ground. My knees went weak. Nausea churned my insides. It was Night Sky's blood! How fitting I receive the news of their wedding on this very spot! I clutched my bough of myrtle for support. I was not going to give Leah my pride for a wedding present.

Jacob was staring at me when I looked up. But it wasn't the same man I had known and loved gazing at me from behind those vacant shifting eyes. The Jacob before me was a dull sorry victim caught in a treacherous web of deceit. When he spoke I shuddered. His words had lost their magic lustre. They were no longer connected to his heart. His charismatic spirit was buried in his besotted flesh. My beloved was nowhere to be found. His heart had hardened under father's tutelage. Jacob didn't want a Naditu Priestess for a wife. He had accepted a breed cow. Yes! Father and Leah had succeeded. Jacob had become one of them. Not until I confronted Jacob did I realize how fully I had lost him. To confirm the awful truth, he squirmed before my gaze afraid to meet my eyes.

I was engulfed in disappointment. We had been so close. We had shared all each other's hopes and dreams. Now Jacob couldn't even look me in the eye. It had taken only one glance at me for him to see he'd betrayed me, and all the ideals we once had shared. Oh, Jacob could still look father and Leah in the eye. That was easy. They didn't ask the truth from him. Now his shame, his self-deceit, and powerlessness, would be between us just as Leah always would.

Father took the seal from around his neck, and commanded Eschol to bring him the marriage contract he and his Brothers had prepared. When it arrived, he pressed his seal into the clay tablet, declaring, "This is the moment you have both been waiting for. Here is the marriage contract with my seal affixed. Have it with my blessing. You're free to marry Rachel now, Jacob, and should with quick dispatch."

No one moved except Leah, who flew off in an angry huff.

Unable to stand the strained silence, father continued, "You must be tired of festivities, son. So let's dispose of ceremony. Why don't you two lovebirds just retire to the wedding tent? . . . And take the next week off."

Grinning at Jacob, he added chuckling. "You'll make it up to me over the next seven years. Now run along!"

I couldn't move. I was an immoveable mountain, my feet rooted in the ground.

Father raised his voice. "Stop standing there like a stubborn mule, Rachel! Take your husband's hand!"

Ours was a somber wedding, no guests, no toasts, no music, and no laughter. Only strained silence as we walked back to the wedding tent. The pain between us was so palpable, I was crushed beneath it. Neither of us said a word until we reached the tent. I stood before the entrance like a dispirited animal, glancing up at Jacob.

Jacob spoke first, though his words sounded hollow. "I've waited so long for this, Rachel. Aren't you going to invite me into our wedding tent? It's the custom for the bride to ask the groom inside."

Did Jacob expect things to be as they had been before? Avoiding his eyes, I sputtered, "It's not OUR tent! I can't go inside. Nothing's the same between us! I feel like I don't even know you anymore."

Jacob looked at me aghast, strained surprise, then disappointment, taking over his face. "Don't be ridiculous! Nothing's changed! You've only been gone for two weeks. You heard your father! You can't blame ME for what happened! I was following the customs of YOUR region, and YOUR people. I thought you knew, and that was why you left. I had no choice! I had to marry Leah in order to marry you. I did it for YOU!"

"You may have been able to deceive your father, Jacob, but your quick tongue is not going to work with me!" I retorted angrily.

"Is this any way to speak to your husband?" cried Jacob in dismay. "Your father's right! You are far too outspoken, and you think too much!"

"You expect me to go in there?" I said looking at Jacob in disbelief. "I can't go in that tent with you! Why! The bed's probably still warm from you and Leah . . . And please . . . don't dishonor me any further! Though we labored on the tent together, don't refer to it as ours. It's not OURS any longer. You've already shared it with my sister, your first wife!"

Jacob stepped back, his face filled with consternation. This was no lover's spat that was going to blow over quickly. My blood was boiling. Afraid I'd say something irreparably damaging, I turned on my heels and walked away.

Jacob came after me. Grabbing my arm, he spun me round. His eyes were softened with sorrow, as he said, "Please, Rachel! Let's not quarrel! My love for you is as strong as ever. You know I have no great affection for Leah. I feel sorry for her because you show her up so. Please try to understand, she's been put in a very awkward position."

I looked at Jacob, disappointment then fear mounting in my soul. "Are you completely blind? Leah put herself in this position! She and father had seven years to plan for this. That was plenty of time to marry her off to someone else. My sister had other choices. But she prefers to be your first wife so she can lord it over me for the rest of my life."

Fire flashed in Jacob's eyes. "That's not true! Leah loves me. I won't have you saying such things! I'm not the one who's changed, Rachel! You are! You're sick with jealousy, and it ill becomes you! This has to stop, or there'll be no peace in our home."

I was boiling mad. "Peace in our home? I've been humiliated enough! I'll have my say! Father tricked you, just like you tricked your own father. Then he uses some ridiculous law the Brotherhood concocted to cover himself. I warned you he would try to come between us. But you said I was only looking for trouble. Now it's too late! Father **has** come between us. And you let him!"

"You said I was the only one!" I continued, breaking into sobs. "You said there could be no other! You spoke of a Higher Marriage to evolve our spirits as well as hearts. But when it comes right down to it, all you want is a breed cow! Don't you realize one of our children would be worth more than a hundred of hers?"

Jacob's face paled at my words. He started fidgeting, and looked away. "That's quite enough!" he said finally. "You're my wife! This is our wedding week! You shall do as I say! What's transpired is between me and my God. I won't have you judging me. Besides, it's ridiculous for you to place all the blame on me! Where were you these past two weeks when I needed you?"

I wiped my eyes and looked directly up at Jacob. "I was at the Eye Temple in Brak. Father sent me there to prepare for our marriage. He said it was a wedding gift."

Jacob's eyes were on fire, as he bellowed, "You were at that heathen Goddess temple! And how dare you act so sanctimonious when you yourself were tricked!"

Jacob touched a sensitive chord in me, and I turned on myself. "It's true! I have made mistakes." I said sobbing. "You're right! How can I be so angry with you when I was also taken in? We have to stop fighting! That's what they want us to do."

"Who's they?" inquired Jacob impatiently. "Who wants us to fight?"

"Father and the Black Hand, that's who!"

"The Brotherhood?" said Jacob aghast. "What have they to do with this?"

I stopped crying and looked Jacob in the eye, as I continued, "The Black Hand has everything to do with it! They were at the wedding feast, weren't they?"

Jacob looked surprised, but answered thoughtfully. "They were all there that night. But they were only there because they're your father's cronies."

"The Black Hand is behind everything that happens in Haran." I insisted. "You should know that by now! Father does nothing on his own. He's their puppet. They're all dominated by Sin. He has possession of all their leaders, even father. I've seen it in his eyes!"

"You have a very fertile imagination, Rachel!" said Jacob incredulously. "What possible interest could the Brotherhood have in our marriage?"

"Doesn't Yahweh tell you anything?" I asked in exasperation. "The Black Hand is very interested in you, Jacob! Think how their flocks have flourished since you've been here. Marrying you off to Leah means they'll have you another seven years. But it's even more insidious than that! The Brotherhood's goal is to corrupt the righteous. You are the bearer of Yahweh's blessing. You carry the blessing of a great new spiritual tradition. With all your potential you're a great challenge for them. They'd do anything to dim your spirit and win you over to their side!"

Jacob was silent when I finished speaking, but his eyes shone again with an inner glow. I had passed the light of truth on to him.

"Maybe you're right!" he replied after a few moments. "I'll have to protect myself against them more diligently in the future. . . . And I'll ponder all you've said. I have no desire to play into their hands, or fight with you, my angel."

"But enough serious talk! This is our wedding week! Come! Let's go to our special place beside the Balikh. You're hot and dusty from the road. A swim will do you good. What need have we for a wedding tent? The vault of heaven will be our wedding canopy."

The Balikh had always been my comfort. A dip in the river would lift my spirits. I'd never step foot inside that wedding tent. "Fine idea! Let's go! I need to get away from all of this." I said looking around me.

"That's my angel!" said Jacob in relief.

Taking hold of Jacob's hand, I told myself that I too had made mistakes. Our marriage would work. We could put all this behind us. But walking to the river the devastation from the frost was everywhere. How could I smile and pretend everything would be alright when I had brought on this devastation?

Hoping to break the silence which encased me, I inquired, "What did you think of the hailstorm, and that bitter frost on the night of the eclipse?"

Jacob looked at me with a bemused smile. "You don't think the eclipse had anything to do with the frost, do you?"

"I think it had everything to do with it!" I said adamantly.

"Now you're the one sounding like Laban!" said Jacob chuckling. "The stars of heaven don't influence what happens here below! I wish there was something I could have done. At least the wheat and barley crop has been spared. They can take a cold wind when they've filled out with starch. Let's pray the hamsin winds don't come in the next few weeks. That would spell their ruin."

It was as though Jacob were speaking to me from across an enormous chasm. I felt defeated. Even this innocent attempt to contact Jacob with my true concerns had failed. Would things ever be the same? How could so much have changed in two short weeks?

The words of the En Priestess thundered in my mind. I'd been unable to heed her wise words at the Eye Temple. Now I couldn't get them out of my mind. Was there any hope for me? I felt like a pariah at the Eye Temple. Now at home with Jacob I was even more estranged. Would I always feel like a stranger, or an outcast? Despair engulfed me. Perhaps I did think too much.

I was relieved to finally arrive at the Balikh. I couldn't wait to take a plunge and wash my anguish away. The river was running fast from the melting snow up in the mountains. The blessed thistle Jacob and I planted had taken over the banks, reseeding itself year after year. It survived the frost due to its proximity to the river. We were both relieved to see it come through so well. While Jacob went to check on the blessed thistle, I removed my clothing and stepped into the river. It felt good to drift away in the swift current. The strain of the last two weeks dimmed as I closed my eyes and let myself be carried by the river.

My heart was heavy. Father's callous words echoed in my mind, and I couldn't forget Leah's gloating face. All my disappointments rushed in on me, crushing my spirits. I don't know how long I had let myself be carried by the river, but when I opened my eyes Jacob was a tiny figure waving frantically in the distance. I didn't want to go back to him. I needed time alone to recover. Coming around a bend in the river, I spied some soaproot on the bank and stopped to cleanse myself. The soaproot smelled sweet and fresh, and lathered up quickly in my hands. After I washed my hair and rinsed it, I began to feel better.

There was loud splashing behind me. I turned to find Jacob, frisky as a lamb in springtime. He dove between my legs, disappearing like one of the Goddess's golden perch. I laughed out loud at his playfulness.

Taking me in his arms, he declared, "There's no getting away from me, my angel!" After caressing my cheek, he continued, "Nothing's changed between us! We love each other too much for that to happen. Besides, you need me! You're far too serious. I'm the only one who can make you laugh."

The exuberance of a child was still so much alive in Jacob. He possessed a magic that could turn even the most onerous chore into fun. I had been sobered since mother's death, and he WAS the only one who could make me laugh. When I looked into his eyes my burdens began to lift. Did I have to carry the weight of the entire world on my shoulders? No one could be serious all the time. There was no sense holding on to how things once had been. I had to make the best of my life, or be miserable forever.

Jacob smiled to see me relax. "You wouldn't invite me into your arms back at the tent. But what about making love with me here beside the river? Afterall, this is our river. Even the blessed thistle was protected here. If those plants can make it through the frost, then so can we! Come! I'll race you back to our special spot."

Jacob's eyes were beaming, his skin tan and wet glistening in the sunlight. He was wearing that special look he always saved for me. How could I resist him? "What a splendid idea! Let's see who can get there first!"

We were off in a flash, laughing and swimming against the current. As we got closer to our special bathing place, Jacob slowed his stroke to let me win. I looked over at him, saying laughingly, "You must really want me in a good humor. You've never let me win before."

Jacob laughed out loud playfully. "You're the most incredible wife! Not only are you beautiful, you're clever too! I can't wait to make you mine. But first let me bring you flowers. I want to honor my wife."

The magic was starting all over again. Jacob was captivating me, as he had that first day at the well. In no time he was back his arms laden with sweet spring flowers. Crimson poppies with pale lavender hearts, purple anemones with dark centers, and heavenly smelling rock roses from the riverbank. They still had some color, even if they were a bit bedraggled from the frost. Best of all, Jacob was carrying my bough of myrtle. He lifted it proudly and planted it in the bank behind us, saying, "Let's not forget this, my angel! I was intrigued with this bough the moment I saw you carrying it. Let's plant it here behind us."

As he finished watering the myrtle, he said, "The sky shall be our wedding canopy! This bough shall be our tent! It's ours and no one else's! No one has ever loved as we do. Why should we do things the way they've always been done. We'll be the first couple to have such a fine canopy, and wedding bed! Come to me, my angel! I've had enough of darkness! Let's wed here in the full light of day. I've waited so long for you."

We were finding our way back together again. Jacob was speaking what was in my heart. His smile and his words were enchanting and drew me in. Before I knew it all the barriers I'd erected against him came tumbling down. I was young and full of life. The fire of springtime was in my veins, warming all that had been frozen and dead inside me since the eclipse.

Jacob took me in his arms. His touch unleashed a glow, that melted my heart. We had waited seven long years for this moment. I wanted to surrender to his embrace. But could I trust this man? We were fine here alone in our special place. But how would we fare back at the farm with father and Leah?

I looked searchingly in his eyes. With all my heart I wanted this to be a new beginning. But all I could say was, "I missed you, Jacob."

That was enough. Jacob's hungry mouth was on mine, his eager tongue parting my lips, probing the mystery inside me. A warm glow welled up deep in me, spreading like wildfire on a summer prairie. Jacob wasn't holding back the way he used to. His breathing was quickening and deepening. Time thickened to a honeyed slowness, everything receding except for Jacob. His strong hands were all over me, caressing my breasts, and enjoying every soft curve of my body. The fire of his touch beneath the cool liquid blanket of the water was exciting, and invigorating. It took my breath away, and with it went my fears.

Jacob used his penis like a magic stylus rubbing my thighs and drawing mystical symbols on my belly to make me his. I went soft and weak with pleasure. His penis was warm and hard and communicated with thrilling urgency. I leaned against him swooning gently, and swaying my hips. We moved together in life's primal dance. Our hearts and bodies one. Every surface of us melting together, as the water surged around us.

Then he picked me up and laid me down on the riverbank beside the myrtle. After surrounding me with flowers, he leaned over me and said, "You are an angel, Rachel! Your body is heaven to me."

I flowed into Jacob, more enraptured with every kiss. Heat rising inside my belly, I opened like a flower to the sun inside his heart. My legs were trembling. Streamings of pleasure coursed through me from head to foot. My deepest center began to throb awakening unknown depths inside me craving to be filled. I had been close to Jacob before, but this new intimacy was stirring and broke down all my resistance.

Jacob seemed to understand me perfectly, his every movement an answer to my unspoken desire. When he entered me with his manhood, we were fulfilled in one flesh. The scent of our bodies mingled on the altar of the earth, travelling on spring breezes expanding our love to take in the entire world. The late afternoon sun wrapped us in its warm embrace. Slippery wet, we bathed in each other's sweat and were born anew. This was the Goddess's sacrament, Her precious gift of lovemaking! The estrangement I had been feeling vanished. I didn't know where Jacob began and I left off. Never had I felt so open, or at one before.

Jacob began riding me with an increasing urgency. Waves of bliss took us over, lifting me above my fears and the sharp pain which heralded the end of my virginity. Smiling down at me in triumph, Jacob collapsed into my waiting arms. "You're mine now, darling! Let's lie like this forever! Just let me close my eyes a moment. I'll awake refreshed and hungry for you again."

I closed my eyes in peaceful rapture, too full to speak. It was good to feel the warm blood of my virginity mingle with Jacob's juices as they overflowed the vessel of my body, and trickled down upon the earth. My entire body smiled offering the blood of my virginity to the Goddess for the healing of the Earth.

My heart was full to brimming. Never had I known such peace and joy before. Our lovemaking needed no manmade temple or wedding tent. I received Jacob's seed upon the Earth Mother's fragrant altar in communion with the pulse of life. It was a new form of meditation lying with Jacob in the gathering twilight coupled in such exquisite peace. No longer was I alone or estranged. I was whole at last. I wanted to reach out to Jacob with all the fullness in my heart. But he had fallen asleep, and I could only wonder what he was dreaming of.

13

THE WEDDING WEEK

WE NEVER RETURNED TO THAT ILL-FATED WEDDING TENT WHOSE GOSsamer veils masked such treachery the night of the eclipse. Our marriage night was spent beneath the starry canopy of heaven. I had no need for slumber. I felt as though I was awake for the first time in my life, aglow with the stirring warmth of our lovemaking. There was so much I longed to share with Jacob. But he was sound asleep. His wedding week with Leah had so sated his body and deprived his soul, he was depleted like the waning moon above.

I was just drifting into slumber when Jacob awoke. Even with sleep beginning to enfold me, I could feel the warmth of his smile as he tried to rouse me. How quickly I could be ignited. Though disappointment from lying awake all night alone, still hung on me like a well worn cloak. But this was no time for petulance. The morning matched the brilliance of Jacob's smile. I loved to awake outside upon the bosom of the Mother with the sky above. I couldn't help but smile at the splendor of the morning. The earth was lush with spring and glimmering in a mantle of fresh morning dew. Even the air seemed to sparkle, as gentle breezes caressed the trees and played tricks with the damp ringlets of my hair.

Two snow white doves circled overhead, their song a lover's enchantment heralding the rising sun. My heart took wing to watch them soar. Were they an omen? Had the Goddess forgiven me? Was She Who Watches smiling on us again? The sky poured forth a golden radiance, a breath taking backdrop to their graceful flight. Soon scarlet, and rose tongues of fire lit the sky, expressing all the passion trapped inside me the whole long night.

Entwined in each other's arms, we watched the sun, a golden ball, climb over the distant mountains in the east. The dew drenched fields came alive to its radiance, glistening like a carpet of jewels in the early morning light. There wasn't a cloud in the sky. With the promise of such a beautiful day, I put thoughts of sleep away.

"Look above us, Rachel! Our wedding guests have arrived! Your friends the doves are here. Do they wake you every morning? " inquired Jacob laughing.

"They're here to celebrate our marriage." I said smiling.

"What is this special rapport you have with doves, my angel?" inquired Jacob.

My spirits were high, and so I ventured, "Doves are the animal spirits of the Naditu Sisterhood, because they're sacred to the Goddess. They serve as messengers between the different temple sites."

I expected Jacob to be annoyed at my mere mention of the Goddess, but he wasn't paying attention to what I said. He was ready to resume where we'd left off the previous evening. "The early morning light is caressing every soft curve of your body, my angel, and making your face glow. How long have I waited for the pleasure of rising with you beside me! This is going to be a glorious day!"

Blushing as deep as the rosy sky, I said, "You're a flatterer, Jacob!"

"I'm not flattering you! I'm telling you the truth, my dove. You have no idea how much it means to waken with you beside me!"

Sighing deeply, he looked away. "It helps me forget the bitter disappointment of awakening to Leah, that grim morning after our wedding feast. How my head ached from the potent wine your father pressed on me! It was such a cold dreary morning. It could have been winter. And a ghastly spell seemed to hover over everything draining its life away."

"But enough of that, my angel!" he said turning back to me. "How can I be morose today? I've been waiting seven long years for this moment. Come closer! I need to make sure this is not some wondrous dream."

Jacob was melting me again, his honeyed words drawing me to him like a charm. I was helpless to resist. My heart was so full, my tongue was tied. Even at my best, I could only stumble over words in comparison with Jacob. His words wove a subtle yet compelling kind of magic. This time they were quickening my breathing, and making my blood run hot. There was no time to respond. Jacob was on top of me, communicating with his tongue and hands. His breathing quickened uniting with mine, until we seemed to merge and expand beyond our bodies out into the countryside.

I was surrendering to the full sweep of Jacob's desire, when out of nowhere came the piercing sound of a female voice. Through the flutter of the doves departure, I recognized the voice. It was Leah, acting oblivious to the intimate scene she was intruding on.

Her words cut through the peaceful stillness like a magpie's shrill cry. "Oh! There you are! I couldn't sleep a wink all night. Father and I were so worried when you didn't come home last night. You never went to the wedding tent. We didn't know what had become of you."

Leah's voice trailed off into ponderous silence. But she was not about to be put off so easily. "Please excuse me! I don't mean to interfere." she continued undaunted. "But it's a wife's duty to look after her husband. Someone has to! You didn't take a thing from the fire hut yesterday. You must be famished, Jacob."

Jacob grinned sheepishly, then sat up like an obedient child, releasing me from his arms. I struggled to regain my composure. When I sat up, Jacob looked at me helplessly. Then he looked back across the river at Leah.

Not in the least dismayed by our lack of welcome, she said going on and on. "Someone has to think of you! Rachel's never been much of a cook. You can't depend on her. It's a good thing you have me to look after you, Jacob."

I looked at Jacob in quiet desperation. Leah was Jacob's first wife. There were elaborate codes of conduct that had to be followed. It was for Jacob to put Leah in her place, not me. And given Jacob's silence, Leah had full rein.

Assuming the power of first wife, she addressed me in a haughty scolding tone. "You should have provided for Jacob, Rachel! This is no way to treat our husband!"

Feeling better after having admonished me, she spread a meal out on a blanket on the grass. Jacob didn't know what to do, and just sat there looking bewildered. A mixture of fear, then outrage, came over me as I regarded him. Such passivity was an open invitation to a woman like Leah. I was glad we were across the river. Or I feared Leah would have come and sat between us, serving him herself.

My thoughts were intruded upon by Leah's cloying voice. "Come see what I've brought you, dear husband! Here's some bread still hot from the oven. The kind with the poppy seeds you loved during our wedding week. And I've brought sheep cheese, olives, and some delicious dried fruit to go with it."

"At least I know how to please my husband." she said looking at me with a scornful face.

Receiving no response from Jacob, she continued, "Now don't you worry Jacob. I'll be on my way. I don't mean to interfere. I'll be back at lunchtime with more goodies."

Leah was going to intrude on us again! I was irate, and glanced over at Jacob, hoping her last remark would mobilize him into action. But he just continued sitting there looking stupefied. I knew I should wait to see what Jacob would do, but I couldn't bear the position I'd been forced into.

Anger boiling up inside me, I nudged Jacob in desperation. But he just continued to sit there in silence. Enraged by his failure to act, I poked him sharply with my elbow. Jacob turned and frowned at me in annoyance.

Then he looked across the river, and said awkwardly, "You needn't have gone to so much trouble, Leah."

"It's no trouble, Jacob." said Leah responding in the same obsequious tone she used with father. "As your wife it's my pleasure and my honor to serve you. You can always count on me having your best interests at heart."

Jacob nodded smiling.

179

Pleased to see she'd taken Jacob in, Leah grew more bold. Turning toward me with a leering smile, she said, "At least I know how to treat a husband!"

I turned toward Jacob hoping he would come to my defense. But Jacob was smiling, his face aglow at the scent of the bread wafting across the river. His white teeth gleamed in the sunlight, as he called out, "It smells delicious, Leah! Thank you for all your thoughtfulness! Now run along! We'll see you later!"

My body stiffened at Jacob's response. I felt as though I'd been stung by a serpent. Leah knew she had succeeded. She stood there gloating at me, knowing full well she'd spoiled our romance. I was furious to have to see her triumphant face.

Once she was out of earshot, I said, "It was bad enough Leah had to spoil our first morning together. Did you have to invite her to return? This is supposed to be our private wedding week!"

Jacob ignored my question. Getting up he started across the river toward the blanket spread with delicacies. Only with reluctance, did he finally turn around and ask, "What did you say?"

With impatience building, I repeated myself. "I said, how could you have invited Leah to return?"

"What do you mean?" inquired Jacob in surprise.

His behavior was infuriating. I couldn't help myself. "First you invite Leah to return. Then you get up and leave me because you're in such a hurry to fill your stomach."

Jacob replied without even turning around to look at me. "What are you talking about?"

"What am I talking about? I exclaimed. "It was bad enough Leah had to intrude on our first morning together! Did you have to give her an open invitation to return any time she likes!"

"You're making something out of nothing." said Jacob continuing to head across the river.

"No I'm not! This is our wedding week." I shouted. "If you're hungry I'll fix you something."

"You're making too much out of this, Rachel! What harm has Leah done? All she did was bring a lovely meal to grace our first morning together."

Jacob had almost made it to the other side. So I shouted across the river. "Leah interrupted us at a very delicate moment, or don't you remember?"

Jacob regarded me from the opposite river bank. Then glancing over the delicious spread, he said, "Just look at this magnificent fare! Leah's not here! She left! You're the one spoiling our first morning together! Come on over! The bread's still warm! I'd forgotten how hungry I was."

After sampling a piece of bread, Jacob continued. "Leah wasn't intruding. She's my wife. She has every right to serve us breakfast, if she likes. Why make a problem out of it! I think we're fortunate to have our own private cook."

Lured on by the delicious aroma, Jacob continued as he admired the delicacies on the blanket. "Come join me! Don't stay over there by yourself pouting! You must be starving. I hadn't realized how hungry I was until I smelled this bread. Come! Let's have our first meal together as husband and wife!"

Jacob piled his plate with food, not waiting for my response. Tearing off another piece of bread he gestured to me with it in his hand, shouting, "The bread is wonderful! Come try the olives, and stop this ridiculous competition with your sister! Let's not waste this splendid morning arguing!"

I stared at Jacob filling his face. He could have been feasting at the banquet of my body and my soul, but he preferred Leah's bait instead. Though I hadn't eaten since the previous morning, I would rather starve than succumb to Leah's latest ruse.

Jacob ventured on his mouth full of bread and cheese. "It was kind of Leah to think of us. She's an excellent cook. You have to give her that."

"Leah did us no favor!" I exclaimed boiling over. "Everything's changed since her visit? Or don't you remember? You had something very different in mind before she showed up!"

Jacob's mouth was full of food, but suddenly a look of embarrassment came over his face. Flashing me a guilty smile, he attempted to cajole me. "Don't be impatient, Rachel! We have our whole lives ahead of us. There's nothing to get upset about. We'll be alone together all week."

Seeing I was unmoved, Jacob stopped eating for a moment and tried another tact. "Why make a problem out of this? Allow Leah to do all the cooking for us. Spend your time with me instead."

Jacob was showing me just how adroit he was at working all the angles. Perhaps he belonged with father and Leah after all? I had thought he was a man of vision, a seeker after truth. But this man before me was shortsighted and possessed an enormous appetite.

Angry as a hissing cat, I snapped at him, "You're wasting your words on the wrong woman! Save such convincing arguments for Leah!"

"Stop this right now! I won't have you spoiling another moment with your jealousy!" he shouted adamantly from across the river.

"I'm not the one spoiling things! Open your eyes Jacob! It's daylight now. Can't you see what Leah's up to? Given your invitation she's free to come and go whenever she chooses during our wedding week! I know her! She has the uncanny knack of horning in on me at exactly the wrong moment. She's always sneaking around behind my back. As your first wife, you'll tell me she now has the right!"

Jacob replied sharply, "I won't listen to another word about Leah! She was only fulfilling her wifely duty. And frankly, I'm beginning to think you have something to learn from her in that regard!"

My heart plummeted at Jacob's last remark. I was my own person. I couldn't bear him comparing me to her.

Everything went red, and I lashed out. "Father and Leah might have tricked you in the dark on your wedding night. But you have no excuse today! You have to be completely blind not to see what Leah's up to! Or do you simply enjoy playing us against one another for sport? Is that what father taught you while I was away?"

Jacob's face darkened like an angry storm cloud. Without a word he pulled on his pants picked up his plate and stormed off angrily.

I screamed across the river loud enough for him to hear. "Go ahead! Leave in a huff if you like! How quickly you've forgotten that your brother Esau sold out his birthright for a dish of lentils! You and he are just alike!"

I held back the tempest of my emotions for as long as I could. When Jacob was out of sight I burst into a fit of tears. I had said the truth. It was obvious what Leah was up to. Didn't Jacob want to know the truth? Couldn't he see what she was up to? I collapsed on the ground, fury then despair washing over me. What good had the truth done me? Jacob had abandoned me, and I was all alone as usual. For all I knew he was off with Leah at this very minute enjoying breakfast with her. The thought of it was devastating. Maybe it would be too hard for Jacob with me, and he'd come to prefer Leah. She would never challenge him. She'd obey him like a dumb cow. Father liked her fawning obsequiousness. Maybe Jacob would too?

I crawled to the river like a wounded animal and threw myself in. The water was cool from the run off in the mountains. But once I grew accustomed to it, it was exhilarating to give myself over to its powerful surge. The Balikh was my only comfort. It was heinous and cowardly, and against every value I'd been brought up with, but I couldn't help it. I thought of drowning myself. My life was over. Why not offer myself as a willing sacrifice? Perhaps it would make up for my not going through with the sacred rite? She Who Watches must have been protecting me. For at the moment of my deepest despair I was carried to my altar down stream. Out of force of habit, I stopped to sit on the smooth rocks along the riverbank and ponder my cruel fate. My mouth was so dry from crying. I cupped my hands and took a drink.

My ears opened. The spirit of the river began speaking in its babbling tongue. DON'T DESPAIR, RACHEL! PEOPLE SHUT THE TRUTH OUT FOR MANY REASONS. TRUTH IS FOR THE COURAGEOUS AND THE PURE OF HEART. LESSER SOULS SEE MANY TRUTHS, AS MANY AS THERE ARE PEOPLE IN ANY SITUATION. DO NOT LET YOURSELF BE FOOLED. BE GLAD YOU HAVE VISION AND THE PENCHANT FOR TRUTH. TREASURE YOUR GIFT, THOUGH THOSE AROUND YOU MAY NOT. IT'S A SIGN THE GODDESS HAS NOT FORSAKEN YOU, EVEN THOUGH YOU PLACED THE LOVE OF A MORTAL MAN BEFORE THE WILL OF HEAVEN.

DO NOT BE SURPRISED THAT JACOB FAILS YOU NOW. BECAUSE YOU EXALTED HIM ABOVE ALL ELSE, HIS WEAKNESS WILL BE REVEALED TO YOU IN THE STARKEST TERMS. BUT ALL IS NOT LOST. THERE IS GREAT COMPASSION IN THE WOMB OF TIME, AND A SEASON FOR EVERYTHING. THAT WHICH HAS BEEN RAISED UP SHALL FALL DOWN, AND THAT WHICH HAS BEEN EMPTY SHALL BE FILLED. ALL THINGS MUST CHANGE. YOU CAN'T CONTROL THEM. THOUGH YOU CAN INFLUENCE THEM POSITIVELY IF YOU HAVE THE CORRECT ATTITUDE. STAND FOR THE TRUTH, RACHEL. DO NOT DESPAIR. THE TRUTH IS ITS OWN REWARD. YOU ARE BUT

ONE IN THE VAST TAPESTRY OF CREATION, AND CANNOT SEE THE ENTIRE WEAVE.

YOU ARE YOUNG AND HEADSTRONG. DO NOT BE BLINDED BY IMPATIENCE! LOOK ABOUT YOU! EVERYWHERE YOU LOOK YOU SEE THE MERCY OF THE GOD AND GODDESS. THEIR UNDYING LOVE HOLDS THE WEB OF LIFE TOGETHER. MEDITATE ON THE GREAT LAWS OF NATURE. THERE ARE IMPORTANT LESSONS TO BE LEARNED IN WAITING. THE WITHERED VEGETATION WILL REVIVE IN THE FULLNESS OF TIME. YOU TOO, SHALL FLOWER. LIFE FOLLOWS UPON DEATH, AND EVEN DEATH FLOWS BACK INTO RENEWED LIFE.

The words of the great Speaker of the River rang in my ears long after the whirlpool had ceased its hypnotic churning, and the river was silent. My heart was glad. The river spirit was speaking to me again. I rejoiced and savored every word. Slowly I could begin to feel again through the crippling pain in my heart. I gazed about me with new resolve. Everywhere I looked Nature's mysteries were woven like a complex tapestry of truth and love in action. I too had been blind. I was blind to the splendor around me. Spring was here. The earth was rousing from its winter slumber. The sun was strong and high. Soon it would reach its pinnacle in the sky. Life was humming with the busyness of a bee, bent upon renewal.

The oracle was right! Everything was part of a higher plan, the divine plan behind creation. To its universal laws we had to bow. The moon was continually dying and being reborn, a cosmic lesson in the pattern of growth and transformation. Even the mighty sun would reach its zenith in the sky, and then decline. Small wonder, we creatures were destined to experience our own highs and lows. I had to accept my lot in life. I had made my choice. Now I would have to accept my fate.

I climbed out of the Balikh. Navigating on dry land again, exhaustion caught up with me. All I wanted to do was sleep. But first I needed to give thanks to the River Oracle. I took my fire rocks from beneath my altar, and got some frankincense I'd been saving in my secret stash. The sun directly overhead I lit the incense and gave thanks to the wise spirit of the river. With the pungent fragrance still wafting up to heaven, I made myself a bed and laid down beside the altar.

It was a deep peaceful sleep. Unbroken til I heard the sound of a man's voice, and the plaintive bleating of one of my sheep. I awoke with a start, and sat up quickly to have a look around. Jacob was approaching with one of my ewes. I'd kept my shrine a secret. How had he known where to find me?

I could barely hear Jacob over the ewe's cries. She was in the lead and bleating with excitement at the sight of me. She and Jacob made such a ridiculous pair. I burst out laughing. As they got closer I could see it was Jonquil, her pregnant belly was so full it almost touched the ground. It seemed a miracle that she could walk. Jacob too was laden down, equipped with the fixings of a sumptuous meal.

He beamed at me, as he shouted from across the river, "Thank God, I've finally found you! I'd been searching for hours when I happened upon this stray ewe. She was so determined in her path. I knew she'd lead me to you. I'm so relieved! Here! I brought you something to eat. You must be famished."

The nap, coupled with my morning's visit with the oracle, had done me a world of good. So I replied, "I'm glad to see you too! Stay there! I'll swim across!"

"Wonderful! I'll spread supper out for us." called Jacob enthusiastically, glad to find me in such fine spirits."

Waving something in the air, he continued, "I even brought you some clothes. I thought they might prove useful, though I must say I prefer seeing you without them."

Jacob was being his old thoughtful self again. I had to laugh out loud. I had left my robes up river, where we'd spent the night. "Thank you! I'll be right over." I called out gratefully.

The relief on Jacob's face told me he too wanted to put the unpleasantness of the morning's quarrel behind us.

The moon was down and I was filled with a strange apprehension, as we started home the last night of our wedding week. Change was in the air. Even the subtle tides of my body were shifting. Not long into our walk, I felt the first seep of my moon blood. The wind picked up and a strange wistful mood seized hold of me.

I had always welcomed the wise blood of my moon change. It was proud herald of my body's connection to the Moon Goddess. My sensitivity was always heightened during my moon change, and the veil between the worlds grew thin. My Spirit Eyes and Ears were opened illuminating the unseen reaches in my soul. Why did I feel so strange tonight?

I held my skirt down against the wind, musing to myself as we walked side by side in the gathering dusk. Suddenly I heard mother's words in my heart relating the story of creation.

THE GREAT GODDESS NINHURSAG FASHIONED HUMAN BEINGS OUT OF CLAY WITH HER WISE BROTHER ENKI. SHE INFUSED LIFE INTO THE INERT MATTER WITH THE POWER OF HER MOON BLOOD, THE PRECIOUS BLOOD OF LIFE.

SHE WHO WATCHES BLESSED WOMEN WITH THE MIRACULOUS GIFT OF LIFE. SHE MADE SUGUTU WOMEN AS FERTILE BIRTH MOTHERS, PORTALS OF LIFE. SUGUTU WOMEN RETAIN THEIR MOON BLOOD IN THEIR WOMB, SO IT WILL GROW INTO A BABY AFTER INTERCOURSE.

NADITU WOMEN ARE THE SPIRITUAL MOTHERS OF THEIR PEOPLE. THEIR WISE BLOOD FLOWS AT THE DARK OF THE MOON TO PROVIDE THEM ACCESS TO THE SPIRIT REALM. A NADITU WOMAN IS AN UNSOWN FIELD. HER WOMB WAITS UPON THE WILL OF HEAVEN. FOR NADITU WOMEN ARE THE DESTINED MOTHERS OF THE STAR CHILDREN, THE WORLD SERVERS AND SAVIORS OF THEIR PEOPLE.

I was grateful for mother's words. They had illuminated the shadow gathering in my heart. So that was what it was! My moon blood proclaimed that I was not with Jacob's child. Even the thought saddened me, and I was left to wonder. I was a Naditu woman, and not meant for breeding. Why did it bother me I had not conceived? Why this strange wistful mood? I couldn't understand, but I tried not to show my apprehension. Jacob liked to see me happy.

Jacob was staring at me when I looked up. "Why are you frowning, Rachel?"

"It's because our wedding week is over and we're returning home. I wish we didn't have to go back. I had hoped we'd be making a new start alone together in your homeland. Instead we have seven more years under father's stifling control. I'm afraid what may come between us. There's father, Leah, and the Black Hand becoming more powerful all the time."

"I had also hoped to leave, Rachel!" replied Jacob looking at me uncomfortably. "But I have to make the best of it. At least it will give me time to build up wealth, and flocks, so I can return home in a position of power, not of weakness. . . . Don't worry about your father and the Black Hand, Rachel. Yahweh will protect us. . . . And you know how I feel about you. We'll stay together in the wedding tent by ourselves. I'll sleep with you every night to ease your fears."

"I feel better knowing you want it that way." I said smiling at Jacob.

"I do! I promise you!" said Jacob with conviction.

Jacob put his arm around me and we continued walking. I told myself, I didn't have anything to fear. My apprehension was just my dread at returning home. But could I really count on Jacob? My only consolation was to be here upon this land. I looked at the snowcapped Taurus mountains glimmering in the distance like towering angels. This land was my home, my mother. This land and I were one.

It was the dark of the moon and the sun was going down fast now. It would soon be completely black with nothing but the stars to guide our way. It was a long trek home, but the wind was strong and pushing at our backs hurrying us along. We chatted intermittently, sharing a heightened intimacy as we navigated by the stars. Everything was well until a dense cloud cover moved in out of nowhere as we came up over the last ridge behind the farm. My flesh began to crawl. Even the stars of heaven were blocked out as we approached the farm.

Closing the gate behind us a deep foreboding took hold of me. Something ominous was in the air. I didn't have long to wait to find out what I'd been sensing. Leah emerged from the darkness as we made our way to the wedding tent. She ran up to Jacob saying coyly, "Excuse me for disturbing you on your last night, my husband. But I have important news! My moon blood hasn't come with the dark of the moon, as it always does! Father consulted his oracle. I'm with child! Father says it's sure to be a boy! I'm so excited, Jacob! I had to tell you."

Jacob was pleased by the news, but uncomfortable with me there. "That's wonderful, Leah!" he replied guardedly. "But how can you be sure?"

Leah looked at him in surprise, and retorted. "Women's moon blood always comes at the dark of the moon, Jacob. That's why we call it the moon change. It's women's way! Aren't you going to hug me?"

I stood there wishing I could disappear, as Jacob replied, "Of course! Come here!"

Leah walked over proudly and stood between us. After giving me a smug look, she stepped into Jacob's open arms. Jacob looked over at me nervously as they finished their embrace. Hoping to include me, he took my hand and said, "It's wonderful news, isn't it Rachel!"

Pregnancy and childbirth were among the most sacred Mysteries of the Goddess. I didn't want to defile one of the Blood Mysteries with my anger and jealousy. I breathed out slowly hoping to diffuse my irritation at Leah's intrusion. Fighting back the welter of emotions churning inside me, I said. "Congratulations!"

Leah turned toward me with a sly smile. Seeking to make the most of her advantage, she questioned, "This is the dark of the moon. What have you to say for yourself, Rachel? Are you with child? Or has your moon blood begun to flow?"

I was taken aback by the directness of Leah's question. Everything was happening so quickly. I hadn't had a chance to discuss this matter with Jacob yet, and didn't want to have to answer Leah. I stepped back trying to melt into the background. But Leah would not allow me that small courtesy.

Continuing in an urgent tone, her question pursued me in the darkness. "Where are you going, Rachel? I just asked you a question. Has your moon blood begun to flow?"

I was mortified by Leah's insidious questioning and felt completely cornered. What was Leah up to? She'd never questioned me about this before.

I steadied myself before replying, "I don't see why it's any of your business, Leah!"

Fortunately at this point, Jacob must have felt my desperation. Taking pity on me, he intervened, "Rachel's right, Leah! It is none of your business!"

Full of herself, and still gloating with the newfound power of her situation, Leah was not about to be put off. "Don't be angry with me, if I'm not being tactful, Jacob. But today is such a special day. I was hoping that if Rachel had her moon change well . . . you certainly wouldn't want to sleep with her . . . would you?"

My heart sank. I had already seen how poorly Jacob did when he was put on the spot.

Sure enough! Only a stunned silence followed Leah's question.

Turning in my direction, Leah queried, her cloying tone boring into my soul. "If you have your moon change, you'd prefer to be alone. . . . Wouldn't you?"

Leah waited a moment, then turned toward Jacob in my silence. "If Rachel's in her moonchange, couldn't I sleep with you tonight, Jacob? It would mean so much to me."

I was reeling under the intrusive force of Leah's questions and insinuations. I didn't know what to say, but one thing was for sure I wasn't going to remain in the shadows a moment longer. Obviously that was what Leah had planned for me. Gathering my strength I stepped forward, thinking what a busy day father and Leah must have had working out their invasive plan

I returned to Jacob's side just in time to witness Leah's next tactic. Taking full advantage of her condition, she grabbed Jacob's hand and placed it over her womb. Holding it there, she looked up at him adoringly and said, "It's such a special day! Surely you understand how I feel, Jacob. It would be such a comfort to have you with me tonight."

There was a churning nausea in the pit of my stomach. Jacob was such a nurturer. I shuddered at how expertly Leah knew how to play him.

The sensation of Leah's full belly ignited a smile on Jacob's face. Turning toward me, he said, "I know it's the last night of our wedding week, Rachel, and I don't know much about these things. But we have to think of Leah now that she's pregnant. So tell me? Do you have your moon change?"

There was no ignoring the question now. I had to answer. But I was furious I wasn't being granted the privacy of having this conversation alone with my husband. Is this how our married life would be?

I looked down at the ground before answering. I couldn't bear to see the pride on Jacob's face at the thought of Leah being with his child. "I am with my moon change, Jacob."

Jacob took my chin in his hands. After patting my head he turned my face up forcing me to look at him. Then he said in a soft voice, just audible over the wind. "Don't worry, my darling! Your time will come!"

Even Jacob being considerate didn't help. Nothing could have helped me at that moment.

Then he said in a firm voice loud enough for both of us to hear. "That settles it! I can't sleep with you in your unclean state, Rachel. So I'll stay with Leah tonight. It's such a special occasion. I'm sure you'll understand."

No! I didn't understand how Jacob could go back on his word to me so quickly. I also didn't appreciate his thinking my moon change was an unclean state. I could understand his thinking the blood of life as too powerful to get close to. But his thinking of my moon change as unclean was an affront to me, and to the Goddess. Didn't he have any respect for the foundations of life? What was more, he was falling into yet another of father and Leah's traps.

My pride would not allow me to argue with him in front of Leah. Leah was his first wife. Now she would be the first to give him a child as well. I felt powerless and defeated, but I had to rise above the misery I was feeling. I was a Naditu woman. I couldn't let them see how much it rankled me that Leah was pregnant and I was barren.

"Very well, if that's what you wish." I replied, forcing a smile.

Then I disappeared into the darkness without waiting for his reply. The night swallowed me up completely this time. The wind was blowing strong. It whipped my robes about like a sail, but I didn't care. I wanted to be picked up and carried away. All my hopes for our marriage had been dashed to pieces. I had wanted to get away from father and Leah's clutches, but I had been delivered over to them instead.

I went to the tent I had shared with Leah to get my things. The scent of her sickeningly sweet oil filled the air. I couldn't even step inside. I had some old clothes up at my moon lodge beside my altar. I would retire to the safety of my woodland bed. I preferred taking my chances alone out in the wind, rather than stepping one foot inside Leah's tent. At least I could honor the Goddess at my moon lodge and return my wise blood to the earth.

14

THE YEARS OF DROUGHT BEGIN

THE PROMISE OF SPRING DESERTED US THAT YEAR. IT WAS THE SEARING hamsin winds which started up on our return home at the conclusion of our wedding week. Its burning breath continued in a relentless blast for several days consuming all vegetation. Not until Jacob kept his promise, and welcomed me back to his bed, did the shrivelling winds die down. By then it was too late. The fertile earth was scorched into a fine dry powder crying out to heaven for life giving rain. The healing rains never came. What was once rich topsoil was turned into a suffocating dust that blew about relentlessly in the air. It was weeks before the dust clouds finally settled, and we could see well enough to walk about. Then the tragic results were all too visible.

The wheat and barley crop was parched and flattened. Its sorry remains were as crushed and fallen as my downcast heart. For one entire moon the fine dust lingered in the air, filtering out the sun, and obstructing the inspiring view of the Taurus mountains. Such cruel punishment! Even Mt. Ararat was obscured. The people in our region were sick with grief, and forced to question why the Gods ignored their prayers.

The answer was all too clear to me. I was racked with guilt for having shirked my sacred duty. And I was not the only one to blame. Jacob had strayed from the path of his illustrious forbears, diluting his bloodline with a Sugutu wife.

By midsummer all the graze land in our region was completely spent. I was forced to take our flocks far out beyond the distant foothills, where there was still some tender grass. The terrain there was wild and steep, but the air was pure and sparkling. There my vision had room to open and to heal. The danger of marauding wolves and lions didn't frighten me. It was easier defending against them, than the covert assaults at home.

We made an encampment in the heights, and I was not alone. Many of the shepherds in our region were there with their flocks. Eli and his oldest son Jubal had come with me. We had several well trained herding dogs, three ornery donkeys to scare off predators, and our stout crooks and knives. When Bilhah could be spared from her work at home in the fields, she would relieve me. At first it was difficult being away from Jacob for such long stretches at a time. But I fared better on the mountain ridges than I did at home where Leah's pregnancy dominated everything, and Jacob most of all. The time he spent with Leah grew along with the size of her belly, until there seemed nothing left for me.

Being out on my own with the flocks, there was time to ponder and to pray. I had to rise to the occasion. Leah was my sister, and mother would have wanted it that way. Pregnancy and childbirth were important rites of passage in the Goddess Mysteries. For centuries women had pledged to be there for each other to create a circle of protection. Determined to keep faith with the ancient ways, I sought out Leah on my return home.

It was early in the morning of another sweltering day. Jacob was in the fields with the men. The entrance to her tent was open. With that as an invitation I stuck my head inside. "Are you awake? May I come in?"

All was silent inside the tent. I began to feel nervous. Leah had been avoiding me since I returned. This would be our first time alone together since our weddings. I gathered up my courage, and walked inside. The same cloyingly sweet fragrance permeated the tent. Once my eyes adjusted to the dim interior, I could make out Leah's ponderous form lying across her mat. She did not make the least gesture of welcome as I entered.

When she finally deigned to speak, she said, "What do you want?" in a petulant sulky voice.

I could feel myself growing apologetic for merely being there. My heart was heavy, but I told myself not to give up so easily. For the sake of the Sisterhood and the Goddess I had to effect a reconciliation. Perhaps Leah would have a change of heart, now that she was swelling with the precious gift of life.

I put a smile on my sinking spirits, and began, "How are you doing? I brought you some herbs from the mountains to settle your stomach. Mother said mornings could be difficult the first three moons of pregnancy."

Leah examined the herbs without a word. Not even bothering to look up, she announced. "I don't need your herbs! Don't trouble yourself for me! Jacob's nowhere in sight. So you can stop pretending. You don't really care about how I'm feeling."

It was warm out, but the atmosphere was cold and heavy between us. I felt defeated. We should have been great friends. Why did it have to be this way? I wanted to turn and run. But thinking of mother and the Sisterhood, I continued, "That's not true, Leah! How can you say that? You're my sister. Of course I care about you. This is a special time. I came to see if there was anything I could do to help."

A quizzical, slightly vulnerable look crossed her face. Then it was gone. A bemused smirk had already taken its place, when she said, "You expect me to believe that?"

"Why is it so difficult?" I asked in astonishment. "Women have stood by each other during pregnancy and childbirth for untold centuries. Don't you remember the Sisterhood in the Women's Circle? It's the Goddess's will, and women's sacred trust to support each other at this time."

At the mere mention of the Goddess, Leah rolled her eyes and looked away. "The Goddess! The Sisterhood! Won't you ever grow up? You've got to stop holding on to the past! Mother's gone! The Naditu Sisterhood is fading! This is the Age of Abraham and the Fathers!"

My heart sank to hear her words, and I had to struggle to regain my composure. "This may be the Age of Abraham, Leah. But it doesn't mean that we women have to turn our backs on one another. Why abandon the values of the Sisterhood? We need to stand together now more than ever."

"Don't bore me with such nonsense." snapped Leah in irritation.

"You sound like father and Jacob when you say those things." I blurted out. "I feel like I don't even know you anymore. But we've all been under quite a strain. So let's not argue. What can I do to help you? There must be something I can do for you."

Leah was silent for a few moments. Then she looked me coolly in the eyes smiling maliciously. "Come to think of it! There is something you can do. You can continue staying away from Jacob. It suits me having him all to myself."

"What a selfish thing to say! I'm the one who's sharing Jacob with you." I said feeling as though a knife had been thrust into my heart.

The look in Leah's eyes was withering and filled with hate. It took my breath away.

As I turned to go, she said, "What do you expect? Do you think I like having you around taking up Jacob's precious little time. And though you've been excellent at concealing it thus far, you must be absolutely green with envy that I'm pregnant, and you're not. Furthermore I don't need your support! I have father's and Jacob's. What more could I want?"

The stillness in the air was as ponderous as death, and I was forced to question. Had I betrayed myself coming to see her? Hot fingers of shame crawled up my back. I felt sick and wretched. I wanted to say something clever to cloak my misery. But disappointment choked me, and I could find no words.

When I looked at Leah again. She was sitting up on her mat primping herself and looking very self-satisfied. Obviously enjoying my discomfort, she patted her full belly, saying proudly. "I'm doing quite well for myself, as you can see. Maybe there's something I can do for you. You've gone pale. I must say I'm surprised! I thought you liked to hear the truth."

Leah's words seared into me like an ember from the fire. My patience was dwindling. She was mocking me again. Bursting with righteous anger, I said, "Don't you dare speak to me of truth! You and father are both masters of deceit! You wouldn't even be pregnant now, if you hadn't tricked Jacob into sleeping with you. You're just being rude to bolster your pride, but that doesn't change anything. You wouldn't have a man at all, if it wasn't for me. Unless, of course, you think having father is the same as having a husband."

Leah gazed at me with a mischievous glint in her eyes, saying, "Those are very angry words from someone who came to offer help. Say what you will! Rattle on all you like! I have what I want! Just don't speak to me of the Woman's Circle! What good did it ever do me, or you for that matter? And now all times of day and night women show up to discuss their problems with you. Who wants to listen to problems? What's in it for you? I'd think you'd be sick of it by now."

I looked at my sister in dismay. "It's a privilege and an honor to work with those women, Leah! Each time I bring relief to a woman's heart I know that I'm helping the Goddess and furthering the Sisterhood of all women."

"Well, go ahead if you like! But I'm glad I'm a Sugutu woman! And I'm proud of it! Your antiquated Sisterhood is dying out. This is my time to shine, because I'm a real woman and not some . . . freak of nature. Yes! I'm pregnant and you're not. You'll always be barren. That's my just revenge, because Jacob wants sons. Lots of sons to take over the Promised Land! Wait and see! He'll soon tire of you."

"So run along, and take your good intentions with you. I don't believe them for a moment. Not another word about the Sisterhood or the Goddess! Where were the Sisterhood after mother's death? The women in town shunned us just the same as the men. The Goddess didn't give me a husband! Father did! He and the Brotherhood have all the power now. So stay away from me! Or I'll have to tell Jacob about our little chat. You know how he disapproves of the Goddess."

Smarting with the sting of Leah's words, I said, "Very well, if that's what you wish! But the Sisterhood dies with you! No one, not even the Black Hand, could wipe out the Sisterhood if we women stood together!"

I turned around quickly and left, so Leah couldn't see the tears of disappointment and humiliation burning in my eyes. Leah would never change! Why had I been such a fool?

The sunlight was so dazzling outside, my eyes hurt. Luckily neither father nor Jacob were anywhere in sight. Only Bilhah was crossing the yard on her way to the fire hut. She couldn't help see me leaving Leah's tent. Shame welled up in me anew. Hadn't I been humiliated enough? I hated being caught leaving Leah's tent with my eyes wet! I slowed my pace, hoping Bilhah would go on her way. But to my dismay she stopped and waited for me.

When I came into hearing range she inquired, "Is something troubling you this morning, Mistress Rachel? It's so good to have you home again. Let me know if there's anything I can do to help."

Bilhah seemed genuinely pleased to see me. Her words were kind and sympathetic, but I was in no mood to be detained. The isolating sting of shame had me in its grip, making her presence an unwanted intrusion. I rushed past her, shaking my head. Then I took off running for the Balikh. I needed to be alone beside the river. I couldn't bear the thought of any more prying eyes.

The sound of the river water soothed the poison of Leah's words. I had kept faith with the Sisterhood putting my jealousy aside, but Leah wasn't with me. I couldn't heal our relationship alone. With the sun directly overhead, I swore to the Goddess, that this was the last time I'd open myself to her. I would keep my distance. I could hold the Goddess's circle of protection praying for Leah and her baby from afar.

I was relieved to return to the foothills of the Taurus mountains with my flocks. Leah had never been known for the sweetness of her disposition. But during her ripening, she ruled everyone with her voluminous needs and wants. The extreme hardship of the growing season and toil of harvest put some checks upon Leah's unwieldy moods. But once the harvest was in and her time drew near, there was no end to the demands she placed on Jacob.

One cold bleak evening Leah was in one of her moods as we all sat together around the fire after supper. The entire day the north wind had been blowing in from the mountains with tremendous force. It had picked up strength when I returned home that afternoon. Now it was threatening to storm.

Leah was none too pleased to see me. She was pouting in her seat of honor beside father near the hearth. I had begun bracing myself even before she spoke.

"The wind is so angry tonight, Jacob! I'm so sensitive these days. It frightens me. Won't you please stay with me tonight?" she asked petulantly.

Jacob was sitting beside me across from her. I couldn't see his face, but he began fidgeting the moment she started talking. "Come now Leah! Rachel's only gotten home today! There's nothing to worry about. A little snow may fall before daybreak, but we should be grateful for that. We need the moisture."

"I'm sorry, Jacob! But I just can't help myself. The wind's so loud. If I'm alone I'll be up all night." she muttered peevishly.

Jacob leaned over to her and stroked her hand comfortingly. "There's nothing to fret about! Zilpah can sleep in your tent with you if you're worried. And I'll walk you to it and see you're safe and warm inside."

Nothing but my leaving was going to please Leah tonight. At least Jacob wasn't giving in to her so easily this time. I smiled over at him gratefully. Though I was still on guard. Leah was like father. It made her angry not to get her way.

Jacob started speaking to me, but I could hardly listen. Leah was squirming around in her seat, and I was afraid of what his attention might provoke.

Interrupting our conversation, she asked, "Did I tell you the baby started kicking today, Jacob? Come! Sit here beside me! Maybe he'll start again."

"You told me, Leah. Now please, I'm trying to have a conversation with Rachel." said Jacob patiently.

Leah started to glower. Glancing over at me she raised her voice. I held my breath as she began sourly, "I don't understand why you have to stay with Rachel every night she's home, Jacob. I'm your first wife! Your first son will be mine! What do you see in her? She can't give you a child."

The atmosphere was stifling. No one dared speak. Shame began pawing at the back of my neck. My face grew flushed. I tried to calm myself, but nothing worked. I was about to get up and leave the room, when I refrained. Leaving wouldn't solve anything. That was what Leah wanted.

Time stood still. Why wasn't Jacob coming to my defense? I looked over at him, praying he'd say something . . . anything . . . so that I could save face. But he was staring aimlessly at the fire. In utter desperation I turned to father. That was even more disappointing. Father's arm was around Leah. He was speaking to her gently to calm her fears.

The fire hissed and began to sputter. Finally, to break the tension, father stood up. "It's the waning moon. Everyone's a bit on edge. Let's have some wine to cheer us up! It will help you sleep, Leah. What do you say, Jacob?"

Jacob looked up at father gratefully, relieved the silence had been broken. Shaking his head, he said, "That sounds good to me, Laban!"

Jacob glanced over at me as father went to get the wine. I beckoned to him that I wanted to leave. He responded in a whisper. "We'll just have one cup. Leah's upset. She didn't mean what she said."

There was nothing to say. I couldn't be heard over father's booming voice. "Bilhah! Fetch some cups! Be quick about it!"

As soon as Bilhah returned with the cups, father began pouring. 'Have a taste of this, Jacob! It will do you good. Here's some for you Rachel . . . and Leah."

It was unusual for father to serve me. I took the cup from his hand without glancing up. The wine was red and full bodied, the way I liked it. I was beginning to enjoy the warmth spreading inside me, when Leah started up again. This time it was under her breath to father, but loud enough for all to hear. "Why did you have to serve Rachel first? I'm here all the time and I'm neglected. As soon as she shows up everyone makes such a fuss."

I turned away in disgust, and took another sip of wine trying not to pay attention to her. Bilhah caught my eye. Her gaze was compassionate, but shame flared up in me anew. Even my maidservant felt sorry for me. My life was suffocating. I never had any privacy. Why did Bilhah always have to be there when I was at my worst? I was angry and disgruntled, and wanted to lash out at Bilhah to make myself feel better. But I caught myself. That was no solution. I'd only become like Leah. Just the thought of it sent shivers up my spine. I took another sip of wine.

Jacob and father were talking. The same old conversation about the drought and the withered harvest. I knew why we were in drought. Kak.Si.Di. was the dispenser of the rain. We were in drought because Ninhursag was no longer worshipped. But no one would listen to me. No one ever listened to me. I was well skilled in keeping my ideas to myself. Braced by the wine, I looked away and started to ponder. Was it really so terrible Bilhah felt sympathy for me?

I glanced over at Jacob, hoping we could retire early. But father was plying him with another cup of wine. They were engrossed in some heady conversation about the Gods. Jacob had forgotten his promise to me, and was oblivious to my urgings to leave. Leah was stewing beside father. I was afraid she was just waiting to pounce on me again.

After gazing into the fire for a while I looked at Bilhah in the far corner of the room. She smiled at me again warmly. Her unspoken sympathy took some of the sting out of Leah's words. Did I have an ally in Bilhah? It had been so long since I'd known the fellowship of the Women's Circle, I was afraid to trust it. I smiled perfunctorily back at Bilhah, then turned from her gaze. I didn't want any more disappointment. I hoped the storm would blow over quickly. I couldn't wait to return to my mountain retreat with the flocks.

The storm hit very hard up in the mountains. A pack of hungry wolves had descended on our camp and devoured several sheep. They'd also killed Danu, our best herding dog. The shepherd who found them in the morning had killed one of the wolves, and been wounded himself in turn. There was a trail of blood leading up into the mountains.

From then on we were on constant alert. Eli and his son took turns sleeping out beside the flocks with Zack and a pack of dogs. As winter came on in earnest, we had to move further up into the wolves' territory in search of grass. As frightening as it was to enter the wild steep terrain of the mountains, there were numerous gifts as well.

The air grew thinner the higher up we went. It seemed to sparkle and crackle with heightened life. The rarefied mountain air proved a heady wine, and I was relieved to see the farm, a tiny speck out in the distance. The expansive vistas caused my mind to reel, challenging the boundaries of my spirit and my senses. It was thrilling sleeping out under the bright canopy of stars. Strange lights would arch across the sky, and I could feel the presence of the Nefilim, the Shining Ones who from heaven came. Dreams were crystal clear at these heights. Many a night the Shining Ones would appear to me in my dreams. One particular face was always beckoning. Feelings of wonder and longing were stirred in me I could not understand. How I wished I had the terafim! I might have been able to call the Nefilim down, and fulfill the Higher Marriage after all!

Of course, I still thought of Jacob from time to time, but I no longer missed him. How could I miss the jealousy and competitiveness always in his wake? I longed for the idealistic Jacob of our early years. My husband was not the man he once had been. Attempting to juggle his many duties and responsibilities to those around him, Jacob had lost himself. Now the light in him was also dim.

One night at sunset when the moon was a slender boat upon the horizon, the sky turned blood red sending shivers through my soul. A thick wall of fog came rolling in from the distant plains around Haran. By the the following morning it had arrived. Bilhah appeared in the afternoon with Nathan and Amos to relieve me. One more night in the peace of my mountain retreat was all I had to sustain me before the onslaught of the birth.

There was a farewell gift for me when I awoke the next morning. During the night the fog had deposited a glistening mantle of frost over everything. My mountain retreat had been transformed into a treasure trove, sparkling magically in the early morning light. It took my breath away to see the stately trees dressed in their fine white lace. Even the bushes and tall grasses were feathered out, glimmering like jewels in the morning light. Winter was setting in.

I sat down to our usual breakfast around the campfire with Bilhah, Eli and the men. Bilhah's eyes were kind, as I prepared to leave. I packed my few belongings, some supplies for the journey, and started down the mountain reluctantly. The walk with Amos was exhilarating. Cleansing showers fell upon us as the sun melted the frost off the trees. The magic ended by the time we reached the plains. When we arrived in Haran we could hardly see in the dense fog.

A curious fear assailed my heart as we approached the farm. So I sent Amos on ahead to announce our arrival. Sealed in the mysterious gloom of the fog, I hesitated before the gate afraid to enter.

My trepidation was greeted by the sound of father's voice calling to me through the mist. "Are you there, Rachel? What are you doing standing there? Come inside!"

"Why did you come out to greet me, father? Is everything alright?" I inquired cautiously.

"Of course it is!" he replied gruffly. "Leah's Sugutu! There's nothing to worry about! I called you back because your mother would have wanted you here for the birth. But I have to tell you, there have been some changes since your last visit."

"Nothing to fret about, mind you!" he said steering me toward the house. "It's just that Leah's been . . . a bit . . . temperamental these last few days. Jacob's with her and can't be disturbed. He sent me to tell you she's moved into the wedding tent with him. You'll have to stay in your old quarters until after the birth."

My heart sank. Had they called me back just to humiliate me? I wanted to turn and run.

Sensing my distress, father spoke sharply, "Come now, Rachel! Don't be selfish! We have to think of Leah now! Don't make a problem of yourself! You'll still see Jacob at meal times. And of course, after the birth it would be taboo for Jacob to stay with Leah. Everything will go back to the way it was before."

The patronizing tone of father's voice was more than I could bear. I felt trapped. How could I pretend everything was alright? "Why did you bother calling me down from the mountains?" I asked in annoyance. "Was it just to humiliate me? There's no place for me here! You may have been able to fool Jacob, but you can't fool me. Things will never go back to the way they were!"

Then brushing passed him, I made a run for my old tent. At least there I could be alone.

The tent was rank with the scent of Leah's oils as I stepped inside. Her things were strewn around everywhere. I had to pick them up and pack them away just to make a place for myself to sit. After a good cry I got some pungent sage, and went to work making the tent my own. It was harsh and blustery outside, but once I purged the tent it was a cozy haven. At least there I could get away from all of them.

Jacob was run ragged fulfilling Leah's every whim as we waited upon the birth. She was so temperamental and demanding, I couldn't bear to watch the foul display. So I kept my own hours, and ate my morning meal alone. Father made sure I put in an appearance every night at dinner. Then I was forced to sit and watch Leah fuss and fume, devouring Jacob along with her meal.

Eventually even father grew impatient with her. A few days before the birth we were all at the end of our tether.

"Stop fretting, Leah! Can't we eat a meal in peace? I examined you this morning. Everything's as it should be! The baby's dropped into position. It will only be a few more days now." said father in annoyance.

"I feel wretched and crampy!" replied Leah sulkily.

"It's probably something you ate," declared father irritably. "Did you have any leeks or onions? I told you to avoid them now that the birth is close."

"I just had a few!" said Leah peevishly. "You know how I love them. It wasn't my fault! Zilpah put them in the stew. And you told me I had to eat meat to keep my strength up."

"Enough of this infernal whining!" replied father in exasperation. "You brought it on yourself! Stop blaming everyone else! What's all the fuss about? You're a Sugutu woman! Get a grip on yourself! I consulted my oracle and the moon charts, as I told you this morning. The child will come with the full moon. The Gods have all been propitiated! It's sure to be an easy birth! So let us eat in peace."

Leah was crestfallen and agitated. Having lost father's support, she immediately turned to Jacob. "Father's being so cross with me tonight, Jacob. Tell me you love me! Tell me here in front of everyone! Only your love will make me feel better."

Jacob responded perfunctorily, "Don't worry Leah, everything will be alright."

Then looking over at father, he said with a scowl, "Stop filling Leah's head with foolish notions, Laban! We don't need you propitiating Nanna/Sin. Yahweh will guide this birth. And it's important for Leah to notice all the changes going on inside her, and keep us informed. . . . How can you, or anyone else, know when the child will be born?"

Father looked at Jacob in annoyance, saying, "I'm a seasoned moon priest! I know about these things! This is your first child! You may be interested in your wife's indigestion, but I am not! And I would prefer not to be entertained with it at mealtime!"

The atmosphere at the table was suffocating, but Leah wasn't finished yet. Glancing at me out of the corner of her eye, she continued, "Come now, Jacob! Last night you told me you loved me. Tell me here again in front of everyone!"

My head started pounding. Jacob had told Leah he loved her! He told me he was just being kind and dutiful to the mother of his child. He said he only felt sorry for Leah. Who was Jacob deceiving now?

THE YEARS OF DROUGHT BEGIN

Everyone stopped eating. Silence reigned at the table. I kept my eyes on Jacob. After a few minutes he glanced at me, and smiled sheepishly. I was completely unmoved. We were only separated by a table length, but it seemed an unsurmountable gulf. Jacob could smile all he liked. His boyish charm no longer worked its magic on me. His silence spoke more eloquently.

The day of the full moon was biting cold. I left the farm early in the morning and didn't return til sunset. I preferred the frigid blast of nature to the biting chill at home. The moon was a large disc upon the horizon as I opened the creaky old gate and stepped inside, looking around in apprehension. No camels or donkeys were tethered before the house. The Wise Women of Haran had not yet been called, and Leah's cries were piercing the evening's cuiet.

Hearing my sister in travail I remembered the ancient ways, and stopped by the tent to see if there was anything I could do to help. Father, and Tubal, and another of his loathsome brethren from the Black Hand, were in the tent with Leah when I peered inside. Zilpah was also there standing in the corner.

Father glared at me in impatience. "What are you doing here? We don't need you! I'll bring the child in alone."

I was aghast. Noting the look on my face, father cried out, "You heard me! I'll notify you when the child's delivered."

I staggered away from the birth tent in disbelief. This was women's realm! Father was breaking another taboo taking over the midwife's role! Was there nothing sacred anymore? What did father think he was doing usurping the role of midwife? The tree of life was being turned upside down by the Brotherhood. Sin had taken over the feminine lunar realm. Was the Black Hand also going to rob us of our role in birthing? What would become of us, women, when we weren't even accorded our rightful place in the sacred act of lifegiving?

Jacob came up behind me. I hadn't spoken to him since the incident at the supper table two nights before. He was pacing back and forth before the tent like a hungry lion, and didn't even acknowledge me. I went to my tent in tears.

Jacob was exultant the following morning, thrilled with his first born son. Leah never asked for me, and wouldn't even let me see the child. There was nothing for me to do. My life seemed suddenly meaningless.

My arms felt cold and empty as I watched Leah proudly nursing Reuben with Jacob by her side. Jacob was a devoted father. It was winter and there wasn't much work to do about the farm. Breaking all tradition, he took Reuben allowing Leah time to rest. This arrangement delighted Leah. It sealed Jacob's devotion to his son, and didn't allow Zilpah or I to bond with the little one.

Jacob was so swept up in the excitement of his first born son, he no longer had time for me. He only came to see me for short visits when he could spare the time. It didn't matter. His visits were of little consolation. My jealousy was enflamed watching Jacob's face glow as he spoke on and on endlessly about his son. I wanted to be happy for him, but how could I? I felt abandoned and alone. It was no comfort that Jacob still professed his love for me. He had told Leah he loved her too! And he didn't savor my every gesture, or delight in my every sound, as he did with Reuben.

What was worse, I was sure from Reuben's star chart that he'd been conceived on the full moon wedding night. As difficult as the previous months had been this new discovery broke my heart devouring me with jealousy.

15

RETREAT TO THE SACRED MOUNTAINS

I WAITED UNTIL THE NEXT NEW MOON THEN I APPROACHED FATHER with a proposition. Only the misery of my situation could make me brave enough to enter his hideous domain. The air was rank with dragon's blood incense. He was sitting alone in the dark. His pet cobra was coiled around his fiendish skull oracle in its place of honor on the altar. It raised its head unfurling its majestic hood as the sunlight filtered in after me.

"Please father, I can't bear it here a moment longer. Allow me to return to the flocks up in the mountains?" I pleaded.

The directness of my appeal caught father offguard. He studied me carefully before responding. "What possesses you to make such a request? The mountains are no place for a woman this time of year."

"It can't be any worse for me than it is down here." I blurted out. "Please let me go! I'm no use to anyone here."

"But you'll miss Reuben's naming ceremony and his circumcision.

We're going to have a big celebration. I'm sure Jacob would want you there." said father trying to dissuade me.

I averted my eyes. I hadn't even thought about the circumcision. It seemed such a strange barbaric custom to serve as a covenant between Jacob's male descendants and his God. Why was it necessary I be there? I braced myself and continued imploringly, "There will be other celebrations. I have nothing to do down here. At least I can make myself useful up there. I'll return in springtime. It will be a new beginning."

Father took his time contemplating my request, enjoying the full power of his position. When he'd kept me waiting long enough, he replied, "It could be somewhat awkward for you down here these days. I'll consult my oracle for the best time for you to leave."

"Thank you, father." I said, sighing with relief.

Returning to the mountains, I found that Eli had moved the flocks up to our permanent winter encampment there. Winter in the Taurus mountains was freezing cold but also peaceful and serene. A much needed retreat from the emotional turmoil engulfing me at home. Like the frozen earth beneath my feet, I too was spent and exhausted, and needed to draw my forces deep within to renew my sinking spirit.

It was no small challenge living at the top of the world during the cold dark winter months. Life on the plains was much milder in the winter. The cold was treacherous and biting at such heights. Only the resilient sheep could make it on the mountain glens and ridges, pawing through the ice and snow for the grass beneath. The dimwitted cows needed to stay at home and be fed from our meager reserves through the winter. I was proud that like my sheep, I could manage for myself.

I wasn't as lonely and beleaguered in the mountains as I was down on the farm. Beside Eli, Jubal, and Bilhah for company, there was also the magnificent view of Mt. Ararat, and the proximity to the eternal reaches of heaven. The vault of heaven never seemed so close as within the silence of that winter darkness. The anguish of my attachment to Jacob paled before the pristine clarity of the stars.

After having been relegated to the background by Jacob, it gave me new heart to remember the Nefilim's invitation. How could I have been so foolish as to deny that incredible opportunity? It wasn't even a full year since the En Priestess's invitation, yet with all I'd suffered it had gotten buried in my misery and shame. Only now beneath the stars, so close to the roof of heaven could I remember. My spirit was given wings to contemplate the Nefilim. My heart was set aflame with a relentless yearning, which lighted all my nights and warmed my days. The Shining One was always with me. Though I had my flock and many more practical things to think about to offset the fever of my longing.

The privilege of living at such exalted heights exacted quite a price. Atop the world in winter the price was the bitter cold and the purity snow could evoke. More snow fell in the mountains that winter than I'd experienced in my entire life. It fell in deep silent blankets like an enchantment, transforming our world into an ethereal landscape, that exhilarated my soul but put my tired flesh to sleep. Many times that winter my existence was an ordeal of cold and ice, a veritable fight for survival for me and my flock.

There was nothing to do but dig my heels into the frozen ground, and pray to She Who Watches that I be saved. I learned much about survival from my hardy sheep. They taught me to eat the snow for water. As I watched them paw through the snow to find the tender grass beneath, I learned to dig through what had gotten frozen inside me to contact my will to live. Over time swaddled in many layers of clothing, Nature's white blanket came to feel like a soothing cocoon to which I could withdraw to purify and heal myself.

Soon the days began to lengthen, and the earth warmed in welcome of the sun. Overnight the ewes grew round and full. My blood waxed warm and restless as I hiked the mountainsides. Birds appeared out of nowhere, chattering in the branches of the trees. Croci dressed the mountain ridges, and I began peeling off clothing one layer at a time. The driving force of nature was gathering around me. I could feel its urgent call. It was springtime once again.

I was out on the mountainside dreaming of the Nefilim when I heard a call. I turned to see a figure bounding toward me over the mountain glens and ridges. It did not look like Amos. He cried out. "It's you, Rachel! Thank God I've found you! I'm here to take you home, my darling. Come to me! I can't bear to be without you another moment."

Jacob came running toward me, flashing his most beguiling smile. His call startled me out of my reverie, echoing over the silent mountain ridges like a chorus. He had remembered me at last. The flame of his smile made my breath quicken and my heart melt like the fast retreating snow. My entire body warmed to the magic of his touch. Tears came to my eyes. Inside the charmed circle of his embrace hard shackles, like armor, seemed to fall from my body as he pressed me into him. Fire began coursing through my veins. I felt young and alive again. Jacob played me like a lyre, his every touch drawing me back to him. All my misgivings scattered in the wind, which was blowing us together as if by fate.

My mind was racing just ahead of my breath, as I struggled to reign myself in. What was happening to me? How could I open to this man? I couldn't bear any further disappointment. Was this the Jacob I once had known? Could I believe in him? How could he have changed so much? What spell was this that had come over me? Only moments before I had been roaming the mountain ridges with my flock thinking about the Nefilim, and wondering how I could ever leave the glory of the mountains with the spring flowers peeking through the patches of snow.

Could I trust Jacob? Or, was this some springtime fancy that would soon grow cold? His mouth and hands spoke the urgent language of the flesh, but how could I let him in? He had fooled me so many times before. I wasn't ready to leave this hallowed place. I was safe up here and close to the Nefilim. These sacred mountains were my haven. In the dark night of my soul they had been my only refuge. I could lose myself again at home.

Jacob was carrying me over to a boulder at the edge of the clearing. All my resistance vanished in the tide of his desire that came washing over me, capturing me in its wake. His strong warm hands called me back to life. His honeyed words reached into my heart moistening my inner reaches. Before thrusting his manhood into me, he looked me in the eyes. "There's no one in the world like you, Rachel! No one could ever take your place. Not Leah! Not my son! You had but to leave to teach me that bitter lesson. Please forgive me? How I have hungered for you, my angel! I longed for your beauty and the depths of your shining soul."

We spent two glorious days together in the mountains. After that I was Jacob's again, and all thoughts of the Nefilim vanished. But duty called, and we had to return to the farm with the flocks. I was filled with trepidation on the journey down the mountain.

"I promise you, there's nothing to fear, my angel. Leah's pregnant again, and so busy with Reuben, she has little time for me. Everything will be fine. You'll see. We'll be together every night as before. I promise!" he said reassuringly.

"How can I trust you, Jacob? You've disappointed me so many times." I said standing still, and balking at the thought of going any further. "Swear to me by Yahweh, that we'll be together every night!" I demanded, feet rooted in the ground.

Breathless from our descent, Jacob turned too face me. "I'll stay with you every night you're not with your moon change, Rachel. I swear it."

I stood my ground. "Swear to me by Yahweh, Jacob! Swear to me by all you hold as dear, that it will be different this time. You won't give in to Leah, and father all the time."

Jacob's face was serious. Looking me straight in the eyes, he said in a firm voice. "I swear, Rachel! I swear by Yahweh, the God of my fathers, Isaac, and Abraham that I will be the happiest of men having you to look forward to each evening. I missed you, my angel. I was so lonely without you. Don't ever leave me again! I'll make sure it will go well for us this time. Just please don't leave me!"

Jacob was a dutiful father by day, but each night he slept with me circled in his arms. Swept up in his embrace I forgot my yearning for the shining Nefilim. Jacob's arms were warm and close, his lovemaking powerful and intense. My thoughts of the Nefilim were a treasured memory, that couldn't keep me warm at night.

Spring was beautiful down in the valley. The spring wheat and barley crop took the edge off the people's fears. The Balikh was running strong from all the melting snow. The earth yielded to the furrowing plow. Even my flock seemed to cooperate with Jacob's and my reunion. They had mated later than usual due to the conditions up in the mountains, and so the lambing came later too. For once there was time to enjoy spring. It wasn't until early summer that the lambing began in earnest. Then I was busy spinning wool, while Jacob tended the crops for father and the Ehulhul temple.

The great round of the seasons came and went. Though I followed the ancient fertility rites, walking around the fig tree chanting at the new moon and the full hanging it with charms and praying, still my wise blood never ceased to flow. While Leah blossomed out giving birth to three more sons, as easily as rabbits in the springtime.

My womb cried out to see Leah with her four sons. A stone weighed down my heart, growing in size with each of my sister's births. How could life be so unfair? Once it had been an honor to be a Naditu Priestess, but the Eye Temple had long since closed. Ninhursag's time was past. The ranks of the Sisterhood had all moved on. There was no place for a Naditu woman anymore. Father still had the terafim, and was careful to keep them out of sight.

Inanna had taken over Ninhursag's place, just as Leah had eclipsed me. Sin and his bloodthirsty daughter were now the presiding deities in Haran. Their worship was the only one allowed. Kingship no longer came down from heaven nourished by the sweet milk of Ninhursag. Instead, Inanna called her puppet kings to her lap awarding them with riches and great victories in battle. To suit their goals the Brotherhood of the Black Hand made the worship of the power hungry duo the state religion. Their petty wars and exorbitant taxes continued to sap the fat from the land. While every year the tablet of their laws grew, strangling the last remnants of the people's freedom and turning them into a nation of sheep.

Jacob continued to work with the temple flocks at father's behest. His service provided us with many benefits, including immunity from worshipping Sin. Father rose swiftly in the ranks of the Brotherhood, coming to spend most of his time at the Ehulhul temple. Jacob saw to it that Yahweh was the only God prayed to at home. There was no place for a Naditu woman in Yahweh's scheme. Yahweh wanted Jacob to be the prolific father of many sons. Even father came to respect Yahweh after the birth of a son to him by Suzannah. Only I was barren. I was caught between two worlds, my womb crying out to see Leah so richly blessed by Jacob's God.

What did it matter that Jacob swore undying love for me when he buzzed around Leah and their brood all day like a drone around the hive. Leah was triumphant, enshrined amidst her brood of boys, her bovine mark upon them all. It caught my breath to watch the flurry of their constant activity. My own life seemed trivial in comparison. What little strength I had was drained away by Leah's gloating eyes.

First, of course, there was Reuben, Jacob's pride and joy, his privileged eldest son, who resembled him most of all. Young Reuben followed his father about from the time he learned to walk, screaming profusely if

Jacob dared to leave his sight. From early morning until Reuben's bed-time, it was impossible to get a moment alone with Jacob. Wherever we went at home Reuben was in our shadow clamoring for Jacob's regard.

Then came Simeon, followed by Levi. These two were the most troublesome of the lot. Both born under Nergal, the Star of War, they were a red-faced meddling duo, constantly quarrelling between them-selves and vying for their father's attention. Soon after Levi came Judah's birth.

Jacob had to build additional rooms onto the house after Simeon's birth, so Leah and her brood could move into the main house with fa-ther. Even with their separate quarters, these boisterous boys turned our lives upside down and kept it in chaotic turmoil. No peace was to be found at the farm. My only solace was to take the sheep out to pasture to escape the din. Even father moved his study to a dwelling behind the main house to flee the noise. Only Jacob and Leah didn't seem to notice. They swelled with pride revelling in the antics of their raucous brood.

Father came to have several sons by his concubines Suzannah, and Zadia, which sealed his appreciation of Jacob's blessing. My dejection was all the more complete with father thrilled to have a horde of boys to command.

Every time I turned around there was a celebration of some kind. First of course there was the celebration of their births, that was to be expected. Then came their circumcisions, followed by their naming cere-monies. Such a fuss! It never seemed to end. With seven of the little pests it seemed there was always something to be celebrated.

I'd never been fond of father's gala parties. But now that I was seated off by myself at the far end of the banquet table among the concubines, I found them even more disagreeable. As first wife and mother, Leah was in her full glory on these occasions, proudly ensconced on Jacob's right with her brood of boys beside her. Father was of course always at Jacob's left, and beside him were the Brotherhood. Ever the showman, father displayed great pomp and ceremony, beaming with pride amidst his swelling tribe. He read the fates of all the boys amid great fanfare, never tiring of toasting the little men, as he loved to call them.

While as barren second wife, I was seated alone at the far end of the banquet table next to the boys and apart from all the guests. Engulfed by their boyish prattle and annoying pranks, I was cut off from the adults with nothing to bolster my sinking spirits. I felt disgraced in my seat of exile, and feared I made a pitiful sight for all to see. My only relief was when Jacob would catch my eye from time to time, but those were inconsequential gestures in comparison to the enormity of my humiliation.

Judah was the last of Leah's first set of four boys. By the middle of his naming ceremony, I'd had more than I could stand and wanted to leave before father's toast and the anointing of his forehead. What did it matter if I was there? We were almost through the meal, and not a single adult had spoken to me. My head was splitting from all the childish jabber, and I longed to escape the prying eyes of all the guests. I found the perfect excuse, when Simeon spilled his milk all over me.

After drying myself off I stood up to say goodnight to Jacob. Leah was the first to notice my approach. Even busy as she was with her boys, she still watched me like a hawk. As I drew near she placed the infant Judah in Jacob's arms seeking to engross him in conversation. I could hear her plainly as I came up behind them.

"Judah's grasp is strong for one so young! Even now he takes after his father in strength." she said beaming at Jacob. "See how curious he is! He can hardly take his eyes off you."

Enraptured with the squirming bundle in his arms, Jacob hadn't noticed my approach. I was forced to stand by idly waiting my turn, sure the entire crowd was witnessing my neglect.

"We've done well naming this one, Judah. One day he shall give glory to Yahweh, as now he gives it to me." said Jacob proudly.

Glory! For the life of me I couldn't understand what glory this bald ruddy faced infant was giving Jacob. As far as I could see, Judah was just another player in Leah's game. But I had to check myself. Judah was just an infant. This strange lack of sentimentality had to be jealousy.

My spirit vision opened looking down into the baby's eyes. I saw Judah, a grown man. He was still bald and stout, but he did resemble Jacob, though he possessed his mother's earthbound squareness. Now what was this? I had to laugh. This glory of his father was being tricked. He took after Jacob in that way too. For like his father, Judah was being deceived by a faceless woman behind a veil. She was his own kin, though he mistook her for a prostitute. And there was more! Now I could see Judah with a crowd of men. From their looks they had to be his brothers. I could pick out Reuben, Simeon, and Levi, though they were older too. There were more than just these four. Judah was interceding in a pleading voice, imploring them not to slay their brother. Their brother! Such an abomination!!! What did it mean? As the vision faded I smiled down at the squirming infant. At least he had interceded on behalf of what was right.

Was my vision playing tricks on me? No one had invited me to read this child's fate. Why was this being revealed to me? This was the closest I'd ever been to one of Leah's infants, and this quite by accident. Leah kept me away from all her children when they were young. She treated me like the Lamashtu she-demon, who stole the soul of the new born. Well, I had had enough of this. I would make my excuses, and cut the misery of this evening short.

I had to tap Jacob on the shoulder several times before I could catch his attention. "Excuse me, Jacob, but Simeon's had an accident with his milk. I'm dripping wet, and have a bad headache. I'd like to retire early. May I have your permission to go?"

"I'm sorry to hear that, Rachel. The party's only getting started, and I haven't given the blessing yet." said Jacob looking disappointed.

"You don't need me to give the blessing, Jacob." I replied wearily. "Have a look yourself! I'm wet with milk, and don't want to be seen this way."

"Very well! I'll join you when the guests depart." said Jacob sighing.

I smiled at Jacob in relief.

Leah grinned at Jacob, saying, "It's just as well you let her go she adds nothing to the festivities. Simeon's accident is the closest she'll ever get to mother's milk!"

Leah's remark struck me like a dagger in the back as I turned to go. Our company happened to be between courses as I made my way across the courtyard. All eyes were on me. It wasn't just my imagination. Their stares weighed me down as I made my way between the tables. Adah, the town's oldest matriarch and worst gossip, was coming toward me stalking me like a hungry lioness.

Fortunately mother's sister, Tamar, hailed me over just in time. "Is everything alright, dear? You're leaving so early. I haven't had a chance to speak with you yet."

I smiled at Aunt Tamar, grateful she had saved me from Adah. It was always a pleasure to speak with her, but tonight I felt so fragile I had to be on guard. Her sympathy and questions might loosen my tears. So I replied perfunctorily, "You're kind to ask, but it's really nothing, Auntie. I have a gruesome headache, and one of the boys just spilled his milk on me. So I'm retiring early."

Aunt Tamar wasn't satisfied with my reply, but she was not one to pry. Taking my hand she whispered in a low voice. "Why are there so many of the Black Hand here? I've never seen so many of them in one place before."

Looking around furtively, she continued under her breath. "This may not be the best place for us to chat. Let's try to talk in the morning."

Then putting her arm around me, she said, "Take care of yourself, dear! Don't fret! Your time will come. It was the same way with your mother. You're a Naditu woman, and take after her."

Aunt Tamar's remark should have comforted me. But with the way I was feeling, the mere mention of mother threatened to bring on tears. Gulping back tears, I said, "I wish you didn't live so far away and could visit more often. These guests of whom you speak are always around. I'm uncomfortable in my own home."

"I'll try to return in the morning, dear. Have a good rest. You look drawn." said Tamar nodding thoughtfully.

It was hard enough to say goodbye to Aunt Tamar, but as I turned to go Adah came and stood before me blocking my escape. Her massive figure exuded an oppressive heat and her breath reeked of onions, as she cornered me in the narrow passageway between the tables. I stepped back to brace myself for the onslaught of her questions. There was no getting away from her this time.

Her ravenous eyes bored into me, as she inquired, "Where are you going so early? You're not going to leave the party so soon! We haven't had the blessing or the naming ceremony yet."

Adah's intrusive questions had always annoyed me, but tonight I felt defeated at the mere sight of her. I took a deep breath. There was nothing Adah liked better than a good row. Frankly, I didn't have the strength for it.

I smiled politely, hoping to keep things cordial and slip through the snare of her questions. "I'm retiring early, Adah. I have a splitting headache, and one of the boys just spilled milk on me."

A frown crossed Adah's brow at my reply. Looking down her nose at me, she declared as if it were her right. "That's no excuse, Rachel! Change your gown and return! What would your mother say you leaving before the infant's blessed?"

Aunt Tamar must have been following our conversation. At the mention of mother she rose to her feet, interrupting. "How is it that you, a stranger, feel free to speak for Rachel's mother! I am Anna's sister from Brak. I speak for her. If she were here, she'd tell Rachel to take good care of herself. Now step aside! Can't you see that Rachel's wet and uncomfortable? Make way so she can pass!"

Adah stepped back, her fleshy jaw dropping wide in disbelief. I had to stifle a grin. I'd been waiting years for this old busybody to be put in her place. Adah had the power to make, or destroy reputations in Haran. No one ever dared to speak to her that way.

I looked over at Aunt Tamar in gratitude. She smiled and took my hand. All eyes upon us, she escorted me back to my tent.

Before letting go of my hand, she commented. "Things have certainly changed around here since your mother's death. The Black Hand have taken over haven't they? Ninhursag wasn't mentioned once all night."

"It seems the Eye Goddess has been relegated to the same place in your family as you, my dear." she added wryly. "Feel free to visit me anytime. I'm sure you'd like it in Brak though the Sisterhood have all departed. They left when the Eye temple closed down some years back. Still many of us follow the ancient ways, and enjoy the same freedom we had in Sumerian times. But we need young people like you to keep the traditions alive. The Black Hand leaves us alone now that the Eye Temple closed and the Sisterhood is gone. I think they're intimidated by the proximity to Mt. Ararat. Have a good rest! We'll speak further in the morning."

Aunt Tamar was such a darling! But even her kind invitation filled me with sorrow. How could I return to Brak and witness the destruction I had brought on? Nonetheless, it was a relief to be away from the din of the children, and the staring eyes of all the guests. Once alone I could breath again though my head was still splitting. Tears came to my eyes as I lay down.

Leah wasn't pregnant yet, but with her luck there'd be another boy along soon enough. What was wrong with me? First father, then Jacob, now even Yahweh supported Leah. Why was Leah always being raised up while I was being cut down? Who was this Yahweh who blessed deceivers?

Life had been good when mother was alive and we women enjoyed our spiritual freedom. Life was different in the Sisterhood. Justice prevailed because mother and the other Priestesses listened with their heart. There was a sense of joyous participation in nature and with each other. Our code forbade jealous rivalries and encouraged cooperation. Now my spiritual life was as deprived as my womb. But how could it be otherwise? How could I be fertile when the Eye Temple had been closed down and Ninhursag's fertility cult destroyed? The Goddess's pain was in my womb. No wonder I was barren!

Hearing footsteps outside, I wiped my eyes. It wasn't like Jacob to be retiring so early.

"Mistress Rachel, may I come in?" a plaintive voice inquired.

When I looked up, it was Bilhah sticking her head through the narrow opening of the tent. "I'm sorry if I startled you, but I was concerned when you left the party early. Is everything alright?" she inquired sympathetically.

Bilhah's voice was warm and tender. There was no meddlesome prying in her eyes. "Come in, Bilhah!" I said feeling lonely.

Kindness shone in her dark eyes. Bilhah was my maidservant, but she was also a friend. She'd been a real comfort to me up in the mountains. "I'm all right." I replied tearfully. "I just can't bear these parties father puts on to impress all his friends. Jacob and Leah love them, because they delight in showing off their children. While I'm forced to sit alone apart from all the guests."

Bilhah looked at me compassionately and said, "I don't know how you bear it, Mistress Rachel. I can't understand why Jacob doesn't sympathize with your plight and make things easier for you."

At least someone understood. For all the simpleness of her ways, Bilhah really understood. Everything dammed up in me came flooding out. "What can I do, Bilhah! All my hopes are dashed. There's no place for me, because I'm not a mother. My womb aches. I feel as though I'm useless, and my life is through."

Bilhah took me in her strong arms, as she said. "I know all too well the sadness of being childless, Mistress Rachel. You can confide in me.

You're always so thoughtful. You're the only one who's kind to me. Even Zilpah will have nothing to do with me anymore. She copies Leah in everything. Now she's putting on airs."

It took my mind off my own situation to think of Bilhah's plight. I shook my head, saying, "That's ridiculous! I'm sorry it's so difficult for you as well."

We sat together until the last of the guests departed. It was comforting being with Bilhah. She was uncomplicated, and steady as a rock. When I heard Jacob approaching, I gave her ample body one last hug, and said, "Thank you for looking in on me tonight, Bilhah. It's best you leave now. Jacob will soon be in."

"Good night, mistress Rachel! Remember, you have a friend in me."

"Thank you! Good night!" I said warmly.

Jacob's face was flushed when he entered the tent a short time later. Father had been plying him with wine again. He reeked of Leah's cloying scent as he came toward me. "Are you feeling better?"

"I felt better as soon as I could get away from that stuffy gathering." I said irritably.

"What do you mean?" replied Jacob in annoyance. "It was a lovely party. Leah's an excellent hostess. We had magnificent fare. Everyone enjoyed themselves. I don't see why you couldn't. Your father was angry I gave you permission to leave so early. He felt slighted, you didn't wait for his toast."

"He and Adah too!" I said laughing.

"It's not amusing, Rachel! You're my wife. Your place was at the table with me tonight."

Jacob's tone was so infuriating, I broke in. "If my place is with you, why am I always stuck at the far end of the table with all the children? They're not my sons! And Leah never lets me near them otherwise."

Jacob was impatient. "Why do you have to be so petty? We were celebrating Leah's son's naming ceremony. It was only right she sit beside me on such an important occasion. Someone has to sit at the end of the table with all the boys. What would you have me do? Put Laban there instead!"

"I don't care who you put there as long as it isn't me." I snapped in annoyance.

"I'm disappointed to hear you go on so!" retorted Jacob. "Leah wouldn't speak to me like this. First you were jealous of Leah. Now you're jealous of her children. This jealousy of yours has to stop!"

I was getting heated now. "I wouldn't have to be jealous if you thought of me as much as you do Leah and the children. Try looking at things from my point of view for a change! I'm treated worse than a stranger in my own home. Leah doesn't have to speak with you this way, because she's well taken care of. If you're not looking after her and the boys, then father is."

Jacob clenched his fists in irritation. "According to you I never do anything right! You must stop this rivalry, and always making everything my fault! You know the law! It's my right to take another wife because you can't give me any children."

This was the first time Jacob had confronted me with my barrenness. I was exhausted and it was late. I was angry and frustrated and saw red. "Your sons are all you think about! What happened to your dream of a Higher Marriage? Your mother sent you here to find a Naditu wife. But you don't want a priestess for a wife! You want a breed cow to propagate for you like Leah! You don't even care you're weakening your bloodline, like Esau. All you care about is having enough descendants to inherit the land Yahweh promised you. Don't you realize one child of ours would be worth more than all the sons Leah could give you? But you can't see that because you've become obsessed with progeny and material things, and become more like father everyday!"

Jacob's face turned purple. I stepped back out of reach, afraid he'd strike me like father did when I spoke the truth.

Seeing the fear in my eyes, Jacob restrained himself. Angry as a hissing cat he gritted his teeth and turned his back on me. Once he had composed himself, he turned around responding, "You're sick with jealousy, Rachel! Don't ever speak to me like that again!"

Jacob's words stung me with a fatal poison, and I turned against myself. "Maybe I am sick with jealousy, Jacob! But it's you, and father, and the intolerable situation I have to live in that has made me this way! You're not my partner in the truth! You let Leah bamboozle you. You don't want a Higher Marriage! You're not capable of an equal partnership. You'd rather play Leah and I off against each other for sport. There's nothing for me to live for! Give me a child, or I shall die!"

"I'm not in God's place! Only Yahweh can give you a child! It's He who has refused you motherhood . . . not I!" replied Jacob in fury.

Jacob's words tapped into the enormity of my despair. "Everyone's behind Leah! No one stands with me! There's no justice anywhere! Even Yahweh rewards Leah with fertility! If your God favors such willful deception, I want to die! What hope is there of fairness in the world?"

My anger turned to despair and I threw myself down upon the mat sobbing violently. I don't know how long my tempest lasted, but my chest was aching when I looked up. Jacob was in the corner staring at me like a frightened child. The fear in his eyes ignited my desperation further.

When I couldn't bear the silence any longer, I said, "My love for you has all but destroyed me, Jacob! There's no place for me in your world! I've lost the Goddess . . . I've lost you. . . . And I've lost myself. I'm nothing now that I'm not a Naditu Priestess."

"That's enough! Be still!" cried Jacob with fear in his eyes.

Even this attempt to calm me sounded like a command. Jacob didn't want to hear the truth. I could see it in his face. He wanted to close his eyes and hope this would all blow over. I collapsed back on the bed feeling utterly defeated and alone. There was nowhere for me to turn. Everyone had betrayed me . . . Jacob . . . father . . . my sister. Even Yahweh had abandoned me. I had destroyed my chance at the Eye Temple. The Sisterhood was gone. I was in disfavor with Jacob's God. I was finished! What could I do?

Memories of Sisterhood in the woman's circle came to mind bringing with it a faint glimmer of hope. Attempting to save face and find some place for myself, I cried out in desperation, "Very well, Jacob! Since Yahweh won't bless me with a child, and you care more about having great numbers of children than having a Naditu Priestess for a wife, I'll find some measure of respect. I'll make a place for myself. And I'll prove to you that I'm not sick with jealousy. Take Bilhah, my maid servant! Sleep with her! She'll give birth on my knees. I can have a son through her. And you . . . you can have all the sons you crave."

16

BIRTH ON RACHEL'S KNEES

I WAS UP IN THE HIGH PASTURES WITH THE FLOCKS AT MY MOON lodge. The murmur of the Balikh was a soothing tonic for my anguished soul. I rejoiced to hear the oracle's voice and listen to the secret heart of nature. All day I had been on edge with a curious anticipation. Prophetic dreams and utterances had come to me with my wise blood. My moon change was over now, and I was looking forward to returning home to see if my dream was true.

A figure came running toward me on the far horizon. My heart started pounding. It could be Esther. She said she wanted to speak to me about her star chart when the moon grew bright. Or was it Bilhah? Was my dream a portent? Anticipation mounting, I took off at a fast trot.

It was Bilhah!! Her face aglow, she cried out breathlessly. "I couldn't wait to see you! I have important news, Mistress Rachel! Your prayers have been answered. Laban announced tonight is the crescent moon. This makes two moons since I've had my moon change. I didn't mention anything to you last month, because I wanted to be absolutely sure. But now I'm certain that I'm pregnant! Isn't it wonderful?"

Bilhah's words were like the sound of heaven sent rain after years of drought. "Yes, it is wonderful! And I had the most incredible dream last night. We were laughing together in it. We laughed so hard we had to embrace to steady ourselves. Out from that embrace between my knees came a fine strong infant boy. It will be a boy, Bilhah. He will be strong and healthy. We'll call him Dan, because God has judged me and at long last given me a son."

"Whatever you say, Mistress Rachel! I'm so happy . . . and so grateful! You're happy too! I can see it in your face. You haven't been so light hearted since we were young, and your mother was alive."

My heart was pounding. "Yes! It's just like in my dream." I said exuberantly. "After the birth you'll be free according to Sumerian law, Bilhah. You won't be a slave anymore. Though you'll still be my maidservant."

The look on Bilhah's face was dazzling. "I'll be free but I'll still get to be with you! That is wonderful! My son, too?" she responded in a daze.

"Of course!" I said answering joyfully.

"It's everything I could hope for!" said Bilhah enthusiastically. Then suddenly the smile froze on her face, and a troubled frown replaced it.

"Is anything wrong, Bilhah?" I asked expectantly.

"I just got frightened for a moment." Bilhah responded in dismay. "I'm afraid of what Mistress Leah might do when she finds out. I know she'll be furious. She's been watching me like a hawk ever since the night you took me in to Jacob. I'm afraid to even glance at her now. Whenever I do she looks at me with the kiss of death."

I was standing so close to Bilhah, her fear was contagious and a shiver ran down my back. Conjuring up my dream, I responded in a strong voice to steady us both. "Don't think about Leah, Bilhah! This is a joyous occasion. We mustn't let her ruin it for us! Remember my dream! There's nothing to fear so long as we stay close together."

Bilhah tumbled into my arms with relief like an elated child. Joining hands we danced around in a circle with delight. When we were out of breath we collapsed merrily on the ground. It felt good lying there looking up at the sky until the wind began to blow. I was exhilarated and didn't feel the slightest chill. But thinking of Bilhah my protective instincts were aroused. She and her young were in my charge. So I said, "You've had a long walk. Rest here until I get the flocks. I'll be back shortly. We'll go home together. I can't wait to share our news."

Bilhah was relieved, as she said, "Thank you, mistress Rachel! I feel better knowing you'll return with me. Everything will be fine so long as I'm with you." Tears welling in her eyes, she added. "I'm so grateful. I owe our son, and now soon my freedom to you."

The sun had set by the time we reached home. The moon sat like a bowl of light upon the horizon waiting to be filled. Above the moon was the Eye star. I turned toward Bilhah as we approached the gate. "The moon is rising with Kak.Si.Di., Bilhah! That's a powerful omen! The fertile moon is joining forces with the Eye Star. There's nothing to fear. Take the sheep to the east meadow for the night. Make sure there are several donkeys, and Zack to protect them. Then fetch Jubal and don't worry about a thing! I'll make the announcement tonight at dinner when you come to take the supper plates away."

Bilhah beamed up at me as trusting as a child, saying, "Thank you, Mistress Rachel! I'll see you at dinner."

Father, Jacob and Leah were all sitting by the fire surrounded by the boys when I opened the door. Since my winter in the mountains Jacob was never comfortable when I was away for any length of time. He rose as soon as he saw me, almost stumbling over Levi in his eagerness to greet me. "There you are, Rachel! The winds are picking up. I was hoping you'd return tonight. Take off your cloak! You must be tired and hungry. Come! Have a seat beside me at the fire! We're just waiting on dinner."

Jacob and I had been being cautious with each other since our quarrel the night of Judah's naming ceremony. I was pleased by the warmth of his welcome. Yet I wasn't quick to respond to his greeting, and I could see this troubled him. I would have been only too glad to sit in my usual seat beside him at the fire. But behind Jacob's back, Leah had beckoned Simeon to take my seat as soon as I entered.

Jacob stiffened at my reluctance, and all warmth left his face. I was so weary of Leah's ploys. I was cold and tired, and not up to a fight tonight. How should I handle this situation? I stood there frozen with the usual weight descending on my heart. Finally, after smiling at Jacob lamely, I nodded in the direction of the fire. Annoyed and somewhat mystified, Jacob turned around. Catching on to the young rascal, he spoke good naturedly. "What are you doing there, you little scamp? Your Aunt Rachel's tired. She's just returned from the high pastures with the sheep. Be a good boy! Get out of her seat this instant!"

Simeon looked at his mother before responding. Leah turned nonchalantly from his gaze. Taking his cue from her, Simeon continued sitting there with a sheepish look on his face.

Jacob raised his voice impatiently. "How dare you make me have to ask you again! Get up this instant!"

We waited in silence, all eyes except for Leah's fixed upon the willful boy. Simeon had always been a stubborn, demanding child. But this was the first time I'd seen him so defiant of his father. His mother behind him, this must have seemed the perfect opportunity for him to pit his will against Jacob and test the limits.

The silence in the room was deafening. No one dared to move. Even after Jacob's admonition, Simeon still wouldn't budge. His jaw set in fixed determination, he remained seated obviously enjoying being the center of attention.

I was amazed at his audacity. If he was like this now, what would he be like when he grew up? I shifted my weight back and forth between my feet nervously. All the color had drained from Jacob's face when he shouted, "Wipe that foolish grin off your face, Simeon! Get up! Go to bed! There'll be no dinner for you tonight!"

I was pleased by the strength of Jacob's admonition.

Sulky agitation mixed with fear crossed Simeon's face. Without a word he turned and looked at his mother. Leah intervened immediately on his behalf. "Oh, Jacob! Don't be so hard on the boy! He's just a child. He needs to eat to keep his strength up. Come here, Simeon! You can sit on my lap!"

Simeon looked at Jacob smugly, taking his time to rise. Swaggering over to his mother, he seated himself triumphantly in his throne of glory on her lap. Once positioned he made a grimace at Jacob then hid his face in his mother's bosom.

Leah looked at Jacob with a coy smile on her face. "It's been a long day. We're all hungry and a bit on edge. Don't upset the children! Let's have a pleasant dinner. I've prepared your favorite stew. Let's not spoil it."

Before Jacob could respond, Zilpah entered the room surprised at the sight of me. Catching the look on her face, Leah commanded, "Miss Rachel will be joining us for dinner, Zilpah. Set another place at the table!"

Bowing courteously to Leah, she said, "Yes! Of course, Mistress Leah! I was just coming in to say that dinner's ready."

"Very well!" said Leah responding in her most authoritative tone. "We'll be in in just a moment."

Leah was in control of the entire situation, seated like a queen upon her throne with her precious boy a trophy on her lap. Jacob was too embarrassed to even look in my direction. He remained standing in the middle of the room not knowing what to do.

Father rose taking Jacob's arm, and ushered him into the dining room ahead of Leah and the children. As they passed me by I could hear father say. "Simeon's only a child, Jacob! Don't pay him any mind! I heard Zaltan gave you another gold coin yesterday. He believes we have you to thank for the relief from the drought. You'll soon have enough gold to make that prayer bowl you're always talking about. Stay on here with me, son. We're a great team. Together we'll become very rich."

I was aghast, and needed to collect myself before venturing into the treacherous confines of the dining room. How artful Leah was! And how easily Jacob could be unmanned by her manipulations. Where was the undaunted young hero who had rescued me so effortlessly the first day at the well? A stabbing pain pierced my heart, and I felt utterly forlorn. Was there no one to take me from this prison of a home? Jacob's servitude was almost over, but Leah was adamant about not wanting to leave father. Was there any hope for us? Jacob was a pale shadow of his former self. I was not much better. How could this have happened? Where was Jacob's God? Why wasn't He doing something to save him? Jacob was no great religious leader. He was a well fed captive ensnared in father and Leah's deceitful web. Would Jacob be able to regain his former power and take us away from here at the end of these seven years? Would his noble spirit triumph? Or had it been carried away by the deputies of the netherworld like Dumuzi, Inanna's husband?

Tears welled in my eyes. The flame of our love had been as short-lived as springtime. The Brotherhood of the Black Hand was clever and subtle as a serpent. They had spoiled our love, destroying its purity and idealism forever. Jacob and I could have been invincible together. But we were divided, each of us conquered in our own way by father and Leah.

Sighing with resignation I went over to the corner of the room to remove my cloak. This had been some welcome home! My appetite was ruined. How could I get through another dinner with the miserable lot of them?

Zilpah entered the room, interrupting my thoughts. "Dinner is being served. Mistress Leah sent me in to ask you to take your place at table. Everyone's waiting!"

Zilpah's announcement did nothing to soothe me. I grew more agitated hearing her deliver Leah's command. As first wife and mother, Leah ruled my life. Everything was according to her will! Everyone did her bidding!

"Tell them to go ahead without me! I'll be in shortly!" I replied without turning round.

All was silent when I entered the room except for the prattle of the children. Everyone had begun eating. On the surface it seemed like every other night. Father was in his seat of honor at one end of the table. Jacob was at the other. The seat left for me was between Jacob and Simeon. I took a deep breath as I sat down hoping not to meet Jacob's eyes. He kept on eating, and didn't bother to look up. No one seemed to notice I came in.

I was beginning to breathe a sigh of relief, when father said irritably, "Nice of you to finally join us!"

"I've been out for four days. Can't I have a moment to remove my cloak and freshen up? Or must I get your permission to do so?" I replied in annoyance.

"Always a sassy remark from you, Rachel!" exclaimed father. "Perhaps you should have stayed in the high pastures. All you do is create trouble around here."

Simeon began to giggle, and the other children joined in.

I could hardly believe my ears after Simeon's performance. When I looked up Leah was staring at me with a bemused smile on her face. I breathed in deeply attempting to quell my anger. Then I glanced over at Zilpah and beckoned her to bring me the stew. She came toward me with a steaming bowl. Once I finished serving myself. Jacob called her over. She stood before him expectantly, hoping to catch his eye, and smiled seductively as he helped himself to a second steaming portion.

When Jacob finished serving himself, he glanced over at Leah. "My compliments, Leah! It's a wonderful stew tonight!"

I almost choked on my first bite, hearing Jacob's comment. But I caught myself and sat back slowly clearing my throat, while everyone continued eating in silence. I had been gone for five days. But other than father, no one had even bothered acknowledge my presence. I tried to block them all out, fastening on my hunger which had returned with the aroma of the stew.

This was the first home cooked meal I'd had in days. I was determined to enjoy it. Why should I care that no one spoke to me? I didn't want to talk to them anyway. What was there to say? Suddenly I remembered Bilhah. She'd be coming in for the dinner plates. I had promised her I'd make our announcement tonight. Leah would be none too pleased. I smiled to myself. At least there would be one thing she couldn't control. And soon I wouldn't be alone at this table. I'd have Dan beside me. Just the thought of it got me through the meal.

I was fairly glowing by the time Bilhah entered the room. I caught her eye and beckoned her over. With her hand in mine I made an announcement. "I have something important to share with you tonight."

Looking over at Jacob, I continued. "I have wonderful news for you, Jacob."

Jacob looked at me in surprise. I managed a brief smile without looking him in the eye, then continued happily. "Bilhah is with child! She will give birth on my knees. I know from my dreams it will be a boy. Isn't that grand, Jacob?"

The color came flooding back into Jacob's face as he replied, "That is wonderful news! Congratulations! How marvelous! Another son!"

The joy stopped there. Not another sound was uttered in the room. Even the children's prattle ceased. Leah finally broke the stunned silence. Glaring at me across the table, she interjected caustically. "How can you be so sure it will be a boy, Rachel? Only a trained Naditu Priestess with the terafim could be certain of such a thing. You're not a priestess . . . and you don't have the terafim!"

Bilhah's hand tensed in mine as soon as Leah began to speak. Squeezing her hand to lend us both courage, I replied, "I don't need the terafim, Leah! I saw it in a dream up at my moon lodge. My dreams tell me all I need to know."

Leah lashed out. "You and your insubstantial dreams, Rachel! Won't you ever learn?"

Then turning toward Jacob she continued, "I wouldn't count on Rachel's dreams, if I were you Jacob. She's always been a bit daft."

Jacob responded with excitement, clearly strengthened by my news. "Don't be ridiculous, Leah! Dreams are very telling. They can be messages from God. Yahweh often speaks to me through my dreams."

Taking his goblet in hand, he stood up declaring proudly. "Fill your cups! I propose a toast to Rachel!"

Leah's face soured. Immediately, as if on cue, one of her brood started crying. I shut my ears to the red faced screaming brat. I didn't care what Leah thought. Jacob was rising to the occasion. His response made me grin. At least this time Leah would not prevail. Unable to hide my glee, I laughed out loud, a deep belly laugh that was so contagious, first Bilhah, then Jacob chimed in. Together our laughter drowned out the howling child.

Before I could raise my goblet to my lips, father bored into me with one of his fiendish compelling stares. I went feeble, almost dropping my goblet. I felt hot and flushed all over. His stare possessed a curious draining power. It was like a force working against my will . . . bidding me . . . no compelling me to look at him. His piercing snake eyes were rivetted on me. It was a struggle even to breathe. This was the look I had come to dread. I swallowed hard struggling to muster my dwindling reserves. Was it too late? I was beginning to lose contact with what was going on around me. Was father drawing down the power of the dark moon? Or was he using the power of his hideous skull to control me? I called upon the Goddess, visualizing She Who Watches and the Sisterhood in my mind, as I strained to unlock from father's withering stare.

The starry light of She Who Watches came down around me. In the next moment my breathing opened and I was released from the stranglehold of father's grip. I clutched the table reeling from the enormous strain. This was only a small taste of the control father and the Black Hand could wield over their unfortunate victims. Oh the Brotherhood's tactics were clear to me by now. They were masters at stirring up fear in people. They were ingenious at finding ways to get people to fight between themselves, so they stopped paying attention to what was really going on. I wasn't going to be taken in this time. I would keep the mantle of the Goddess down around me.

When I caught my breath I looked for Bilhah. The supper dishes had all been cleared away. She was probably safe in the firehut. I looked over at Jacob seated beside me. Perhaps he too had felt the curious force. To all appearances he had not. His wine goblet was empty, and his face was aglow with my news. He caught my eye smiling proudly.

I sat back tentatively in my chair, not daring to look in father's direction. The crafty old magician hadn't played that loathsome trick on me since Jacob's arrival. Obviously he hadn't liked seeing me take my power, and felt the need to rein me in. In the next moment it was all too clear. Laban was not about to be preempted.

Addressing Jacob, he pronounced wryly. "Dreams can be very telling, Jacob, but don't be rash. You can't rely on Rachel's dreams. Women's dreams can't be trusted, because they don't have the same spiritual power we men have. The crescent moon is an auspicious time for an augury. I'll see to this myself. And of course, if Bilhah is pregnant, I'll preside over the birth. We shouldn't take any chances, should we Jacob?"

Father's offer sent shivers down my spine. I wanted Laban and his evil eye nowhere near the birth. To smooth things over I took Jacob's hand in mine for a show of strength, and replied graciously. "It's kind of you to offer, father. But Bilhah and I have already discussed it. I'll deliver the child in accordance with the instructions from my dream. Don't worry. We'll be fine. Childbirth has been women's domain for countless centuries."

Father raised his voice in a threatening way. "Come now, Rachel! You haven't the slightest experience with childbirth. Don't let your foolish pride risk the life of this child . . . if there even is one."

He continued, glancing over at Jacob. "Rachel may have skill with lambing, but birthing a child is an entirely different matter."

My mind was set. For father, or any man, to deliver the child would be a sacrilege. Father would not have dominion over this birth. Women were the guardians of birth. It should not be controlled by men. Mother would never have allowed it. I closed my eyes in silent prayer and called upon She Who Watches to deflect the self-doubt father was seeking to engender in my mind.

BIRTH ON RACHEL'S KNEES

Father and his Brothers may have presided over Leah's births, but as far as I was concerned that had been just another scheme to break women's solidarity and their power. The miracle of life flowed through women's bodies. I would not be party to such an offense against the wellsprings of life. Bilhah would give birth on my knees. My son's birth would not be controlled by men. It would be a new beginning for me, my offering to Ninhursag. This birth would purge me of my jealousy and grief, and make life bearable again. I had swallowed my pride. This birth was fashioned according to the ancient bonds of Sisterhood. It had the full weight of Sumerian law behind it. Bilhah and I would claim the protection of She Who Watches and take our chances by ourselves.

Looking father in the eye, I said with complete assurance, "This is my child! Bilhah will give birth on my knees according to ancient Sumerian law! I will not have you, or any other man, deliver my son into the world."

Laban looked at Jacob with a snide look on his face. "Rachel's young and headstrong, Jacob. See if you can talk some sense into her! You're not going to risk the life of your child, and allow your wife to make a fool out of herself, are you?"

I clutched Jacob's hand and looked him in the eye, saying in desperation, "You know what this birth means to me, Jacob! Have confidence in me!"

Jacob looked back and forth between father and I.

Finally he said, "The Lord, my God, Yahweh is behind this birth. Rachel and Bilhah have my full protection. They don't need your help, Laban. I only allowed you to officiate at Leah's births, because that was what she wanted. I will not entertain another word about this matter. Is that clear?"

Jacob was standing by me. Could this be a new beginning for us? I smiled at him in appreciation.

Bilhah and I laughed together each day as we watched her belly grow ripe and round like the lush melons the caravan traders brought up from the southern climes. By midspring in the month of Guanna, sacred to the Bull of Heaven, Bilhah was huge with child.

She roused me early one morning in a feverish sweat soon after Jacob had departed. Sticking her head inside the entrance to our tent, she cried, "Forgive me for disturbing you, Mistress Rachel. But I'm so afraid. It happened again. I found another splattered egg outside my tent when I awoke this morning. There's sorcery afoot. This is the second time I've found an egg crushed outside my door."

I was barely awake, and had to collect myself. My heart was wrenching, as I said, "Don't worry, Bilhah! We know who's behind this. Leah's just trying to scare you with those evil spells. Leah doesn't have any real power. The only power she has is what your fear gives her. Come inside while I think this over. We'll find a way through it." I said with determination.

Bilhah was so huge with child, I had to stifle a laugh watching her force her way sideways through the narrow opening to our tent. My laughter was soon dispelled, however, when I saw that she was trembling. Her forehead was drenched in sweat. I spoke to her slowly, as I would to a child. "Don't be afraid, Bilhah! Fear robs you of strength, and splits your heart and mind. It will deliver you into Leah's hands."

Bilhah nodded as I went to get some of my most potent white sage, I kept in a basket in my herb corner. Prayers and the smoke of the aromatic sage would clear away any demon Leah might have conjured up with her spell. The fervor of my prayers, coupled with the pungent smoke, revived Bilhah. I sat down beside her and closed my eyes praying for guidance.

My vision opened. I saw an enormous egg at the center of Mother Earth. It was pulsing spasmodically, pained to see her daughters come to this. I put my hand over Bilhah's belly and invoked the ancient power of Sisterhood. OH GREAT MOTHER NINHURSAG, FILL BILHAH'S WOMB WITH YOUR STARRY LIGHT. FORGIVE LEAH'S CRUEL HEART. SHE'S LOST HER WAY WITHOUT YOU. FATHER'S LOATHSOME TUTELAGE HAS DONE THE REST. PROTECT US FROM FATHER, LEAH, AND THE BLACK HAND. BLESS BILHAH AND LITTLE DAN, AND KEEP THEM SAFE WITHIN YOUR LOVE.

As I finished my prayer, it came to me. "We'll put your tent beside ours for the next few months. That way you'll be safe and close at hand. As Jacob's always the first to rise, he'll come upon any fiendish sorcery that's laid in your path. I'll wager that will put and end to Leah's wicked tricks."

Bilhah smiled, "I'll feel safer close to you."

Pleased by Bilhah's response, I continued, "I'll see to it that you're relieved of your duties at the farm today. That way you can work with me and be out from under Leah's watchful eyes. The shearing and the lambing are almost over. So the work won't be hard. The walking will do you good."

"Thank you, Mistress Rachel!" replied Bilhah gratefully. "I've been longing for the open country. I'll also be pleased to have more time with you these last few weeks."

"It's settled then! I knew we'd find a way through this trickery. Wait and see! Everything will be just fine!" I said smiling with relief.

With Jacob's aversion to sorcery he'd have no trouble seeing my plans were carried out. Sure enough! After hearing of Bilhah's fright Jacob released her from her duties. On the morrow she began accompanying me as I tended the sheep.

Like Leah, Bilhah was a Sugutu woman with broad strong hips. She thrived on the increase in exercise. We began each day with a visit to my altar beside the Balikh. I'd seat her beneath the Ashera tree so she could catch her breath and soak up the Goddess's blessing. After the flocks were watered I'd have her bathe in the potent stream.

Bilhah was a child of Earth with little of the ancient Sumerian blood to attune her to the stars. But her countenance glowed and all her fears were washed away by the time she finished bathing. Then I'd lay her on my altar stone and rub her belly with the protective gum of acacia, and say prayers to keep away the Lamashtu demon that preyed upon pregnant mothers and the newborn. I taught her ancient chants to Ninti, the Great Mother Goddess Ninhursag in her capacity as Womb of Life. We'd sing them together as we walked the foothills with the flocks.

One day close to the full moon, she shrieked with laughter as I applied acacia to her belly. The sound was distinct to my ears. The Goddess Ninti was behind Bilhah's cry pressing to engender new life. In the next moment Bilhah's waters broke, the river of life gushed forth from between her thighs. I climbed atop the altar stone behind her, and held her firmly in my arms. After getting her started in a rhythmic breathing, I spoke to calm her. "It won't be long now. There's nothing to fear. Father and Leah are far away. It's a beautiful day. I have everything we need here. All we have to do is keep on laughing."

Bilhah's answer was a breathless pant. "I felt a few sharp pains this morning just before rising, but these are more acute. They're coming faster too."

"That's a good sign, Bilhah! Just relax in my arms, and trust me! We're on the altar of the Goddess. This is the miracle of life we women are privileged to bear. And just think, it's Dan we're welcoming into life today. Remember my dream! You have only to lie in my arms and feel the joy of this new life and let him come. I'll start breathing with you. Then I'll chant to evoke the Goddess."

I sang to the rhythm of Bilhah's breath. GREAT GODDESS NINTI, LADY OF LIFE, MIDWIFE OF THE GODS, TAKE BILHAH AND DAN TO YOUR HEART. HOLD THEM FIRMLY IN YOUR GRACE.

GREAT LADY NINTI, SHE WHO OPENS THE WOMB, START YOUR BIRTH-GIVING RHYTHMS FLOWING. KEEP BILHAH AND DAN IN YOUR PROTECTION.

GREAT LADY NINTI, MOTHER OF ALL FORM-GIVING, WORKING FROM YOUR DARK PLACE INSIDE THE WOMB. HOLD BILHAH AND DAN IN YOUR EMBRACE.

GREAT MOTHER NINHURSAG, PROTECTOR OF MOTHERS, OPEN BILHAH'S WOMB WHEN THE TIME IS RIPE. KEEP SHE AND DAN SAFE IN YOUR CIRCLE OF LIFE.

Bilhah's breathing intensified along with my prayer, until the urgency of her cries and the speed of her contractions announced it was time for her to start pushing. I positioned myself in front of her on the altar and spread her legs wide. Her face was beaded with sweat, but soft and open. The generosity of the Mother Goddess was shining through her. Never had she looked more beautiful to me.

She put her arms around my neck to steady herself as her breathing deepened. When she started gasping with pain, everything converged around us. The sun peeked through the branches of the Ashera tree beaming directly down on us. Three of the older ewes crowded round the altar bleating loudly. Two grey morning doves appeared out of nowhere singing in the tree beside us.

I positioned Bilhah so the sun wasn't in her eyes, and helped her into the squatting position. She started pushing. Not long after the baby's head began to crown. The portal of life was opening. I put my arms around her shoulders and looked her in the eyes to steady her. "Push, Bilhah, push! Dan's coming! He's almost here! I can see his head! It's crowning!"

Bilhah began laughing through the tears that mingled with the sweat pouring down her cheeks. After a few more moments Dan's entire head was out. Bilhah was faint and had stopped pushing, delirious from the wrenching pain. I shook her firmly, and cried to cheer her on. "Dan's head is out! You push and I'll pull and you can hold him in your arms. Now push!"

Bilhah opened her bloodshot eyes. After a few more moments of laughing and crying together there was a wet squealing infant boy between us. Bilhah collapsed on me weak from exertion. We clung together laughing triumphantly with Dan between us, all of us dripping the blood, sweat, and tears, that are the teeming torrent of the river of life. It felt wonderful and warm holding the healthy infant boy. He looked exactly as he had in my dream. His skin was soft like the underbelly of a newborn lamb. I thrilled to touch it.

I helped Bilhah down and placed the baby on her full warm breast. He immediately groped for the breast and started suckling. Life was taking root. Contentment took me over to see Dan suck Bilhah's great mountain of a breast. I thought of Ninhursag, Lady of the Foothills, and couldn't help but laugh. Bilhah's breast was Dan's first experience of life. Her body was his landscape, his ground of being, the fountain of his life. The circle of life was complete and drawn. All I had to do was to cut the purple cord of life that still pulsed between them.

After tying off the life cord, the inner river of life, I examined the afterbirth. It was all in tact. I buried it in the soil beneath the Ashera as a thanks offering to the Goddess for Bilhah's successful birthing. Then entranced, I watched the gift of life flowing between the happy mother and child. The contentment of their love seemed to alter time making it flow more slowly. A curious glow was all about them. It emanated out toward me making me feel a part of their experience.

I was drawn back to the altar into their circle of love like a moth to a flame. I put my cheek down on Dan's back nestling close to him as he sucked his mother's breast. The world slowed down to the peaceful rhythm of Bilhah's breathing, except for the racing drum beat of Dan's young heart. I could have stayed like that for hours, but finally nature called, and Bilhah had to get up to relieve herself.

I took this chance to take the red squealing baby down to the stream and wash him, calling down the blessing of the God and Goddess as I named him. Having been so many months within the Great Mother's river inside of Bilhah, Dan felt right at home in the invigorating water. I was still saying prayers over him, the blood of his new life mingling in tiny eddies at the stream's edge, when Bilhah called. "Please help me down to the stream, Mistress Rachel. I could use a bath as well."

I returned quickly to her side, little Dan still cradled in my arms. "I'm glad you're feeling strong enough for a bath, Bilhah. It's just the thing for you. Here! Take my arm! I'll help you down."

Bilhah's limbs were still trembling from the exertion of the birth as I helped her down the slippery bank. But she was young and strong and her spirits high. I held onto her arm as she stepped into the water, cradling Dan with my free arm. Supporting the two of them, I felt most poignantly how I had been their bridge to life. There was sunshine in my heart. This was my reward for conquering my jealousy. I was alone no longer. We were all together in the river of life.

Dan's first smile put all thoughts of death behind me. My prayers had been answered. My dream had come true. I felt reborn arriving at this, at least partial, solution to my barrenness. I had been so ashamed after my devastating quarrel with Jacob. Now at least he could see I wasn't jealous. No longer was I marked with Yahweh's disfavor in my husband's eyes. Jacob had stood by me concerning the birth. Even father had more respect for me after the successful delivery.

Dan was different from Leah's boys. He was a contented happy child who rarely ever cried. His unsullied innocence awakened all my hope. His warmth and easy going temperament filled the emptiness and despair that had been my life. From hereon I would no longer be disgraced and set apart from other women. Dan was by my side at every family occasion. He was always underfoot when I least expected, smiling and reaching out to me.

I was so well rewarded for giving Bilhah to Jacob, I gave her to Jacob a second time. Dan had just begun walking when Bilhah was pregnant again. I delighted in the news. Though Leah was devastated, as she'd stopped conceiving after Judah. My sister was not used to being deprived of what she wanted. Her rancor over Bilhah's second pregnancy ran even deeper than the first. She was green with envy seeing Bilhah and I so happy together caring for our little one. She shunned little Dan, and did everything she could as first wife to make our lives more difficult.

Leah couldn't hurt me anymore. My relationship with Bilhah, and our mutual devotion to our son, was a blessing from the Goddess that shielded me from Leah's wrath. Finally, completely beside herself and driven by envious competition, Leah relented and gave Zilpah to Jacob to have another son.

Bilhah's second pregnancy went as smoothly as the first, despite all of Leah's tirades. My womb was closed, but Bilhah gave birth upon my knees to a second healthy boy. Jacob was overjoyed his progeny was on the increase. He needed many sons to take over and govern the land that Yahweh promised him. If Jacob was happy, why should I torment myself? Hadn't I given my husband two fine healthy sons? I had a place now within the patriarchal order of the Father God.

Yet the Goddess was a burning torch within my soul, and I was tormented by relentless questions. I had only to look around to see how successful the Black Hand had been in eradicating all traces of Ninhursag and the Sisterhood. The local religion belonged to Nanna/Sin and his daughter Inanna now.

I prayed the reign of Yahweh would supplant the ancient Dragon of Heaven and his lascivious daughter. I was thankful Yahweh's righteousness was there to counteract the bloodthirsty duo. Yet my heart was torn. The Great Mother Ninhursag protected the Earth. The land would be ravaged, the hearts of humankind untutored, if the Goddess was not revered.

Sin had usurped the Goddess's moon wisdom. The Black Hand was using it to suppress women and steal their power. The Tree of Life was being turned upside down. My womb was clenched and sick with grief. Women were becoming ashamed of their wise blood, and no longer gave it in offering to the earth. While Inanna and Sin demanded greater and greater numbers of bloody sacrifices to fulfill their vile cravings.

Yahweh was our only hope. Yet Yahweh was a jealous God who demanded Jacob's entire allegiance. Wasn't it He, as well as father, who encouraged Jacob to play one wife against the other? For as Yahweh opened one womb, he closed another, fostering women's jealous competition in the race to increase his Chosen People. I must admit the idea of a Chosen People made me uncomfortable as well, even if they were to be my sons. The Goddess loved all Earth's children, which had united us. Wouldn't Yahweh's idea of a chosen race generate distrust and jealousy that would divide the people of Earth, just as my sister and I were now divided?

Of course, who was I to question? The perspective of the Gods was much wiser than my own. Nonetheless, the more I learned, the more difficulty I had with the patriarchal philosophy. Yahweh was a great Warrior God, the sole Master of the Universe. He had given man dominion over the Earth and all its creatures. Mankind was fashioned in His image and His likeness. Like Yahweh man was created to conquer and to rule in solitary splendor. I didn't understand where we women were to fit into his scheme.

The patriarchal philosophy was so different from the ancient Mother Goddess tenets which understood all of Earth's creatures to be one big family, with humanity serving as the wise stewards of the planet and its resources. The matriarchal perspective fostered the harmonious cooperation and interdependence of all people and creatures on Earth. With such fundamental differences between the two philosophies, how could Yahweh understand the yearning and questions in a woman's heart?

When I broached these matters with Jacob, he told me not to bother my pretty little head with such concerns. He said I thought too much. It was for men to understand the will of God. I should be grateful and content that Yahweh heard my prayers. I tried to quell the tempest in my soul and buckle under. I knew what was required of me. Yahweh made it quite clear what He wanted from His daughters. Hadn't He rewarded me for surrendering my pride, just as He'd rewarded Leah from the first for surrendering her pride on her deceitful wedding night?

So I named my second son, Naphtali, which means wrestler, because I had fought Yahweh's fight with my sister and I had won.

PART FIVE

The Marriage of Heaven and Earth

17

THE MAGICAL MANDRAKE

JACOB'S YEARS OF SERVITUDE WERE LONG OVER NOW, YET STILL WE LAN-
guished in father's choking grip. The promise of wealth was father's new
bait to hold Jacob and his blessing fast. Leah was also loathe to go, balking like a stubborn mule at the prospect of leaving father. Thus the years
flew by with Jacob's reasons for staying becoming an ever more ensnaring web.

The Great Drought had begun in earnest. The underground water-
courses dried up when the Eye Temple closed and the Goddess removed
her blessing from the land. The lush Khabur valley, which once had
housed the Temple of She Who Watches, was now as shrivelled as a
prune. Its teeming wildlife were all forced to migrate elsewhere. Even the
levels of the vast Euphrates were going down.

Only our region was strangely blessed. Year after year enormous
storm clouds gathered in the mountains raining their beneficence down
upon our emerald valley. The people were in a state of wonder. The
renowned Skull Oracle at the Ehulhul temple in Haran had spoken after

years of silence, proclaiming Jacob responsible for the blessing of the rain. Once again the rumors started, first in quiet murmurs then with loud acclaim. The great awakening in the townsfolk declared Jacob Shepherd of the People as in days of old. No longer trapped in servitude, my husband was hailed as a prince throughout the land. He was in his full glory working solely with father amassing all the riches that were his due. The Brotherhood still kept a watchful eye on Jacob. They never ceased trying to lure him into their secret fraternal order. But nothing could tempt Jacob away from his steadfast love for Yahweh.

Harvest was abundant for us again that year despite the drought. Our flocks were on the increase. All our storehouses were full. The weather was unseasonably warm and mild. My heart was light, as I was busy with my sons. But as much as I loved the boys and my hallowed homeland, I knew no peace. My dreams were full of warnings. Always the same relentless message, announcing it was time to go. I knew it was time to leave. The Black Hand had dominion over everything, and it was imperative we get out from under father's relentless control. I was waiting for the right moment to speak to Jacob of what was in my heart.

One Sabbath evening was particularly graced. The sowing was in. Jacob's spirits were high. Our tent was warm and softly lit with oil lamps. I had spent the afternoon in prayer and meditation, crushing rose petals for the oil. The fragrance of love was in the air. The star of the Goddess was shining in my heart. I lay quietly on our mat waiting for Jacob to finish his prayers.

He approached me, the last lines of his prayer still a refrain upon his lips.

"COME MY BRIDE, MY PRECIOUS BRIDE, MOST SPARKLING GEM IN THE CROWN OF THY HUSBAND. MAY OUR HEARTS BEAT AS ONE AS WE LIFT THEM UP TO THE ALMIGHTY FATHER.

COME MY BRIDE, MY PRECIOUS BRIDE, ABIDE WITH ME IN PEACE AND LOVE. REJOICE AS I TAKE YOU IN MY ARMS AND OFFER OUR LOVE TO YAHWEH, KING OF KINGS, THE RULER OF THE UNIVERSE.

COME MY BRIDE, MY PRECIOUS BRIDE, FLY WITH ME ON THIS HOLY NIGHT. RECEIVE THE BLESSING OF THE LORD, MY GOD, THE ONE TRUE GOD ON SABBATH.

Gazing down, Jacob smiled saying, "Sometimes when I look at you I still can't believe my good fortune. Forgive me, if I've failed you, darling. You are my one true bride. The only woman who can quench the thirst in my heart and soul."

Jacob was aglow with the fire of his God, as I took his hand and pulled him down upon me. Lifting up my heart to the Goddess I whispered. "MAY OUR LOVE BE A PRAYER THAT OPENS THE HEART AND RIGHTS THE BALANCE HERE ON EARTH."

Our love twice blessed, Jacob's lips were on mine. His hands in eager search of the comfort my body could provide. What was this magic? Was it the wings of angels fluttering in my heart, or the awakening of promises made long ago? Our spirits soared as in the days of our youth, merging together out of time. Had the God and Goddess heard our prayers? It was years since I had felt transported by our love.

The sound of the eternal reaches was in my ears as Jacob removed my clothing piece by piece gazing upon me in delight. There was no high or low, no up or down. My spirit and my body were both exultant as Jacob took me in his arms. Our souls united fully with our bodies as he thrust the power of his manhood in me. Jacob's passion was a bell that tolled, commanding all that had gotten buried between us to rise. Had all the years of pain been necessary to arrive at this new depth of love? The hallowed communion of man and woman lit my soul with a compelling fire. My love was reawakened, rekindled from the ashes of a pledge deeper than the suffering which had been my life.

Such wondrous power has love to cleanse the wounds of pain, and lift the human heart above its grief. Our breath was synchronized in the streamings of pleasure that swept over us in joyous profusion. This great explosion of love lifted me above my sorrow. The Goddess was right, the power of transformation is in the human heart. Love is the great healer, the unifying force behind creation. The end to separation came as we became one, enfolded in the waves of ecstatic orgasm. Riding its swell I prayed for Yahweh to know the goodness of our love, and tasting the harvest in our hearts relent in his estrangement from the Goddess.

We collapsed together, one heart, one mind, breathless and smiling, down upon our pillow. The tidal surge of love was spent, but its afterglow remained a golden blanket of warmth to nurture the healing of our lives. My heart and soul were renewed as we lay back in joyous peace listening to the secrets of the night. The wind was a gentle whisper. The crickets a jubilant chorus bidding their farewell to the day. All of nature seemed to be rejoicing in our love's renewal.

The trill of a dove sounded forth my joy. I listened to its music for some time before inquiring, "Isn't it late to hear the song of a dove?"

Stars were in Jacob's eyes, as he said, "Tonight I've learned it's never too late to open the heart and let it sing. What's so special about this evening, Rachel? Where have I been all these years? How has this magic eluded us? It was there in our youth, but somehow it slipped away. It hasn't felt like this between us since before our marriage."

The Goddess's grace was still between us. Jacob had never asked questions like this before. Had our lovemaking melted the armor in his heart? This was the moment I had been praying for. But I had to be careful. I didn't want to spoil the new openness between us. Jacob always got so impatient with me, when I spoke of leaving.

I looked into his eyes. They were soft and unguarded like a child's. At least tonight he didn't have to have all the answers. I put the rancor of my grievances behind me, and responded tactfully. "Many factors have contributed to our estrangement. What's important is that we've found each other again. We're older and wiser now . . . and you're free. We don't have to let anything come between us anymore."

Gratitude shone in Jacob's eyes. "Your words are a soothing balm for my soul, Rachel. Yes! Thank God I am free! I'm no longer a captive of your father! But there are still so many things that weigh me down."

"Unburden your heart with me Jacob." I responded gently. "I want to be your friend as well as your wife."

Jacob sighed deeply. "I could use a friend. There are so many I have to provide for. Leah asks so much of me. Whatever I give her, it's never enough. There's always something more she wants. There's no end to her list of wants and needs."

Chuckling softly he shook his head. "You're different! You've always been so different, Rachel! All you've ever wanted is for me to be my highest self." He continued smiling wryly, "But that's not easy either! God knows it's a full time job! I can never hide a thing from you! You read me as easily as you do the tea leaves in your mother's divination cup. And when Laban had his hooks in me . . . it took all I had to hold my own. Then, of course, there's always been the Brotherhood. Just keeping out of that confounded Ehuhul Temple for the fourteen years of my service was a major feat. Thank God, it's not a problem any longer. Though that detestable Brotherhood still clamors after me. They're always looking for some new ruse to lure me in."

I responded sympathetically. "I know how hard its been for you, Jacob. You're the only man I know with the integrity not to be drawn into their ranks. We need to put them behind us, and make a new start in your homeland. You have Yahweh's blessing. Wherever we go you'll prosper. Wherever you go you'll be a success."

"It's not that easy! The Black Hand is everywhere." said Jacob sighing. "They have control of all the land between the two great rivers, the Tigris and Euphrates. There's no escaping them! I want to leave, but Leah refuses to go. She insists on staying with your father. She's threatened to keep our sons here, as well. I can't go without my sons, Rachel. Then again, I've made a place for myself here. The townspeople depend on me. I'm all they have against the drought. And I'm the only one who dares to stand up to the Black Hand. What would happen to them if I leave?"

I took a deep breath then began, "You take too much on yourself, Jacob. You can't be responsible for everyone and everything. Your presence here is a blessing, but the drought began in earnest when the Eye Temple closed down. Everything's gotten out of balance because the Goddess is no longer revered. The Earth is neglected because the ancient rites are not performed. How can there be balance when the Goddess isn't worshipped?"

Jacob had begun frowning at the mention of the Goddess. "That's just a coincidence! I don't want to hear another word about the Goddess, Rachel!"

I continued on, thinking of my sons. "You're strong Jacob, but you can't fight the Black Hand alone. Especially not while we're living with father. They're always around. I don't understand how you tolerate that dreadful Nimah tutoring your boys? Aren't you afraid he'll corrupt them with the Brotherhood's teachings? We must leave! I can't bear the thought of Dan and Naphtali being exposed to such a man as Nimah."

"I'm not alone. I have my sons." said Jacob interrupting. "And Nimah doesn't teach the boys religion! I'm the only one who teaches my sons about God. But I can't be with them all the time! I have other duties. And there's no one else to teach them!"

"That's just the point, Jacob! There is no one else! Haran is the stronghold of the Black Hand. The situation is worsening all the time, and father's a master of persuasion. I'm afraid we'll be stuck here. You mustn't let anyone deter you from returning to your homeland. Ask the boys if they'd stay here with Leah, or go with you to the Promised Land."

"Yahweh will let me know when it's time to go!" declared Jacob with annoyance.

Then with a crestfallen look he lay back upon the pillow folding his hands under his head. "I want to go home, but I have to consolidate things here first. Would you have me return home a pauper? I want to return in a position of strength, not of weakness. I've worked hard for your father. I'm just starting to reap the benefits. In a few more years I can return home a wealthy man."

I lay back on my pillow. Our love making had softened Jacob's heart. I hoped I hadn't pushed him too hard. When I could speak again from my heart, I said, "Forgive me, Jacob! I didn't mean to offend you. It's just that the Brotherhood scare me! They're such masters of deceit and discord. All they sow is distrust and jealousy. They're experts at fragmenting people. It's they who have come between us."

Jacob took me in his arms. "Don't worry your pretty head about them, my darling! Yahweh will protect us. Now close your eyes. It must be late. And we both have to work in the morning."

It was time to separate the ewes from the rams. They'd mated early last year. The lambing had come during the winter season, and we'd lost several of our older ewes as a result. I was taking the ewes down to a meadow that hadn't been grazed since early springtime. Then it had been carpeted with anemones and wild flowers. A smile crossed my lips to think of the multitude of flowers.

It was harvest now. I gave thanks for the different faces of nature's bounty, as I gazed about me at the high meadow. There was enough grass here to keep the flock happy for some time. A gentle breeze rippled through the grass which was shining like gold in the afternoon light. Stately moriah plants dotted the landscape. They swayed in the breeze like elegant candelabra bowing to the sun. My heart opened at the splendor of the meadow. Filled with reverence I sat down on a large sunbaked boulder at the meadow's edge. The heat of the rock penetrated me, helping to relieve the cramping from my moon change.

Gazing at the harvested wheat field I was stirred into a recollection of the rites when I was young. My reverie was like an ancient echo, it seemed so long ago. I nestled back on my sun warmed throne to remember. Those were the days before my first moonchange, when women's wise blood was still a profound mystery. Nonetheless, the scene in all its vividness came back to me again. Pungent clouds of incense mingled with the smoke of the first fruit offered here upon this boulder. Giant plumes of smoke rose proudly to the sky underscoring the fervor of the women's chants. I could still see the women lift their skirts and squat down giving their wise blood to the harvested fields, as proud offering to Nisaba, the Mother of the Grain.

Too soon my vision was over and there was only emptiness in its wake. I took off my sandals and ventured over to the harvested field. The rich brown soil was warm beneath my feet, sending ripples of pleasure streaming up my legs. I raised my voice in thanksgiving for the harvest. The ancient chant moved my spirit and before I knew it, I was squatting down offering my wise blood to the depleted earth.

Drawing the cross of the virgin on the field in my moon blood, I prayed, GREAT MOTHER NINHURSAG, AUGUST LADY OF THE FOOTHILLS, FECUND MOTHER OF THE EARTH, RECEIVE MY MOON BLOOD AS IN THE DAYS OF OLD. ACCEPT IT IN THANKSGIVING FOR YOUR CEASELESS TOIL THAT WILL NOURISH US THROUGH THE WINTER MONTHS AHEAD. MAY THIS BLOOD OF LIFE REPLENISH THE FIELDS AND BRING THEM TO INCREASED LIFE NEXT SPRING.

My prayer finished, I returned to my rock perch sitting in deep attunement with the Earth. When I looked up the sun was beginning to set and someone was calling out to me. It was young Reuben, a vivacious gangly twelve year old, waving to me from across the field on his way home from harvesting. Impetuous, proud, and temperamental, like all of Leah's boys, Reuben was the one who most clearly resembled Jacob. Of course, I attributed this to the unusual circumstances of his conception. Reuben had been conceived on the eclipse wedding night, when his

mother had dared to wear my dress, my veil, and precious oils consecrated to Ninhursag. Reuben had a connection to the Goddess. I could
see it plainly with my inner sight. It was in the timbre of his voice, the
glimmer in his eye and the way his feet rested firmly yet gently upon the
earth.

Reuben had always been drawn to me. His unwitting connection to
the Goddess bound us with a rapport that only increased with age, much
to Leah's chagrin. He often joined us when I took walks with Dan and
Naphtali teaching them about the joys and mysteries of nature. An inquisitive, passionate boy, whose senses were attuned to subtleties,
Reuben was curious about all the wonders around him. I took him under
my wing and taught him to take pleasure in the things his mother ignored. His appreciation of nature finally won me over, so that in the end
he was the only one of Leah's boys I was really fond of.

Delight lit up Reuben's face at the prospect of finding me alone. Immediately changing his path, he came running full speed in my direction.
His ebullient presence punctured the last vestiges of trance lingering
about me.

I was in my moonchange. It was taboo for Reuben to approach me. I
tried signalling him to go home, but the impetuous youth was blind to
my gestures. His exuberance rendering him incapable of understanding
my directives.

As he came bounding toward me my attention was drawn back to
the field I had seeded earlier with my moon blood. The entire area was
glowing with a rosy light. My heart was thundering at the mystery before me, and I forgot about the heedless boy. One particular spot, where
rays of light were rising our of the ground, riveted my attention.

I caught Reuben's eye as he approached. Using the strength of my
will I directed him over to the enigmatic spot. I was in the glory of my
moonchange, my senses aglow with the Goddess's power. Magic was in
the air. I peered into the dark rich soil connecting myself with the primal
power at the center of the Earth. Then I sent it on to the curious boy. It
worked like a charm. Reuben bent to my will as easily as the moriah
plants swaying in the breeze.

The young lad's face took on a fierce determination. Pulling with all
his might, after a few moments he wrestled a treasure from Mother

Earth. Even from this distance I could see the wondrous light emanating from the prize in Reuben's hand.

Jubilant from the reward of his efforts, Reuben came bounding toward me. A few feet away he exclaimed breathlessly, "Look at this root, Auntie! I've never seen anything like it. Do you know what it is?"

"Bring it here! Let me have a look." I replied, my body quivering with excitement.

Drunk with power from the potent root, Reuben was transformed by the time he stood before me. Dangling the enormous root between his legs, he strutted back and forth parading like a cock.

It was taboo that we were even speaking. Yet all I could do was laugh, as he cried out, "Look at me, Auntie! I'm full of luck today! See what I've found! It was glowing in the earth like a flame. What is it?"

Shrugging off his boyish cockiness, I examined the root he dangled teasingly before me. Light was beginning to fade from the leafy plant, but the forked fleshy root still pulsed as if it was alive. Never had I seen such an enormous root! It was black on the outside, soft and white on the inside, and looked like a man's body. It had two legs with another subsidiary root between them which resembled the male member. Incredible power was emanating from the root. No wonder Reuben had become so cocky.

I'd heard incredible stories in my childhood in the women's circle of the mandrake, the magical root in the shape of a man.

"It must be a mandrake, Reuben! The stem is hairy and the flowers are all gone. But look at those golden apples. They're the much touted love apples of the mandrake, prized for their fertilizing powers."

Reuben was bursting with curiosity and impatience. "Is it special, Auntie?"

"Of course, it's special, dear! Doesn't it look like a magic little man? Let me hold it!"

"Alright!" said Reuben petulantly. "But I want it back!"

My womb leapt with joy, as Reuben placed the mandrake in my hand. I was transfixed for a moment. Then said, "You have found a treasure, Reuben! Mandrakes are the dark phallic root powers of Mother Earth. Did you see the light it was giving off, and the way it continued pulsing after you picked it? My mother once told me that spirits from the stars are attracted to these plants. An unusual foam is said to adhere to the plant giving it increased life. That must have been the ruby light we saw."

When I looked up Reuben's face had paled. All his cockiness was gone. He stepped back awkwardly, saying in a faltering voice, "If it's connected to the Earth Mother, I don't think father would approve of my having it. Here! You take it. Just don't tell father I gave it to you."

"Thank you, Reuben!" I said elated.

The mandrake had appeared at a most auspicious time. In less than two weeks it would be the full moon of harvest. Did the Goddess have something planned?

My joy was suddenly interrupted by a shrill female voice calling me from behind me. "What do you have there, Rachel? And what are you doing with my son?"

As Leah's smothering weight descended upon us, Reuben giggled nervously. Then stepped back away from the two of us sheepishly.

"What did Reuben give you?" Leah demanded, grabbing the precious root from my hand.

"How many times must I tell you to stay away from my son?" she screamed, glaring at me.

"Give that back to me, Leah! It's none of your concern!" I cried out indignantly.

"You're out alone with my son during your moonchange, but it's none of my concern!" said Leah shouting.

Looking over at Reuben, she continued screaming as she shook the mandrake in his face. "This is no place for you! I told you I don't want you out cavorting with your Aunt Rachel! She's only going to get you in trouble. Look at this! Now she's teaching you earth magic. Run along! Don't let me catch you with her again!"

When Reuben was out of earshot, Leah turned on me with fury. "You have your own sons! Why can't you leave mine alone?"

"I don't go after Reuben!" I replied testily. "He follows me around."

Taken aback by the truth of my words, she replied sulkily, "Isn't it enough you've taken my husband? Must you also take my son's mandrakes?"

Leah's words were like an evil wind blowing through me, and I shivered. My entire flock had become agitated when she raised her voice. A few of the older ewes came crowding around me protectively. I eyed the mandrake in Leah's hands with determination. I wasn't going to let Leah have what was intended for me a second time.

I stood firmly on the ground of my entitlement. I had guided Reuben over to that spot, and prepared it with my moon blood.

Leah stood before me like a frenzied bull. Her nostrils flaring in anger, as she grasped the mandrake with all her might.

I was so tired of the endless struggle. I modulated my breathing to quell my anger before responding. Leah had been to the Women's Circles. She recognized the mandrake. I knew why she wanted it. Leah hadn't conceived for many years. She was as desperate as I to have a child, and would try anything.

Looking into Leah's eyes at this close range I saw her pain. I knew the ache of an empty womb. My sister's pain was no different than my own. The ancient dictate of the Sisterhood came to mind. 'The Goddess is all women, and all women are the Goddess'. I dropped down a level inside myself, and entered a place where I knew the pain of all women. I was in the circle of life, a link in the vast female chain of being, carried along by the great river of life and death, that flowed backward to my ancestors and forward into the generations of women yet to come. Within that enormous surge I could feel the pain and joy of all women flowing in my veins. My heart went out to all women whose wombs cried out to be filled. I could feel the wrenching pain of childbirth, and the hideous grief of watching one's child die. How could I be indifferent to this suffering? It was the Goddess crying out behind the pain of women. With the Goddess's presence so close, I knew what to do.

I was tired of wrestling with Leah in accordance with the dictates of the patriarchal Father God. Since the birth of my sons I had a place within our tribe. Yet my spirit couldn't flourish as long as I was engaged in such futile rivalry with my sister. Touching the pain of all women, I was born anew in the Goddess. I would no longer pit myself against my sister. Our struggle was fruitless and sundered the chain of life, diminishing the power of all women. Our maidservants had given birth, while we were caught in the barren web of envy.

My vision had been restored remembering the ancient formula of the Sisterhood. She Who Watches was overshadowing me. One of us had to break through the futile bonds of this rivalry. I would forgive Leah, even if she could not forgive me. To regain my power as a woman,

I had to stop feeling sorry for myself and become accountable for my own actions. What use was it to blame Jacob, father, or the patriarchal Father God for our suppression? If we women had stuck together and maintained our allegiance to the Goddess, the patriarchy never would have succeeded. I'd reach out to Leah. It was the only hope for reconstituting the chain of life which was the Goddess.

I didn't take up the challenge of Leah's angry rebuttal. Instead I looked her in the eyes, and responded with compassion. "I know why you want the mandrake, Leah. I know how much it means to you, because I want it too. I'm glad you remember the mandrake from the Women's Circle. Do you recall how mother used it to open Esther's womb?"

Caught offguard, Leah replied in wonderment. "Esther was over thirty years old. She'd given up all hope for a child. . . . But we mustn't speak of such things! Father and Jacob would be furious if they heard us!"

The mandrake truly was magical! Leah hadn't been so unguarded with me in years. Encouraged, I continued in a soothing voice. "Don't allow father to spoil this for you. He wants to suppress women's wisdom and convince us that we're powerless. There are four love apples. That's enough for both of us."

"My son found the mandrake. Why should I share them with you?" demanded Leah.

I breathed in deeply not wanting to become distracted by her tone. 'I guided Reuben, Leah. You know these roots. They're almost impossible to wrestle from the ground. They can only be taken if a woman's wise blood has been poured on the ground. Reuben would never have been able to get it without my help."

Leah stared at me in horror, stepping backward.

"Don't be upset, Leah! Reuben never saw my moon blood. I seeded the field in the afternoon while he was at work."

Leah continued gazing at me in revulsion.

"Why are you so squeamish about moonblood, Leah? The blood of life is good! . . . It's full of power like this plant."

Leah's face relaxed, as I continued, "Here, sister! You take two love apples, and I'll take two. If you give me the entire root, we'll make a trade."

Leah was silent, but I continued on undaunted. "Share your son's mandrake with me, and I'll trade Jacob with you for one night."

Leah's interest was piqued. "I'll share the mandrake with you, but only if you agree to trade Jacob for the night of the next full moon. That way I'll be sure to conceive." she responded shrewdly.

Leah drove a hard bargain. The next full moon was the harvest moon. But I told myself there would be other full moons. I'd waited this long to have a child. At least we were talking, and had actually agreed on something. The idea of Leah and Jacob together was more palatable when I thought of returning here to watch the moon come up.

"It's a deal!" I said shaking Leah's hand. "You can have two of the love apples and Jacob for the night. If I can have the rest."

Not so much interested in the root as the love apples, Leah nodded her assent.

The mandrake root was my constant companion. I fashioned a leather pouch for it and wore it around my neck. Its presence was so invigorating, my entire body strengthened. The love apples were potent too, but in a different way. I secreted them away beneath my pillow, but there was no hiding their stimulating effect. Even with the heavy toil of harvest upon him, Jacob's romantic fires were ablaze. Vibrant new life infused our lovemaking.

The magical effect of the mandrake's fruit was not wasted on Leah, either. The harvest moon was a majestic evening. I was on my way out to the fields when I chanced to spy Leah in her best finery waiting for Jacob beside the gate. I laughed to see her resembling one of the Goddess's sacred prostitutes who used to stand outside the temple when we were young.

"I've come to fetch you for the night, Jacob!" said Leah greeting Jacob boldly.

"What's the occasion?" inquired Jacob with a surprised look upon his face.

Leah sauntered over to Jacob, smiling seductively. "I've hired you from Rachel for the night."

Jacob was flustered for a moment, then replied good naturedly, "You've hired me for the night, have you? If that's the price of peace between you two sisters, so be it! It's about time you and Rachel made up.

Just don't ask too much of me tonight! I've had a long gruelling day out in the fields."

Jealousy singed my heart as I watched Jacob walk away with Leah. Holding onto the mandrake root for strength, I prayed the flames would subside. I told myself that Jacob and I had come to a new level of under-standing. But such noble thoughts were of little consolation, as I saw Leah fawning all over Jacob.

I walked away still being burnt up by invisible flames. Walking to-ward the field I told myself that Jacob couldn't have what he had with me with anyone else. Certainly not with Leah! But that didn't diminish the fire in my soul.

It got a little easier when I took off at a fast trot putting plenty of distance between us. The tranquility of the open vistas was a healing balm for my enflamed soul. My cares were always diminished when I was running with the wind at my back. When the farm was a mere speck in the distance, what was happening between Jacob and Leah didn't con-sume me anymore.

I was out of breath by the time I neared the mandrake field. My ewes had moved on to greener pastures the day before. I smiled to see the quick work they had made of all the lush grass. Reuben was with the sheep. He was good with the flock. At least I didn't have to worry about them tonight.

18

THE HIGHER MARRIAGE

THE SUN WAS SETTING AS I SAT DOWN ON MY ROCK THRONE AT THE edge of the well trimmed meadow where I'd found the mandrake. The western sky was a palette of brilliant coral and gold. Its sublime peace called to me, a stirring reminder of a higher purer way. The eternal truth of heaven had not felt so close since my retreat up in the mountains years ago. I turned toward the east to wait upon the moon's arrival. The boulder on which I sat still emanated the precious heat of the day. Pleased by its warm welcome, I took the love apples from my pocket. Their color matched the sky, appearing luminous in the twilight.

I removed the mandrake from its pouch around my neck, and held it close to my heart as I began musing. Why was I alone on this special night? . . . Why did I always feel so different and alone? . . . Would anyone ever understand me? . . . What evil had I done to deserve my family? . . . Would there ever be relief?

I was choked with feeling, when I spied the bright orange moon peeking up over the horizon. My heart suddenly opened and I was lifted above the consuming anguish of my thoughts. The personal drama of my life seemed far away staring at the moon's shining surface. A light went on inside me as I gazed upon the brilliant orb. The moon had done no wrong to be stolen from the Goddess and taken over by Nanna/Sin. Perhaps I too was innocent, and did not deserve my father or my sister.

Pleased by these thoughts I took out my fire rocks and some braided sweetgrass. Its fragrant smoke rising up to heaven, I lifted my arms in prayer to drown out the aching loneliness in my heart. GREAT MOTHER NINHURSAG! QUEEN OF HEAVEN! SHE WHO WATCHES FROM HER STARRY THRONE IN KAK.SI.DI. LONG AND HARD HAVE I WORKED TO CONQUER THE JEALOUS POISON THAT HAS FOULED MY HEART AND SPOILED MY CONNECTION WITH YOU. YOU ARE MY TRUE MOTHER. DO NOT FORSAKE ME!

I LONG TO BE WITH YOU AND MOTHER IN THE STARRY REACHES. MY TRUE HOME IS THERE WITH YOU! DON'T LEAVE ME ALONE IN THIS WORLD OF ENDLESS SORROW AND DISAPPOINTMENT, WHERE NO ONE WANTS TO HEAR YOUR TRUTH. TAKE ME TO YOUR BOSOM. NOURISH ME WITH YOUR SWEET MILK THAT LIGHTS THE NIGHT IN THE GREAT MILKY WAY OF STARS.

FORGIVE ME FOR STRAYING FROM YOUR HOLY PURPOSE AND IN YOUR MERCY GRANT ME ANOTHER CHANCE. I AM OLDER AND WISER NOW AND WILL NOT DISAPPOINT YOU.

By the time my prayer was over the full moon was a golden orb dancing on the horizon. Taking up the braided sweetgrass and my mandrake root, I strolled over to the harvested wheat field. As if guided by some unseen power, I walked the same path I had two weeks earlier with my moonblood. When I reached the center of the cross I placed the mandrake root back in the earth.

Returning to the boulder I saw another moon, a blue moon, rising from behind a cloud. My mind reeled, as my eyes travelled back and forth between the two orbs in the sky. Looking down in a state of bewilderment, I saw the love apples beside me were blazing like the sun. What was happening? Had She Who Watches heard my prayer? My eyes didn't lie. Something curious was going on. The blue orb seemed to be coming toward me, speeding like lightning across the sky.

Rose light glowed leaping about the harvested field. Cold fear began running down my spine. Was the field on fire? I had to think fast. No heat was emanating from the field, and there wasn't the slightest trace of smoke. The field couldn't be on fire. Nonetheless the rosy light was spreading out like tongues of flame. When I was finally able to decipher it's pattern, I gasped out loud in wonder. Painted across the field in the rosy light was the Cross of the Virgin. Now what was this? The blue lightning was coming closer, heading for the cross emblazoned on the ground. It was moving quickly and emitted a deep humming sound.

Never had I seen or heard anything like it before. I stared in wonder at the lightning streak that was coming closer and closer all the time. When it aligned itself with the cross, the curious humming grew louder. Suddenly a blue flame descended on the center of the glowing cross. The humming entered my heart. All my fear was swept away, replaced by a gentle warmth spreading throughout my body. I started feeling weightless. When I looked down again my body was aglow with an unearthly light. The love apples had disappeared.

When I looked up, there in the center of the cross stood the most amazing being I had ever seen. Beside him was an enormous winged lion. Who were they? What was happening? Was this the answer to my prayer? Had She Who Watches sent this shining angel down to me? When the humming ceased my entire body was filled with starry light. Was this the milk of Ninhursag's stars, that nourished the kings of old? Never had I felt so vital or at peace before.

My blood racing, I gasped out loud unable to contain myself. The incredible being coming toward me was no stranger. As if waking from a dream, at last I could remember. It was his shining face that had graced my dreams when I was up in the mountains years ago. Yes! It was the same shining angel presence. I would have known him anywhere. He had haunted me for years, ever out of reach, pervading all my thoughts and dreams since my blunder at the EyeTemple. He was here now, and coming toward me in broad confident strides, a blonde golden being, taller than a man. The winged lion reached me first looking me straight in the eye. He seemed to be able to look right through me. There was wisdom and compassion in his gaze. The shining being beside him had to be one of the Nefilim, the Elohim, the God/men mother had talked about, and Jacob had seen in his vision of the ladder. But I thought they had all departed.

My heart warmed and opened in his presence. An ancient knowing wakened deep inside me and I was not afraid. The Shining One coming toward me was a pure and noble spirit. So much so, that to be in his presence my body took on light. I felt unworthy in comparison to the brilliance of his spirit. What was I to do, or say? Overwhelmed by the splendor of his presence, I gazed at him in awe until a disturbing thought came to me. Was he the one I was to have mated with on the Goddess's golden couch years ago? If so, how could I face him? Would he be angry with me? I was consumed with guilt.

The angel coming toward me was the most beautiful being I had ever seen. His hair was the color of gold and flowed down around his shoulders like the sun's rays. A dazzling white light surrounded him. His eyes were a penetrating blue violet flame, resembling the furthest reaches of the sky which was his home. I knew immediately they could read my heart and mind.

The winged lion beside him possessed a regal dignity. His emerald eyes bore into me, assessing my strengths and weaknesses. In the face of such awesome majesty all I could do was prostrate myself.

The shining stranger never uttered a word. He transferred his thoughts to me and I could hear them in my heart. "Daughter of Man, arise that I may see you! I come at your invitation, because at last you have remembered who you are."

I rose trembling to face the Shining One. It was awesome gazing into his eyes, that could encompass the heights of heaven yet see into a woman's heart.

The Angel of Heaven continued. "Do not be afraid, Rachel! I am no stranger to you. I come in peace and friendship, the answer to your fervent prayers."

Astounded by his exalted presence, I said aloud, "How is it that you know my prayers, oh Shining One?"

As he gazed into my eyes his words resounded in my heart. "I know all about you, Rachel. I have been watching you ever since the beginning of your sojourn here on Earth."

Even more confused, I inquired, "How is it you are interested in one so lowly?"

The radiant one smiled. "There is a high purpose to our meeting, Rachel. Didn't your mother ever speak to you of her connection with the Nefilim?"

I shook my head in wonder, and he continued. "Allow me to introduce myself. I am Zandar, one of the Watchers from Kak.Si.Di. This is Ariel. He is one of the Cherubim, the noble Lion People also from our star system. We travel together. You are the star child of my father, Rachel. Your mother Anna was a great Naditu Priestesses, a pure and special soul beloved by Ninhursag. She was chosen to climb the great ladder to the stars and become the Nindingir. She came together with my father in the Sacred Mating rite at the Eye Temple. You are the fruit of that union, Rachel, and one of the Family of Light. You carry the blood of the Star People, which is why you were chosen to mate with me at the Eye Temple years ago. Though you failed to fulfill that higher purpose."

The mere mention of that tragic night filled me with shame, I looked away unable to respond.

I heard a thundering in my heart. "Do not turn your face from me, Rachel! Look me in the eyes, and tell me why you chose not to come to me on that fateful night!"

The Nefilim's eyes were the blazing heart of the sun, as I responded, "I am sorry, oh Great One! Please forgive me! There's no excuse for my behavior! But it was long ago and I was young and foolish. I was betrothed to my cousin, Jacob, and had come to the Eye Temple to prepare for our marriage. He had great plans for us in those days. My virginity was so important to Jacob. I was afraid he wouldn't understand, and would hold it against me forever."

"Like Laban did your mother?"

The Nefilim's statement set my mind aglow, and I was unable to go on. His words put so much in perspective that had always troubled me. Laban knew I was not his child! So that was why he hated me! Why had I not been told? At last I could understand the gaping void between my parents. It also explained Laban's loathing for Ninhursag, the Naditu Sisterhood, and the Eye Temple. A weight lifted from my heart. I was exhilarated knowing that Laban was not my father.

The great being before me was a Sky Teacher. His light of truth had illumined the darkness of my life. I was still quivering with the power of his revelation when he continued on.

"Your truthfulness earned you that revelation, Rachel. It also shows me that you are one of Ninhursag's own. Earthlings rarely admit their mistakes, or say they're sorry. The universe is merciful. I did not come to chide you for your past mistakes. It's self-defeating to live in guilt about one's past failings. There is no misstep that can not be turned to a good purpose by a noble heart. And I know how much you have already suffered for your youthful folly. What's important is that you have remembered who you are and called me down."

Not understanding, I inquired, "Remembered who I am? I called you down? Pray tell, my Lord, by what means did I call you down? I didn't think you Star People came to Earth anymore."

The Nefilim flashed me a smile so bright it took my breath away. "You remembered your true home is in the stars, Rachel. Please do not call me, Lord! Don't think of me as a god. We are all children of the Prime Creator, which makes us cosmic brothers and sisters. Think of me as a wise older brother."

"The Earth's energy field has become so dense, we Star Beings can no longer come down to Earth unless summoned by those of our lineage with a pure heart, who keep faith with the ancient practices. I come from the star system Kak.Si.Di., the Eye Star of the Lion People, the sun behind your sun, great star of the Goddess, and of women. Its holy emanations have given life to gods and men, and many living things upon your planet. Kak.Si.Di. is the great seat of wisdom, the dispenser of rain, and cosmic regulator of the waters. Star Beings from Kak.Si.Di. brought knowledge of the stars, crystals, and many of the precious grains to Earth in the ancient times."

"We are the Starry Watchers, the ancient guardians of Earth. Our purpose is to uplift humankind and stimulate the spiritual evolution on your planet. We cannot assist however, unless we are summoned, as it is not our way to interfere. We have guided the Naditu Sisterhood and the great White Brotherhood for untold centuries. The sign for our star is the cross of the virgin, the insignia of the Naditu order. You called me down just now with the mandrake, and prepared the ground with the cross you emblazoned in your moonblood. And I came because at last you have risen above the dynamics of your earthly drama and remembered who you are. Your true origin is from the Stars. You are one of the Family of Light who has come down to uplift your Brothers and Sisters upon this planet. You are a Naditu Priestess and have taken up the ancient mysteries once again. Consecrating this field earned you possession of the mandrake, Rachel. You might have called me down much sooner with the terafim, but Laban prevented that."

"Do Laban and the Brotherhood of the Black Hand know the power of the terafim, oh Wise One!."

The Nefilim scrutinized me before responding. "Laban and his Brotherhood know the terafim have great power and can be used to communicate with us, but they will never fathom their secret. The terafim would burn to cinders anyone unworthy of their use. Only the most select initiates of the Eye Temple know how to use them. Laban went to great lengths to seize them in order to prevent you from having contact with us. He would do anything to suppress the ancient Star Wisdom and the Naditu order. If earthlings remember their ancestry from the stars they will begin to regain their ancient power and will not be so easy to control."

"You see it is not enough to have the terafim in your possession. You must be of pure heart and possess the Ancient Eyes and Ears to tap their power. Then you have to connect with the serpent power at the base of the spine, which is asleep now in most humans. For those who can make the connection, the terafim will take them spiralling out into the universe. Even then they will only work if they are used in accordance with the vibrations of love. the great music of the spheres. As you have already seen, they bring on disasters such as earthquakes, drought, even madness, if they are in the wrong possession."

Light seemed to enter every pore of my body as I listened to the wisdom of the Shining One. The Nefilim's superior knowledge opened vistas to my inner sight. My spirit expanded and I was filled with questions.

"Forgive my questions, Oh Wise One, but there is so much I need to understand. How did you get here?"

"The miracles of Earth are the Laws of Heaven, Rachel. I came here by what we Star Beings call teleportation. That is the ability to depart from one point and reappear in another with the speed of thought. Not all the Sons and Daughters of Heaven can do this. The Anunnaki and many others require their space ships. It's only possible to teleport a solid body when there is a perfectly balanced interchange between spirit and matter. Only one who has touched the galactic center can teleport, as spirit and matter are united at the center."

Deep peace enveloped me as I listened to the blessing of his truth. "Please tell me of Earth's history? Is it true that Gods once walked with man upon the Earth?"

The Nefilim looked at me with shining eyes. There was no separation between us as I heard his answer in my heart. "It is good to hear your questions, Rachel! Through them I see you are a genuine seeker after truth, and wish to penetrate the Mysteries that lie hidden behind the veil of forgetfulness which enshrouds your planet. Would that there were more earnest seekers at this time! But the time is not yet ripe. That time will not come for many aeons yet. Not until your solar system enters the photon belt in the Age of Aquarius in the far distant future, will there be enough seekers after truth gathered to ask the right questions that unlock Earth's secrets. But listen now, and I will tell you truly as most of the ancient history of Earth has been destroyed in the Great Flood. And there are few records left of what came before."

"There once was a time, a true Golden Age upon this planet, when the Ancient Ones from Heaven, the great Sky Teachers lived and walked upon the Earth sharing their prodigious knowledge with the earthlings. This is no great mystery. It is self-evident though humanity has entered a sleep of forgetfulness. It is apparent to any genuine seeker after truth. For it is far from coincidental that the power of all Earth's ancient high civilizations was always greatest at their inception. This, of course, is because they were all seeded from on high. Their slow steady decline occurred when the Star Beings receded."

"Many high civilizations have already come to birth and been destroyed upon your planet. Atlantis, Lemuria, and Mu, to name but a few. Angels, devils, creatures of light, and even enormous reptiles have taken part in the history of Earth. The founders of all the ancient civilizations came from the Apsu, the great primordial abyss of outer space. During the Golden Age, long since past, the beings on your planet were not divided into male or female. They were magnificent beings of light whole unto themselves, and seeded by a variety of different Star Peoples, who came to Earth to share their prodigious gifts and knowledge.

"For millennia successive waves of Star Beings, you call angels, have come to Earth from Athtar/Venus, Sirius, which you know as Kak.Si.Di., the Pleiades, Lyra, and Orion just to name a few. They came to assist humankind in their development and to gain experience on the physical plane. Long ago, during the Golden Age of your planet, inhabitants of Earth were called the Family of Light. These light beings enjoyed a sublime and what would now seem magical relationship of Oneness with the Prime Creator, the universe, and we Star People.

"This glorious state of Oneness was humankind's true and rightful condition until the Fall. The Fall was not instantaneous, Rachel. It was brought on gradually by fear and a lack of faith. Over time as the early light beings grew attached to Earth, they took on greater and greater degrees of materiality, until they began to identify with a sense of separateness and forgot their primal Oneness with the Creator. In the early time you know as the Garden of Eden, the Family of Light inhabited your planet and participated in the great Oneness. They walked and talked with the Prime Creator, and could create by the power of their own thoughts like the Creator."

"The spirit and the heart are heavenly, Rachel, the product of divine creation. The body was fashioned here on Earth, and is thus handicapped by weight and the downward pulling force of gravity. Gravity is not only felt on the physical plane on Earth. Its heavy drawing force is felt on the emotional and mental planes as well. Overtime the early light beings seeded by the Star People fell in love with the materiality of Earth and became more dense. The force of gravity taught them limitation and they gradually became conditioned to fear—the fear of death, and the fear of separation. These fears incited them with the wish to become as great as the Prime Creator. But in so desiring, they fell out of harmony with the Divine Plan, and lost their original state of Oneness with the Creator. From hereon they were locked in flesh and had to toil by the sweat of their brow to survive. Thus did Earth's beings come to know disease, aging, and death."

"Not all the Sons of Heaven who have come to Earth have had the best interests of humankind in mind. You live at the end of the Bronze Age, in the death throws of the Sumerian civilization founded by the Anunnaki, the sons and daughters of Anu whose abode is in the highest heaven. The Anunnaki come from the planet Nibiru, the twelfth and hidden planet in your solar system. Nibiru is the Great Traveller in the sky. Its orbit reaches beyond the farthest limits of your solar system where light and darkness meet. The Anunnaki are part human and part reptile. This is why they live for thousands of years. They are intelligent beings who taught the ancient Sumerians the arts of civilization. They travel your solar system with their advanced space craft and weaponry, but do not be fooled. They are not gods, though they want earthlings to believe so. And their hearts are cold. They have little regard for earthlings. Sumer was blown up in a catastrophic disaster brought on by their constant wars and fighting.

When the Anunnaki came to Earth approximately 500,000 years ago, they were primarily interested in the mining and exploitation of Earth. Great wars were fought as the Anunnaki unleashed their weapons to establish control of Earth. These explosions tore the Earth asunder. The Family of Light was defeated and forced to depart. To secure ownership of Earth, the Anunnaki tampered with the original genetic codes of Earth's creatures in an effort to control them. Thanks to their tampering, human beings have a distinctly reptilian level to their brain and nervous system. The Anunnaki sealed off the vast majority of the brain of your species. This was a tragic loss. Full brain access supported the Family of Light's original multidimensional awareness which maintained contact with their lineages from our star, Lyra, the Pleiades, and various other star systems throughout the universe. The Anunnaki's tampering also deprived earthlings of more than 85% of their brain capacity, confining them to a limited three dimensional awareness, which cut them off from their spirit, their vast intuitive faculties, and the cosmic light of the stars. Your Ancient Eyes and Ears are a mere vestige of what the Family of Light once possessed."

"Tampering with the original makeup of the Family of Light was not the Anunnaki's only offense. They fashioned primitive slave workers from primates found here to work their mines. But when the reptilian Anunnaki combined their genes with the primitive humanoids on Earth they could not reproduce. So they turned to us on Kak.Si.Di. to help them solve the problem. Ninhursag and Enki volunteered to come to Earth in the employ of the Anunnaki to temper their rapacious power strivings, and foster the spiritual evolution of the primitive earth beings in any way they could."

"Before the Black Hand's suppression of the Goddess, Ninhursag was revered throughout all of Mesopotamia as the Great Mother Goddess, because she had given birth to the Adam, the Anunnaki's first primitive worker. She also instituted the Naditu Sisterhood, the order of the Chosen Women, and its central rite the Sacred Marriage, so that Star Beings could mate with selected Daughters of Earth to accelerate human evolution. All the ancient kings and great men of the past, such as Gilgamesh of Uruk, were progeny of the Sons of Heaven through the Naditu Sisterhood. As your myths relate they were nourished by the milk of Ninhursag, the great light of heaven, which is the stars."

"Enki gave the primitive Adam the knowledge of good and evil, which infuriated Enlil. The cold hearted reptilian leader did not want his slaves having the power of discernment. But that is not all Enki did. Unbeknownst to the Anunnaki, Enki and Ninhursag inserted a latent DNA code in the primitive earthlings. During the Age of Aquarius when the Earth and your solar system passes through the photon belt, its starry light will unleash that latent DNA code. That code will unlock the enormous brain capacity given humans by the Prime Creator, and help earthlings to reconnect with their intuitive faculties and their ancient Star lineages, so they can remember who they are and regain their original spiritual evolution."

Staggered by the revelations of the Starry One, I exclaimed, "So this is why the sleep of forgetfulness enshrouds our planet and so few wish to know the truth. . . . It also explains man's inhumanity to man . . . the heartlessness of the gods . . . and all the bloody wars and fighting that go on here."

The shining Nefilim looked me in the eyes, smiling with great compassion. "Yes, Rachel! The Anunnaki are not gods, though they want humankind to believe so. They are the cruel reptilian warlords of your planet. Great wars have the Anunnaki fought in heaven and on Earth using men as pawns to establish their control. Wily Enlil, first son of their head God Anu, was made chief of all the Anunnaki here. He possessed the Tablets of Destiny and other objects of power which enforced the Anunnaki's dominion. Enlil ruled Sumer from the city of Nippur, where he maintained the Dur.An.Ki., the sacred Bond uniting Heaven and Earth. But the craving for power is bound to corrupt, and there was great strife within the ranks of the Anunnaki."

"Enlil and Enki locked horns. This was inevitable due to Enlil's lust for power and his callous disregard for human life. Enlil and Enki's progeny continued the battle taking up arms. Brother fought against brother, and sister, as the Anunnaki sought to dominate the Earth, and steal power from the Goddess. Ninhursag and Enki went south to Magan to establish the Egyptian civilization in righteousness. Magan is the great repository of star wisdom from Kak.Si.Di. There Enki is known as Ptah, and Ninhursag is called Hathor."

"Nanna/Sin was one of the worst of the Anunnaki. Nothing was ever enough for that great deceiver. After he usurped the Moon power from the Goddess, he dared betray his own father Enlil. Sin stole the Tablets of Destiny and the objects of power from Enlil at Nippur to fulfill his ruthless power strivings."

"The Anunnaki fled the Earth with Nanna/Sin's rebellion. Only Ninurta, first son of Enlil by Ninhursag, dared take up battle against Sin and his fallen angels. Ninurta recovered the Tablets of Destiny and the other sacred objects, and returned them to his father. The Assembly of the Anunnaki voted to unleash their greatest weapon in retaliation to destroy Ur, Sin's stronghold. The destructive power got out of control and all of Sumer was laid waste by the explosion. Great mushroom shaped clouds poisoned the air, the water, even the ground. Sin and his dark angels were wounded and vanquished. They were exiled from heaven as punishment, and cast down to Earth. Now they require the blood of men and animals for their survival. Thus was evil, and human and animal sacrifice, entrenched upon the Earth."

My flesh crawled to think of such abominations, but I continued listening intently.

"After his exile Sin took up residence here in Haran at the Ehulhul temple, which is the exact replica of the one in Ur. Like the original, it's the stronghold of the Brotherhood of the Black Hand, known in other times and places as the Brotherhood of the Snake or the Brotherhood of the Dragon, after that scheming reptile Sin. These same conspiratorial forces that brought down Sumer, once conspired to construct the Tower of Babel. Fortunately they failed in that attempt to set up a secret one world government. The Black Hand are the puppets of Sin, and the other exiles from heaven."

"There are other exiles?" I inquired in amazement.

"In the ancient past a giant star exploded within a triangle of stars formed by Zeta Puppis, Gamma Velorum, and Lambda Velorum in the

Southern Sky. The star that exploded was called Lucifer, the Shining One. Its remnants are known as the Asteroid Belt. Knowledge was worshipped on that lost world and placed above the wisdom of the heart. This is what eventually brought on their demise. Their science and technology got the best of them, and they blew themselves up. The explosion of Lucifer caused great catastrophes on other worlds as well. Earth still suffers as a result of this event. Many of their most powerful leaders and minds, including Lucifer himself, escaped the final devastation and came here. His rebel horde are still on Earth today living underground. Nanna/Sin joined forces with Lucifer, and his remnant from the lost world, when he was exiled here. We Watchers were powerless to prevent it, as we were not called upon to help and it's against the universal law to interfere."

My heart sank. So this was the root of evil on Earth.

The Shining One continued on. "After Sin's exile here all the Star People departed, due to the widespread degeneration he and his minions engendered on your beautiful planet. Earth's vibrations have now become so dense, even the Anunnaki have been forced to retreat to Nibiru, their throne in heaven. We ancient Sky Teachers who seeded Earth and were once in constant contact with you earthlings can only come at times of dire need, when called upon by the righteous and the pure of heart."

"Imagine how we feel to know that Ninhursag, the Great Mother of All, is suppressed on Earth, and even our star, the great star of the Goddess is called the Star of Ninurta. And one so low as your so-called father is in possession of the terafim! One day I fear it will be said that the Eye Temple at Brak belonged to Inanna/Ishtar. This is the level of depravity which has befallen your once glorious planet."

"It will only worsen as you move into the Age of Iron. The workings of the Black Hand now envelop this land like an invidious plague draining away its spiritual lifeblood. The closing of the Eye Temple at Brak, our stronghold in the north, was a great triumph for Sin and the Brotherhood. Vanquishing the Great Mother Goddess and her traditions will hamper human beings' emotional development. Thus foiling their ability to re-integrate the masculine and feminine polarity which could unlock humankind's enormous brain capacity, and lead them back into their light bodies."

"Truth and Love are the greatest forces in the universe. Love promotes the spirit of Oneness which presides on all the liberated planets throughout the universe. The heart is humankind's link with spirit and the Prime Creator. When the mind works alone it becomes demonic. What happened on Lucifer is proof of that! The Goddess is the Opener of the Heart. For centuries Her teachings promoted love, the greatest civilizing tool on Earth. The suppression of the Goddess will bring on a decline in culture. Gross imbalances will plague the Earth. The overwhelming predominance of the masculine will result in an increased emphasis on war and bloody conquest, and will usher in what shall be called the Age of Iron."

"Sin and his dark angels seek control of Earth. The only Goddess who fits in with their plans is the bloodthirsty Inanna. Though in time even She will be forgotten. Nanna/Sin's daughter, Inanna, is a ferocious warrior. Her lust and enormous craving for power cannot be tempered. When ancient divine kings, such as Gilgamesh, turned up their noses at Inanna, the sly reptile went after an Assyrian named Sargon with none of the blue blood of the Star People in his veins. Using him as her battleaxe, Inanna has devastated the land of Sumer and taken over Ninhursag's place. Now thanks to Inanna, kingship no longer comes down from heaven nurtured by the sweet milk of Ninhursag. Instead the lascivious reptile chooses kings according to who pleases her in bed. Inanna has given the Goddess a bad name. Of course, this pleases her father, as Sin lives off the energy released by violence, grief, and chaos."

"All is not lost, however. Yahweh has risen up. Jacob's presence here in the north has helped him to take over Mt. Ararat. Yahweh has been sent into this time of darkness by the Star Beings of the Pleiades to fight the evil forces of Sin. Yahweh will resist Inanna's seductive persuasions, and put an end to the sacrificial killing of human beings, which Sin and his evil minions feed upon to keep themselves strong. Yahweh will institute the Ten Commandments, which are in accord with the Laws of Heaven, to help thwart Sin's corruption of humankind."

"But alas, the Pleiadeans are tricksters and very power oriented, and even Yahweh will be a product of these warring times. He will go down in history as a jealous wrathful God, a dividing sword that shall cut his people off from the Oneness of All that Is. Yahweh will insist on complete and absolute power, thus denying the Goddess and Her worship.

Without a consort, in the end I fear even his Lordship will become a vehicle of war encouraging heroic combat and aggression, albeit against the forces of darkness."

"Yahweh and the Age of Iron will require warrior/priests to subdue the Black Hand and its demonic leader Sin. Your husband Jacob's forbear, Abraham, was originally from Nippur the spiritual capital of ancient Sumer. Abraham was the progeny of the Anunnaki, and a great warrior/priest. He and his cavalry of men halted the forces of the Black Hand when they tried to take over the Anunnaki's spaceport on the Sinai peninsula. Jacob will take up the fight once more, but for this he needs you and our star child Joseph."

"Jacob is in Haran to come to know the Brotherhood and resist them in their own stronghold before returning home to Canaan, the land of his fathers. Jacob's mother, Rebekah, was a Priestess of the Eye Goddess, and a woman of vision, though she's fallen away from the Goddess teachings. She realized how important the integration of the Feminine would be for the man with Yahweh's blessing. That is why she sent Jacob to you. Our son Joseph will strengthen the tribe of Jacob against the corruption of the Brotherhood of the Snake, the Black Hand. If they will but listen to our son, he will institute a new Kingdom of Heaven on Earth.

"But the Black Hand is expert at keeping humankind in a state of materialist trance. The Brotherhood knows how to feed into each person's dark side. They can blind even the purest souls with their arts of sexual persuasion and corruption. As you well know, Jacob has compromised much of what he once was in his lust for wealth, and the engendering of progeny to take over his homeland. Laban and the Black Hand have so far duped Jacob, he lingers on here forgetting his Higher Purpose. The Brotherhood always seeks to destroy those of noble character to hold back human evolution."

"Look how well they succeeded in ensnaring you in their insidious plot through envy. You came to Earth to serve, but having been deprived of your spiritual lineage and being so abused, even you lost your way. Leah represents your lower nature, your shadow, the enemy within, greedy for personal power and progeny. Your rivalry with Leah cost you your connection with the Goddess and your Higher Self, your angel spirit. But finally you have ceased your envious rivalry with your sister, and remembered who you are. You have your own destiny! You are a Naditu Priestess! Your Higher Purpose is to carry the bloodline of the Starry Ones into Yahweh's new dispensation. Keep your eyes on heaven, Rachel! Do not allow yourself to be distracted by Leah and Jacob. Like seeks like. Jacob and Leah belong together, both having gotten where they are through treachery, deception, and playing off the blindness of others. Marriage with Jacob has brought you low. Our union will lift you up and help heal the imbalance inflicted on this planet through the suppression of the Goddess and women."

My heart and mind expanded with the Nefililm's vision. This was the truth I had yearned for all my life, though most poignantly during my retreat up in the mountains. To be with the light of his truth was all that I desired. The thought of losing it was more than I could bear. I gathered up my courage. "Oh Great One, you know how lonely I am, and how much I have suffered. Take me with you! Please take me with you!! I will not be missed here."

The Nefilim looked at me with compassion. "I'm sorry, Rachel, but that is not possible! Your work is here. But never fear! Distance will be no barrier to our love. When the spirit is wedded there can be no separation. The Earth is now a dark and troubled place. I know how much you have suffered. Your eyes are full of sorrow for one so young, and beautiful. Nonetheless I cannot take you with me."

"You are a World Server. You volunteered to come to Earth to partner me in the Higher Marriage. We must salvage what we can of our plan to help humankind. You must remain here to give birth to our Star Child, and help Jacob and his progeny by your example. It hurts me to see how you have been abused. But it is ever thus. When the Family of Light shine upon Earth they illumine the darkness all around them, and the darkness rises up in an attempt to destroy them."

"You are a Naditu Priestess, one of the Family of Light still upon this planet. Now that you have remembered who you are, your presence will connect Heaven and Earth. Our son will bring truth and light into these troubled times. He is sorely needed to counter the influence of the Black Hand and redeem Earth from the demoralizing materialism into which humankind has fallen. Only the son of a Nefilim with you to guide him, will have the strength and love necessary to ransom his brothers from the darkness into which they will descend. He shall be an example to them in the fight against the forces of darkness and degradation upon the Earth."

"Our son's mission is an important one, but onerous. His task is to preserve his own people, by serving as an Opener of the Way fostering brotherhood between the nations of Enlil and Enki. To do this he may have to follow the Eye Temple down to Magan/Egypt, the channel for the Star Teachings from Kak.Si.Di. Our son will not only effect a healing between nations. He will effect a healing between the God and Goddess traditions. He shall be tempted, but he will not be seduced. He shall succeed where Jacob failed and marry a Priestess of the Goddess to foster balance upon Earth. His great wisdom and compassion will preserve his brothers, and his entire people. He shall unite two great cultures upon Earth, saving them both. Though our son's own brothers may plot to kill him, so long as there is another Son of Heaven who sits upon the throne of the Goddess on Earth, our son is destined to find him. Yes! Our son will be recognized by he, who is called Pharaoh, the God/King of Magan, and raised up to become his right hand. Together their joint righteousness will preserve both their peoples against the imbalances wrought by the suppression of the Goddess and the Brotherhood of the Black Hand."

"Our son shall be called Joseph, because he will increase the light, the love, and wisdom upon the Earth. His righteousness shall maintain the sacred bond between Heaven and Earth, uniting two great peoples. Through Joseph it will be remembered in future times, that Magan/Egypt and the Holy Land of Jacob are not enemies, but meant to hold the light together against the Black Hand that aims to control the entire world. Joseph's sojourn in Magan will open the way for Moses, another great leader of people, and for Jesus the Christ, Son of the Most High and Savior of the World, who will come to Earth at the beginning of the next Great Age, the Age of Pisces."

"Joseph will be keeper of the wisdom of the Star People. He will pass that knowledge on to his children, so that the word's of angels may be written down and carried into the future for the children of Aquarius."

"I come from Kak.Si.Di., Star of the Watchers, the guardians of Earth, the great Arrow Star poised against the enemies of light in the universe. The cycle of our work here is over for a time. The Earth is in bloody turmoil. We can only watch and come if called, as it is not our way to impose our will upon anyone. But we are the Starry Watchers, and we shall be watching over the Ages. We shall return one day when the Great Ages move into Aquarius, when humankind will face its greatest test. Humanity will have to choose between the seductive antics of the Black Hand, mascerading as "peacemakers of nations" and great "corporate leaders", the secret government behind all governments, or taking a giant leap forward, open their hearts and minds and claim their sovereign heritage from the stars. When humanity remembers who they are and chooses the latter, they will be ready to join the other liberated planets and come to know the Universal Brotherhood and Sisterhood we enjoy. Then we shall return and institute a new Golden Age of freedom and true Brotherhood and Sisterhood on Earth."

My entire being stretched to the enormous task this great Angel of Heaven had shared with me.

The Shining One looked me in the eyes. "Much have you suffered, Rachel. But you volunteered knowing that when the Goddess was suppressed women would become confused and turn against each other. You knew they would be brought low and lose their connection with their Higher Self. Yet you came to hold the light of heaven through the darkness and show that love could conquer all, even envy. You are the Spiritual Mother of a great people, Rachel. Though young in body, you shoulder an immense burden for humankind. Your eyes are filled with tears. But in your tear-filled eyes many will remember the Primordial Mother of All, She Who Watches, who laments the suffering of her children from Her throne in heaven."

When the Nefilim took my hand brilliant white light entered through the crown of my head igniting my entire being. My heart beat was tuned into the heart beat of the Universe. All pain and sorrow left me. No longer was I a separate entity, but part of God's glorious creation, at one with the Oneness of All that Is.

Tremendous forces passed between us, as the Radiant One sent me the power to fulfill my purpose. When the Shining One finished his blessing, my entire body pulsed with light.

Seeing this he said, "Come to me, Rachel! Our embrace shall heal the world and open you to the wisdom of the Stars. You shall conceive a Star Child, and be alone no longer."

"Shouldn't we be inside the temple on Ninhursag's golden couch?" I inquired, taken aback by the suddenness of his request.

"What need have we for a manmade temple, when we have the whole starry vault of heaven?" replied the Shining One with a smile.

The Nefilim had already entered my heart and mind. But when he took me in his arms, I melted into the vastness of his shining being as we soared throughout the Milky Way.

19

BIRTH OF THE STAR CHILD

THE SHINING NEFILIM DEPARTED IN HIS BALL OF LIGHT AS MYSTERIOUSLY as he had arrived, bringing light to the night as easily as he had the depths of my soul. I was left to ponder the miracle which had befallen me inside the enchanted circle of the mandrake's light. Always had I longed for a transcendent love that would lift me to the stars. I couldn't remember when that secret yearning had not burned within my soul. My deepest longing had been fulfilled. I was filled with peace and would never be the same.

The Shining One's brilliant insight had opened my eyes and given meaning and purpose to all the suffering and estrangement I'd endured. I would never forget the brilliance of his eyes. Gazing up into the azure reaches of the sky, I could feel his shining presence smiling down on me. Deep within the silence of my womb his starborne seed was spreading out his love as Joseph made his home in me. She Who Watches had not forgotten me. The Universe was merciful. Finally I had been seen and known, and in that process reconstituted and reborn. All my years of neglect and humiliation melted away in the angel fire of his recognition.

Amazed at my good fortune, I bubbled over with gratitude and delight the whole way home. Laban and Leah were chatting together when I arrived, lingering over breakfast with a few of the younger children. Their conversation dropped off suddenly at the sight of me. As usual, I felt as though I was interrupting.

My first thought was to turn and leave. But my stomach grumbled loudly catching sight of the bowl of porridge in the center of the table. Leah didn't say a word to me as I sat down. Though she stared at me with probing eyes, as she sat guarding the morning fare.

After eying me in silence for some time, she ventured, "You certainly look full of yourself this morning, Rachel!" Then she added smugly. "But that won't last for long! Jacob's angry with you! And rightly so! Where were you last night? He said you hadn't slept in the tent. Don't you know better than to go traipsing around the countryside in the dead of night?"

This morning I could not be goaded. The new life tucked inside me was like a magic shield deflecting Leah's ill will. Helping myself to a heaping bowl of porridge, I responded casually, "All this concern for me! I didn't think I'd be missed, or I would have left a note. It was such a glorious evening. I wanted to be outside to enjoy it."

Replacing the bowl in the center of the table, I gazed at Leah warmly and said, "I hope you had a pleasant night!" Then I started eating.

Leah stared at me in amazement, not knowing what to say. My good will had not been part of the bargain we'd made in sharing Jacob. The porridge was still warm, and sweetened with date honey for the children. It would take more than Leah to upset me today.

Leah was beside herself. She hadn't seen me this undaunted in years. Clearly perplexed at the good-natured ease of my reply, she sat back glaring at me in silence.

Bilhah entered the room with a pitcher of milk for the children. Pleased to see me eating with such relish, she smiled approvingly.

"Good morning, mistress Rachel! I'm glad to see you with such a fine appetite today. You usually eat like a bird. Here! Have some milk with your porridge. It's still warm from the cow."

I smiled at Bilhah and took the milk from her hand, glancing over at Laban. Sure enough! His serpent stare was fastened on me. Usually such a penetrating look would send chills up my spine, but not today. An enormous grin spread across my face at the thought that I was not his child.

This was too much for Laban, and he began interrogating. "What's come over you, Rachel? You're not yourself today. You're acting very strange."

Almost giddy with laughter I responded, "I'm more myself than ever. I'm just happy, that's all. The weather is beautiful, the harvest abundant. You should be pleased as well."

Pleasure was the last thing on Laban's mind. He stared at me trying to intimidate me with his flashing eyes. The old fox's acumen was amazing. He usually never gave me a second look, but this morning he couldn't take his eyes off me. Afraid that he was not going to be put off so easily, I finished my porridge quickly and rose to leave. After taking a few pieces of bread for my afternoon meal, I started for the door.

"I must be off! It's my turn to relieve Reuben. I'll see you tonight at dinner. Should I send Reuben to Jacob, or do you want him here today?"

Getting down to the matters at hand took Laban's attention off me.

"Take some bread and cheese along for Reuben. Send him out to the wheat fields with Jacob. The weather's been good but I want to get all the wheat and barley in before it changes." he replied in his usual gruff voice.

"Very well! I'll see you later!" I said closing the door behind me. Then I was off like an arrow shot from the bow.

Laban and Leah kept a vigilant eye on me the next few weeks. But even their joint scrutiny couldn't effect me. The revelations the Angel from Heaven had shared with me was an inner shield that grew stronger with each day. It served me well at the next new moon.

I hadn't seen Jacob all day and was fairly bursting to share my news. Drawing him aside after the dinner plates were removed, I said, "Let's go for a walk, Jacob! I have the most wonderful news. I'd like to share it with you in private."

I had been keeping to myself of late, and Jacob was pleased by my invitation. "Good news? Fine! Take your cloak! The wind was starting up on my way here."

Leah was pregnant. She'd announced it at dinner amid the usual fanfare. Now she leered at me. "Must you two be off so early tonight? I haven't seen you all day, Jacob. I hoped you'd stay and have some wine with us to celebrate our new child." she said between sobs as we started toward the door.

Caught between Leah and I, Jacob didn't know what to say and fumbled nervously.

Leah was still sobbing as she continued in her intrusive way. "It's the dark of the moon, Rachel! Shouldn't you be going up to your moon lodge?"

I breathed in deeply, resenting her intrusion. I had wanted to share the news of my pregnancy with Jacob privately, but I could see that would be impossible now. Smiling directly at Leah, which caught her offguard, I said, "I didn't want to take away from your announcement tonight, Leah. But since you've asked, I won't be going to my moon lodge."

I turned and looked Jacob in the eyes smiling warmly. "I'm with child, Jacob! My time has finally come!"

Jacob stared at me in amazement. Thrilled by my announcement, he took me in his arms and whispered softly so that only I could hear. "This is the most wonderful news I could hope for, dearest! I'm so happy, and so proud!"

I glanced over at Leah with bated breath, not knowing what fury my announcement might unleash. Sure enough! Her face had darkened into an angry scowl. I prepared myself for the worst, praying the storm on her face would pass.

Father was the first to speak. "Well! This certainly is a surprise! You being a Naditu woman and all, Rachel! I thought you had been acting strange of late."

Noticing Leah's disgruntled look, he announced trying to cajole her. "Tonight's a special night! There's much to celebrate. Don't rush off, Jacob! This deserves a special toast! It's quite remarkable that both my daughters are pregnant at the same time. Come have a seat here beside the fire! Let's have some wine!"

My heart sank. Laban and Leah were the last people I wanted to celebrate my good news with. I glanced over at Jacob hoping he'd find some excuse. But Jacob was beaming proudly, hand outstretched to receive his goblet. I felt trapped, the usual suffocating weight descending on my heart. I sat next to Jacob beside the fire and looked down, hoping to avoid an ugly confrontation with Leah. It was difficult, however. Leah was seated across from me seething with emotion. I was afraid she'd erupt at any moment.

I felt for the mandrake root in its pouch around my neck, and placed it over my heart. It was just in time. Leah was starting to blow. Her words spewed forth with angry venom. "How fortunate we are that you deign to join us this evening, Rachel! There'll be no end to your arrogance once you have a child of your own."

The rancor of Leah's tone made my lip start to quiver, but I was determined not to be goaded. Too much had already been ruined by her envious spoiling. I put my hand on my abdomen hoping to shield my son. It was always easier for me to be strong for someone else. I breathed in deeply. I could see it was going to be quite a challenge raising a Starchild in this household.

I looked over at Jacob for support, but he was choosing to ignore Leah's comment.

Laban came toward me with a full goblet of wine. Just the thought of wine was repugnant to me now that I was pregnant.

"Congratulations, Rachel." said Laban, pressing the goblet on me. "This is quite a surprise after all these years. I'll have to consult my oracle about it. And you'll have to take it easy. You know how dangerous birthing can be for a Naditu woman."

I took the goblet from his hand, trying to force a smile. Though after seeing the look he'd just given Leah, I wouldn't have been surprised if he'd put poison in it.

I was putting the goblet down, when Leah started up. "Father's right, Rachel! You may have conceived, but I wouldn't get too excited about it. This is your first child . . . you're older . . . and well . . . as a Naditu woman there's no telling what could go wrong."

Refusing to expose myself to another moment of their negativity, I rose, grabbed my cloak and left without a word. It didn't occur to me to look at Jacob. Long ago I had given up on his coming to my defense.

Leah was sobbing. I could hear her complaining as I opened the door to leave. "Now that Rachel's pregnant I'll never get a moment alone with you, Jacob."

Laban's booming voice cried out. "Just where do you think you're going? Come back here this instant!"

As I slammed the door behind me a gust of wind rushed up to greet me, swallowing his words. Bracing myself against the wind, I thought of Jacob. He was right. A storm was brewing. How could he be so wise about so many things, yet so dense when it came to father and Leah. I pulled my cloak down around me. I preferred to battle the wind, rather than the fear and doubts Laban and Leah were trying to infect me with.

I lingered for a moment outside the door, hoping Jacob would follow. But he didn't come. Even the wind was against me as I made my way through the darkness to our tent. What a family they were! Let Jacob stay with them, if he wanted. I'd had enough!

I smiled wryly as I reached our tent and stepped inside. Perhaps it was more than riches Jacob wanted to amass. Maybe he enjoyed Laban and Leah's company. I sat down heavily on our bed.

I don't know how long I sat there staring in the darkness, but after what seemed like an eternity the tent flap opened and Jacob stepped inside. "Are you here, Rachel?"

"Yes." I answered calling through the darkness.

Jacob approached the oil lamp, and lit it. "What are you doing sitting here alone in the dark?" he inquired cautiously.

"I'd rather sit here alone than be in that house! How could you stay with them after the way father and Leah spoke to me?"

Annoyance building inside him, Jacob replied, "Please Rachel, don't be unreasonable! It's been so much better between us. I don't want to quarrel. Your father and Leah are only thinking of you! You are a Naditu woman! And you do have to be careful!"

"Really Jacob!! Can't you see through them? They only want to spoil my joy. I'll be fine so long as you keep them away from me!"

"You're being too hard on them Rachel!" said Jacob sighing heavily.

"Oh Jacob! Can't you see? Leah isn't happy for me! You saw her face when she heard I was pregnant."

"How can you say such a thing, Rachel? Leah's your sister, and the mother of my children. She's experienced in child birth and very worried about you. She and your father were only expressing their concern. You were very ungrateful. It hurt their feelings your leaving the way you did."

"Ungrateful! Concern! If that's concern, why does it feel so awful?" I retorted testily. "That may be your idea of concern, but it feels to me like they only want to frighten me and have me doubt myself!"

"Don't be so suspicious!" replied Jacob in exasperation. "You're looking for problems! This is a special occasion for all of us! It's only right we share it with your family."

"I've shared enough with my sister!" I declared in exasperation. "Must I share this with her as well?"

"Don't be so petty, Rachel!"

"I'm not being petty. I'm being truthful. I shared my good news with them and it didn't bring me any joy. This pregnancy is very special to me. I've waited many years for it. I don't want it spoiled."

"They're just worried about you. Let them get used to it. They'll come around. It was a surprise for all of us after so many years." said Jacob, his voice deepening with emotion as he spoke.

My heart went out to him. "Were you surprised, Jacob? Are you pleased?"

Jacob's face softened. He came over to me at once and rubbed my belly proudly. "Of course, I am! I'm absolutely ecstatic! This is the child I have always longed for! I want to shout the glad news to the stars. There's so much to be thankful for. I finished the harvesting today. Return with me a while? I'll take tomorrow off. We can be alone all day. Laban, the old miser, said he's going to open his best wine. Please join us? It would make it such a special party! Do it for me!"

Listening to Jacob I had to smile. He could coax me into anything. Softened by the look in his eye, I nodded in acquiescence putting on my cloak. "Alright! I'll return with you, if it will make you happy. But I warn you, I'm going to leave the moment they give me any trouble."

The storm had begun in earnest. Lightning crackled lighting up the night. The rain was coming down in torrents. We were drenched by the time we got inside.

Jacob opened wide the door, so all could see the thundering sky. He called Laban excitedly. "Look at that storm, Laban! It hasn't rained like this in years. It's Yahweh's blessing! Praise be to God! We brought in the last of the harvest before it began!"

Laban came and stood beside Jacob grinning, without so much as a glance at me. Putting his arm around Jacob's shoulders, he said, "You may call it your God, or mine, what does it matter? It was good timing and fine work, son! We're an excellent team!"

Then he ushered Jacob over to the corner of the room where he kept his special stash of wine. I stood just inside the door dripping wet. Alone once more, I had to ask myself what I was doing here. Father had Jacob locked in conversation. Neither of them showed the least concern for me. Leah was sitting alone sulking beside the fire. All the children had gone to bed.

I turned in resignation, and closed the door against the menacing storm. I was just about to take my cloak off, when Bilhah appeared. Spying me, she came rushing over.

"Congratulations, Mistress Rachel! I just heard the wonderful news. I'm so happy for you. But look here, you're dripping wet. Let me have your cloak. Go stand by the fire. Then I want a big hug."

It was a pleasant relief to see Bilhah. I needed her generous hug to take the chill off the room. No sooner had our embrace ended, than Zilpah called her to tuck the children in bed. With Bilhah gone, I was left alone again standing awkwardly beside the fire. I looked around hoping for something to distract me. Mother's copper mirror gleamed in the corner of the room catching my eye. To avoid having to sit beside Leah, I walked over to its shining surface and peered within.

I hadn't seen my reflection since the Nefilim's visit. The change was startling. There was a new happiness in my eyes, that made me smile. With nothing else to do I continued gazing into the mirror's burnished surface. I could see the entire room in it. Leah was still pouting beside the fire, but the storm of her rage appeared to have passed. Laban had Jacob engrossed in conversation, expounding on his plans for their future. The old fox had had a bit too much wine, and in his enthusiasm his voice swelled. "Don't be a fool! Stay on with me, son! Why go home a pauper with your tail between your legs? Our flocks have increased fortyfold. The wheat and the barley crop have been excellent again this year. With the drought going on everywhere around us, we can get anything we ask for it. The stable is full of camels, and we have all the donkeys we could use."

"But there's more to wealth than livestock! I started purchasing gold some years back. The new coins aren't worth a thing any more. Let the lame brains hold on to that devalued coinage. I collect only the purest gold and silver. Gold is a useful tool for those wise enough to possess it, and an object of envy for those who don't. Gold fixes the rate of all the other values and currencies. You can hold men at your mercy with gold and become their master. Gold can buy anyone, even the most independent and rebellious of men. I only take payment in the purest gold and silver for all my services."

"Still it's wise not to put all your eggs in one basket. So I increase my land holdings whenever I can. This year I'm taking over old Jessup's farm. The poor fool hasn't been able to keep up on his payments. I'm getting it for a song thanks to my connections with the Brotherhood. I tell you they're smart. They know just what to do. They call it the peaceful conquest of a nation through debt."

"Oh! Livestock are fine, but they're too much work. It's gold and land that bring influence and power. Stay on with me and we'll become great landowners. With your blessing and my connections there's no end to what we can achieve together. We'll both be stinking rich."

Jacob was listening to Laban with fascination. "That may be true, uncle. But there are more important things." he said thoughtfully.

"More important things! Like what?" asked Laban incredulously. "You can't be serious!"

"Like following the will of Yahweh . . . and walking in the footsteps of my forebears!" said Jacob proudly.

Laban looked disappointed for a moment. Then he added. "Well, of course! But you can't rely on the Gods for everything. A man has to help himself. I know you have to leave someday. But why be in a hurry to face your brother's wrath? Gold and riches would improve your status, son. With them your brother would have to respect you, and you'll be better able to accomplish the will of your God."

Slapping Jacob on the back, Laban continued in a lower voice. "Consider your future wisely. You have many mouths to feed, and more on the way. You have your Lord's blessing, but you have to be well connected in this life as well. I have some important friends I'd like you to meet. Oh, you know Zaltan, Nimah, Ham, and the others, but there are those even higher up who have taken an interest in you on account of the oracle at the temple. Prosperity is in the air! I can smell it. If you're wise you'll meet them soon. It's necessary to be on good terms with them, if you want to be wealthy . . . really wealthy."

A chill went through me to see Jacob so intent on Laban's words. Who were these important friends? As if to confirm my own worst fears Laban suddenly looked around suspiciously, then continued in a whisper.

This was Laban's idea of a festive party to welcome my son into the world! Now that I was pregnant I was more determined than ever to leave.

When I looked back in the mirror, a veil of smoke seemed to cover its gleaming surface. I tried to wipe it off, but it was to no avail. The haze seemed to be on the inside of the mirror. Did mother's mirror have magical properties? Staring into it a scene opened up within. The mirror had darkened, but the scene was clear. It was Laban's private study behind the house. The one he had built on after his sons' birth. His fiendish oracle was glowing in its place on the altar. Laban entered and knelt before the demonic skull. How strange! The old fox was in the room behind me. I could hear him offering Jacob another cup of wine. Nonetheless, I could see him in the mirror lifting up a wooden plank from the floor in front of his ghoulish skull. He was removing something from a hiding place beneath the floor. I gasped out loud. It was the terafim!

The scene faded at the sound of my cry. Now all I could see in the mirror was the reflection of Laban and Jacob behind me. They looked alarmed. I turned around to face Laban's questions.

"What are you doing at the mirror, you vain girl? Why did you cry out? Get away from there this instant!" he insisted.

Glancing at Jacob, he continued, "You can't be too careful with these Naditu when they're pregnant. Anything can set them off."

I moved away from the mirror. This had been an important get together after all! I'd finally learned where the crafty old magician hid the terafim. Laban rose, looking annoyed.

"Don't worry about me." I said, struggling to formulate an answer. "I'm just a bit on edge. I'm tired and a little sensitive these days."

Jacob came and stood beside me. Putting his arm around my shoulder, he said to Laban. "Don't be hard on Rachel, Laban! You know women's ways."

"Well said, son!" father replied in a jovial voice slapping Jacob on the back.

"But stay away from that mirror, Rachel! I don't want you getting yourself all riled up." said Laban with a patronizing smile.

It was a mild winter that year. Jacob insisted that Reuben was old enough to take over the flocks. I missed the peace and freedom of roaming the hillsides with the sheep. Though I had more time with Bilhah and the boys. When I began feeling nauseous in the morning and the weather cooled, I was glad for the change in my routine. There was a new kind of freedom. One day flowed into the next, each one possessing its own unique rhythm and character. When the weather was favorable, I took long walks to my favorite places along the Balikh. When the weather was foul I remained inside spinning, and weaving, and dreaming of my son. When I closed my eyes I could feel the Shining One smiling down on me.

The months of my ripening were a sweet hallowed time filled with surprises, expectancy, and hope. The primordial process of life bearing, the Goddess's most potent initiation, was taking root. No longer was my body my own. I had to learn to move over and make room inside, as my bodily functions seemed to take on a new self-will and determination all their own. I learned to follow the dictates of my instincts, and listen to the wisdom of the Ancient One who wakened deep inside me.

I was one with the pulse of life, taken over by my body which spoke to me in insistent moods and urges. My senses were sharpened. Many a time my awareness would be carried away in a waking dream state as I learned to resonate with the nascent life within. Never had I possessed so vital a connection to the Mother of all Life. I was one with the river of life, drifting to a primordial rhythm and song.

More than ever I longed for the camaraderie of the women's circle. But Laban and Jacob were both adamant I not get involved in such foolish antiquated practices. They wouldn't even let me visit my Aunt Tamar in Brak. Still the wisdom of the Mother could not be denied. It surfaced in my dreams and reveries, directing me in the specific use of a plant, or stone to aid me.

My ripening mirrored the great cycle of nature. The long winter months of my pregnancy were the most bittersweet, coinciding with the moons of my morning sickness. But I knew that, like winter, my nausea was a purification process discharging toxins and slowing me down to nurture the life within. When spring arrived I too was showing off my budding fruit. Never had the passage of time seemed so sacred, as day by day my body swelled with life, rounding like the moon.

As my time approached the Great Mother blessed me with the marks of initiation, writing in magic script upon my body. Tiny white circles blossomed forth, like a legion of full moons on my swelling breasts, to announce the presence of my milk. When my belly rounded the Goddess drew a line the color of dark rich earth from my navel down to the gate of life, outlining the path my son would take into this world.

Joseph was with me always. I could feel the sweetness of his presence as I fashioned his swaddling blankets and baby clothes from the softest virgin wool. Jacob and I built a birthing tent adjoining ours. From the seventh moon I spoke to him in the cooing language of a dove as I rubbed my belly. He would answer in a kicking language all his own. The crest of my excitement came during the final moon of my pregnancy. It seemed then I never slept. I lay awake in bed each night in ecstatic oneness with my son.

But every crest has its trough, and in the wee hours of the morning the wise women call the hour of the wolf, I would lie awake contemplating Joseph's birth. Sometimes a shadow would cross my heart like an ominous cloud blocking out the sun. In those shadowed moments Leah and Laban's fearsome muttering would echo in my mind, and I would remember the tales told in the women's circle in my youth. I could hear the whispers, like the hiss of an ancient fire blowing in the wind, repeating over and over. BIRTHING FOR A NADITU WOMAN IS LIKE TRYING TO CATCH A STAR.

The bright of day would soothe my fears away. Hadn't the Shining One told me my higher purpose was to raise our son? A wrestling match with death was a small price to pay for bringing a Star child into the world. All the more so, when it was dear Joseph tucked beneath my heart.

As we approached the scorching heat of summer Leah was the first to give birth. Wavy lines of heat rose above the torrid ground on her birthing day. Of course Laban was delivering her child. All seemed to be going well, when I heard a blood curdling scream issue from her tent. Fearing for my sister's life I ran to see what was the matter.

Father and his Brothers from the temple were just departing. Laban pushed his way past me without a word, wiping his dripping brow. His Brothers followed murmuring beneath their breath. "Glad that's over! Such a temperament that woman has! Takes after her father."

I entered the birth tent in time to catch the end of Leah's fit. Her face contorted in disgust, she was shoving her precious bundle at Zilpah. "Here! You take her!"

Seeing me at the door merely fanned her fire.

"Look who's here! How dare you show your face! The very culprit who's responsible! It's all your fault I had a girl! You talked me into taking the mandrake. Why did I listen to you? The Goddess has never favored me. After all this all I get for my travail is a worthless daughter. Take her away, Zilpah! Get her out of my sight. She's a reminder of my foolishness. I never should have taken that mandrake!"

Zilpah's face was pale and drawn, as she looked back and forth between us, not knowing what to do. At last in desperation, she pleaded, "Don't make me take the child away, Mistress Leah. You're her mother! You haven't even named her yet."

"I'll name her! If you promise to get her out of my sight!" Leah replied in anger.

Zilpah nodded obediently.

"I'll call her, Dinah which means judged, because Yahweh has judged me harshly giving me a girl. He's punishing me for the mandrake. Now take her away! I don't want to look at her! All she is is a reminder to me of Yahweh's punishment! Now go!"

Futile as it seemed, I approached Leah's bed hoping to reason with her. "Please reconsider! Take her to your breast. The baby needs you."

"How dare you speak to me about her?" she bellowed. "Get out! Get out of here this instant! You did this to me!"

I continued in desperation. "Look how beautiful and healthy she is. And you already have four boys!"

Leah turned on me in fury, "What makes you think I want another beauty around? Leave me in peace! Get out here both of you!"

Zilpah fled with the little one, who had begun screaming. The infant's cries pierced my heart, and I couldn't resist. "She's crying for you." I pleaded.

Leah turned her back on me screaming at the top of her lungs. "Leave me alone!"

"Then let me have her?" I asked imploringly. "I'll care for her as though she were my own."

Leah turned around to look at me, her face contorted with rage. "You'll do nothing of the kind! Don't you dare touch her! You've done enough to ruin things! Now get out of my sight! Curses on you and your little brat!"

Leah already had four sons. I couldn't understand why she was so unhappy to have a daughter? Dinah had been conceived using the mandrake. The mark of the Goddess was all about her. I was thrilled to have such a girl in the family at last. I prayed Leah would relent. But she was filled with bitterness and so depressed, she covered herself in ashes begging Yahweh's forgiveness. Jacob was too concerned with the irrigation of the summer crops, and Joseph's forthcoming birth to give the matter much heed. All my protective instincts were aroused on behalf of the tiny girl. It broke my heart to see a child of the Goddess treated so poorly. I wanted to take Dinah to my breast, but Leah watched me like an owl with eyes at the back of her head.

Finally, even Jacob chafed under the strain of Leah's moods. His temper began flaring with the heat, as Laban and Leah instilled fear and doubt in him, packing his mind full of frightening birth stories about Naditu women.

I was confident all would go well and Joseph would be born with the rising of Kak.Si.Di. As the time drew near She Who Watches whispered in my ear. HAVE FAITH, MY DAUGHTER! COURAGE AND LOVE BELONG TOGETHER. MOTHERHOOD WILL TEACH YOU JUST HOW CLOSELY THEY'RE INTERTWINED. MOTHERHOOD DEMANDS THE STRENGTH AND CONSTANT VIGILANCE OF THE WARRIOR. THE WARRIOR WOMAN IS THE OTHER SIDE OF THE COMPASSIONATE MOTHER FULL OF LOVE.

The Goddess's words rang with truth, stirring my primal depths and jolting me into a new awareness. With the warrior in me aroused, Laban and Leah's stories couldn't touch me. What did it matter that father wouldn't allow the wise women to deliver my son? I stood ready. She Who Watches was guiding this birth. Joseph would come the day the light came down, and Kak.Si.Di. rose along with the sun. This year the rising of the brightest star of heaven coincided with the full moon. In my bones I knew this was the day my son would be born. As the time approached a bevy of doves began clustering around Joseph's birth tent.

The sharp pains of labor began in the wee hours of that glorious day. Jolted awake, I knew the time had come. Like a warrior preparing for battle, I began the panting breath familiar to me from helping Bilhah.

When the pain intensified I went to fetch her, and we moved into the birthing tent. There was no point in waking Jacob. My waters were still intact and this could go on for hours. I was ecstatic through the wrenching spasms. For with every pain I knew that Joseph was making his way to me.

Jacob awoke with an anguished start. Finding I was missing, he came running into the birthing tent. I was dripping with sweat, and must have looked ghastly, as. Jacob cried out. "You're pale as the moon, Rachel! Why didn't you wake me? Let me get your father! He's experienced in these matters."

I gritted my teeth in determination. "Don't you dare call my father! Everything will go well, if you leave him out of it!"

I reached out to Jacob pleading. "Promise me you won't let Laban near me all day! Promise me, Jacob, or I'll never forgive you!"

Beads of sweat broke out on Jacob's face to see me so distressed. "Very well!"

I smiled gratefully. "There's one more thing, Jacob. Would you please roll up the side of the tent? I could use some fresh air, and the sunrise would be an inspiration."

Jacob rolled up the tent. The sight of the stars renewed my courage. Jacob kissed me on the forehead, gladdened by my expression."

"It's just a matter of time now, Jacob. There's nothing to worry about. All will go well. I promise. Please go peacefully about your day, just keep Laban and Leah away from me. Bilhah will call for you when it's time to see our son."

Jacob looked none too reassured. "I don't want to leave you, Rachel. I couldn't bear it if anything went wrong. There must be something I can do!"

"You can believe in me, Jacob!" I said looking him directly in the eye. "And have faith that you will see our son today."

Jacob bent over me, kissing me tenderly on the forehead. "I believe in you, Rachel. It's just that I've been hearing such frightful stories about Naditu women giving birth."

I started frowning.

"I'll put them out of my mind this minute if it will please you." said Jacob patting my hand. "And I'll pray to Yahweh that all will go well."

A burden lifted to hear Jacob. "That's right! There's no use fretting! It just makes for strain between us. And that's what Laban and Leah want."

"Don't worry! Leave everything to me. I know how I can get Laban away from here. He's been after me for several moons to meet with some of his cronies. I'll tell him I will go with him this very morning. That way we can keep your labor a secret until after the birth. Would that please you?"

I was anything but pleased to hear that Jacob would be meeting more of Laban's Brothers. But at least it would keep Laban at a safe distance. He had the most uncanny way of knowing what was going on. I didn't want him or his cronies anywhere near this birth. So I nodded, my labor pains intensifying.

Seeing my difficulty, Bilhah took Jacob by the arm and steered him out of the tent. Dawn was glimmering in the eastern sky. A gentle breeze came wafting in, cooling down my heated brow. A white dove followed it, and perched on my herb chest in the corner.

"You have a guest, Mistress Rachel, and it's not dawn yet." said Bilhah brightly.

I nodded as she rubbed me down with a cool cloth.

"It's going to be a beautiful day to welcome your little one!"

I looked up at the sky. I always felt better when I could see the starry reaches. I was not alone. Kak.Si.Di. was gleaming on the horizon, as I said my prayer. HAIL KAK.SI.DI., YOUR BLESSING IS UPON ME. EVER VIRGIN GATE OF HEAVEN, BRIGHTEST OF THE STARS, I OPEN MY WOMB TO THEE. GUARDIAN OF THE WATERS, MEASURER OF THE SEA, RELEASE MY BIRTH WATERS, AND BRING MY PRECIOUS SON TO LIFE IN THEE.

Soon after my waters broke and a peaceful calm came over my entire body. Even the pain of labor receded for a time.

"That was a beautiful prayer." said Bilhah glowing. "Allow me to rub you with this water from the Balikh. I got it for you yesterday. I wanted you to have some for your labor. I'll never forget what that water meant to me in my hour of need."

Sharp pains were taking over again, and I was unable to respond. I looked up at the mandrake root hanging over the bed. It was glowing with a rosy light. Everything was going to be alright. The sun was up now and Kak.Si.Di. was beginning to fade from view. I blew a farewell salute to the Goddess's star. I was no stranger to pain. And this time the pain had meaning. I was in service to Ninhursag, Her holy warrior, fulfilling Her purpose on Earth. Mother had taught me not to resist pain, but to go with it. The Goddess would do the rest, like when I swam in the Balikh allowing the current to carry me. These birth pains were the rapids in the great river of life bringing Joseph to me.

The pain of labor stretched me on every level, heightening my sensitivity to fever pitch. I deepened my breathing to steady myself. Joseph and I were in good hands. Bilhah was devoted to me. She stood beside me steady as a rock attuned to my every breath. Gratitude and love were in her every gesture.

Aunt Tamar arrived mid morning, sailing into my birth tent like an angel sent from on high.

"Dear child, I've been dreaming of you for days. You were calling out to me, and I knew that I was needed. I came as soon as I could get away."

Aunt Tamar had arrived at the perfect moment. I was too weak to talk, but I looked up at her with gratitude as she took my hand.

The Goddess was shining through her eyes, when she said, "I told you your time would come. Don't weary yourself trying to speak. I brought some herbs from the Mountain of the Gods. They'll open your womb."

Spying the dove in the corner of the tent, she continued, "I see the Goddess watches over you. There's nothing to fear. Kak.Si.Di. rose with the sun this morning. Today is the full moon, and the longest day of the year. With so much light issuing from heaven, it's bound to be a most auspicious day. This child of yours must be very special!"

The intensity of my labor increased with the sun as it climbed higher in the sky. I kept my eye on the dove in the corner of the tent, until the light became so blinding it appeared to vanish.

"The sun is so intense, Mistress Rachel. Shall I close down the tent? I fear it's too much for you." inquired Bilhah solicitously.

I was riding the pain but motioned Bilhah to leave things as they were. The light was blinding, but I didn't want it dimmed. In the blinding light I could feel the presence of the Shining Nefilim. The light became so intense it seemed to penetrate my flesh. My entire body began to vibrate.

BIRTH OF THE STAR CHILD

As Aunt Tamar stroked my brow with a cool wet cloth, I heard Bilhah cry. "You're dilating quickly now! It won't be long!"

I struggled to lift my head. The rosy light of the mandrake was shining in a perfect circle around my bed. My breathing deepened, as Bilhah helped me up onto my haunches. I squatted down resting on her shoulders for support. I started feeling faint and weightless like I was drifting away. Aunt Tamar stroked my back bringing me back to Earth. Then she put her arms around me. Bilhah pressed down on my shoulders. Stuffing a rag in my mouth, she shouted, "Push, Mistress Rachel! Push! Your baby's coming! But you have to fight for him!"

The Goddess was speaking to me through Bilhah's words. The warrior in me was aroused. I bit down hard on the rag in my mouth to relieve the tension. I was glad to have it. It gave me something to focus on. This was the Goddess's wrestling match, the greatest struggle of my life. It took every bit of strength and heart that I could muster.

I don't know how long I remained straining with all my might between Tamar and Bilhah. But suddenly, I heard the flutter of a great many wings and Bilhah cry. "I can see the baby's head! It's crowning! . . . It's a boy, Mistress Rachel! . . . A fine healthy boy!"

I collapsed back on the bed, and Bilhah held Joseph up so I could see him. The sun was at its zenith. Doves were flying around like angels everywhere inside the tent. Light glowed around the squirming infant like a halo. My heart stretched just to see him.

Opening wide my arms, I cried, "Welcome, Joseph! Welcome! I love you! Thank the God and Goddess that you're finally here!"

When I held Joseph to my heart, a dove hovered directly above us in the air. I could hear the words of the Shining Nefilim inside my heart. "Well done, Rachel! Peace and blessings to you and our child of light."

"All is well, Mistress Rachel! The birth sack has been delivered. It's all intact." cried Bilhah through tears of joy.

"Congratulations, Rachel! Your mother would be so proud. This bevy of doves. And look! There's a rainbow of many colors arched over the tent. Never have I seen such signs and wonders at a birth!" exclaimed Aunt Tamar.

"Good God!" she continued, her face growing pale. "Your baby doesn't have a shadow! What does it mean, Rachel, that your son doesn't make a shadow!"

Joseph was here at last. He was a miracle of otherness, yet strangely familiar as he squealed with glee inside my arms. Holding him to my heart, I melted into his purity and innocence giving thanks to She Who Watches, and the Shining One. Then we fell asleep together in the radiant light.

PART SIX

Patriarchal Legacy

20

FATHERS AND SONS

THE MANY SIGNS AND WONDERS ACCOMPANYING JOSEPH'S BIRTH DID not go unnoticed. Jacob arrived home with Laban shortly after the birth, scattering the angelic bevy of doves and marvelling at the multicolored rainbow arching over the birth tent. Inquisitive Brother Nimah, and all of father's concubines, had already been drawn by the spectacular sights. Luckily, Aunt Tamar was standing guard outside the tent. I was grateful Bilhah had turned its sides down when we went to sleep, or it would have been impossible to hold back the swarm of intrusive onlookers.

I awoke to the sound of arguing outside our tent. Laban's voice was sharp and quite insistent. "I don't care about any fool promise! You should know better than to make promises to a woman on her birthing bed! They're half-crazed at such times, which is why we men have to take over. Look at this rainbow and those doves! You heard Brother

Nimah. The planets are forming a mystic cross in the sky today. I have to see the child who gives rise to such extravagant displays. He's my own flesh and blood. How dare you keep me from him?"

Joseph was sleeping peacefully on my breast, though my flesh crawled at Laban's insistence. Spent and weak, I gazed up at the mandrake root above my bed and prayed Jacob would find the strength to resist him.

Jacob spoke with new authority. "Rachel is my beloved wife! I fully intend to honor her request. We've waited many long years for this blessing, Laban. You can wait another day. Now I'm going in to see my son. No visitors are allowed until tomorrow. Will you please see to that, Tamar?"

Brother Nimah was the next to speak. "Come now Jacob, the moon is full! There's a mystic cross in the sky today. Rachel's a Naditu woman, like her mother. With such signs you don't have to be a seer to realize the child is special. He shall be a World Server. He belongs to the entire world, not just to you. I shall be his mentor. Laban and I have the right to see him. We want to give him our blessing."

My blood ran cold. Joseph whimpered softly in his sleep. I stroked his back and continued praying.

"You shall do no such thing, Nimah!" responded Jacob angrily. "Yahweh's blessing is upon this child! He needs no other! You may be my sons' teacher, but you are not mine! And I will not have you telling me what to do."

"But you'll follow the dictates of a woman!" interrupted Laban hotly. "You weren't the least bit interested in the proposal my friends made to you in town today. What's the matter with you? Are you getting soft?"

"I'm not getting soft." said Jacob irritably. " I'm getting angry! I could be in there visiting my new son, but I have to be out here instead arguing with the two of you. Now get out of my way! I'm going in to bless my son. If you want to see him tomorrow, you will cease detaining me now."

"Very well!" said Laban in an angry huff. "But I must say my patience is wearing thin."

What was this new intractability in Jacob? I was so proud of him. I was smiling brightly when he entered the tent. His face was strong and glowing as it had in our youth. I looked up at him gratefully as he approached my bed. "I overheard what was going on outside. Thank you, Jacob."

"No, my dearest! It is I who must thank you." said Jacob bending over to look at his son. "Thank you for this wonderful boy, and for standing by me all these years. Laban must be put in his place! Everything came clear to me today. Just about noontime the most amazing thing happened. I was talking to some of your father's cronies from the Black Hand. Ham was there, the High Priest Zaltan, and others I had never met before. Zaltan took out his oracle in an attempt to bully me. It was a hideous glowing skull with ghoulish powers. This sounds incredible, but I think it was connected to demonic beings. When Zaltan spoke to me with his hand on it, he changed right before my eyes. It was like he was possessed. I could hardly breath and my willpower turned to butter. Only calling upon Yahweh returned my strength to me."

"You once mentioned this, Rachel. But I didn't believe it. I knew the Brotherhood was corrupted by greed and power, but I couldn't believe it was an instrument of demonic power. I thank the Lord, my God, that He was with me today. At high noon suddenly an incredible light and grace came flooding down on me. Everything became clear. We must leave here, Rachel! There's no way of dealing with the Black Hand. Those in the higher ranks are all possessed by demons. The underlings are possessed by greed. Dealing with these men is like walking on quicksand. They're always trying to suck you in. First they flatter you, then they lure you in with promises of prestige and wealth, while all the time they sap your spirit dry. I've given the best years of my life to your father, but it's not enough. No matter what I do it's never enough. And in the end everything is always for him, little or nothing for me or anyone else."

Just then Joseph awoke. Jacob took him proudly in his arms and kissed him on both cheeks. Looking into his eyes, he said, "This child is special, Rachel. His birth is quickening my spirit. I can feel it. What shall we call him?"

"Let's call him Joseph, because he shall increase the light and goodness on Earth." I said glowing with love.

Jacob responded his eyes filled with tears of joy. "Then Joseph it shall be, my dearest! I have already been touched by his grace."

As Jacob raised Joseph up to give him his blessing, the rosy light of the mandrake glowed like a circle of protection all around us. BLESSED

ART THOU OH LORD MY GOD, KING OF THE UNIVERSE, GOD OF MY FATHERS ABRAHAM, AND ISAAC. RECEIVE MY NEW SON JOSEPH. BLESS HIM THAT HE MAY ALWAYS GROW IN THE POWER AND WISDOM OF YOUR LOVE. HOLD HIM IN YOUR PROTECTION AND MAKE HIM STRONG THAT HE TOO MAY RESIST THE BROTHERHOOD OF THE BLACK HAND.

When Jacob returned Joseph to me, I held him to my heart, praying silently. OH GREAT MOTHER NINHURSAG, YOU WHO ARE THE EYE OF HEAVEN, WATCH OVER MY DEAR SON JOSEPH AND HOLD HIM IN YOUR LOVE. NOURISH HIM WITH THE SWEET MILK OF YOUR STARS, AS YOU DID THE GREAT KINGS OF OLD. INSPIRE HIM WITH YOUR PASSION FOR TRUTH AND LOVE. KEEP HIM SAFE FROM THE BLACK HAND, AND SPARE HIM FROM THE RIVALRY AND ENVY OF HIS BROTHERS.

GREAT FATHER ENKI, LORD OF WISDOM, COMPASSIONATE TEACHER OF HUMANKIND. BLESS JOSEPH WITH YOUR WISDOM AND GOOD JUDGEMENT. HELP HIM TO BE AN INSPIRED SEER, AND A TRUE HELPER OF HUMANKIND.

NINURTA, GREAT CHAMPION OF HEAVEN AND SON OF SHE WHO WATCHES, BLESS JOSEPH WITH YOUR STRENGTH AND COURAGE. FILL HIM WITH YOUR POWER THAT HE MAY BE A RESOLUTE PROTECTOR OF HUMANKIND.

GREAT FATHER GOD, YAHWEH, LORD OF MY HUSBAND JACOB AND HIS FOREBEARS, BLESS MY SON JOSEPH. MAKE HIM A TOOL OF YOUR RIGHTEOUSNESS IN THE TRADITION OF ABRAHAM YOUR PROPHET. INSPIRE HIM TO BE A POSITIVE EXAMPLE TO HIS BROTHERS.

The struggle of my entire lifetime had brought me to this. Joseph was my precious gift from on high, my long awaited Star child. My spirit soared even to look at him. Into my son I would pour the best I could provide. So there would be at least one patriarchal man whose heart was balanced in the wisdom and love of the God and Goddess. One man of honor above the seductions of wealth, power, and the momentary pleasures of the flesh.

Joseph truly was a magical child. Unspeakable love flowed from his deep pools of eyes. His bright spirit, his brilliant wit, and gentle heart revealed to me the wisdom of the stars, that I too might remember from

whence I came. Mischievous little imp! Wise little sage! Child of spirit as
well as flesh, Joseph embodied the best of both worlds. Fruit of the harvest moon and the magical mandrake, Joseph's feet were planted firmly
on the earth, though his profound attunement to spirit caused him ever
to seek the stars. Offspring of the shining Nefilim, Joseph's angel spirit
shone through all his deeds. Like a fine gem reflecting the cosmic rays of
heaven, he fascinated all those who came to know him. Drawing out of
each their best, or worst, according to the fault lines of their character.

Heaven knows, it isn't easy to be a priest or priestess called to serve
the Gods as their connecting link. You are in the hands of Higher Powers and must ever seek to be attentive to their will and purpose, not your
own. Yet to be a priestess and a mother is a greater burden still. Your
inner vision soars upon the vigilant wings of a mother's heart, and cou-
ples with the protective fears etched inside a mother's bones. The trials
of motherhood alone are more than ample challenge. Each mother is the
Goddess's tool that fashions her child's flesh and blood. She is also her
child's instrument of fate, their ground of being, and primary experience
of the world. Already carrying such an enormous weight of responsibility, what mother would also seek to know in advance the trials and tribu-
lations her young must face?

Having lived within the treacherous bosom of my family, I did not
need the Nefilim to tell me that Joseph's life would be difficult and haz-
ardous. I already knew quite well the burden his difference would exact. I
had been the victim of enormous awe and admiration, and knew quite
well that such extravagant love was ravenous and carried envy and hatred in its wake. Armed with such hard won knowledge, how was I to
prepare my son for the hardships of life? All I could do was to strengthen
Joseph's will and affirm his belief in himself. I also trained him in the art
of inner sight from the time that he was young. Knowing full well the
gift of sight was a double edged sword that could heal or maim its pos-
sessor. Then I sought to build in him a faith in the Divine Plan.

From the very first it was evident that Joseph was Jacob's favorite,
which of course, bred enormous rivalry and contention among Jacob's
many sons. Every evening when we sat down to table, Reuben, Levi,
Simeon, and Judah fought bitterly between themselves about who would
sit at Jacob's right. As everyone knew the seat to his left was always saved

for Joseph. I watched with a heavy heart the beginnings of yet another envious rivalry growing in our midst.

My rivalry with Leah had been healed. Though Leah's rivalry intensified to fever pitch, when Dinah's birth was followed by the birth of such a son to me. Joseph so far outshone Leah's boys, their shadows were revealed in the starkest terms. All Leah could do was glower at me with envy at the end of her long line of sons. While I, with Joseph on my lap, was given the most favored status beside Jacob. With little to play off from me, Leah now carried on her vicious rivalry through her sons.

One evening when Joseph was almost four Simeon started in with his usual gripes after we finished the dinner blessing. "There you go again, father, always giving Joseph the choicest piece of meat. He's only a baby on his mother's lap, yet you always give him the finest portion."

"This refrain of yours has to stop, Simeon!" answered Jacob wearily. "Everyone receives equal portions in this family. It's only your imagination that sees disparity. Be grateful there's enough for everyone, and stop this petty bickering!"

A grim silence came over the table.

Joseph pushed his plate across to Simeon. "Here brother! You can have my meat. I'll have yours."

The triumphant look on Simeon's face was more than I could bear, as he snatched up Joseph's plate and began eating. I was afraid Joseph's noble nature put him at a disadvantage with his self-serving brothers. But I remained silent, afraid to make matters worse.

Jacob looked over at Joseph, saying, "That wasn't necessary, Joseph."

"Oh father, please don't be cross with me. It doesn't matter what piece I get. I want my brother to be happy."

Smirking disbelief covered the faces of Leah's sons. Making no attempt to cover their malice, they all began, as if on cue, exchanging plates like in a game laughing and making fun of Joseph. I looked away hoping to avoid their mischief.

While Jacob exclaimed, "You find this so amusing! I'm ashamed of all of you! Your foolish antics only make Joseph's heart appear the larger."

Jacob's remark was answered by an embarrassed silence. The boys' plates stopped rotating.

I had started eating again, when Joseph inquired innocently. "What does disparity mean, father?"

Jacob turned toward Joseph with a smile. As he answered Joseph's question, Leah's boys began laughing and whispering among themselves. "Disparity is when things are not equal, son."

Jacob loved teaching his sons. It was wonderful seeing his loving patience finally being turned to one who appreciated it. The noise the older boys were making made it impossible for Joseph to hear.

Jacob was forced to repeat himself. "Disparity is when things are not equal."

"Then there must be a lot of disparity in the world, father. No two things are ever exactly equal, are they?" inquired Joseph thoughtfully.

His brothers howled with laughter.

Jacob turned toward Leah's sons, and bellowed, "Quiet down! We're trying to converse!"

Then smiling down at Joseph, he said, "You certainly are the little sage."

"What's a sage, father?"

"A sage is one distinguished by wisdom, and sound judgment, son." replied Jacob with pleasure.

"Then I want to be a sage when I grow up." said Joseph with enthusiasm. "For I love to learn and ponder things."

Jacob chuckled at Joseph's reply. His pleasure was more than the older boys could bear. Immediately they began making silly odd noises to distract the conversation. Jacob was infuriated. Staring at Simeon, their ringleader, he raised his voice, "Settle down! Can't there ever be any polite conversation at this table? Why don't you stop laughing, and listen to your brother? You might learn something. We were talking about disparity. And if you ask me there's a great disparity between Joseph and you older boys, and it's not merely one of age! You should all be ashamed of yourselves! Joseph is better behaved at the table than the whole lot of you! You act like asses!"

Leah's boys quieted down, and sat with sullen looks of hatred on their faces. No one said a word, but Simeon and Levi glared resentfully at Joseph.

Joseph started wilting before my eyes. I put my arms around him, and glared at Simeon and Levi hoping to shame them. Suddenly my vision narrowed. Everything felt as though it was slowing down. I saw Simeon and Levi as grown men. They were splattered with blood and dipping a rainbow colored garment in a pool of blood. I began to feel sick, and a shudder went through my entire body. Joseph felt it, and looked up at me with piercing eyes.

Trying to force a smile I whispered softly so no one could hear. "Don't let your brothers' mean spirits make you sad, Joseph. The God and Goddess love you."

Leah was fuming at the far end of the table. She stood up and began venting in a shrill voice. "You're not being fair, Jacob! Rachel can whisper all she wants to Joseph, but my boys are not allowed. You always take Joseph's side. Come boys! Let's go! Why should we take this kind of treatment in our own home?"

I was relieved to see Leah's boys file out behind her one by one like meek little lambs. I wanted to laugh, but Jacob had stopped eating and was looking despondent, his head in his hands.

Laban had been observing all of this in silence. When Leah left he said, "Don't take it so hard, Jacob! The moon is down, and Leah's in a foul mood today. In a day or two she'll have her moon change, and that will be the end of it. You know how women are! They're as ill tempered and changeable as the wind."

"It's more than just her moonchange, Laban!" replied Jacob with a downcast face.

"Perhaps you're right!" said Laban shaking his head. "Even I'm finding it hard having her around these days. It's impossible to have a peaceful meal in this house anymore. I'll have to have a conversation with her. Hopefully, I can talk some sense into her."

It vexed me to hear Laban go on so about women in front of the children. But at least he was admitting the truth about Leah for once. Jacob was relieved by Laban's remark, and resumed eating.

I looked around the table to my right. Dan and Naphtali had such simple good natures, they didn't even appear to have noticed what had happened. I squeezed Joseph's hand in mine, whispering in his ear. "Don't act the way Leah's boys do with your father, Joseph!

And you already know better than Laban. You know to judge a person by what's in their heart, not by whether they're a man or a woman."

Joseph looked at me with his wise eyes. "Of course, mother!" Then he resumed eating.

I looked over at Dinah. Poor Dinah! No one ever paid attention to her. Her pretty face had paled, and she was looking forlorn. But when I smiled at her she perked up like a flower given water. I beckoned her to continue eating, and spoke in a soothing voice. "Don't worry, dear! I'll put you to bed after dinner. I'll bring Joseph. We'll have story time together."

If Leah found out she'd be furious, but I didn't care. The joy and gratitude on Dinah's face were my reward.

Leah and her boys were not the only ones with eyes fastened on my son. Laban was interested in him as well. Joseph's gifted nature was something the old magician could not fail to see. He called it an alignment of the stars and watched Joseph's development with a careful musing eye. I was thankful Laban never had much time for children, or I fear he might have tried to take Joseph under his wing.

Fortunately Laban wasn't around much anymore. He'd stay at the Sin temple for days at a time, carrying with him a dark smoky crystal in the shape of a human hand. When he was home he kept it on a shelf inside his private chapel beside his fearsome skull. It was always a relief when he was gone, but there was still much cause to worry. Rumors were spreading like wildfire throughout town. Curious rumors of a miracle that hadn't occurred since the days of old. Rumor said Sin would be returning. The very idea spread terror in my soul. Sin and his fallen angels had been instigators of the wars of gods and men, and contributed to the demise of Sumer. Would he ruin Haran as well?

For as long as I could remember, Zaltan, father, and the other priests, had been praying for Sin's return. But now when Laban was in his cups he boasted that when the coffers of the Ehulhul temple were full, Sin would be returning. Was it possible? Would the Brotherhood's prayers be answered? I had to speak to Jacob. He had Laban's confidence, perhaps he would know.

Jacob had languished on at the farm with no clear sense of direction until Joseph's birth. His responsibility as a provider enslaving him. Over the years his visionary side had suffered great neglect. But Jacob was inspired by Joseph's birth. Contact with his new son fired his spirit, and he now spoke of our departure. Jacob could see his own spiritual promise in Joseph. All his hopes and dreams were renewed through the little one. Jacob had many sons, but it was plain to see Joseph was the only one who shone with the light of heaven. Jacob regarded me differently now.

He no longer spoke of the Naditu Sisterhood with disdain. He even sought me out to discuss things with instead of Laban, and listened with interest as he'd done when we were young.

Joseph was drawn to the stars from the time that he could walk. Like me, he felt most at home beneath the canopy of heaven. The winter of his seventh year was unusually mild, giving us ample opportunity to study Kak.Si.Di. Every evening after dinner Joseph and I would sit out in what had once been mother's garden and watch the brightest star of heaven. We enjoyed sitting there and talking, perusing the sky until he fell asleep. Always a quick learner, Joseph could identify the entire zodiac of stars by the time he was five, pointing out all the constellations under the changing sky from Nisannu to Addaru.

Jacob came upon us as we sat outside one evening. Spying us in the garden, he called out. "Is that you and Joseph, Rachel? I've been looking for you everywhere."

"Yes! We're here!" I said smiling as he approached.

"Would you like me to carry him to bed for you?" Jacob inquired, noticing Joseph was fast asleep.

"In a little while." I said. "Come sit with me a spell. It's been so long since we sat here together under the stars."

Pleased by my invitation, Jacob sat down beside me on our old familiar bench. Sitting together there awakened pleasant memories. I looked into Jacob's eyes. They were filled with deep yearning and touched my heart. I couldn't help but reminisce. "Do you remember when we used to sit here every night, so we could be alone together? It's been too long since we sat here under the stars."

"Yes! It has been too long since we've had time like that." said Jacob sighing. "There's always something that needs to be done. These days I'm spending all my time trying to figure out how to leave here. Do you remember how we used to sit here together night after night sharing all our hopes and dreams?"

It was delightful to hear Jacob musing. There was so much I could have said, but motherhood and age had taught me to be patient and gentle.

"One of our dreams is asleep beside us now." I said smiling. "But I know what you mean, Jacob. We've stayed on here too long."

I held my breath, afraid Jacob would get defensive.

Jacob only sighed. "I've been thinking the same thing, Rachel. I've wanted to leave ever since Joseph's birth. But your father knows how to play on my sympathies. He's an expert at finding ways to keep me here for one more season. It's curious! Haran for all its given me, has also taken something away. Please understand! I'm glad I came! What would I ever do without you and Joseph? But I've allowed myself to get too comfortable here."

There were tears of joy in my eyes, as I said, "You have Yahweh's blessing, Jacob. That's all you need! Joseph and I are ready to leave with you any time."

Jacob looked at me with relief. "You don't know how glad I am to hear that. It's taken me too long to understand what I'm up against here. Of course, I still have to convince Leah. But there's great foment in Haran these days. Those higher up in the Brotherhood say Nanna/Sin is returning. Laban and his cronies are all busy preparing for his coming. They've asked me to speak to the people to get them ready for their Lord of Darkness. I've begun instructing the people in the ways of the Lord, my God instead. There's a group of them who want to come with me. Yahweh's their only hope. He's been preparing me for battle with the Evil One."

"Laban's no longer happy with me now that I'm not carrying out his wishes. It's amazing that even though I never stepped inside the Ehulhul temple all these years, he's continued to hope he'd someday reel me in. Now that he senses I'm not going to capitulate, he and the Brotherhood are turning against me. My entire life has led to this decision, Rachel. I have no doubt that what I'm doing is the right thing. But it hurts to see the change in Laban now that he realizes I'm not clay in his hands."

Jacob looked crestfallen. So I said. "Don't allow Laban to distract you! I'm proud you'll stand up to Nanna/ Sin. You're the only one who can. The Brotherhood owns everyone in town through usury. You were wise never to take anything you didn't work for, though father always tried to lure you into debt. Don't take Laban to heart. He's not like other men. Sin's taken him over. Laban no longer has a heart. He merely uses people to augment his power. If he's changed toward you, it's because he can no longer control you, or has outgrown his use for you. He can't tolerate having people around him who think and act for themselves."

Jacob's face brightened. "You're not only beautiful, Rachel, you're wise too. You speak the truth! I would have seen it sooner had my father not abandoned me to my mother. Esau was always father's favorite. He had no use for me. That's why I was taken in by Laban. But now I'm beginning to see the limitations of our relationship."

Kak.Si.Di. twinkled above the crown of Jacob's head. He'd been studying Joseph in the moonlight as he spoke. There were tears in his eyes. Joseph smiled sweetly in his sleep. Had this new clarity been Joseph's gift to his father? I had to smile to think of all the truths our children helped us see.

Never had Jacob admitted his failings to me before. I took his hand in mine, saying tenderly, "You can put Laban behind you. You're stronger now for seeing the truth. Yahweh is with you. You are His chosen one. And fortunately, you're not like your father. You have vision and can see which of your sons is most blessed."

Jacob regarded me with appreciation, relieved that I had been able to receive his vulnerability while still acknowledging his special gifts. I smiled back at him. Who was I to sit in judgment? I knew how hard it was to admit our own mistakes. I had tread that path. The Eye Star was shining brightly in the sky. The blessing of the God and Goddess was upon us. Together we could see the entire picture. Both of us being aligned with the truth would make us stronger. That was why the Higher Marriage was the way to regain the ancient sight.

Jacob opened his heart to me. He put his head on my shoulder, and we cried together in the healing womb of night. If I could forgive Jacob for being taken in by father, perhaps I could also forgive myself.

When our tears were spent, I inquired, "Sin returning strikes fear in me. Do you think it's possible? Could it happen soon?"

Jacob looked me in the eyes. "I only listen to your father to appease him, Rachel! But I've had troubling dreams of late, which speak of tyrannical changes in the town. And in all my dreams Yahweh is preparing me for battle."

"I've also had warning dreams." I confessed.

"You have?" Jacob's face went pale. "It's curious we speak of this tonight. With all this talk of Sin returning I've been remembering scraps of ancestral history from my childhood. Bits and pieces of information mother and father would share with me from time to time. Today I remembered my grandfather Abraham left Ur to escape the forces of Sin. But they pursued him here, which is why he left for Canaan."

"That's very interesting!" I said listening intently.

"Yes! Today in prayer I remembered Abraham would not allow my father to come to Haran to choose a bride for himself. He wouldn't allow my father anywhere near this place. That's why he sent Eleazar, his most trusted steward, in his stead. My eyes are being opened, Rachel. I'm being groomed for a holy purpose. I can feel it in my bones."

"We have to leave for Joseph's sake!" I said gazing down at him on my lap.

It took Jacob only a moment to reply. "I'll speak to Laban tomorrow. The situation must be very grave when we are both having such dreams."

I put my hand on Joseph's head and nodded. I had to keep my son out of harm's way. Jacob had Yahweh's blessing. There was no one else who could stand up to Sin. Gazing up at the Eye Star I prayed Jacob wouldn't let me down this time.

Jacob rose early the next morning to pray before going in to confront Laban. I waited anxiously in bed for his report.

My husband returned a new man. The heaviness of all the years of compromise had fallen from his shoulders. Renewed purpose was in its stead. Increased vigor marked his step, and a newfound lightness was in his heart.

He threw himself down beside me on the bed, and began, "The old fox was still in bed with one of his concubines when I arrived. I was not about to be put off however. I knocked insistently upon his door. He was irate to be awakened so early, but eventually he responded in his hoarse morning voice. After much fuss and bluster he agreed to meet me in the dining room. You know how incapable he is of getting moving in the morning."

Despite the seriousness of our leavetaking, I had to chuckle at Jacob rustling Laban out of bed.

Jacob continued humorously. "The moaning and groaning was endless getting him there. First I had to assure him, that it was indeed important enough to warrant his attention at this time of day. Then I had to bribe him with some of that special coffee the traders brought me from the south. Laban was unshaven and looked like the devil himself when he showed up. But once he had a cup of coffee we got down to the matters at hand."

Jacob sighed heavily as he continued, "I don't know how the old fox does it, but as usual he managed to put me on the defensive. Nonetheless, I got to the point and demanded my release. I told him it was time for me to return home. I reminded him of how well he'd prospered since I came, and how hard I've worked for him. Then I rubbed in the fact that I had stayed on long past the agreed time."

"The old fox fussed and fumed. He even had the audacity to act as though you, and Leah, and all my sons were his. When I would have none of that, he tried intimidating me with Esau's rage. I held my ground. Finally he confessed his oracle had told him Yahweh blessed him on my account. He said he didn't want to anger Yahweh. So he asked me to name my wages, and said I could leave when it was time!"

"I'm so proud of you, Jacob." I said with eyes shining.

"I'm proud of me as well." said Jacob beaming. "I've wanted to leave ever since Joseph's birth. I knew you were right about that revolting tutor, Brother Nimah. God only knows what foul treachery he's imbued in my sons. I can't bear the thought of him getting near Joseph. I've had all I can stand of the Black Hand. The townsfolk are spineless, now that they're owned by them. The Brotherhood of the Black Hand produces nothing of value. Everyone does the work for them and they live off the people like parasites. They overgraze the land, and are cutting down all the trees. There'll be nothing left in a few years. I swear they'd sell the clouds if they could. Yahweh has spoken. Last night after our talk I had a dream. He told me to leave by the spring equinox next year."

I breathed a sigh of relief. The end was in sight. "It means so much to me that we're united in vision and purpose again. We'll be stronger for it! You'll see!"

Jacob's face reddened with embarrassment, as he said, "I can feel it already!"

"What did you ask for your wages?" I inquired looking into his eyes.

Jacob responded wryly. "It's not me, it's my blessing that Laban will miss. So I tried to make it easier on the old miser. I agreed to be his shepherd for one more year if he would go through the entire flock with me today, and take out every black sheep, and every speckled or spotted goat. I told him that I'd mate them together, and they and all their off-spring would be my wages."

"He agreed, and we shook hands on it. He said he wanted us to part as friends."

I smiled at him with pride. Jacob was no longer the naive youth, who had hidden behind his mother and come to Laban seeking refuge against his brother. Requesting the black and speckled sheep and goats, he was acknowledging that he also was not unblemished.

But Laban, the old deceiver, was no friend to any man, nor could he honor any bargain. While we were talking, he went out to the flocks and removed all the striped and speckled goats, and all the black sheep. Then he called his oldest son, and commanded him to secret away the entire motley herd, putting three days' journey between them and Jacob.

Jacob was not duped however. He noted all the missing sheep and goats, and prayed to Yahweh. The Lord sent him instructions in a dream. When the mating season came Jacob gathered sap filled branches of poplar, almond, and plane trees, and peeled them in strips laying bare the soft white of their branches. He put these branches in front of the animals in the troughs, and in the channels where they came to drink. When the animals mated in front of these branches they produced striped and spotted young with Yahweh's magic.

Jacob built up his droves this way, keeping them separate from Laban's flock. Whenever the strongest and healthiest animals mated, Jacob positioned these branches where they could view them. Laban's animals were weak and feeble, while Jacob's prospered and gathered strength. Thus Jacob outsmarted the old trickster and grew very rich, coming to own a large flock of healthy sheep and goats.

21

ESCAPE FROM THE BLACK HAND

ANOTHER YEAR HAD PASSED AND IT WAS SPRING AGAIN, THE TIME OF new beginnings. All the world was ripe for change. The lambing was over and the shearing had all been done. The earth was returning to life after its long winter sleep. The wildflowers had awakened on the hillsides, gifts of promise from the underworld Gods. A fine mist hung like a veil upon the air suiting my wistful mood, as I journeyed up to the high meadows for the secret meeting Jacob had called with Leah and me.

The mist conjured up fond memories as I walked along reminiscing about my childhood. It was a privilege to have grown up nestled in the shadow of the Taurus mountains, where the atmosphere was steeped in light and power. This was Goddess country, sacred to Ninhursag, Lady of the Foothills. Even the Nefilim deigned to come down here. Mother was alive for me when I walked these hallowed hills. Her spirit breathed through all the changes in the rolling countryside, reminding me of the many times we'd trod this ground together.

My favorite knoll was coming up before me. It was a rounded breast of a hill, that possessed a commanding view of the entire region. I smiled thinking of how enormous it had seemed to me when I was young, and the many times I had used it as a lookout in my search for a strayed lamb. From this vantage point above the mist, I could see Jacob and Leah waiting for me, two mute grey shadows on the plains. A curious detachment seized me as I viewed them from this far distance. It was a new found freedom seeing those two together without having to experience the pangs of jealousy which used to steal my heart.

What would this meeting be like? I hoped it wouldn't turn into just another ugly scene. As I stood there praying for a peaceful accord, the mist suddenly parted. There between Jacob and Leah was the boulder I had sat upon the evening of the Shining One's arrival. Was it a sign of providence that Jacob had chosen the mandrake field for our meeting? All my trepidation vanished.

The mist was starting to burn off. I glanced back wistfully at the farm before continuing on. A wisp of smoke was coming up from the fire hut. Zilpah must have been making bread. I turned and looked out past the sea of rolling foothills toward the snowcapped mountains in the north. My entire life had been framed by the strength and beauty of this noble land. How could I leave this wondrous place with the hillsides greening and the breezes gentle and warm? I knew why Jacob called this meeting. Hadn't I been encouraging him to go? But now that the reality of our departure was at hand, it pierced me like a sword. Though it only took one thought of Laban and the Brotherhood to urge me on.

Leah was grumbling as I approached. "You've been acting differently of late, Jacob. You're always so busy and intractable. Why did you call us here? What's all the mystery about? It's not right I'm here at the appointed hour, yet you keep me in suspense. It's just like Rachel to keep us waiting. She never thinks of anyone but herself."

I stepped out of the mist and stood before them apologetically. "I'm sorry to have kept you waiting. I had the hardest time getting Joseph down for a nap today. He wants to be up and about with the older boys."

"No need to apologize." said Jacob warmly.

Leah rolled her eyes petulantly, stepping backward toward the boulder away from me. I knew she would be out of sorts. She hated being out of doors when the weather wasn't fair.

Leah spoke up before Jacob could begin. "What's this meeting about?"

"I won't mince my words with you." replied Jacob thoughtfully. "It's plain to see I'm out of favor with your father. He tried to trick me with the flocks. He's such a schemer! He doesn't want to part with a single animal."

"But the God of my fathers is with me. Yahweh has blessed my work, bringing forth abundance and showering blessings upon me. You know how hard I have worked for your father, though he tricked me over and over again. It's only by the grace of God that he has not harmed me."

"When Laban said, 'the spotted ones will be your wages', all the animals produced spotted offspring. When he said, 'the striped ones shall be your wages', all the animals produced striped young. When the animals were in heat, Yahweh sent me a dream. I saw the males covering the females of the flock were all striped or spotted. God called to me in my dream saying, 'Jacob! I will take Laban's livestock and give them to you. I am the God of Bethel where you poured oil on the monument, and made your vow. Make ready! It is time for you to leave this country and return to the land of your birth.'"

"Yahweh has spoken. It's time for us to go. We leave in the dark of the next new moon. I expect you and all the children to come with me. The Brotherhood will soon begin persecuting all those who do not worship Sin."

"Never shall we bow to the Evil One! Yahweh has timed our move just right. The animals are all shorn and ready for travel. What do you say, Rachel? Are you with me?"

I placed my hand upon the boulder, saying, "I am with you, Jacob! I too have received warnings in my dreams. Joseph and I will be ready."

"Thank you, Rachel!" said Jacob with relief.

Then he smiled and turned to Leah. "We've spoken of this before, Leah, and you were not willing to leave. I can appreciate that you will miss your father. But there's trouble brewing in Haran, and I can stay here no longer. A great future awaits us in the Promised Land. Are you coming?"

Leah's face looked suddenly old and tired. She paled visibly as she said, "It's true! I have been reluctant to go, Jacob. But now that I am faced with your departure, I have to ask myself. Have I any share left in the inheritance of my father's house? No! And I too have noticed the change in him in regard to you. You are not the only one he has changed toward. Am I not treated as a foreigner by him as well? Now that he has the sons he's always longed for, I am nothing to him. He sold me and went on to use the money for himself. All the riches Yahweh has taken from him belong to us and to our children. I will go with you, Jacob! We shall go forth and reap the promise of your God together. Our sons will become wealthy landowners as Yahweh has foretold."

Jacob was stunned Leah had acquiesced so easily. He had expected an argument, or at the least a heated debate. He smiled with relief, saying, "Very well! I'm glad you see it that way. We leave at the dark of the moon. Laban will be away at an important meeting at that time. Don't breathe a word of this to anyone, not the children, nor your friends, or relations! Not even Bilhah or Zilpah are to know until its time to go. Don't speak a word of this to the women who come to consult you from town, Rachel! There's no telling what Laban and his Brotherhood would do if they got wind of our departure."

I nodded my agreement.

Leah's words hung in the air like a swarm of buzzards over a dying carcass. So much for her attachment to father! Nonetheless, she'd always be Laban's daughter—self-concerned, practical and pragmatic to the end. Like Laban, everything boiled down to some bullheaded material concern with her. Her decision was nothing more than a shrewd assessment of where the greatest profit lay. But at least Leah was right this time! We had no choice. There was no telling how long we'd continue to be safe here with the Black Hand.

Leah and Jacob returned to the farm so as not to be missed. I lingered on not to arouse suspicion. Jacob nodded, giving me a big hug as he took his leave.

I had always longed to escape Laban's strangle hold. But now that the time was here, I was gripped with a sense of deep foreboding. This land was a part of me. My heart ached to think of leaving it. This was my matriarchal root source. Ninhursag had walked this ground. She had been invoked here for untold centuries. From this land had sprung the most powerful Naditu Priestesses down through the ages.

I headed for the Balikh to ponder this momentous move. It was time to go. The signs were clear. I had received my holy orders in my dreams.

And I couldn't bear the thought of Joseph being influenced by Laban and the Brotherhood. My dreams foretold that chaos would soon reign here. But oh, how it hurt to think of leaving my precious homeland, the root source of the Naditu Sisterhood.

Questions began spinning around in my head. Would the Shining One know where we had gone? I had been deprived of the Eye Temple all these years, but could I survive without my beloved homeland? Approaching the Balikh, my mind was racing as swift as the current. Looking around at the hillsides rising from the mist, I couldn't help but ponder all that I had lost. I had lost my mother, my family, my stature as a Naditu Priestess, my connection to the Eye Temple, the Sisterhood, and the hope of a Higher Marriage with Jacob. Now I was to lose my homeland. Would my departure mean that I would be cut off from the Nefilim as well?

I had to do something. I had to take the Goddess with me. I couldn't allow the Naditu lineage to die out. In the midst of all my confusion I heard the great Speaker of the River.

GRIEVE NOT, RACHEL! THE GREAT AGES HAVE MOVED INTO THE SIGN OF THE RAM. IT IS FOR JOSEPH TO CARRY THE TRADITION OF THE GOD AND GODDESS ONWARD. LABAN AND HIS BROTHERHOOD PREPARE THE WAY FOR THE RETURN OF SIN. IT IS NO LONGER SAFE IN HARAN.

YOU ARE THE SPIRITUAL MOTHER OF YOUR PEOPLE. YOU ARE THE BEARER OF THE STAR WISDOM, THE LAST OF A DYING TRADITION HERE! THE NADITU SISTERHOOD AND THE GREAT WHITE BROTHERHOOD WHO MAINTAIN THE CONNECTION TO KAK.SI.DI. HAVE ALL MOVED ON.

SEIZE THE TERAFIM! DO WHAT MUST BE DONE OR COMMUNICATION WITH KAK.SI.DI. WILL CEASE, AND HUMANKIND'S KNOWLEDGE OF THEIR ANCESTORS FROM THE STARS WILL BE LOST FOREVER. DO NOT LEAVE THE ORACLE BEHIND. THE TERAFIM WILL GUIDE YOU IN WISDOM AND PRESERVE YOUR CONNECTION WITH THE NEFILIM ONCE YOU LEAVE THIS HALLOWED PLACE. IT IS ESSENTIAL YOU TAKE THE TERAFIM WITH YOU TO MAINTAIN THE SACRED BOND BETWEEN HEAVEN AND EARTH IN JACOB'S HOMELAND, WHICH IS A PLACE OF STRIFE.

ESCAPE FROM THE BLACK HAND

HAVE NO FEAR! THE TERAFIM BELONG TO YOU. BUT YOU MUST HAVE THE COURAGE AND THE WIT TO SEIZE THEM FROM LABAN. DO NOT ALLOW THEM TO FALL INTO THE HANDS OF SIN. REMEMBER ALL THAT I HAVE SAID! AND WHEN IN DOUBT LISTEN TO YOUR HEART! IT WILL TELL YOU WHAT TO DO.

I was shaking with fear and excitement when the oracle's voice faded into the roar of the Balikh. So it was true! The terafim were my only hope of preserving my connection with the Shining One. The prospect of entering father's study filled me with dread. But I had no choice. I would risk anything for my connection with Zandar, and to keep the channel with the stars open within the Patriarchy. I might have to face Laban's cobra, or his skull oracle, but I would not shun this sacred duty. I had to seize the terafim and move them forward with me into Jacob's homeland. It would be a way of holding the power of the Goddess and Kak.Si.Di. within the patriarchy. I had to do it for the sake of balance. I had failed once with the terafim. I would not fail again this time.

A veil lifted from my eyes, and the pathos of my entire life suddenly came clear to me. Oh Sin, and his Black Hand were very clever! They had exalted the power hungry Inanna, and suppressed Ninhursag, just as they had raised Leah up putting her ahead of me. Inanna already had taken over the Eye Temple in Brak. I could not allow the connection with Kak.Si.Di. and the Starry Ones to die out, or humanity would forget their starry ancestry. And the bloodthirsty daughter of Nanna/Sin would be the only Goddess remembered in the violent Age of Iron.

Sitting there beside the river, my Ancient Eyes were opened and my vision given wings. I could see the tragic results of the suppression of the star wisdom from Kak.Si.Di., and the Great Mother Ninhursag, guardian of Earth and all her children. The Earth would be devastated in the Age of Iron. Yes! In the panorama of centuries flashing before my eyes I could see war upon bloody war being fought, both sides always secretly armed and supported by the Black Hand. The players changed. The apparent reasons for the wars always varied, but one thing remained true. The Brotherhood of the Black Hand was the unseen hand behind all the wars, always pushing toward a One World Government to strengthen the control of the ancient Dragon of Heaven.

I saw a vast landscape in an ancient land. The spoils of war were all around. Dark pools of the black blood of Mother Earth exuded tall plumes of smoke and fire rising to heaven, an infernal offering from the Brotherhood to Sin. Entire forests were felled, leaving not a tree to root the ground. Landslides fell into the river courses smothering all the fish and wildlife. Rivers, lakes, even seas and mighty oceans were fouled. Huge tracts of fertile crop land were sacrificed to make crowded cities, that sparkled so bright at night, they eclipsed the stars of heaven. I was breathless with despair, tears running down my cheeks as I gazed into the future of the Age of Iron. But how could it be otherwise? How could there be peace and love if there was no Great Mother to nourish and protect the Earth?

A piece of my heart died with every vision, but the blue flame of the Naditu Sisterhood was ignited in me. I would take the terafim, but faced with the ravages of the future, I feared it was not enough. I had to mark my leavetaking with yet another important act. Hadn't the Speaker of the River told me to listen to my heart? My heart cried out to conceive another child, a daughter, here in the foothills of the World Mountain to carry on the Naditu Sisterhood. It didn't feel right to leave the birthplace of the Sisterhood without conceiving a daughter. The Nefilim had once come down here. Such an opportunity might never come again!

Yet my heart was filled with trepidation. It had been a blessing to be residing here in the Goddess's protection throughout my pregnancy with Joseph. How would it be to give birth in a land where Ninhursag was not revered? Joseph's birth had been a difficult one. I had lost enormous quantities of blood, and I was older now. Yesterday was the first full moon of spring. If I wanted to call the Nefilim down and conceive a daughter, I would have to try tonight.

I was in sight of the stables. Laban had just returned from town. Joab, his eldest son, was taking the saddle off his camel, when the idea struck me. I could keep the terafim inside my camel's litter while travelling. That way I could sit in the lap of the Goddess as I rode about. But how was I to call the Nefilim down? I couldn't take the terafim while Laban was here. I would have to make due with the old dried out mandrake that was left.

Joseph was already up from his nap when I returned home. He spoke excitedly, as I rifled through my old trunk. "What are you looking for mother? . . . I just had the most interesting dream. I dreamt we were all going on a long journey. We were riding camels. Everyone was coming with us, and there were great herds of animals as well!"

I chuckled, as I shook my head. "That journey was to be kept a secret, you the little scamp! Promise me you won't breathe a word of it to anyone."

Joseph's eyes opened wide. "I promise I won't say a thing, mother. Just tell me where we're going."

I looked up from my search, and whispered, "We're going to Jacob's homeland, the land promised to Abraham, Isaac, and Jacob by Yahweh, son. It's time to leave Haran. I warned you about Laban, Nimah, and the Brotherhood of the Black Hand. We have to get away from them while we still can. Don't say a word of this to anyone, not even to your brothers. If Laban gets wind of our departure there could be trouble."

Joseph replied excitedly, "I understand, mother! I'll keep it to myself. But I'm glad my dream told me we would be going. It will give me time to say goodbye to the foothills and the mountains. I'll miss them, mother, but I'm excited to see the world. This will be my first big adventure."

Joseph's exuberance was catching and I had to laugh, as I too began to contemplate the journey with excitement.

Joseph came and stood beside me as I rifled through the trunk. "What are you looking for mother?"

"I was looking for this!" I said excitedly, finding the mandrake root wrapped inside the wedding veil I had never worn.

As I tied the pouch with the mandrake around my neck, Joseph stared at it, and inquired, "What is that, mother? I've never seen anything like it before."

Had it been that long since I'd worn the mandrake root? It must have been, if it was wrapped inside my bridal veil. It always filled me with such grief to see that sorry remnant of my broken dreams. But today the veil looked beautiful to me as I admired the potent fertility charms in its embroidery. Gazing at it gave me an idea.

"You haven't answered me, mother." said Joseph interrupting my thoughts. "What is that around your neck?"

I looked up at him startled. In time I had planned to tell Joseph about the Nefilim. But he was still so young, and he'd had enough excitement for one day. So I replied, "It's a pouch I keep some special herbs in, darling. I'll tell you all about it when you get a little older."

"Please, mother! Tell me now! There may not be enough time for all I need to learn!"

I removed the magical root from its pouch and handed it to my son.

"It looks like a little man! What is it, mother?"

"It's a mandrake, a very rare and special root!" I said, inspired by his exuberance. "The Star People from Kak.Si.Di. brought it to Earth in ancient times."

Joseph's eyes had a distant look in them as he said, "I know about the Star People. They speak to me in my dreams. I love the stars, mother. I know they're far away, but somehow they always feel so close to me."

"They are home to you, my son." I said, looking into his eyes. "Your true father is one of the shining Nefilim. The Nefilim are those who come down from heaven. His name is Zandar. He is a son of Ninhursag, and came from Kak.Si.Di., the great Star of the Goddess, the sun behind our sun. I used this Mandrake root to call him down."

"Then I'm a child of the Star People, mother?"

"Yes, my dear." I said softly as I rubbed his back.

"Is that why I'm so different from my brothers? . . . And why I sometimes feel so lonely?"

I could hardly believe the wisdom of the little one. "Yes, my dear! You are a child of heaven and of earth. You have the Ancient Eyes and Ears of the Family of Light, the Star People. One day they will make you a great prophet and seer for your people, but you must beware. Such a teacher is not always welcome in his own home. But never fear! Your Angel Father in heaven watches over you. He and She Who Watches will always be with you."

Joseph continued questioning me, his eyes narrowing. "Are the Star People all good, mother?"

I continued with care. "Many came from the stars in ancient times, my son. Most came to help Earth, but there were others who came strictly to help themselves. Great wars were fought in heaven and on Earth for control of this planet. One of these great wars resulted in Sin and his dark angels being exiled here as punishment for their rebellion."

"Zaltan, Laban, and those higher up in the Black Hand can be taken over by Sin. In that state they are instruments of the Evil One. We must leave so that Yahweh may guide Jacob, as he did Abraham before him, in the struggle against Sin and the Black Hand."

Joseph was still bubbling over with questions, when I said, "That's enough for today, Joseph! Now run along! Not a word of this to anyone!"

When Jacob fell asleep that night, I gathered up a few things and slipped quietly out of our tent. Anticipation building with every step, I hurried to the field where I had encountered the Starry One. My eagerness made the trip seem short, and before long I could see the great rock shining in the moonlight near the mandrake field.

I sat down beneath the stars to wait. Taking the mandrake root from its pouch, I placed it down beside me. When I took up my bridal veil, it's silver charms and embroidery glistened in the moonlight. Tears came to my eyes to think that such a beautiful thing had been used as the instrument of treachery. The years had been kind to the exquisite veil. It was as lovely as ever. I slipped it on and gazed up at the eternal reaches of the sky. Trembling with feeling, I began to chant out loud.

OH SHINING ONE, BRIDEGROOM OF MY HEART, PLEASE HEAR MY PRAYERS AND COME DOWN TO ME AGAIN.

I don't know how long I continued in this rapturous litany, when I heard a voice. "Rachel! Oh, Rachel, there you are! What are you doing dressed like that baying at the moon?"

My heart started beating wildly and my breathing ceased. This was not my celestial bridegroom! It was Jacob emerging in the moonlight.

"I was just saying goodbye to my homeland, Jacob." I replied evasively, feeling suddenly foolish sitting there in my bridal veil. "What are you doing here? You were fast asleep when I left the tent."

Jacob came over and leaned against the rock. "I was awakened by a dream. You were calling out to me in it. When I saw you were missing I was concerned and had to find you. What are you doing in that veil?"

A strange look had come over Jacob's face, when he recognized the bridal veil.

I responded in a halting voice, "Sadness came over me, when I found it going through my things to pack. You know I never got to wear it."

Jacob's face paled. "I know how hard it is to leave your homeland. But there's something strange about you sitting here all alone in your bridal veil."

He looked at me remorsefully. "You've always been my true bride,

Rachel, though you never got to wear that veil. You're not having second thoughts about leaving, are you? I couldn't bear it if you didn't come with me."

I shook my head. "I'm not having second thoughts, Jacob. I'm just feeling wistful tonight."

"Thank God!" said Jacob in relief.

Then he removed the bridal veil and took me in his arms, kissing me hard upon the lips as he carried me away from the boulder . "This will be a new beginning for us. I'll make up for the past. You'll see! Just promise not to shut me out. Let's lie here under the stars as we did our first night together."

I had taken the bridal veil out to this distant meadow unsure of what might happen. I had been calling the Nefilim, my celestial bridegroom. What did it mean that Jacob had heard my call? My head was spinning with Jacob's kiss. The heavens seemed cold and far away as I glanced down at the mandrake root. It wasn't glowing. There was no rosy light to be seen, and no sign of the Shining One. For all I knew he had not received my call.

My spirit cried out for the Shining One, but Jacob's arms were warm and close. He was kissing me all over, the way he did when we were young. I didn't know what to think, or how to feel, but my breathing hastened and a deep warmth began rising up inside me. Jacob disrobed me slowly. He reached for the veil and tossed it aside. It fell atop the mandrake as he entered me.

There was no time to understand what had happened between us as we prepared for our departure. Our brief encounter seemed to fade with the moon's light, as each day the pace became more hectic. There was so much to do and so little time with Laban still at home. His serpent stare seemed to follow us everywhere.

Our one brief night of romance seemed but a dream, as Jacob moved into the warrior mode with all the scores of things he had to do. Even Joseph felt the strain. I couldn't move about without his clinging to me. The only crack of relief came when Laban left for his annual meeting with the Brotherhood. We were to leave in the wee hours of the following morning. There was only one short day to alert Bilhah and prepare for our departure.

The thought of entering Laban's office in the dark of a moonless night put terror in my soul. Yet it was almost dinnertime before I could make my move. Joseph was with Bilhah and our boys. Jacob was out with the livestock making sure they were ready. The sun was low in the sky when I started for Laban's ghoulish study.

Filled with trepidation, I stood for a moment on the threshold which was hung with talisman and charms. I said a quick prayer to gather my courage, then pulled open the heavy wooden door. It's ancient hinges let out a fiendish screech as I stepped inside. An acrid smell lingered in the air burning my nostrils as I closed the door behind me. My eyes soon began to smart. This was my first time alone in Laban's private enclave. My flesh began to crawl. You never knew what foul demon Laban had been conjuring up. There was hardly enough light filtering through the narrow windows to illumine the musty shelves. Bones, rocks, piles of herbs and feathers littered the floor. But thankfully the dreaded skull and the dark crystal hand were absent from their central place upon the altar.

I was just about to breathe a sigh of relief when Laban's guardian snake appeared out of nowhere rising up as if to strike. My blood ran so cold I could hardly breath. My heart was in my throat, but I struggled to quell my fear. It would only incite the clever serpent further.

I stepped back just in time to grab the divining rod beside the door. The cobra came lurching at me. Its fiendish eyes boring into me, as it unfurled its regal hood. I called upon the Starry Ones as I raised the rod and struck it on the head with all my might. It skulked away hiding inside the wall.

My hands were still shaking as I made my way over to the terafim's hiding place beneath the floor. Dust billowed everywhere. Suddenly afraid of unseen eyes, I turned around to check behind me. All was quiet. Only my footprints could be seen outlined in the dust on the floor. I would have to remember to erase them before I left.

I felt around the floorboards until I found a crack. When I pushed in the floorboard, it gave way with ease. There below on the earthen floor were the terafim.

It had been years since I'd seen the awesome oracle. I took a moment to say a prayer of thanks and admire the beauty of their intricate detail. The coiled tails of the serpent and lion oracles were fashioned in concentric bands of gold, silver, and copper. The innermost coil was of the rare heavy metal from Kak.Si.Di., which I'd never seen anywhere else. Emeralds fashioned the serpent's eyes. Two star rubies gleamed in the lion's eyes. I smiled to see them glow with the same uncanny rose colored light as the mandrake.

My heart stood still, and I gasped out loud. It was fortunate I had taken my time before grasping hold of the precious oracle. For there wrapped in the innermost coils of the terafim was its guardian, an enormous female scorpion her young riding triumphantly on her back. The imposing mother raised her tail, positioning herself to strike.

I addressed her as I would one of the kiribu guardians at the Eye Temple. HAIL FIERCE ONE! I AM GRATEFUL THE TERAFIM HAS BEEN IN YOUR CHARGE. THANK YOU FOR PROTECTING THE PRECIOUS ORACLES. I WISH YOU AND YOUR YOUNG NO HARM. GRANT ME YOUR PERMISSION TO REMOVE THE TERAFIM. MY MOTHER BEQUEATHED THEM TO ME. THEY ARE MINE BY RIGHT. IT'S TIME FOR ME TO CLAIM THEM.

When I finished speaking the proud scorpion unfurled her tail, then moved with her young back into the dark reaches beneath the floor. Breathing a sigh of relief I resumed my inspection of the awesome terafim. A pleasant warmth travelled up my arm moving throughout my entire body, as I took them from their hiding place. The room suddenly came alive with a rosy light, reminiscent of the events surrounding my encounter with the Shining One.

After enjoying the incredible show of light for a time, a disturbing thought came to me. How would I be able to secret away this glowing treasure? Luckily I still had the black silk cloth mother had kept them in. When I placed the terafim in the black silk and put them in my saddle bags, the wondrous light disappeared.

I was just about to replace the floorboard and depart, when the mother scorpion appeared again. To my inner sight it appeared as if she were trying to catch my eye. I gazed at her intently. She seemed to be leading my attention to the inner recesses of the next floorboard.

I stooped down out of curiosity and lifted up the floorboard. There to my delight was my eyebead necklace. I thanked the scorpion and placed it in my saddlebag beside the terafim. Then I quickly replaced the floor board, grabbed the broom behind the door and brushed away my footprints. Once I was satisfied I had left no trace of my visit, I departed.

I was flooded with relief to be outside again. The sun had just set sending forth a ruby glow, that matched the light of the terafim. The heavens were smiling upon my deed.

I hurried to the stable, trying to temper my excitement. Reuben was just leaving. He closed the stable door smiling over at me. "Good evening, Aunt Rachel!"

I had hoped there would be no one at the stables, but I did my best not to show my disappointment. 'And a very good evening it is, Reuben!."

Reuben looked around before responding in a whisper. "All the camels are ready. I just heard the dinner bell. Shall I wait and go with you?"

"Run along! We don't want to make your mother angry. I'll pack these last things on my camel, and be up shortly."

"Very well! I'll see you at dinner." said Reuben turning to go.

There was no moon in the sky, nor the slightest trace of wind, to grace our departure from my homeland. The odor of blood was heavy in the air from Jacob's sacrifice imploring Yahweh's blessing on our journey. There was no farewell celebration. No chance to say goodbye to relatives or friends, or the women who consulted with me from town. Even Kak.Si.Di. had disappeared below the horizon.

We fled like thieves in the night with all our servants, livestock, and worldly goods. Seated high upon our mounts in the steeping darkness, we had to trust our camels' surefooted sense of direction to take us over the foothills to Carchemish and the great Euphrates River. Jacob rode at the front of the long line with Reuben close behind. We ventured into the great unknown, never stopping once the whole long night. We travelled by the outskirts of Carchemish reaching the great Euphrates River in the heat of the nooday sun.

Leah was complaining to Jacob as we regrouped before forging the great river. "I'm exhausted! We've been travelling all night and all day without stopping. Have some mercy! Can't we rest here before crossing?"

"There shall be no rest until this river is between us and your father. When we reach the other side we'll stop for refreshments and a brief rest." replied Jacob impatiently.

Leah continued, "I don't see why we can't spend one day in Carchemish. There are so many things I could use for the journey . . . and the children haven't slept all night."

Jacob was resolute. "The Black Hand will be upon us, if we stop here. We're also going to have to skirt Aleppo and Ebla on our way south. All the cities are under Black Hand control."

As Leah rode away grumbling, Jacob came over to Joseph and I. "How are you this morning, Joseph?" he asked in greeting.

"I am well, father. I'm so excited. I'm not the least bit tired." declared Joseph with enthusiasm.

Jacob came up along side me on his camel, smiling warmly as he said, "That boy is an inspiration to me, Rachel! His enthusiasm and faith give me strength I never knew I had. How are you holding up?"

I slackened the reins in my hand. "I'm well, thank you! But I'll feel better once we have the Euphrates between us and the Black Hand."

"At least I can depend on you and Joseph to lift my spirits!" said Jacob with a smile. "Put Joseph with you on your camel when you cross the river. I want you behind Eli and in front of Nathan. You'll be safe with them. Thankfully the drought keeps the river low. It would usually be impossible to cross in springtime. May God protect you both! We'll stop to regroup for one hour on the other side. I want you at the front of the line. That way you'll have more time to rest. From hereon it will be easier going. We'll be heading straight down the valley for Mt. Gilead."

Before I could respond Jacob was off to oversee the enormous line.

Waiting our turn to cross the river, I put my arms around Joseph and prayed. GREAT FATHER GOD AND MOTHER GODDESS, TAKE US ALL UNDER YOUR WING AND PROTECT US AT THIS CROSS-ING. SLOW THE WATERS DOWN AND SPEED US ON OUR WAY. LEND COURAGE TO THE FAINT OF HEART. MAY THE WATERS OF THIS GREAT RIVER PURIFY OUR SPIRIT AND FORTIFY US FOR WHAT LIES AHEAD.

I looked back wistfully at the Taurus mountains, as we waited our turn to plunge into the river's surging course. My heart was heavy to be leaving my motherland, the cradle of life since the Great Flood. Never again would I walk these hallowed foothills where so many of the Naditu Sisterhood had come to birth. How could I say farewell to these familiar foothills rising like fertile waves upon the horizon?

GREAT MOTHER NINHURSAG, THIS IS NO GOOD BYE.

ESCAPE FROM THE BLACK HAND

THOUGH I BID A SAD FAREWELL TO YOUR HALLOWED
FOOTHILLS, YOU ARE ALWAYS IN MY HEART. THIS LAND IS
PART OF ME. IT GOES WITH ME WHEREVER I GO.

My hand on Joseph's shoulder, I said, "Say goodbye to Ninhursag's
foothills, Joseph. Remember She Who Watches as we move into
Canaan, the land of your Fathers. She will always be with you, watching
from Kak.Si.Di., heaven's brightest star."

I had one hand on the camel litter and my other arm around Joseph
as we stepped off the bank into the vast Euphrates river. The river was
cold and deep, but the terafim lent me courage. Whenever I touched it,
even through the litter, it connected me with a lion's share of courage.
We had no trouble getting across. Some of the animals who were slow
swimmers drifted far downstream, however, and it took longer than expected to regroup our numbers. But no loss occurred to any of our company.

Jacob took it as a positive omen and thanked his God. We rested for
an hour, then pressed on once more with spirits high. The speed of our
flight made it difficult to take in the varied richness of all the places we
traversed. Far flung landscapes passed before us like an exotic tapestry
pleasing to the eye. I never felt homesick, or estranged. Wherever we
went familiar wildflowers and foliage greeted us. Only spring bloomed
earlier the further south we went, and stately date and palm trees replaced the towering cedars of the north.

It was a tiring yet breathtaking journey seated atop my surefooted
camel. Whenever I placed my hand upon the terafim, the Nefilim spoke
to me within my heart recounting the history of all the places we traversed. With such companionship how could I feel homesick or alone?
Each day I met new aspects of Mother Earth, who smiled at me with different faces in all the landscapes we traversed, showing me her many
moods.

We travelled by night and slept for only a few brief hours during the
noonday heat. Ten days passed before Jacob gave in to Leah's pleas to
stop and camp the night. We pitched our tents on the highest of the
foothills near Mount Gilead and went to sleep.

Zachariah, Nathan's boy, was on watch. Just before dawn he ran
from tent to tent slapping it with his shepherd's crook, and shouting.
"Wake up! Get your weapons ready! Armed strangers are coming!"

His voice was like a blast of frigid air, rousing me from a dream in which I was seated upon my camel's litter like a throne. I rose only half awake, and sought my camel litter with its precious prize beside the door.

Zachariah pulled back the flap to Jacob's tent next to mine. He caught his breath, and then began, "Ten dark robed men are riding in from the north. They're armed, master. Each one carries a large staff, and wears a sword."

Jacob had slept fitfully through the night. I'd heard him pacing back and forth inside his tent like a hungry lion. His command came with alacrity. "Wake my sons! Call all the men to arms!"

Jacob and the men were gathering as the strangers reached our camp. They charged up the steep hillside, like bellicose marauders, swooping in upon us like a storm. Laban rode proudly into the center of our camp, his staff raised high, accompanied by Zaltan and his men. They made a fiendish sight in their black gloves and ceremonial capes, and spread out quickly surrounding our camp like a raging tide.

Laban cried out, when he spied Jacob. "There you are, you coward!"

Simeon and Levi sprung forth shoving Laban off his camel with their sticks, hearing their father so addressed. Laban fell to the ground with a heavy thud, screaming out abominations. The two boys were undaunted, and continued holding the old wizard prisoner on the ground with their swords poised at his throat.

Leah came tearing out of her tent half undressed, hair streaming down her back. "Simeon! Levi! What are you doing? Stop it this instant! That's your grandfather!" she cried out in disbelief.

The boys looked at Jacob, neither of them moving.

Throwing herself over Laban, Leah looked up at Jacob screaming, "Have you all gone mad? Call them off, Jacob! This is my father, and your uncle!"

Jacob stepped forward, his hand signalling them to relax their swords. Laban's Brothers closed in, brandishing their swords, surrounding us on all sides. Leah was still crying, and Laban fuming, as she helped him to his feet.

Laban dusted himself off. Then he gave his men the signal to circle in upon us even tighter. "Is this any way to treat your kinsman?" he bellowed threateningly.

ESCAPE FROM THE BLACK HAND

Smoothing out his clothing, he regarded Jacob haughtily. "Did you really think you could get away from me that easily? You should know by now there's no escaping the Black Hand!"

Joseph and I were peering at what transpired from our tent. Joseph turned to me and said, "You were right, mother! Laban did follow us! And look at how many of the Brotherhood are with him."

I threw something over me, and returned to gaze out of the tent with Joseph, praying all the while that Laban hadn't noticed the terafim were gone. Zaltan, Shahor, Nimah, Ham and the five others were surrounding us in an ever-tightening circle. Laban stood in the east blocking out the sun rising behind his back, as he spoke to Jacob with disdain.

Jacob had to shield his eyes to look at him directly. Gesturing with his other hand at Laban's men, he said, "Never mind my sons' behavior, Laban! What's the meaning of this armed assault upon our camp?"

Laban raised his eyebrows, speaking in his most sarcastic tone, "You ask what I'm doing here when you ran off with my sons and daughters like prisoners of war!"

Laban was shaking his stick in the air, his face contorted in rage, as he continued, "You may have been able to trick your father and your brother, Jacob, but did you really think you were going to get away with my children, my servants, and so many of my animals without a word. Now speak to me like a man! Why did you sneak off like a thief in the night without telling me you were leaving? I would have sent you on your way with feasting and music. But you have behaved like a fool! You didn't even have the decency to let me kiss my sons and daughters good-bye."

"You have insulted me and the Brotherhood. It is in our power to do you harm. But the God of your fathers came to me last night in a dream, and said, "On no account say or do anything to Jacob. Now it may be that you are leaving because you have a longing to be in your father's house. That I can understand! But why did you have to steal my household gods?"

Sweat began pouring from my brow at the mention of the terafim. I had to clutch Joseph's hand to steady myself. That Laban was amazing! Even after Yahweh's warning he would still exact his own form of retribution, trying to make us all feel guilty for claiming the freedom he never would have granted willingly.

Jacob's face brightened at the mention of the warning in Laban's dream. Looking the old conniver in the eyes, he said evenly. "You know why I didn't tell you! I didn't tell you because you'd try to cheat me out of my wives and children. The same way you tried to cheat me out of my livestock, you old miser! And let me assure you,, no one here has taken your gods. I swear to you by Yahweh, if your gods are found in the possession of anyone in my company, they shall die. Now go ahead! Examine if you must. Take what is yours! But leave all that is mine! Yahweh has spoken!"

Jacob's oath struck me with the weight of a stone mallet. My vision blurred, my knees went weak, and I couldn't hear the last of his pronouncement. Struggling to regain my composure I leaned against my camel litter for support. With my last bit of strength I climbed atop its hallowed seat.

Then I beckoned Joseph. "Tie the tent flap back! I want to be able to see out, but I have to sit down. I'm not feeling well, and I need some fresh air."

Joseph looked at me with worry written on his face. "What's wrong mother? You look very pale suddenly! Are you ill?"

Not wanting to upset him, I said, "Don't worry, son! I'll be fine in a moment. Just tie back the tent flap. I want to keep my eye on Laban and his Brothers."

"Of course, mother!" said Joseph as he quickly set to work.

When I could see out again Laban had already begun to search the camp. Our eyes met by chance as he went into Jacob's tent.

"I'll get to you soon enough!" he threatened menacingly.

I hadn't fully recovered from Jacob's pronouncement, when the look in Laban's eyes cut me through. I struggled for breath, fearing he had cursed me. The fabled power of Laban's evil eye was legendary. All Haran knew his malicious gaze could blight or curse.

Laban knew I had the terafim, but he took his sweet time coming to my tent. The old buzzard was relishing this chance to snoop into all our personal belongings.

Laban entered my tent as if it was his private domain. Jacob waited outside the entrance with Zaltan.

When Laban stepped inside Jacob summoned Joseph. "Come out here with me, son!"

Joseph gazed at me with a troubled look. Though I waved him out with my hand, he pleaded with his father. "Please allow me to stay with mother?"

"Get out here this instant!" Jacob replied with irritation.

Joseph refused to budge. He stood by me protectively, until Jacob had to come and pull him out.

When they were both outside, Laban gave me a sly look then got to work sifting through my belongings. I wasn't surprised he took the longest time rifling through my things, but Jacob eventually got impatient.

Stepping back inside my tent for a moment, Jacob cried, "You've been through Rachel's belongings twice now, Laban. What is it that interests you so in women's wear?"

The atmosphere inside the tent was stifling. I sat upon my camel litter hardly daring to breath.

When Jacob left Laban came and stood before me. Snarling under his breath, he glared at me in exasperation. "I know you have them, Rachel! Stand up so I can search you!"

Laban moved in closer.

"There's nothing of yours in this tent!" I declared emphatically, looking him in the eye.

Laban was not about to be put off, and started edging toward me.

"Don't you dare touch me! You haven't laid a finger on anyone else!" I shouted gripping hold of my camel litter.

A lion's share of strength and courage entered me. The thought of Laban putting his hands on me mobilized all my strength. I was filled with a lifetime's worth of fury. I had taken all I would from Laban. He would not lay a finger on me, or move me from my seat. I pressed my thighs into the area of my saddle which housed the terafim. Fire began coursing through my veins.

With this as ballast, I called down the Goddess's mantle of protection staring him directly in the eyes, and saying, "Excuse me, if I do not rise. But I am as women are from time to time."

A look of consternation, then fury, spread across Laban's face. Glowering at me, he said, "How can that be it's not the dark of the moon?"

"All this travelling has confused my cycle." I declared, looking him straight in the eye.

The old fox stepped away cautiously. Even the fearsome Laban in all his greed and righteous anger was afraid to touch me now. Narrowing his beady snake eyes, he peered into me trying to assess the truth of my statement.

Gazing into my eyes, he knew I was in deadly earnest. The mantle of the Goddess was upon me, and I was filled with the lion power of the terafim. Even Laban was afraid to take me on. Moonblood was something to be taken seriously. He knew full well the sovereignty of women's blood, and the power of a Naditu Priestess in her moontide. Laban was no fool! This was one Taboo even he was afraid to break. The crusty old magician would not dare lock horns with the Lioness during her bleeding time.

Laban knew I had the terafim, but he could see I was no longer a naive child he could bend to his will. As he stood in silence trying to assess the full extent of my power, I heard the Starry One in my heart reminding me of the magic mirror of the Goddess. Concentrating all my life force in the fertile cauldron of my belly, I connected up with the fire at the center of the Earth. Visualizing an enormous mirror all around me, I called down the power of the winged lion cherubim. Then I started breathing rhythmically to center myself. It was essential I remain in full control of my emotions, and merely reflect back to him his own foul energies.

The old magician began looking scared. He stepped back cautiously no longer able to meet my gaze. Crafty Laban knew what I was doing. He knew I was reflecting back to him his own negativity and foulness. He dared not look me in the eyes, afraid I would lock his will and drain his life away.

Still he would posture. "You can't fool me, Rachel. I know you have them!" he snarled.

When I looked him in the eye, he paled. The Magic Mirror was working. He was losing the power to back up his threats. I focused all my concentration until he finally left my tent in desperation, relieved to be out from under my stare.

It was high noon. The sun was scorching. It was Jacob's turn to be riled and his temper flared. "What is our crime, that you and your Brothers have set upon me and my family like this? You've been through all our belongings, and haven't found a single thing that belongs to you.

You are the one who has cheated and tricked us! First you deceived me on my wedding night, and cheated me out of another seven years of labor, after I had fulfilled all my promises. Then, when I spoke to you of leaving, you tried to trick me out of my hard earned livestock."

"This is how you treat me after more than twenty years of service! I gave you my best years. In all those years your ewes, and she-goats, never miscarried. I allowed you to drag me around to your so-called Brothers, using my blessing to increase your status. Never once have I eaten the rams from your flock. Any time your animals were mauled by a wild beast, I bore the loss myself. And you claimed it from me, you old miser. In the daytime I was consumed by heat, at night the cold gnawed my bones until sleep fled my eyes. That is how hard I have worked for you."

"Ten times you have changed my wages. If the God of my father, the God of Abraham, had not been with me, you would have sent me away empty-handed. But God has seen my weariness and all the work done by my hands. Last night He delivered judgment in your dream. You had best heed it now. Because by the word of Yahweh, I am losing patience."

Laban sighed heavily under the weight of Jacob's speech. I knew he was also feeling the pressure of my stare, as I continued glaring at him from my throne inside the tent. Even as Jacob spoke, he turned around in agitation to see if I was watching.

Finally Laban responded in a weary voice, "Your wives are my daughters! Your sons are my sons!"

I grabbed Joseph and held him to me, as he continued, "These sheep are my sheep. All you see belongs to me. But what can I do about my daughters, and the sons they have borne? Let's make a covenant, you and I. We'll set a stone cairn up here as witness between us."

Jacob took up the first stone, saying, "Now you take up a rock Laban, and you Zaltan, Nimah, Ham, Shahor, Zebulin, Mikah, Ahmed, Zedidia, and Mikala."

As each man got down from his camel to gather their stones, Jacob addressed his sons. "Now you go find a stone, Reuben, Levi, Judah, Simeon, Dan, Naphtali, Gad, Asher, Issachar, and Zebulun. Bring them here to place upon this pile."

I bade Joseph go to his father.

When he arrived Jacob said, "Find a large stone, Joseph! Bring it here to put with mine that we may set up a monument between us and your grandfather."

Jacob called Leah. "Make us a fine meal to seal our covenant!"

"Nathan, you go slay our largest fatted calf, and take it to Leah. We shall make a covenant here today upon this cairn, and seal it with a feast."

When the men returned with their stones they made a cairn, and sat together in silence until the meal arrived.

Laban rose with great ceremony. "May this cairn bear witness, Jacob. May Yahweh watch between us when we are out of sight of one another. If you ill-treat my daughters or marry other women in addition to them, beware. Though I am not with you, Nanna/Sin is watching. Both our Gods are witness to this!"

"This cairn shall establish a boundary between us. From this day forward I will not pass this marker to attack you, and you will not pass this monument to attack me. Nanna/Sin, and the God of Abraham will be our judges!"

Leah began serving the men. Jacob, his eleven sons, Laban and all his Brothers sat down together around the monument to seal their oath with a meal. I was considered unclean, and ate within the confines of my tent. Though several times during the course of the meal Laban glanced in my direction, he never dared to bring the subject of the terafim up again.

Laban and his Brothers left our camp at twilight and pitched their tent on Mt. Gilead. I didn't sleep a wink that night afraid Zaltan, Laban, and his Brothers would all team up and assault me in my dreams. I sat atop my camel throne until the heartless deceiver departed camp at first light.

Only Zaltan's farewell echoed in my ears sounding an ominous note. "Fare thee well, Jacob. You shall see us no more as we have sworn. This is a family affair, and ends here. But the day will soon come that Sin returns. Do not be surprised if He looks in on you! You and your sons, your entire lineage, has caught the attention of Nanna/Sin."

22

JACOB WRESTLES WITH
THE DARK ANGEL

NO LONGER WAS I THE NAIVE CHILD I ONCE HAD BEEN. WITH THE HELP of the Starry Ones I had stood against Laban and regained the terafim. The black hearted trickster was gone. I would not miss him, his fiendish skull, or his petrifying stare. As I watched him depart our camp my whole world seemed to brighten. The skies were not completely clear however. There would always be Leah to contend with. But we were on patriarchal soil now, and Leah's power would diminish without Laban to back her up.

The old deceiver's visit had not been without its grim consequences, however. Once again he had come between me and the unsuspecting Jacob. I was still reeling from Jacob's benighted curse. Jacob's blessing was strong, and so were his curses. A pain as sharp as an arrow was lodged behind my heart. And I found myself having to struggle against an ever increasing sense of doom, which was all the more poignant as Jacob's curse had come upon the heels of my realizing I was pregnant.

The surge of this new life was already awakening my tender breasts. I wanted to reach out to Jacob with this joyous news. But since his curse, Jacob was not only my husband, he was also my executioner. More than ever before Jacob's denial of the Goddess was between us. My intuition told me I would be going it alone throughout this pregnancy and birth.

There were further surprises to reckon with as well. Jacob was becoming a different person right before my eyes. The change in him was incredible as we approached his homeland. The closer we came to Canaan the more the warrior took him over. Jacob was serious all the time, and his actions revealed a new grim determination. He rarely spoke to me. We travelled caravan style sleeping in separate tents, and never had time alone. It was weeks before I had the chance to share my glad news with him.

When we were only a few days away from Esau's home in Edom, Jacob sent messengers on ahead to announce our arrival. They galloped back into camp one evening as we sat around the fire finishing our evening meal. Bounding breathlessly into our midst, they addressed Jacob at the central fire, their faces strained from the journey.

Jacob greeted his men with a worried look. "What news have you of my brother?"

After they dismounted and their camels were led away, Joshua, Jacob's most trusted man, spoke up. "We've rode straight here without stopping to rest. Your brother Esau is on his way to meet you. He brings with him an army of four hundred men."

A hush came over the campfire. Jacob's face paled, as he repeated, "Four hundred men! Esau is on his way here with four hundred men!"

"Yes, sir! Your brother is a great leader in his country. He called his men together as soon as he learned of your arrival. We returned as fast as we could. We thought you'd want to know."

Jacob gazed at Joshua, and forced a smile. "Thank you for bringing me this news with speed, Joshua. Your loyalty will not be forgotten."

The sun had set, and a murky darkness was mixing with the heavy silence around the campfire, creating a somber mood.

Jacob rose, saying, "My brother Esau has a furious rage. Leah! Zilpah! You and the children will ride with Aaron, Nathan, Zachariah and Samuel. Form one large company taking with you all the cows, the bulls, the she-asses and the donkeys."

"Rachel, you and Bilhah and your sons will ride with Ethan, Joshua, Jedidiah, Bethuel and Eli. You will form a second company, taking with you all the sheep, the goats, and camels. That way if Esau attacks one of our companies, the other might be able to escape."

I nodded at Jacob, thankful he wasn't putting Leah and I together.

Jacob called Nathan to him as the weary messengers sat down to eat. "Bring me the largest black ram from the flock, Nathan, and be quick!"

When Nathan returned with the ram, Jacob dismissed the servants for the night, and called his sons together in a circle around the campfire. As always, Joseph was on his left and Reuben on his right. I stood behind Joseph. Leah, Zilpah and Bilhah stood behind their eldest sons.

Jacob raised up his sacrificial knife. It's gleaming blade reflected menacingly in the hot light of the campfire. The ram's cries echoed along with Jacob's prayer, as he reached up to heaven hands red with blood.

BLESSED ART THOU MY LORD YAHWEH, KING OF THE UNIVERSE, GOD OF ISAAC, AND ABRAHAM, YOU WHO SAID 'RETURN TO YOUR HOMELAND WITH YOUR FAMILY, AND I SHALL MAKE YOU PROSPER. PLEASE HEAR MY PRAYER. WHEN I CROSSED THE JORDAN MANY YEARS AGO, I HAD ONLY MY STAFF. NOW THANKS TO YOUR BLESSING I HAVE MANY SONS AND ALL THE GREAT WEALTH YOU PROVIDED.

YOU HEARD ME WHEN I CALLED UPON YOU AT BETHEL. HEAR ME NOW AGAIN AND GRANT US YOUR PROTECTION. KEEP US SAFE FROM MY BROTHER ESAU'S WRATH. I FEAR HE AIMS TO KILL US, EVEN THE WOMEN AND CHILDREN.

MY FAITH IN YOU IS SOLID AS A ROCK. I BELIEVED YOU WHEN YOU SAID, 'I SHALL MAKE OF YOU A GREAT NATION. YOUR DESCENDANTS SHALL BE AS NUMEROUS AS THE GRAINS OF SAND ON THE SEASHORE, SO MANY THEY CANNOT BE COUNTED.' YOU ARE A GREAT AND MERCIFUL FATHER. YOU WHO HAVE BEEN WITH ME IN ALL MY ENDEAVORS. YOU HAVE DELIVERED ME FROM LABAN AND HIS BROTHERS. BLESS ME NOW AND MY ENTIRE FAMILY. PROTECT US FROM MY BROTHER ESAU'S RAGE.

HELP US TO BE STRONG AND FEAR NO MAN AS WE WALK AS THE RIGHTEOUS ARM OF YOUR LAW ON EARTH.

When I awoke early the next morning, Jacob was nowhere in sight. After searching the camp, I saw him out in the fields with his servants among the herds. As I went to him, Leah followed close behind, her grumbling mounting with every step.

Jacob was busy giving orders when we arrived, and didn't have a moment to acknowledge us.

The men's eyes were glowing with admiration, as they listened to him.

"I didn't mention you men last night, because I have a special task for you. I'm sending you on ahead with gifts for my brother Esau. Malachai, I want you to go on ahead with these two hundred she-goats and twenty he-goats. Josiah, follow behind Malachai with these two hundred ewes and twenty rams. Move ahead in droves, careful to leave a space between you. Aaron, follow behind Josiah taking with you these thirty camels and their calves. Saul, you follow behind him with these forty cows and ten bulls. Avi, you take these twenty she-asses, and ten donkeys. Remember to pace yourselves, always leaving plenty of space between the herds!"

"When you find Esau tell him these animals are a gift to him from his brother Jacob, his servant, who is following."

Leah had been listening as Jacob directed the men. Silent up til now, her face reddened and she burst out interrupting. "What are you doing, Jacob? Have you gone mad giving so much of our livestock away? You must listen to me, or you'll regret it later!"

Jacob stared at Leah, irate she had interrupted him in front of his men. "How dare you speak to me this way! What are you even doing here? This is none of your concern! Get back to the tents with the children, and see about the morning meal."

Leah was flabbergasted by Jacob's retort. Yet stubborn as ever she persisted. "Please, Jacob! Don't be rash! You're being too generous. We'll have nothing left."

Jacob's eyes flashed. "Silence woman! You don't know my brother's rage. What good will these beasts be to us, if we're lying dead?"

Jacob had never spoken like this to Leah before. Her face whitened. She stared at him in disbelief, then turned on her heels departing without another word.

Obviously Jacob had come into his own. Things would be different from now on.

Thinking it best not to trouble Jacob after this outburst, I joined Leah on her way back to camp. She was walking briskly, still fuming about Jacob's response.

Catching sight of me, she muttered, "Did you hear how Jacob spoke to me? He never would have dared speak to me that way when father was around!"

I couldn't remember when Leah had spoken to me in such a confidential way. Hoping this could be a new beginning for us, I ventured. "Jacob's changing, Leah. We're in his territory now. It's a new land with different ways and customs. It will go better for us, if we can learn to stand together."

Leah stared at me with her dull cow eyes, my remarks having caught her off guard. We reached camp and stood together in silence, watching the herds move out across the valley.

"It's not right that we have no say!" said Leah petulantly. "First father takes our bride price! Now Jacob gives away one third our herd! And we have nothing to say in these matters!"

Perhaps there was hope for us yet! Was Leah beginning to open her eyes? She had moved off toward the campfire, but was still within earshot when Jacob returned to camp.

Catching sight of me, he approached me inquiring hurriedly, "Was there something you wanted, Rachel?"

I replied quickly sensing his impatience. "I just came out to see if there was something I could do to help."

Jacob answered matter of factly not paying attention to Leah's snooping presence. "Everything's ready! Now promise me! I want you and Joseph at the very end of the line for safety."

"I promise!" I declared nodding.

Jacob took my hand and stood with me for one brief moment. Holding his hand I could feel the fear gnawing at the pit of his stomach. But there was new determination in his eyes.

"Have faith, Jacob! Yahweh is with you! All will go as well with your brother, as it did with Laban." I said encouragingly.

Jacob smiled grimly. "We shall see! But at least we are free of Laban! I only wish it was the last of the Brotherhood! They're everywhere a profit is to be made. I'm glad I'm a shepherd so we can avoid the cities."

Then relaxing his stance, he continued. "I haven't been able to appreciate getting Laban off my back, because I still have Esau to face. It's taken me twenty years to get up the courage to confront my brother. That he comes with four hundred men, I fear he means to kill me. May the Lord be with us! Promise you'll keep to the rear, Rachel. I want you and Joseph to be able to escape if things don't go well."

Then he kissed me hurriedly and left.

Leah sauntered over when Jacob was out of earshot. Gazing at me with renewed animosity, she declared, "Jacob hasn't changed all that much! You're still the only one he cares for!"

Then she stormed off before I could reply.

It was a long sobering day with Esau looming over us like a giant specter. A scorching wind came up out of the eastern desert, assaulting us in waves. By noon day clouds of dust appeared, parching our throats and burning our eyes. Jacob was not deterred. We pressed on through the relentless heat. By mid afternoon our camels were our only eyes.

When we stopped to rest I tied Joseph's camel to mine, and we huddled together using them as a windbreak.

Joseph's voice was a thin whisper, when he said, "There's something wrong here, mother. I can feel it. We never had storms like this at home."

"Don't worry, darling! Our trusty camels will see us through this storm. Now close your eyes and take a nap, and I'll tell you what my nurse related to me in my childhood."

"Alright, mother!"

"Old Hannah used to say that the camel was the first creature made by the Gods. She said they fashioned them from the clouds in the sky, which is why they are so large and graceful. She said that after the Gods created them, they were so pleased with the beasts, they made the entire Earth just for them. Have no fear! You can trust in your surefooted camel, Joseph."

When we awoke, the duststorm had ended. But as the clouds of dust cleared a new grief assailed my spirit. We were travelling at a slower pace now, and I could see that many of the ancient hilltop shrines to the Goddess had been desecrated and dismantled. Primeval groves of Ashera were being felled. My spirit was sick to see what man had done. Vast hill tops had been denuded, their ancient stone pillars fallen down. Shepherds were living in houses built from the hallowed rocks.

No wonder we had been blasted by duststorms! I wanted to shout

out in anger for the holy balance being lost. Didn't the people here understand the relationship between trees and the soil? This was windy country and without the forests rooting the soil dust storms would rage, consuming everything This land would become one vast desert.

After we had passed several of these tragic scenes, Joseph began asking questions. There was shock and confusion on his face. "What's happened here, mother? Why have all the trees been cut? It's as though the skin has been torn off the earth."

"It has been torn away!" I replied grimly. "This is tragic! Not long ago people still thought of themselves as children of the Earth Mother, Joseph. They considered the Earth a noble being steeped in holiness, and were grateful for her bounty. Every tree, every rock, every body of water was sacred and important then."

"Oracular trees, called Asheras, dotted all the high places in honor of the Goddess Asherah, forming groves where people came to worship. Trees are the arms of the Earth Mother aspiring to heaven, Joseph. The Ashera trees used to be dressed with charms, the people's prayer offerings to maintain the sacred bond between Heaven and Earth."

"Trees are essential and very nurturing, my son. Every part of a tree is useful. It's leaves build up the topsoil keeping the soil fertile. The roots keep the earth from eroding, and blowing away in storms. Trees offer food and shelter for all of Earth's children. Some of their barks are even used in healing."

"The people here have forgotten nature's holy law. They no longer walk the sacred path with the Earth, or live in harmony with its rhythms. I fear for these people, son. They are destroying the very ground under their feet, and ruining the high places dedicated to the Goddess."

Joseph had listened intently to my every word, and was brimming over with questions. "Why are they doing this, mother?"

"It's because they seek to destroy the Goddess and her worship". I said with a heavy heart. "We live at a time of great transition. The Mother Goddess is being supplanted by the Father God."

Joseph broke in with a look of worry on his face. "But everyone needs a mother and a father! Don't the people understand they need both a Father God and a Mother Goddess? It's not right the Mother be forgotten!"

Nodding in agreement, I continued, "These hilltops were once proud altars to the Mother Goddess, Joseph. Fires were lit on these high places at special times of year hoping to bring the light of the stars down to Earth. The desecration of the Goddess's groves and altars is to suppress the ancient star wisdom of the Eye Goddess and her traditions. The Brotherhood of the Black Hand is behind this! They have vowed to stamp out Ninhursag and with Her all knowledge of humankind's ancestry from the stars."

"The Brotherhood sell the trees to rich foreign kings with gold to spend. They live only for today and to fill their purses. Soon the great cedars of Lebanon will exist only in story. There will be nothing left for their children. What they don't understand is that they are destroying the very balance in nature! Famines, droughts, and natural disasters will be the result."

Joseph interrupted in his excitement. "Yahweh will correct this, won't He mother?"

"Yahweh is a mighty warrior, the Father of a proud nation." I said, looking Joseph in the eyes. "But He is a wrathful jealous God and will not allow his people to worship any other God but him."

Joseph looked at me with his wise deep eyes. "Father says Yahweh is the great hope of the future, mother. Please continue. I must understand."

I continued thoughtfully, "In the movement of the Great Ages the solar Ram of Aries has taken the place of the great lunar Mother Goddess of Taurus. In the cycle of time there is a season for everything, my son. Now it is time for the Father God to claim ascendancy over the Goddess. But it is wrong the Goddess and all Her worship be denied. It is right for you to give your allegiance to Yahweh, Joseph. He is the Great Warrior God called up by the great archons behind the universe to fight the evil Sin. But never forget the Earth Mother, the Star People from Kak.Si.Di., or the Goddess Ninhursag, who watches over you from Her throne in heaven! Walk the sacred path understanding the Earth is your Mother, though your spirit if from the stars."

Joseph nodded saying, "I won't forget! I will carry the Goddess in my heart, and seek to live in harmony with the Earth, as Mother, and Yahweh, as my Great Father."

"That's right, son! Fruitfulness is the product of the harmonious cooperation of the male and female poles of being. There will be no fruit-fulness or balance on Earth, if that important truth is lost."

Joseph's eyes had been downcast, but now they were sparkling with the truth I had revealed. He nodded gravely. "I will love the Goddess with an upright heart, mother. And, even as my spirit is directed toward the Father God Yahweh, I will not forget this beloved Earth, or Ninhur-sag, and Her shining star Kak.Si.Di., which directs the course of my destiny."

The pain in my heart lessened to hear Joseph speak. "Very good, my son. We are all part of the Earth Mother, as She is part of us. Just as we are all one with the Great Spirit behind the universe, who is the Prime Creator. If we remember who we are and live in harmony seeking balance, the Earth will be in harmony and balance. Though we think we are wise, we are fools if we think we alone direct the course of our destiny. Be true to Yahweh, Joseph, but never forget your lineage from Kak.Si.Di. The Star People shall guide you."

"How will they guide me, mother?"

"The Earth will speak to you through the babbling tongue of Her rivers, the rhythms of the weather, the winds and the animals. The Eye Goddess will open your Ancient Eyes and Ears so you will understand the language of nature. She and the Star People will tell you what you need to know through your dreams, as you have already seen."

We had arrived at a river and stopped to drink. Jacob was shouting instructions to his men. The strain of knowing he would soon meet his brother was etched upon his face. He rode toward us stopping to say, "This is the river Jabbok. We will cross at this ford. You'll spend the night atop that hill over there. It has a commanding view of the entire region, and will keep you safe from attack."

Looking up at the top of the hill I was aghast.

"But Jacob, it wouldn't be right to spend the night there. It's a dese-crated shrine." I said beseechingly.

Jacob looked at me in exasperation. "Who's in charge here? I give the orders! I had just about all I could stand from your sister this morning. Don't you become contrary! I don't care what it was! It shall be your camp tonight! It's the safest place around. I'll stay here below on the op-posite side of the river. That way if Esau comes I can lead them away."

Joseph looked at me sadly as Jacob rode away. "What shall we do, mother?"

"There's nothing we can do, but obey, dear. I'll say prayers for the healing of this place tonight."

It was an eerie night huddled amid the hallowed rocks which lay strewn about the ancient hilltop shrine. I made a sacred fire using the remains of one of the felled cedars, the mother tree, reciting prayers to the Goddess under my breath. There was a peculiar stillness in the air which had us all on edge. Leah and her boys ate their meal in silence seated around the campfire. Sobered by the stricken look on Jacob's face, they all went silently off to bed.

I stayed up pleased to have the time alone to pray. I sat atop my camel litter stoking the fire waiting for the moon to rise. The pain of the earth weighed heavily on my heart. Everything was quiet except for the rushing of the river and the choir of bullfrogs, whose cries echoed through the stillness of the night. Only a small fire marked Jacob's camp across the river.

When I closed my eyes an ancient chant bubbled up inside me. I sang soft and low, my song merging with the throaty sound of the bullfrogs' mating calls. As I finished my song a mysterious voice cried out to me from the river's surge.

RACHEL! RACHEL! YOU HAVE RELIT THE SACRED FIRE. ALL OF NATURE REJOICES AND SINGS WITH YOU TONIGHT. I AM THE SPIRIT OF THE RIVER JABBOK, THE GUARDIAN OF THESE WATERS. ONLY THOSE WITH THE ANCIENT EARS CAN HEAR ME. YOUR HEART IS HEAVY FROM THE DEVASTATION AROUND YOU. DO NOT BE DOWNCAST. YOU CAN HEAL THIS HOLY SHRINE. TAKE THE TERAFIM DOWN TO THE RIVER'S EDGE TO REVIVE THIS SACRED SITE. THE TERAFIM CAN HEAL THE WOUNDS TO NATURE.

TO YOUR RIGHT YOU'LL FIND A STONE PATH LEADING DOWN THE HILLSIDE. FOLLOW IT. BRING THE TERAFIM AND A WATERSKIN WITH YOU. PLACE THE TERAFIM IN THE SHALLOWS. WHEN THE RIVER STARTS TO BUBBLE FILL THE SKIN WITH THE MAGIC WATER. RETURN THE SAME WAY STOPPING AT THE OLD CEDAR TREE WHICH GROWS OUT OF THE LARGE BOULDER NEAR THE TOP. PLACE THE TERAFIM ON THE

EARTH, AND SPRINKLE THE HILLTOP WITH WATER WHILE RECITING YOUR PRAYER.

My heart was pounding when the Speaker of the River's words died away. I fetched a large goatskin and removed the terafim from my camel litter. No sooner had I taken hold of the oracle than the moon rose up over the horizon to light my way. The path was waiting. Its stone steps shining brightly in the moonlight, reminding me of those who had trod this same path before me in their devotion to the Goddess. I glanced at the campfire across the river. Jacob was nowhere in sight. The river beckoned me in the moonlight shimmering like a ribbon of stars. It's melodious roar increased as I descended. The path led directly across from Jacob's camp. I sat down by the river's edge and peered across. All was quiet. Jacob must have gone to sleep.

I was about to take the terafim from its silken shroud when a hot wind rose up out of nowhere. Above the rushing of the river I could hear a mighty roar. My heart stopped when I looked up. An enormous spirit bird was thundering in the sky, hovering just above the river. Its great eyes searched the night, illuminating the landscape all around.

My heart was pounding wildly as the enormous bird touched down on the opposite side of the river. Jacob came out and stood beside his tent, spear poised, shielding his eyes against the glaring light. I was trembling in fear. Though it was the dark of night, Jacob's camp was as bright as day. Jacob's men scattered in every direction. What evil had befallen us?

The beams of the mighty spirit bird fastened in on Jacob. He looked startled, but held his ground. The roar of the great bird soon ceased and a tall demonic looking creature with flashing red eyes, scaly skin, and wings stepped out of the thundering bird.

"Who are you? What do you want of me?" shouted Jacob.

The hideous creature smiled slyly. "I thought you would recognize me! Zaltan told you I had my eye on you. You must not be as clever as I thought, Jacob."

Jacob stepped back in amazement, surprised the gruesome creature knew his name.

The dark angel continued with a smirk. "I know all about you, Jacob. You are the son of Isaac. You carry Abraham's blessing. You are on your way to meet your twin brother Esau. He waits for you out in the valley with an army of four hundred men. I know you for the schemer you are, Jacob. I know why you had to leave your fatherland and take up residence in Haran. And I know how Laban tricked you in the dark on your wedding night, when you were driven by your lust. I thought we'd gotten you for sure that night!"

Jacob's face turned red at the demon's words and his lips tightened.

The demonic reptile continued on, obviously enjoying the rise he was getting out of Jacob. "You wouldn't listen to Laban or the Black Hand. But you are going to have to listen to me now."

The dark angel's remarks were more than he could bear. Overtaken with rage, Jacob struck out at the Fallen One with all the fury he could muster. Though the flailing of his spear could not erase the biting truth of the intruder's words.

The Evil One was poised ready to block Jacob's every thrust. He stood like a tower of strength undaunted by Jacob's furious assault. The futility of Jacob's rage increased with every blow that failed to make its mark. Until finally spear broken, Jacob attempted to wrestle the dark angel to the ground.

The hideous reptile hovered over Jacob, like a fiendish screech owl toying with a tiny mouse. Jacob lurched at the Evil One, like a charging ram in rut. His perseverance was astounding, but after an hour his energy began to wane.

Jacob needed assistance. Something had to be done. While the two opponents were locked in combat, I took the terafim from its silk wrapping. The moonlight fell upon it, playing it like a lyre. Its rosy light spread out quickly like tongues of fire in the darkness. With Jacob wrestling across the river, I crept up to the river's edge and placed the terafim and my goatskin in the shallows, and prayed.

WONDROUS TERAFIM, CARRY MY PRAYER ON WINGS TO KAK.SI.DI. BRING STRENGTH TO JACOB ON YOUR TONGUES OF FIRE, THAT HE MAY BE SAFE AND PREVAIL AGAINST THE EVIL ONE. GRANT JACOB THE STRENGTH TO DEFEAT NANNA/SIN.

With each recitation of my prayer the ruby glow of the terafim brightened until it completely surrounded Jacob. He bounded forth, his strength visibly increased, refusing to give in. I left the terafim in the shallows of the river, and continued my prayer.

JACOB WRESTLES WITH THE DARK ANGEL

The great battle raged on and on all night. I never ceased my simple prayer.

Finally just before daybreak, Jacob gasped out while in a deadly hold. "What vile creature are you that engages me with such superhuman strength?"

"Who do you think I am, Jacob?" replied the Evil One smiling slyly.

"You are Nanna/Sin, the Fallen Dragon of Heaven." declared Jacob, refusing to relax the fury of his hold.

"You learn fast! You're tenacious too! I could use a resourceful man like you in my service. We have much in common. I too stole from my father. Forget Yahweh! I will give you greater riches than He . . . power . . . women . . . anything your heart desires." said Sin.

"I have one Lord, His name is Yahweh! Never will I serve you, you hideous reptile!" cried Jacob adamantly.

Light entered my heart to hear a man speak with such integrity and courage. Dawn was breaking. But even after struggling the whole long night Jacob would not give in.

"Let go of me, Jacob! I cannot bear the light of day!" cried Sin with an evil smirk. "Enough of this futile rage! Save your strength for your brother! You still have four hundred men to face."

"I will not let you go until you bless me and promise to go on your way." replied Jacob stubbornly.

Sin smiled wryly. Then striking Jacob a deft blow in the socket of his hip, he replied, "Here! Take this as my blessing! Carry it with you all the days of your life as a token of your blind lust!"

Jacob winced in pain at the Evil One's blow.

"Never will I surrender to you!" said Jacob refusing to give in.

Nanna/Sin looked toward the east. "Very well then! You and your lineage will struggle against me all your days! From hereon you will no longer be called Jacob. You shall be called Israel, because you stayed with your God and did not succumb to me. Because you have striven with me, your seed shall be called upon time and again to struggle against me and my right arm, the Brotherhood of the Black Hand."

Jacob relaxed his grip and the Dragon of Heaven departed in his great spirit bird with its flashing eyes.

The Evil One had fled. Truth and goodness would prevail. A man's heart had triumphed over the darkness of heaven. Tears of joy and relief rushed to my eyes, as the dawn's light spread out across the landscape.

Looking down at the terafim, I said a prayer of gratitude to heaven. The combined strength of the God and Goddess had been able to stave off the Evil One. Jacob and his lineage would stem the tide of corruption in the coming Age of Iron.

Jacob fell to his knees. Raising his hands to heaven, he prayed aloud. "GREAT LORD OF HEAVEN, THE ONE TRUE GOD OF MY FA-THERS, THANK YOU FOR STANDING BY ME THAT I MIGHT PREVAIL AGAINST THAT EVIL REPTILE. BE WITH ME AND MY LINEAGE ALL THE DAYS OF OUR LIFE. AND STAND BY ME AGAIN TODAY AS I MEET MY BROTHER ESAU.

Then he dropped to the ground and lay looking up at the sky.

Jacob was still in prayer, when I filled my waterskin giving thanks to the God and Goddess, and climbed silently up the ancient steps. When I reached the top of the hill I poured water on the cedar tree as directed. Then I lit a sacred fire and laid the terafim on the ground. As I prayed while watering the ground atop the ancient hilltop shrine, snow white doves appeared out of nowhere perching on the ruins of the altar.

Awakened by their song, Joseph stuck his head outside his tent. Spying the doves, he cried out joyfully, "Good morning, mother! Your prayers last night were answered. The hilltop sparkles with new life this morning. And look who's here! The Goddess's birds have come to thank you!"

I smiled at Joseph happily. "Yes, dear! The Speaker of the River told me what to do."

"Can rivers speak?" Joseph asked in surprise.

"Of course, my darling! Nature is alive and always communicating with us, but only those who listen with their heart can hear."

While Joseph went off to dress I slipped the terafim back in its silk cloth and placed them inside my saddle bags.

When Joseph reappeared, I said, "There's nothing to fear today! She Who Watches is with us! The last time I saw this many doves was at your birth, my darling. We're the first ones up. Come! Sit here with me beside the fire. It's a special fire. I made it with acacia branches I gathered down by the river. Let's ask for a blessing and protection on us all. Today's an important day! Today Jacob meets his brother Esau!"

JACOB WRESTLES WITH THE DARK ANGEL

Jacob appeared over the hilltop limping toward the central fire, as the others began gathering around the hearth. His face was lined with exhaustion, but he was beaming with pride as he called us all together.

I ran and put my arms around him.

Leah came toward us, inquiring solicitously, "Are you alright, Jacob? You're limping! What happened to your leg?"

A hush came over everyone. Jacob dismissed Leah's question with a gesture of impatience. "It's nothing!" he exclaimed, taking a bowl of porridge from Zilpah. "We have more important things to discuss. An incredible thing happened here last night."

Spying the doves, he smiled down at me and drew me closer, declaring, "What a glorious sight!"

"I'm so proud of you, Jacob!" I whispered softly.

He looked over at me quizzically, and was about to say something, when he was interrupted by one of Leah's boys. "What happened to your leg, father? Did you fight your brother here last night?'

"No, son!" declared Jacob proudly. "From hereon this place shall be called Peniel, because I wrestled with Nanna/Sin here last night and I survived. Yes! I persevered against the Evil One, because of Yahweh's blessing. Don't feel sorry for me! This limp is my battle scar. I shall wear it proudly. Henceforth, I shall be called, Israel, because I stayed with God and held off the Evil One. And as I have been strong against Sin, I shall prevail against men."

Looking around at his boys, Jacob continued, "You too, and your sons, and your sons' sons, shall have to take up the fight against Sin. We are Yahweh's Chosen People, His bastion of righteousness against the Evil One and his Brotherhood of the Black Hand. We shall be a great and mighty people!"

Tears came to my eyes. Murmurs started up around the campfire. The fear of God was in Reuben's voice as he inquired, "Nanna/Sin was here last night battling with you, father?"

Israel looked him squarely in the eye, and answered, "Yahweh stood by me all night as I wrestled with the ancient Dragon of Heaven. Nanna/Sin came after me as Zaltan said he would. He sailed the sky in a great boat with eyes that flashed lightning in the night. I wrestled with him until the break of day. This limp is the mark of my valor. Glory be to God!"

No one dared say another word. We all stood gazing in awe at Jacob as he ate his porridge.

When Jacob finished his bowl, he limped to the edge of the hill. Looking out over the valley in the direction in which we'd be headed, he said, "Esau and his men are not far away. I can see them out in the far distance. Our flocks will be reaching them soon. There's no time to waste. I don't want to meet my brother down below among these narrow passes. I want to encounter him in the open valley. So let's hurry!"

"Dan, Naphtali, Gad, and Asher, follow behind me with Zilpah and Bilhah. Reuben, Simeon, Levi, Judah, Issachar, and Zebulun, you follow behind them with Leah. Rachel, you and Joseph take up the rear. That's the order! Keep to it! Now finish eating. Then pack up the camp. I'm going to direct the men and see about the animals. I'll wait for you below."

As Israel turned to go, Leah exclaimed, "I think it's only right that I and my children have the position of greatest safety at the rear of the caravan, Jacob. Afterall, I am your first wife, and Reuben is your first-born."

Israel sighed wearily. "Last night I fought with Nanna/Sin! Must I fight you now? We're no longer in your father's house, Leah. My name is Israel. You shall call me by that name from here on and bow to my wishes! Now bow!"

The color draining from her face, Leah bowed meekly. When Jacob left Leah's face contorted into an angry grimace as she gathered her sons together. Abuzz with contention, they sputtered under their breath seething with fury as they finished their morning meal. I took Joseph's hand and led him as far away from Leah and her boys as I could to eat our porridge. After they finished packing up camp Simeon and Levi directed angry glances at us, then hurried to meet Jacob at the base of the hill.

Today of all days this behavior of their's was appalling. Brother against brother, sister against sister, would this senseless vying ever cease? What would become of us as a people? We were all in this together. We had greater foes. But even at this crucial juncture every one of my movements was met by some form of their resistance. If we couldn't stand together now, how would we ever be able to stand against Sin and the Black Hand?

The climb down this side of the hill was steep and difficult. The erosion on the barren hilltop caused the ground to crumble away beneath our feet as we descended. Joseph had run on ahead when I heard a dove cry out frantically. I hurried in the direction of its call. Drawing near I heard a child crying. Looking over the edge of a steep crevice, I saw Joseph crouched below crying.

"Are you alright, Joseph?" I called out in alarm.

From where I stood it appeared he'd fallen and missed an enormous boulder by only a hand's length. I called Dan and Napthali, and they pulled Joseph out of the deep ravine together. Joseph was torn and bleeding when they dragged him from the pit. His limbs were sound but he was cut all over, and weak from shock. I sat him down on the terafim inside my saddle bag. He was silent as I bathed his cuts and gave him water from my goatskin to drink.

The water soon revived him. Clutching me, he said in a weak voice. "Thank you for saving me, mother."

"What happened, Joseph, you're such an able climber?"

A dazed faraway look came into his eyes. "It was Simeon and Levi, mother. They tripped me. They were hiding over there behind that rock, and called me over. Then they tripped me and pushed me into the ravine. They did it on purpose, mother! You should have seen the look on their faces."

Joseph broke into anguished sobs. I stroked his head and held him to me as he cried. Closing my eyes I heard the Nefilim's warning echo in my heart. 'Though your son's own people may plot to kill him."

I had to get ahold of myself. I couldn't let Joseph see how disturbed I was. But looking at his face was like tearing the scab off the wounds of my past. I knew the shock, the disbelief, and ravaging grief that was in his heart. I knew how frightful the whole world could seem when your own family plotted against you. It wasn't the bruises to Joseph's arms and legs that made him cry. It wasn't the sudden fall which catapulted him into this disoriented state. It was the brutal reality of knowing his own family wished him harm.

What words are there to describe a mother's grief at her child's loss of innocence? The disappointment of my own life was as nothing in comparison to this assault on Joseph's trust. No wonder the Family of

Light had fled this wondrous Earth. It was awful having to witness man's inhumanity to man.

I crushed some resin from one of the fallen trees nearby, and applied it to Joseph's wounds to staunch the bleeding. But there was nothing I could do to stop the bleeding in his heart. These were the Chosen People? Esau hated Jacob. Joseph's brothers hated him. Leah hated me. This was a patriarchal family! How would we survive such rampant hatred? How could we stand against Sin and the Black Hand, when we couldn't even stand together? The Goddess was the instructor of the human heart. Couldn't Yahweh see this was the grim result of His suppression of the Goddess?

"You have had some very difficult lessons of late, Joseph. Don't lose heart! Yesterday you saw how the earth has been ravished. This morning your own brothers attacked you. These are hard lessons for one so young. But what can we expect from a people who cannot tolerate the Goddess of Love, whose throne should be in every heart? Don't let your heart be poisoned, darling! Though your brothers hurt you intentionally don't take their hatred into your heart. If you do you will be letting them get the best of you. For you'll become like them."

"Never fear! The God and Goddess will protect you. Did you see how the Goddess's dove was watching over you? It called me to your side."

Joseph looked up at me with soulful eyes. Nodding thoughtfully, he wiped away his tears. "I have some joyful news. You'll be the first to know." I said hoping to lift his spirits.

Joseph looked at me in anticipation.

"You won't be alone for long, Joseph. I'm going to have baby. Won't that be grand?"

Joseph caught his breath. "You're going to have a baby, mother?"

I nodded happily.

The light was returning to Joseph's eyes as he said, "Really?"

"Yes! By the time winter's here you'll have your very own sister, or brother. Now, come! We must hurry. We don't want to keep Jacob waiting."

We were both still shaken when we arrived at the base of the hill. Jacob was too busy to notice. Everyone was mounted and ready to go. The animals had already departed. Jacob was impatient to leave. As soon as we appeared he gave the signal and the caravan started off. I wanted him to know what happened. I wanted justice to be done. But Jacob was preoccupied with the impending confrontation with his own brother. Simeon and Levi were already leaving.

Where was Jacob's blessing now? The envious sister knot! The murderous brother knot! Rivalrous brothers and sisters! Such a futile destructive dance! Where would it all end? Why did Yahweh seem to foster such rivalry and jealousy in His wake? But there wasn't any time. We weren't being blessed by Israel, the great patriarch. We were being pushed on from one great confrontation to the next.

Jacob was riding at the head of the caravan. Unless Joseph and I mounted now, we'd be left behind. I helped Joseph up and handed him the reins. When I looked to my amazement the wounds on his hands were gone.

With a wide grin on my face, I said, "Look, Joseph! Your wounds have been healed by the resin from the Ashera tree. See how much the God and Goddess love you. They'll always be with you Joseph."

Joseph's face was hot and flushed, but he was smiling when he said, "I'm not worried, mother. Look! Here come the doves!"

As I put my saddlebag under my camel litter and mounted, the angelic birds billed and cooed exhorting us on our way. They accompanied us like a heavenly banner of protection as we made our way through the narrow passes.

The sun was directly overhead when we entered the lush Jordan valley. I breathed a sigh of relief as the long line of our company spread out. On the broad plains of the Jordan valley our vision opened, and travel was easier. A great cloud of dust soon became visible on the horizon. Four hundred men! The number reverberated in my mind as the heat made the plains appear to ripple in the noonday sun.

Jacob signalled us to halt. We gathered round him. Shouting out orders, he directed all of us women and children inside the protective circle of the camels. War cries assailed my ears as my feet touched ground. The earth shook with the thunder of many hooves. Jacob's face went pale as he gazed at the huge body of men fast approaching. The camels got frightened and ran off in the direction of our herds. I couldn't blame the noble creatures for being afraid of the horrific sight coming toward us.

Jacob's face was tense as he commanded us to take our assigned positions in the retinue. The doves were still hovering directly above us, as Joseph and I took our position in the rear. Jacob stood at the front of the line. With arms raised high he cried out to Yahweh to deliver His promise.

My eyes were drawn to a large striking man with a great shock of flaming red hair. This had to be Esau, riding at the forefront of his company. His fierce look and determined bearing caused him to stand out above all the rest. This was a leader of men. His company moved in unison with him alert to his every move. As he came closer I could see how he resembled Jacob, only with coarser features. I kept ahold of Joseph's hand and prayed to She Who Watches and her valiant son Ninurta.

The vast sea of men were upon us. Esau rode up proudly and gave the signal for his men to surround us. Jacob ran out ahead of our procession. Throwing himself to the ground, he bowed before his brother seven times.

Esau sat high in his saddle, a look of deep satisfaction on his face to see his brother grovelling. Grinning broadly, he pulled out his sword holding it over Jacob's head.

The doves rose in a tall pillar formation fluttering wildly above Joseph and I.

A dark Hittite woman let out a trilling cry and rode up from the rear pointing at the doves. "Wait, Esau! Wait!" she cried passionately.

The men parted before her like sheaves of wheat in a driving wind. Coming up beside Esau, she continued shouting and pointing in our direction. "Please reconsider! Look at those doves, Esau! They're protected!"

Silence spread over the multitude like ever expanding rings in a pool of water. Still cringing on the ground, a cautious Jacob turned his head in the direction the woman was pointing. All eyes turned to view the doves hovering in their remarkable pillar formation above us.

Esau was visibly moved by the spiralling pillar of doves. After staring in amazement at the doves for some time, a quizzical smile formed on his face. He laid down his sword and dismounted. Approaching Jacob, he took him in his arms and wept.

After parting from their embrace, he looked in our direction again, and queried, "Who are those two the heaven's so favor?"

"They are the wives and children God has bestowed upon me, your servant." answered Jacob.

"I can see that! But who is that woman and child attended by the doves?" inquired Esau again impatiently.

"That is my wife, Rachel, and my son, Joseph, my lord. Shall I bring them to you?"

"Please, do! But first, allow me. This is my wife, Judith. She is a Hittite priestess."

Jacob bowed, and beckoned for us. Half expecting Leah to trip me on my way up to the front of the line, I approached cautiously. But Leah wasn't the least concerned with me this once. Her eyes were fastened on Esau, taking in every bit of his virile frame. So fascinated was she with Esau, she hadn't even noticed that I'd been favored.

The doves maintained their remarkable formation moving in unison with Joseph and I as we moved forward.

Esau took my hand and bowed, as he addressed me. "Hail, Rachel, dove of Haran! My brother is indeed blessed to have such a wife!"

"Hail to you, Esau." I said smiling. "You too are blessed to have such a fine wife."

Gazing into Esau's eyes I saw we had no further need of protection. Esau was a man of vision. Perhaps Isaac had not been so blind after all. Esau was a great leader of men, yet not too proud to heed the wisdom of his Hittite wife. I was impressed with Jacob's brother. It took great control as well as reverence for a higher power to conquer the fury of a lifetime's worth of rage so quickly.

I turned to greet Judith, and smiled with pleasure to see a Sister there. Taking up my hand as I had done so often in my youth, I drew the spiral of the Goddess on her forehead in recognition.

She gazed at me with heartfelt warmth and admiration in her eyes. "Welcome, Rachel! It is an honor to be in the company of one of the Goddess's chosen. Her blessing overshadows you. May you and your son find peace and great happiness in our land!"

Jacob and Esau shook hands. Time and distance had healed the old wounds of the rivalrous twins. No longer were they boys competing for the same prize. They were two distinctly different men pursuing their own unique destinies. There was no man in all Haran who could compare with Jacob. But here in the bosom of his family was Jacob's match. Much could be learned by observing Jacob with his twin brother.

I glanced over at Leah. Her countenance had softened from her brief introduction to Esau. I wanted to reach out and hug my sister. I wanted to shake hands with her and tell her that I wished we'd had the same good fortune as these two brothers.

When I glanced at Leah again, she was looking at me as well. It was usually uncomfortable when our eyes met, but it was different this time. Had Leah also been touched by Esau and Jacob's reunion and given cause to think? Just then Leah noticed the warmth which had developed between Judith and me, and her face hardened back into the same cold mask she always wore with me. In the next moment there was fire in her eyes. Only this time her jealousy was aimed at Judith. The very one who had saved her husband's life.

I put my arm around Judith protectively.

Jacob was fawning all over Esau. Beneath his obsequiousness I could sense he was ill at ease, as he inquired, "If it pleases you, my lord, do you remember the prayer that was written on the ancient scroll that was passed down from Abraham?"

Esau shrugged his shoulders. "No! Why should I? That scroll was given to you along with the blessing. You should have committed it to memory. Now tell me, why did you send all that livestock on ahead of you, brother?"

"They are gifts to win my lord's favor." replied Jacob bowing low.

"Keep your gifts, brother! I have plenty." answered Esau proudly.

"Please accept these gifts if I have found favor in your eyes." insisted Jacob. "I come into your presence as if into the presence of God, and you have received me kindly. God has been generous with me. I have all I need."

Only with Jacob's persistent urging did Esau finally reply. "Very well then! But please allow me to escort you to my home. I will lead you."

Jacob threw his head back with an anxious start, as if the mere thought of Esau leading him was distasteful. Shifting his weight back and forth between his feet nervously, he finally found a worthy excuse. Continuing in the same obsequious tone he had adopted earlier, he said, "May it please my lord to go on ahead of his servant. I shall meet you in Seir. But first I must stop to thank Yahweh properly for your generous and peaceful welcome."

"At least allow me to leave a guide with you." responded Esau with concern.

"There's no need for that." replied Jacob. "All I desire is to win your favor."

"Very well then!" said Esau, not wishing to offend his brother. "But don't be long! We have much to catch up on when we meet again in Seir."

When Esau and his men were out of sight, wily Jacob refused to follow. He turned west instead of south toward Succoth. There we stayed while he nursed his wounded pride.

PART SEVEN

Life in the Promised Land

23

ARRIVAL IN CANAAN

SUCCOTH WAS TRANQUIL LUSH AND GREEN WHERE WE PITCHED OUR tents and made booths for our livestock, so we could rest. The confrontations with Laban and Esau had resulted in accord. I should have felt profound relief to put the life of a wanderer behind me. Yet my heart was not at peace. Jacob was a different man. I no longer knew my husband. Overnight his hair was streaked with grey. His limp and the new lines on his face told the story of his encounters with Laban, Esau, and the Evil One.

Jacob was Israel now. Israel wore his scars like the battle ribbons of a warrior. Father of a great people, and sworn enemy of Nanna/Sin, Israel preferred to be alone or in the company of His God. He no longer had time to confide the secrets in his heart to a woman. Leah and Laban were no longer between us, now it was Yahweh. Israel was His torch, His sword, the bearer of His holy truth. I could see it in the passion in his eyes even as they avoided me.

I was in turmoil, consumed by one smoldering question. Did Israel suspect I had the terafim? He was a stranger to my tent. He kept away from all women, just as Yahweh did. We were in Succoth one whole moon before I was able to speak with him.

It was a beautiful morning I sought him out, following him to the fields after breakfast. After he had given instructions to his men for the day, I approached him. Though seeing me coming, he hastened his step in the opposite direction.

When I caught up with him, he regarded me impatiently. "What are you doing here, Rachel? You should be back at camp with Joseph."

This was not the same man who used to delight in my company. Though his greeting was curt and none too inviting, I began, "It's a lovely morning, Jacob. I hoped we could take a walk together. We haven't had a moment alone since we left Haran."

He regarded me with the cold eyes of a stranger. "My name has changed! You are to call me Israel, like everyone else, Rachel!"

My face reddened to be scolded like a child. "Forgive me, Israel! But it's quite a change after all these years. And there's been so much to adjust to since we left Haran."

Israel had only been half listening as we walked along, but the mention of Haran got his attention. "Enough talk of Haran! You can't look back! We have to move forward!"

I stopped and looked at him inquisitively. Israel halted and fixed his eyes on me, as I tried to explain. "I'm not looking backward, Israel. It's just hard to take in all that's happened. I'm glad we've settled for a while. How long do you intend for us to stay here?"

"Only long enough to regroup." replied Israel. "Then we leave for Shechem. It's just a day or two's journey across the river."

"Shechem?" I exclaimed in dismay, thinking of Judith. "I thought you told your brother we would meet with him in Seir."

Israel was irritated at the mere mention of Esau, and replied sternly, "I have no intention of following Esau! I walk behind no man! I walk with the Lord my God in the footsteps of my grandfather Abraham. I only told Esau I would follow him to avoid any ugliness on his part."

"Won't our failure to visit irritate him all the more? I asked cautiously.

Israel chose not to respond, and began walking away. I had to hasten my step to catch up with him. We were on patriarchal soil, and Jacob was changing into Israel right before my eyes. Israel was a man possessed by God. Though, like Jacob, he could resort to deception to get his way.

"That's too bad!" I said with a note of regret in my voice. "I had hoped to see Judith again."

"Judith!" he repeated impatiently. "That's another good reason not to follow Esau. I don't want you fraternizing with Hittite or Canaanite women, Rachel! Their heads are filled with superstitious ideas, and they worship foreign gods. Stay away from all of them!"

I took a deep breath. Israel was beginning to sound like Laban. My blood was getting heated when I declared, "That Hittite woman saved your life!"

Israel gave me a sharp look. "Don't be foolish, Rachel! Yahweh saved my life! That Hittite woman had nothing to do with it! Yahweh stretched out his hand to save me. With a strong arm He delivered me from the wrath of my enemies, because I am His chosen one. The doves were a sign of His presence! Even someone as blind as Esau could see that!"

There was no use trying to argue with Israel. He was even less Rachel's husband, than Jacob had been. "Very well!" I said, swallowing my irritation. "There is something I'd like to tell you."

Israel had started walking away again. He turned back looking at me impatiently. "What is it?" he asked sharply.

"I'm pregnant!" I responded smiling happily.

Israel's mouth dropped wide open, as he stared at me in amazement. "Yet another of Yahweh's blessings! How wonderful! I shall need many sons to accomplish all the Lord has planned for me!"

Then suddenly looking me in the eyes, he inquired suspiciously, "But how can that be, Rachel? We haven't been together since Laban searched your tent. And you said you were in your moonchange."

My face was flushed as I replied, "My cycles have become confused with all this travel. Nevertheless, I'm quite certain that I'm pregnant!"

Israel pursed his mouth and chose his words carefully. "Since we've camped here, Leah has been insinuating that it was you who took Laban's household gods. I must say she's made some convincing arguments. This is a serious accusation, Rachel. I am the sworn enemy of Sin. So please answer truthfully! Did you take them?"

Looking Israel straight in the eye, I declared, "I swear to you I have nothing of Laban's! You of all people should know how I feel about Sin!"

"I'm glad to hear that, Rachel," replied Israel, sighing with relief. "But now I really must go. Please excuse me. I must be alone to commune with the Lord."

I was taken aback. This wasn't the old Jacob, who relished celebrating his new progeny.

Incredulous, I stammered forth, "But surely you have a few minutes to spare, Israel. Or must you always be alone? . . . Does this mean you will not be coming to my tent anymore?"

Israel stopped in his tracks to see me so downcast. "I'm sorry to disappoint you, Rachel. But I will not be staying in your tent any longer. I must be vigilant. I am Yahweh's dedicated warrior. I have stood in the burning light of His holy truth. He saved me from the Evil One. With a strong arm He has delivered me from the hardness of Laban's heart, and lifted me above my brother's wrath. Yahweh has great need of me. Night and day He speaks to me. My heart, my soul, my life, everything belongs to Him."

"I am pleased for your spiritual awakening, Israel. But why must you shut me out?" I inquired beseechingly. "Allow me to assist you in the service to your God? Man was not meant to be alone. On the spiritual plane, as well as the physical, a man needs the Feminine to be fruitful."

"You don't understand the ways of my God, Rachel! But it's not your fault. How can you? Woman was created to serve man and be submissive. If you want to be of service to Yahweh you have to do it through me. If you want to pray to Yahweh you can do that by yourself. If you wish to win the Lord's favor give me time to myself, and don't disturb me." declared Jacob walking away.

My mind was in turmoil as I watched him limp away. Israel was so serious and brooding. Since his confrontation with Sin, he spent all his time communing with Yahweh and giving spiritual instruction to his sons. Even the fact that I was to have his child was something more between him and his God, than between the two of us.

My blood was boiling as I watched him go. Israel was making it very clear. He and his sons were the chosen ones. There was no place in his Promised Land for me. I was a mere distraction that might take him away from his God. The En Priestess had been right many years ago when she said that Jacob would never truly be able to partner me, or regard me with respect.

I had given up my homeland to follow this man. Once again he had disappointed me. Only this time it was for his God. Was my premonition true? Would I be going it alone throughout this pregnancy?

By the time I returned to camp my mind was filled with dark foreboding. Yahweh was a jealous God to take Israel away from the ones he loved. Did the patriarchal Father God intend to make Jacob like Himself, powerful, but lone and solitary? I would leave Israel alone. It had never been my intention to come between him and his God. But I feared his neglect would resound well beyond us into future generations. What would the future be like for patriarchal women?

Of course, the Goddess could also pull you into solitude and seclusion to commune with Her at times. That was the whole purpose of the moon lodge. But the Goddess also fostered love and the understanding of the interdependence of all life. I prayed those values not be lost in the clash of metals, and the force of arms in Yahweh's holy wars.

The vale of Shechem was an enchanting place steeped in power and mystery at the crossroads of ancient trade routes which dissected the land. In Shechem's valley every rock was alive with power, every breeze caused the trees to whisper long forgotten wisdom. Even the air was a pungent incense to the gods. Shechem was overshadowed by two large mountains, Mt. Ebal on the north and Mt. Gerizim on the south. These two majestic guardians protected Shechem, providing the verdant valley with amazing acoustical properties that rendered every tree an oracle. I found peace in the shadow of the holy mountains. There the Nefilim spoke to me fulfilling the yearning in my heart.

Israel was also exhilarated by the magic and beauty of this sacred place. Shortly after we arrived he gathered his sons together in the shade of Mt. Gerizim to recount their greatgrandfather Abraham's experiences there. His story travelled on the wind between the mountains rallying the ancient spirits and re-consecrating the land. "This is the Promised Land, my sons! Yahweh spoke to your great grandfather Abraham here. He repeated to me what he first said to Abraham here in Shechem. 'Leave your country, your family, and your father's house for the land that I will show you. I will make of you a great nation. I will bless you. Your name will become so famous all the world will remember it as a blessing. And all the tribes of Earth shall bless themselves by you.'"

"Abraham left Haran when he was seventy five to follow the will of the Lord. He followed Yahweh as we have done. Abraham took with him his wife Sarah, his nephew Lot, and a company of fighting men. They came to Shechem in search of the Oak of Moreh. The Canaanites were here then just as they are today. Yahweh appeared to Abraham in this lush green valley saying, 'This land I give to you and your descendants'. Abraham built an altar here in gratitude, as we shall do, in thanksgiving for Yahweh's promise and protection."

"Abraham continued on to Bethel. The very place where Yahweh showed me His great ladder to heaven with angels ascending and descending. God's voice may be heard here. The angels of the Lord still come in great numbers, my sons. This is sacred land. Abraham pitched his tent in Bethel, and built an altar to Yahweh invoking His holy name. Abraham received his holy orders in Bethel. There he was told to go down to the Sinai with his cavalry to protect the spaceport for the Elohim, the Nefilim, the great Angels of Heaven."

"We will rest here. The Lord will lead us to the oak of Moreh, and Abraham's altar. I shall anoint it with oil this very day and pray to find land here for us to purchase. Then we'll build our own altar and await instructions from on high."

Israel's words echoed throughout the verdant valley announcing his arrival. The boys' eyes were wide with wonder. Brimming over with questions, they raised their hands waiting for their turn to speak.

Simeon was the first to gain his father's attention.

"If this land was bequeathed to us by Yahweh through our great-grandfather Abraham, why do we need to purchase it? This land already belongs to us!" declared Simeon arrogantly.

Israel looked upon his son with patience, saying, "This is the Promised Land. It belongs to us. But we are newcomers, and there are many here before us. We must live in peace with our neighbors, until Yahweh announces it is time for us to claim dominion over all the land."

"Save your silver, father!" interrupted Simeon in his excitement. "If Yahweh has given us this land, we can easily conquer it with our swords."

"Keep your sword in its scabbard, son!" commanded Israel. "We come in peace, one small tribe against the many Canaanites already here.

Only Yahweh can tell us when it is time to take up swords. Until that time we live here in peace with our neighbors. You've been listening to Abraham's story, Simeon, but you have not understood its meaning. We are in God's hands. It is His will that shall be done. It is for Him to guide us. He shall lead us as He did Abraham, as we are His Chosen People."

"Alright, father." replied Simeon, crestfallen.

Israel nodded at Joseph's upraised hand. Young as he was, Joseph turned to face his brothers as he spoke. "Do not speak of bloodshed in this beautiful land, brothers. Let us carry love in our hearts and be an example to our neighbors of Yahweh's holy law."

Leah's sons responded by snickering at Joseph. When he turned to face Israel, they all made faces behind his back. "When do we go in search of the holy Oak of Moreh, father?" inquired Joseph. "Perhaps Yahweh will speak to me there."

"Who do you think you are?" spouted Reuben in annoyance. "You're just a child! I'm the first born! If Yahweh speaks to anyone besides father, He'll speak to me."

"Enough of this petty squabbling!" cried Israel above the din of all the boys. "There's one more thing I want you all to remember! You're going to be surrounded by strangers here. You must beware of these Canaanites with their false gods, and their foolish superstitions. Blessed is the Lord Our God! The Lord is One! Yahweh will have no other Gods before Him!"

Yahweh did indeed guide Israel and his sons. Taking them upon His shoulders, we were led directly to the altar of Abraham and the Oak of Moreh in the shadow of Mt. Gerizim. And the Lord saw to it that Israel was able to purchase a tract of land there from Hamor, prince of Shechem, who welcomed us and treated us fairly.

I was at home in Shechem. My spirit was at peace knowing this was a place the angels still visited. As my body grew heavy with child, I took long walks absorbing the hallowed power of the region. And I built an altar near a brook, beside one of the Goddess's groves.

In the vale of Shechem I came to see that Israel's neglect had its advantages. Left alone I was free to devote myself to the Goddess, and prepare for the forthcoming birth. My inner vision led me to all the ancient power centers in the region. Joseph often accompanied me on my visits to these sacred places. There I instructed him in the ancient art of divination, teaching him to listen to the wind as it rustled through the trees, and interpret the flight of the sacred birds. I also taught him to read the patterns of the leaves in mother's silver divination cup.

Joseph was wise beyond his years. A mere eleven years old, he was a natural priest and diviner, and gifted with the inner sight. He revelled in all the knowledge I had to give him. His questions helped me see things I had never thought about before. We enjoyed each other's company so much Joseph usually preferred to spend his time with me rather than with his older brothers. He had so little in common with his older brothers and with each day their differences swelled.

Leah's boys enjoyed tormenting animals for sport. Animals were not the only creatures Leah's sons loved to torment. They also gloried in harassing Joseph, and their little sister Dinah. Whenever Joseph spent time with his brothers, he always came away with a bruise and his feelings hurt. I tried speaking about this with Israel, but he'd hear none of it, insisting it was what all brothers did.

One afternoon during the wheat harvest, as we walked by our neighbors' threshing floors piled high with golden mounds of grain, I heard the Nefilim in my heart telling me it was time to speak to Joseph about the miracle of his conception at the harvest moon. We sat down amid the heaping piles of grain and spoke for hours. I told Joseph all I knew of Kak.Si.Di. from whence his father came.

The season rounded like my belly, and there was much to be thankful for. The wheat and grape harvests were abundant that year. One day when the crops had been brought in for winter storage, Joseph and I set out for a walk through the countryside. We had just turned toward the Oak of Moreh, when Joseph cried, "Look, mother! See how many people are gathered at the holy tree. They're hanging ornaments on it. Why are they moaning?"

I smiled gazing over at a woman making a wheat dolly. Remembering the rites of my childhood, I said. "That doll represents the spirit of the wheat, Joseph. The people call her the Wheat Mother. They must be praying for next year's crops."

"Why are the people groaning after such an abundant harvest, mother?"

I pointed down at the cracked dry ground beneath our feet. "Do you see how parched the soil is, Joseph? It's dried out after the long hot summer.

Joseph nodded his head, as I continued, "The people are praying for rain to moisten the soil, so they can prepare the ground for next spring's crop. If the rains don't come soon the growing season will be too short for the spring wheat crop."

Joseph's brow was furrowed, as he asked, "Is there anything we can do, mother?"

"Take my divination cup! Fill it with water from the stream beside the sacred oak. Then bring it to me." I said after thinking for a moment. "I'll wait for you here beside Abraham's altar. Now go, and be careful not to disturb the people's prayer."

"Yes, mother!" said Joseph obediently.

I waited beside the altar watching. The chanting died down to a soft murmur when Joseph went to the stream to fill the silver cup with water. On his return he smiled and bowed his head in respect to the people, then hastened to me with the cup.

"Thank you, son! Now stand with me, and as I say the prayer pour the water in the center of the altar."

DEAR FATHER GOD, YAHWEH, GOD OF ABRAHAM, ISAAC, ISRAEL, AND JOSEPH, AND DEAR MOTHER GODDESS, NIN-HURSAG, LADY OF THE FERTILE EARTH, PLEASE HEAR OUR HUMBLE PRAYER. JOIN HANDS IN PEACE AND LOVE. OPEN WIDE THE VAULT OF HEAVEN SENDING FORTH YOUR GIFT OF RAIN.

When Joseph finished pouring the water, he came and stood beside me. We continued the litany, our two voices merging into one.

The wind died down. Suddenly a celestial music sounded forth like a host of bells. Fire started dancing on the treetops in the grove about us.

Gasping at the awesome sight, we stepped back away from the trees. People started flocking around us gazing in reverent awe at the fire dancing on the trees' canopes.

"What is this magic?" a woman cried. "Not a single leaf or branch is being scorched."

Great clouds began amassing overhead. I took Joseph's hand in mine and we continued our prayer until the sound of the bells grew so loud it drowned our voices out. Soon the heavens opened up putting out the mysterious fire. As the rain intensified the people shouted out their praises to the gods falling into each others arms. Then they swarmed about us, clasping hands and dancing in jubilation.

The rain was falling hard and we were getting soaked. I grabbed Joseph's hand. We stepped through the circle of dancers taking cover beneath a tree, as the rain started down in earnest. The people pranced and leapt about in ecstatic dance.

I could barely hear Joseph above the laughter of the dancers when he said, "Look at Abraham's altar, mother! Though it's raining everywhere else, not a single drop has fallen on it."

The people danced and sang in jubilation until the rain abated. Then happy and exhausted they came and bowed to us in appreciation before they left.

A wise woman approached the altar stopping at a respectful distance. Bowing low, she exclaimed, "The altar is dry. What miracle is this?"

Looking up she addressed us respectfuly, "Greetings! I am Zara, Wise Woman of our tribe. To whom did you pray for this rain? I wish to send them our thanks. Astarte and Baal, have abandoned us."

I stepped through the dripping branches as through a purifying veil. Gazing into her dark proud eyes, I saw only heartfelt respect and curiosity, so I responded, "We were praying to Ninhursag, Great Mother of the Sumerians, and to the Father God Yahweh. He is the God of Abraham, our forbear, who built this altar when he travelled through your land many years ago. I am Rachel, the wife of Israel. This is my son Joseph. We are new here, and were grateful to have been able to purchase this land which was so special to our ancestor. I come from Haran a town to the far north on the Balikh, a tributary of the great Euphrates river."

The woman bowed saying, "Welcome." as the others crowded round. "I have heard of Haran. It's on the caravan route near Carcamesh."

I nodded, smiling broadly. Zara continued as her people's spokeswoman. "Many thanks for the wonders you have wrought! You are a great priestess to have called down such a rain. Would you honor us with your presence at our harvest celebration next week? Bring your whole family, if you wish. We shall offer the first fruits of harvest to our Gods and make our usual harvest sacrifice."

I bowed my head to Zara. "Thank you. I'd be pleased to attend."

The freedom of being out from under Laban's watchful eye made me bold. I went to Leah's tent that evening. Dinah was sitting at the entrance to her mother's tent when I arrived. She was sorting out laundry in the late afternoon light Her face brightened at the sight of me.

Smiling warmly, she stood up greeting me with a kiss. "Good evening, Aunt Rachel. Ill tell mother you are here. I'll just be a moment."

I could see Leah grimace through the dim light of the tent, as she snapped at Dinah. "All right! Get back to work! You should have finished sorting those clothes long ago. Hurry! They must soak overnight."

Leah came to the door of the tent. "What do you want?" she inquired begrudgingly.

Not having been invited in, I stood outside the entrance gazing at Leah's sour face. I felt like turning on my heels, but I saw Dinah's smiling face gazing up at me. 'Hello, Leah! I came to see how you are getting along. Do you like Shechem?"

Leah sighed heavily and cast her eyes down at the floor. Hands on her hips barring my entrance, she said, "I don't have time for small talk, Rachel. If Israel is content here, then so am I. It's just awkward not knowing anyone. It reminds me of the years after mother's death."

Leah hadn't mentioned mother in years. Glad for the opening I said, "Those were lonesome years! That's exactly why I've come, Leah. There's an interesting circle of women in town. They're preparing a harvest celebration next week. We're invited. Would you and Dinah like to come?"

Leah shook her head disapprovingly. "Won't you ever do as you're told? You heard Israel say he didn't want us fraternizing with these Canaanites, and getting involved in their rites?"

"Are we supposed to become hermits?" I asked sighing loudly.

"There you go again always looking for trouble." said Leah irritably. "I have no wish to return to a Goddess circle. It's the Goddess I have to thank for that good for nothing over there. If that's all you came about, I wish you'd leave."

I was only too happy to leave. But poor Dinah! There was no escape for her. It was foolish of me to think that Leah might have changed, because Israel was no longer paying attention to me.

Later that evening I heard someone outside my tent. I sprang up defensively, half expecting it was Leah wanting to start a row. But to my surprise it was Dinah. She looked worried, the poor dear, and kept turning around to look behind her at the slightest sound, frightened her mother would see her with me.

I took her hand and invited her into my tent. "Come in, dear! How are you? It's good to see you."

Dinah's face was as wilted as a flower. Breaking into tears, she said, "I hope you don't mind my coming to talk to you, Aunt Rachel. But sometimes I think you're the only one who cares about me."

I patted her on the back until she could go on.

Continuing to sob, she said, "I was listening to your conversation with mother today. It's awful how she treats you. She treats you almost as badly as she treats me. Mother takes all her grievances out on me. She never lets me have any fun. The boys can do no wrong in her eyes. I can do no right."

My heart went out to the sobbing child. She was the same age I was when my mother died. Looking at her was like looking at my young self. I put my arms around her stroking her long silky hair, hoping to dispel her misery. "All you say is true, dear! You're a wonderful girl and don't deserve that kind of treatment. I know it's difficult, but try not to let the injustice hurt you and make you bitter."

Dinah stopped sobbing, and looked up at me with her beautiful dark eyes. "Why is mother so mean, Auntie? You're her sister, and you're so kind."

Dinah's question brought up all my grief. I wanted to turn away. But the child's eyes were intent upon the truth, and I had to answer.

"Your mother's gotten lost, Dinah."

"Lost?" asked Dinah with a puzzled look.

I breathed in against the sharp pain rising in my heart. How could I explain the tragedy of our lives to this young girl? "I suppose it began with our mother's death. Mother died so young. Your grandmother was a wonderful woman, Dinah, and a wise priestess."

Dinah interrupted in her excitement, "My grandmother was a priestess? I didn't know women could be priestesses, Auntie."

Guilt tore at my heart to hear the child's statement. Tears welled in my eyes, and I heard the words of the En Priestess resound in my heart. 'If you don't go through with the Sacred Mating Rite, I fear it will mark the beginning of the end of a great and noble tradition.'

"Why are you crying, Auntie?" inquired Dinah interrupting my reverie.

"I'm crying for all women, Dinah. I'm crying because women can no longer be priestesses and serve the Goddess. We can only worship the Father God Yahweh. But to answer your question. Women can be priestesses! Until quite recently there were women priestesses. Even now in Shechem there are holy women. Wise Women who serve the Goddess and the God, and speak to them on behalf of the people."

Dinah's eyes glowed with wonder to hear of such a marvel, and in her excitement she questioned further, "Will there be priestesses at the harvest festival?"

"Yes, my dear!"

Never had I seen Dinah so excited as when she asked, "May I come with you, Auntie. It would mean so much to me to see a real priestess."

The longing on Dinah's face was moving. She had been neglected by her mother all her life, and treated more like a maid-servant than a daughter. I had been powerless to remedy it. Here was something meaningful I could do for her. But if Leah or Israel found out, there could be serious repercussions. And I didn't want to make our lives any more difficult than they already were.

Dinah's enthusiasm broke into my thoughts. "Take me with you! Please take me with you, Auntie! I won't be any trouble. I so long to see a priestess. If you don't take me, I may never get a chance to see one. Mother and father never take me anywhere."

Gazing into Dinah's pleading eyes, I could see she was a Goddess child. Conceived with the mandrake, the Goddess's blessing could not be denied. She was a rare beauty, possessing a mysterious magnetism that shone all around her. How could I deny Dinah her birthright? I had to give her at least one glimpse of the love and respect women possessed in a culture that still worshipped the Goddess.

Smiling down at Dinah, I said, "Very well, dear! I'll take you with me. We'll leave right after the noonday meal. But I don't want anyone to find out where we're going. So I'll meet you in the clearing behind Bilhah and Zilpah's tents. Dress in your best white robe, and bring an offering for the Goddess that you'll leave at the sacred oak. Remember to be careful! We don't want anyone to find out where we're going."

24

THE WHEAT MOTHER
AND THE WHEAT MAIDEN

THE DAY OF THE HARVEST FESTIVAL DAWNED CRISP AND BRIGHT, THE perfect day for plowing. Israel and the boys were out in the fields, too busy to notice our departure. Dinah was careful to do everything I told her. She finished her chores by noontime, and stood dressed in white waiting for me in the clearing. Her smile was radiant as she greeted me. 'I'm ready, Auntie! I'm so excited! Today I'm going to see a real priestess! What's that necklace you're wearing? I've never seen it before. It's beautiful."

"Thank you, dear! My mother left it to me." I said smiling. "You look lovely. The Goddess shines in your face today! Did you remember to bring an offering to leave at the holy tree?"

"Yes, Auntie!" said Dinah proffering a white shell. "I brought this. It's my favorite shell, but I wanted to bring something special. One of grandfather's traders gave it to me."

"That's a lovely offering!" I said approvingly.

Dinah's eyes returned to my necklace.

"My necklace appeals to you." I said. "It's very special. It's an eye bead necklace. My mother used to wear it in her role as priestess. That's why I only wear it on ritual occasions."

Dinah's excitement was palpable as we started on our way. Her enthusiasm reminded me of my youth, bringing up the young girl inside me. I felt full and blessed walking along beside Dinah. The living presence of the triple Goddess, maiden, mother and crone was overshadowing us. Dinah was abud in the flower of her maidenhood. I was a proud mother for the second time, and we were walking through the harvested fields reminiscent of the crone. With my womb full I felt closer than ever to the fecund Goddess of harvest.

Women were dressing the holy tree with offerings when we arrived. My gaze was drawn to an ancient crone shrouded in black, skin as brown as the earth, in the shadow of the Oak of Moreh. She was worn as the hills and seemed to beckon me with a knowing smile. A shiver ran down my back. Was she real or just a figment of my inner sight? What did it mean that death was in the shadow of the Tree of Life? Was this an omen?

I put these thoughts aside as Zara approached me with a retinue of women, and I was swept up in the joyous warmth of their presence.

Zara greeted me with the customary Goddess salute, drawing a spiral on my forehead. Her keen eyes were admiring my necklace, as she said, "Welcome, Rachel! I'm so pleased you joined us. Who is this young beauty with you? You were both in my dream last night."

Dinah purred with pleasure at Zara's salutation.

"This is my niece, Dinah." I announced proudly. "This is her first time in the circle of women."

Zara smiled at Dinah warmly and beckoned to some young maidens, as she said, "Welcome, Dinah! I am Zara, priestess of the Goddess Asherah, and guardian of this holy tree. This is Sarai, princess of Shechem, daughter of Prince Hamor. These are Miri, Devi, Shana, Amar and Mista. Did you bring an offering for the Goddess's tree?"

"Yes! I brought this shell." said Dinah proudly.

"Splendid!" said Zara nodding her approval. "Shells are sacred to Astarte, the Goddess of Love. She will reward you for your generosity! Why don't you join the other young maidens, and place your offering beside theirs on the holy tree? They'll introduce you to all the young people here."

When Dinah went off with the young women Zara looked more closely at my necklace. "What an exquisite necklace! You were wearing it last night in my dream, Rachel. I've heard of eye bead necklaces, but I've never seen one before. Where's it from?"

"It's from the Eye Temple of She Who Watches in Brak. It was a gift from my mother, who trained there. She was a Naditu Priestess of the Eye Goddess. She left this necklace to me at her passing. It's very special to me. The eye beads are very old and were made at the Temple."

"What's that in the center?" asked Zara admiringly.

"This bead is made of An.Bar., the sky fire, which falls from heaven."

Zara looked at me thoughtfully as she replied, "My dream was right! You are a priestess of the olden ways! You must be from the Sumerian Sisterhood around the World Mountain."

I nodded, astounded by her recognition of my lineage.

Zara continued. "I have thought a great deal about you since last we met, Rachel. Your prayers the other day had great power. When did you and your family arrive here? We've been in drought for many years now. But it lifted suddenly early last summer."

"We arrived at the beginning of summer!" I said smiling.

Zara's eyes were wide with wonder, as she said, "Just as I suspected! We have an ancient custom that hasn't been practiced for many years. It's so old I'm uncertain of its origins. But it's a way of honoring strangers to our parts. It feels right I extend it to you after my dream last night. Would you do us the honor of being the Wheat Mother in our ritual today, Rachel? Your niece could be the Wheat Maiden."

I looked into this stranger's eyes. The reverence I saw in them was touching, and melted away my resistance. Still I had to think before daring to reply. This ancient custom had grown out of visits from the Nefilim, the great Angels of Heaven, who had come to Earth in olden times to instruct the people. Was I worthy of such an honor? I was still pondering her invitation when I recalled the consequences of my not having participated in the Goddess' rites before.

"I would be pleased to be the Wheat Mother in your ritual today. As for Dinah, she will have to answer for herself." I replied.

THE WHEAT MOTHER AND THE WHEAT MAIDEN

Delighted with my acceptance, Zara said, "Wonderful! Has Dinah made a wheat dolly before?"

"No!"

"Very well then! We'll let her get familiarized before I ask her. We'll be teaching all the young women the art of making wheat dollies today. After we're finished I'll ask Dinah if she'd like to be our Wheat Maiden. I'm so glad you've agreed, Rachel. You'll make a most auspicious Wheat Mother being full with new life."

Dinah was radiant standing in the midst of a crowd of young people, when I came to escort her to the altar in front of the sacred tree. Never had I seen her so animated before. She was speaking to an attractive young man, as I drew near.

A bell tolled and a hush came over the entire gathering. Zara announced, "Mothers and daughters take your places around the altar! It's time to honor the Goddess by making our wheat dolls!"

Dinah was so enthralled in her conversation she hadn't noticed my approach. She looked up in dismay at Zara's announcement. A look of panic, then sadness, swept over her face, as she saw the other girls disperse to meet their mothers around the altar. I came up behind Dinah taking her arm, and we went to join the others.

As we approached the altar Dinah said, "I wish you were my real mother, Auntie! Thank you so much for bringing me here today."

I squeezed her hand. Taking our places around the altar, I said, "The Goddess of Harvest is your true mother, Dinah! It was She who provided the mandrake."

When we were positioned, I put our sheaf of wheat upon the altar piled high with mounds of golden wheat and wild flowers.

Zara spoke above the sonorous chanting of the Wise Women of the tribe. "I am pleased to introduce two special guests the Goddess has sent to grace our day. This is Rachel, a Naditu Priestess from Haran. This is her lovely niece, Dinah. We are very pleased to have you with us. Thank you all for remembering the bounty of the Earth Mother and bringing your last sheaves of wheat to the altar of the Goddess Asherah, the Tree of Life, and sustainer of Her people."

"Lift your voices in thanksgiving for the harvest. Reach out in love to the women beside you. Remember the Goddess shines through all women."

After exchanging embraces our circle felt warm and close. Zara announced, "Today we will introduce you maidens to an ancient rite women have been practicing on threshing floors and harvest fields for untold centuries, the art of making a Wheat Mother dolly. You may take it home with you today to honor your fields and bless next year's crop."

"The Wheat Mother represents the bounty of the Goddess Asherah, the Staff of Life. The Wheat Mother is always made from the last sheaf of wheat to be cut to represent the spirit of the wheat which sacrifices itself so that we may be nourished. Each mother will instruct her daughter in fashioning the Wheat Dolly, as her mother did with her before the altar of the Great Mother."

"Today we shall choose a Wheat Mother and a Wheat Maiden, who will remain beside the altar for the entire ritual. The rest of you may return home to place your Wheat Dollies in your fields and sow the seeds of the new wheat, that will rise again next spring."

"Rachel has consented to be our Wheat Mother this year. She will embody the Goddess of Harvest and dig the furrow around the sacred Oak. The Wheat Maiden will be chosen when you finish your wheat dollies. The Wheat Maiden will be adorned to step inside the furrowed circle and embody the Virgin Goddess. She will offer the unsown field of her virginity, in the Sacred Mating with prince Shechem, anointed priest of Asherah. The Wheat Mother will make the traditional harvest sacrifice to the Goddess to assure our crops next spring."

"Now let's begin!"

Harvest sacrifice?? Was this the shadow of death I saw lurking around the holy tree?

My thoughts were interrupted by Dinah. Turning to me in flushed excitement, she exclaimed, "It's wonderful that you've been chosen for such an honor, Auntie. Is there any chance I too might be selected? What an honor it would be! That was Prince Shechem I was speaking to when you came to get me. I'd love to be his partner in the rite."

As I showed Dinah how to plait the wheat and fasten it together to make our doll, we continued talking. "There's a good chance you'll be chosen, Dinah, but you have to give it great thought. You'd be partaking in a rite considered unclean by your father and mother."

"Oh, but do you really think I have a chance?"

Dinah was beaming, when I said, "There's a very good chance! But this is an important decision, and you're very young. You don't even know what the ritual entails."

"Please tell me?" Dinah asked imploringly.

I continued very seriously, "You would be offering your virginity to the Goddess, Dinah!"

She was regarding me with wonder in her eyes, as I continued, "The Sacred Mating is an ancient rite performed to ensure the fertility of the land. The king, or in this case the young prince, makes love with a Priestess of the Goddess beneath the Ashera tree to call a blessing down on the land. The consummation of their love is a sexual rite to mirror the Sacred Mating of the God and Goddess in heaven. The Sacred Mating rite is to promote harmony, and balance the Male and Female forces here on Earth. It aligns the land and all its people with the divine mating to fructify the land. Your body would become an altar for the Goddess. You would be consecrating your sexuality to Her."

Dinah had stopped plaiting the wheat dolly, and looked at me in starstruck wonder. "I've never dreamed of such a thing. To think that making love could help the Earth and all its people. What a beautiful thought! Why have father and mother never mentioned this to me before?"

A weight descended on my heart, as I responded, "Your father doesn't believe in the Goddess, Dinah. He worships only one God, the Father God Yahweh. Yahweh is a lone God, and has no partner for a mate. Yahweh is a great God, but jealous. He forbids his worshippers to believe in any other God. That is why the Goddess is never mentioned at home. And without the Goddess there can be no sacred mating."

Dinah's face was downcast, as she said, "That's very sad! You were right the other night. Something important has been lost! My mother doesn't believe in the Goddess, does she?"

Dinah's eyes were earnest and searching, as we continued wrapping strands to make our dolly. "You heard your mother the other day when I came to your tent. She was angry at me for even bringing up the Goddess. We were both raised in the Goddess tradition, but your mother has abandoned it."

"Your mother is a Sugutu woman, Dinah, which means a fertile birth mother. I was selected to become a Naditu Priestess of the Eye Goddess Ninhursag. But when our mother died Laban no longer allowed Leah and

I to go to celebrations at the Eye temple. He also forbade us to go to the circle of women in our town."

"Thank you for telling me all this, Auntie! It explains so much."

"I cannot speak for your mother, Dinah." I said looking her in the eyes. "But I know women would have been treated with more respect in our home if the Goddess had not been denied. Women were very different in my youth. They were happier, more independent, possessed greater self-determination, and received more respect. My mother, your grandmother, was a great Naditu Priestess. She belonged to an ancient Sisterhood of Seerers, who were sworn to stand by one another, and assist all women. It made for a spiritual closeness and bonding that you do not find between women today. My mother had her own chapel in our home, and ministered to all the people of Haran. She was renowned in our entire region. I wanted to follow in her footsteps, but your father and Laban would not allow it."

"Father and Grandfather did not allow it!" said Dinah with indignation. "How sad!"

"The Black Hand got in the way as well. The Brotherhood has sworn to put an end to the Sisterhood. They made life so difficult the Naditu Sisterhood was forced to leave the Eye Temple in Brak and go south to Magan. The Black Hand is bent on keeping power in the hands of men. They seek dominion over all the realms of the Goddess. They've made enormous inroads since my childhood."

"This was possible because the Sumerian religion had been on the decline since the Assyrian conquest hundreds of years ago. Your great great grandfather Terah, Abraham's father, was one of the last great priests from Nippur, Sumer's ancient spiritual center. Abraham and Terah were warned to move to Ur before the warring started. Later Yahweh instructed them to leave for Haran to escape the great Storm of Fire unleashed by the Anunnaki. That storm brought on the fall of Ur and most of Sumer."

"There's much to be proud of in your lineage, Dinah. On your father's side you have great Sumerian priests. On your mother's side you have great Sumerian priestesses. The Sumerian culture of our forbears is the root source of all the great religions. Before its demise it even fueled this Canaanite culture."

"The Sumerians worshipped the Goddess and the God. Consequently Sumerian women were highly respected. They could become priestesses, and enjoyed many more rights and privileges than we do today. Sumerian women could hold property of their own, engage in business, and choose who they wanted to marry. Once married they could even divorce their husbands, if they didn't like the way they were being treated."

Dinah looked me straight in the eyes, as she inquired, "The women here all worship the Goddess don't they?"

I nodded.

"Is that why they're so different? They seem so happy and self-possessed."

"I'm sure it has a great deal to do with it." I said candidly. "But enough talk! We have our wheat dolly to finish, and you have to decide whether you want to be the Harvest Maiden in today's rite. Think carefully! If you enact the Sacred Mating rite with Shechem, prince of this land, your parents would consider it a sacrilege. Your decision could have grave consequences on your future."

Dinah's face had become downcast, but it began to glow again at my mention of the Sacred Mating rite. "After what you've just shared with me, I feel even more strongly than before that I want to be the Harvest Maiden. There's so little fairness in our household. I'd do anything to help bring more harmony and balance between men and women. If only I am chosen!"

Zara was walking among the mothers and daughters making their dolls. I beckoned her with a smile.

She put her arms around us when she arrived, saying, "I can see you've both been busy. You're almost finished. Well done!"

Looking up at Zara, I said, "Thank you! It's been many years since I've made one of these."

Zara regarded me with a quizzical expression.

Then I said, "I've been speaking of the harvest ritual with Dinah, Zara. She says she'd love to be your Harvest Maiden."

Zara smiled at Dinah. "Wonderful! We'll prepare you both as soon as everyone finishes their dolls."

Dinah was ecstatic to be chosen. She could hardly contain her excitement as we put the finishing touches on our Wheat Dolly and placed it on the altar beside the others.

When all the Wheat Dollies were finished, Zara blessed them. Then exclaimed, "Not since the before the Great Flood has a stranger been chosen to enact the rite of the Harvest Mating. But last night I was told in my dreams that a new and potent magic is required to counteract the drought. So it is with great pleasure that I announce Dinah will be our Wheat Maiden today. She will perform the sacred mating ritual with prince Shechem to bring the blessing of the God and Goddess down upon our land."

The women raised their voices to heaven when Zara finished. As the chant rose up they swarmed about us carrying us over to the sacred tree. The women's excitement was contagious. How differently we were being treated in comparison to life in our patriarchal family, where woman had to vie against woman for any scrap of attention! I was overwhelmed at first that these so-called strangers would treat Dinah and I with so much warmth and respect. I hadn't known such treatment since I was young.

In the midst of all the exhilaration the Goddess overshadowed me. I stood poised within Her starry light, one foot inside the circle of the Goddess, the other foot without. With my inner vision I saw my position clearly. There was no going back. The En Priestess had been right. I was one of the last of the Naditu Sisterhood. We were a dying breed. Though I prayed the child growing within my womb would continue on.

Israel had not merely been languishing in Haran amassing great wealth. He had been Yahweh's spiritual warrior all along. Hadn't Yahweh taken over Mt. Ararat? It wasn't only the Black Hand. Yahweh had also had His own reasons for enticing Leah and I into His wrestling match for power. It suited Yahweh's purpose that we were both married to His chosen. If Leah and I, the matriarchs of the new tradition, were divided in competition over the same man, the way would be open for subsequent patriarchal women to also be divided. With the Goddess tradition destroyed from within, the Sisterhood could easily be conquered and overthrown.

Yes! In the future to be steered by the patriarchal Father God, there would be no sacred rites celebrating the mating of the God and Goddess. There would be no more love feasts like the one today to promote the fertility of nature. There would only be male priests and the worship of the Father God, with woman vying against woman for any bit of recognition to be had.

THE WHEAT MOTHER AND THE WHEAT MAIDEN

As the women dressed me in the wheat consecrated to the Goddess, I became the Wheat Mother. The anguish of the Earth was in my heart stretching me, until my inner vision opened and I was carried into the future. The great love feasts and celebrations were replaced by centuries of violence and warring over the sacred land on which I stood. I saw the sublime face of a gentle Man of Light, who had come down from heaven to teach the people love and forgiveness. He was being nailed to a cross and called out to his Father in heaven to hear him. There were inquisitions, bloody inquisitions with vast tribunals of men pointing their finger in judgment against women. And great hosts of women, keepers of the ancient faith of the Goddess, guardians of the Earth, being tied to stakes and burned to death as they cried out their innocence. I saw men, women, and children, shunted about like animals in fire breathing cages that ran on iron tracks, then sealed into metal ovens to be killed.

I saw an elderly man, whom the people addressed as the Holy Father. He was dressed in white and stepping out of an ornate palace to rail against his daughters who had remembered the Goddess and assembled to speak to him of the woes which beset the Earth. But this man was no great Holy Father, for he could not hear his daughters. He sent them away, calling them heretics and infidels for wanting to be priestesses, and caring for the Earth. He returned to his ornate palace, closing the door behind him on the poor, the sick, and starving people without. While clouds of black smoke filled the skies and people choked, and even the children's tears were blackened.

I saw enormous forests being levelled, and huge seas covered in a thick black slimy substance which was carried to the beaches full of dead, and dying fish, birds, and other creatures. When my legs were trembling and I was afraid I could stand no more, I saw a blood bath in the town of Shechem, and myself writhing in pain inside an ever-widening pool of blood, disappointment on my face.

My skin was crawling from these grim visions when the women finished dressing me. The old familiar weight was on my heart, and my shoulders ached. Tears welled within my eyes. Was this to be our children's future? I didn't want to cry. But how could I hold my tears back after what I'd seen?

The women dressing me were all laughing and singing. The harvest had been good despite the drought. Joyous music sounded forth. This was Dinah's special time. It wasn't right that I should spoil it with dread thoughts of the future. I was Priestess of She Who Watches. This vision was Her gift. I had to be strong enough to bear it. When the time was right I would bring Her message to the people.

My eyes searched about for Dinah. We were forging something special here today. She was completing something for me, which I'd been unable to do when I was young. Dinah made a splendid Virgin of the Wheat. I thanked the Goddess for this second chance, and vowed to be strong for Dinah, the women present, and the women yet to come.

Dinah was wearing a diaphanous robe the color of golden wheat, which set off the dark luster of her hair and the blush of her tender cheeks. Her breasts were painted with henna and looked soft and round. The dark V of her pubic mound could just be seen peeking through the sheerness of her gown. As the women put the finishing touches on Dinah's hair, the Goddess overshadowed her. She looked amazingly mature and self-possessed for one so young, like the bud of a flower opening to the morning sun. Zara took Dinah aside to converse with her, initiating her in the secrets of the Goddess's art of lovemaking.

The women came and stood before me, each taking their turn to receive my blessing. When they gazed at me they bowed reverently their eyes rejoicing. Then they went off to the altar taking their wheat dollies home to bless their fields. After Zara finished conferring with Dinah, the young maidens approached her winking and giggling merrily. Many of the older women also stopped to kiss her on the cheek. Then they left for home and the evening rites with their own partners.

Dinah was aglow from all the heartfelt salutations when they brought her over to me. Overcome by the women's love she turned and looked at me. Standing before the sacred oak she asked in a voice full of feeling, "Is it the Goddess's love for Her daughters that I am feeling, Auntie? Never have I experienced such love before! Thank you for bringing me here today! I never would have known this!"

I looked at Dinah. "This love is your's and every woman's birthright from the Goddess." I said smiling. "There's no need to thank me. The happiness on your face is my reward."

Zara returned with a young boy garlanded all over in sheaves of golden wheat. After placing him on a large baetyl rock in the center of a circle of stones, she positioned Dinah in prayer beneath the sacred oak.

Then she handed me the copper trowel to renew the furrow of the Goddess's circle of protection around the sacred tree. As I circled the holy oak drawing the furrow, I prayed.

GREAT GODDESS NINHURSAG, GUARDIAN OF THIS BLESSED EARTH, RECEIVE OUR THANKS FOR THIS ABUNDANT HARVEST. OPEN THE GATES OF HEAVEN AND HEAL THIS DROUGHT STRICKEN LAND. BLESS THOSE WHO WALK THE PATH OF HARMONIOUS CREATIVE COOPERATION WITH THE EARTH. SHOWER THEM WITH LOVE AND PEACE.

GREAT GODDESS ASHERAH, BLESSED TREE OF LIFE, MISTRESS OF LOVE AND FERTILITY, BLESS THIS UNION IN YOUR HONOR HERE TODAY. INSPIRE US WITH YOUR GREAT MYSTERY OF LOVE THAT DINAH AND SHECHEM'S UNION MAY BRING YOUR BLESSINGS TO EARTH TO RESTORE THIS PARCHED LAND. MAY THEIR LOVE RISE UP TO HEAVEN, A SWEET INCENSE, TO RELIEVE THE DROUGHT. SEND FORTH YOUR HEALING RAINS TO MOISTEN THE EARTH, AND MAKE IT READY TO RECEIVE THE SEEDS PLANTED TODAY. OPEN THE PEOPLE'S HEARTS AND MINDS. AND MAKE GREEN THESE FIELDS AND MEADOWS NEXT SPRING.

GREAT FATHER YAHWEH, LORD OF HEAVEN, GOD OF ABRAHAM, ISAAC, AND ISRAEL, WHO PUTS THE EVIL SIN TO SHAME. OPEN YOUR HEART TO YOUR DAUGHTERS AND BLESS THIS UNION IN YOUR HONOR HERE TODAY. BLESS DINAH AND SHECHEM THAT THEY MAY COME TO KNOW THE STRENGTH AND POWER OF YOUR LOVE. HAVE MERCY ON US AND OPEN WIDE THE GATES OF HEAVEN TO NOURISH THIS DROUGHT RIDDEN LAND.

When my prayer was over and the sacred furrow drawn, prince Shechem stepped forth dressed in white wearing a gold belt detailed in wheat. Brandishing a large sheaf of wheat, he prostrated himself before me. The fervor of his devotion to the God and Goddess, and the steadfastness of his dedication to the land shone in his every movement. His noble face was aglow with sublime light as he bowed before me to begin his prayer. "I TAKE MY PLACE BEFORE THE SACRED OAK AS ORDAINED BY THE GODS OF HEAVEN SINCE THE DAYS OF OLD. I COME BEFORE THE HOLY TREE OF LIFE, GARDENER IN THE

GARDEN OF THE GODDESS, AS MY FATHER HAMOR AND HIS
FATHER DID, BEFORE HIM, BACK INTO THE FAR HISTORY OF
MY FAMILY. "

"HAIL BEAUTIFUL STRANGER, PROLIFIC MOTHER OF THE
HARVEST, THE FACE THE GODDESS SUD ASSUMES ON EARTH
TODAY. I THANK YOU GREAT MOTHER OF THE GRAIN FOR
THE FRUITS OF YOUR LABOR THAT SUSTAIN OUR LIVES. RE-
CEIVE OUR GRATITUDE FOR THIS ABUNDANT HARVEST!"

"LET MY PRAYERS RISE TO HEAVEN. MAY THE GOD AND
GODDESS REJOICE AND FIND ME DESERVING TO ENACT THIS
SACRED RITE. MAY THEY OVERSHADOW ME SO I BE A WOR-
THY CONDUIT TO BRING THEIR LOVE TO EARTH. MAY AN
ABUNDANT FATE BE DECREED FOR THE CROPS NEXT SPRING.
MAY OUR UNION BE A SOURCE OF PROSPERITY AND FERTIL-
ITY THROUGHOUT THE LAND I LOVE. TO THIS I DEDICATE
MY LIFE."

After bowing one last time Shechem crossed the furrow stepping
into the circle of the God and Goddess's bliss. Dinah rose to meet his
ardor as the full moon rises to receive the blessing of the sun's light.
Shechem took her in his arms and laid her down on the green velvet
moss beneath the oak. Smiling proudly he raised his sheaf of wheat shaking it over her. The grains of wheat caught the sun's rays, showering
down on Dinah like a golden rain as he sang his praises to her as the Virgin Earth.

GREAT GODDESS SUD, EVER-VIRGIN GODDESS OF THE
HARVEST, MAY OUR BRIDAL BED REJOICE YOUR HEART AND
EXALT YOUR SPIRIT ALLOWING YOUR BLESSINGS TO FLOW
DOWN TO THIS LAND AND ALL ITS PEOPLE.

Once Shechem seated himself beside Dinah on their moss throne,
first Hamor, then all the elders of the tribe filed by to pay their respects
to the young couple and deposit their offerings within the magic circle.
As reigning prince, Hamor was first to place his offering before the
young lovers. He brought honeyed wine in golden goblets saying. MAY
THIS UNION BE BLESSED THAT THE DATE PALMS FLOURISH,
AND THE GRAPES BE LUSH UPON THE VINE NEXT SPRING.

Hamor was followed by his wife carrying a tray of sweetmeats. She
deposited them inside the circle saying. MAY THIS UNION BE

BLESSED, THAT OUR STALLS BE FILLED TO OVERFLOWING WITH SHEEP, COWS, AND GOATS. MAY THEY BE STRONG AND MULTIPLY THROUGHOUT THE LAND.

Then each of the elders of the tribe filed by placing their offering within the circle and reciting their prayers. They carried fruit, bread, cheese, and flowers to ornament the circle. When all the offerings had been made, Shechem and Dinah were left to sip their wine in privacy. As the elders left the young lovers laughed gaily in anticipation.

Shechem opened Dinah's robe, and began stroking her tender breasts, her waist, the soft curve of her belly all the way down to the sacred mound which marked the entrance to the gate of life. Dinah's cheeks flushed with each caress until her body came alive harkening to the ancient call that welled up within the temple of her body. She became a woman awakening to Shechem's touch sheltered by the Tree of Life.

Delighted by her movements, the prince removed his clothes placing his golden wheat belt arching like a rainbow around Dinah on the ground. He stood proudly before her his member erect praying aloud. MAY THE GREAT GOD AND GODDESS, BLESS OUR HOLY UNION AND SHOWER THEIR GRACE DOWN UPON THIS LAND. MAY THE COFFERS OF MY PEOPLE BE FULL. MAY THEIR FIELDS BE RICH WITH THE GOLD OF WHEAT AND BARLEY NEXT SPRING. MAY THE DROUGHT BE PUT BEHIND US, AND MAY WE LIVE IN PEACE UPON THIS SACRED LAND.

When Shechem took Dinah in his arms her face glowed. She spoke the ancient words of the Goddess, that Zara taught her.

MAY YOU PLOW MY VULVA LIKE THE GOOD FARMER TILLS HIS FIELDS.

MAY YOU PLOW MY VULVA LIKE THE GOOD SHEPHERD WHO MAKES HIS FOLDS TEEM.

MAY MY GARDEN BE WELL WATERED AND PRODUCE MUCH HONEY AND WINE FOR THE PEOPLE.

MAY MY WELL WATERED GARDEN BRING FORTH ABUNDANT WHEAT AND BARLEY.

MAY THE RIVERS RUN HIGH AND FULL WITH SCHOOLS OF CARP.

MAY THE FISH AND BIRDS BE PROLIFIC IN THE MARSHES.

MAY THE DEER AND WILD GOATS MULTIPLY IN THE FOREST.

MAY THE SHRUBS GROW LUSH IN THE HIGH DESERT.

MAY THIS LAND AND ALL ITS PEOPLE LIVE IN PEACE AND HARMONY.

Shechem smiled radiantly and lay Dinah down upon the soft moss carpet beneath the Ashera. Mounting her he began the ancient dance which brings joy to the heart, and first stirred the waters of the great deep calling life into being.

The elders turned and left the couple to rejoice in the fulfillment of the sacred rite. Moving toward the stone circle with the young boy, they began the ancient song of Lamentation for Tammuz husband of the Goddess.

Zara came and escorted me to the stone circle. Handing me a shining metal sickle, she said solemnly, "The Goddess gives life and the Goddess takes it away. The Bounteous Goddess of Harvest is also the Grim Reaper of Death. The earth is thirsty for renewal. Perform the sacrifice! Draw the blessing of the Goddess down upon Earth."

I stared at the young boy seated solemnly on the baetyl rock. He was the same age as Joseph. I was appalled to see him decked in wheat, eyes closed in prayer, waiting to receive the tragic blow.

Revolted by the gruesome task, I stepped back in loathing, asking, "In whose name do you perform this human sacrifice?"

Startled murmurs rose up from all the elders.

Zara spoke with the voice of authority. "We do this sacrifice in the name of Astarte, and her consort Baal. These are desperate times. The earth cries out for blood."

"The earth does not cry out for blood!" I said with determination. "The earth cries out for love, and righteousness! There is enough senseless war and killing upon Earth thanks to the Brotherhood of the Black Hand!"

"The Black Hand??" Zarah exclaimed.

"They call themselves the Black Hand because their dealings are cloaked in darkness. They are a secret society of men, also known as the Brotherhood of the Serpent or the Dragon. They have vowed to destroy the Goddess and her worship. You will know them by their evil deeds and the black gloves and aprons they wear. They are tools of Nanna/Sin, the ancient Dragon of Heaven. Astarte, who we call Inanna, or Ishtar, is his daughter. She gives the Goddess a bad name, and will be known in history as the great Whore of Babylon for her lascivious cravings and her bloodthirsty powerlust."

"I will not lift my hand against this innocent boy for her, or for any other God or Goddess! The earth does not cry out for blood! It is Sin and Astarte who crave it! The earth cries out for rain! Kak.Si.Di., the Eye Star of the Goddess Ninhursag is the dispenser of the waters. But in their lust for power Sin and his daughter Inanna have eclipsed Ninhursag. It is because the Eye Goddess is no longer revered that your land suffers drought!"

The mantle of the Goddess had come down upon me as I spoke. I could feel it in tingling sensations streaming down my arms and legs, and see it in the eyes of all the elders.

Zara stepped forward to address the elders of Shechem. "Some of you were here last week when the heavens opened in response to Rachel's prayer. Fire came down from the sky and danced upon the trees. We have seen the wonders Rachel's gods have wrought. We had a good harvest this year after years of want! The drought lifted when Rachel and her family arrived. Rachel is a great priestess. She is one of the Naditu Priestesses from the region around Mt. Ararat, the World Mountain. Last night I was told in a dream that she has much to teach us. I say we listen to Rachel and try her ways."

Hamor came forward next to speak to his people. "I know the men of whom Rachel speaks. They spread fear and terror throughout the land and tax the people so heavily they can no longer buy bread for their children. The drought speaks to us most eloquently. It says the ancient ways no longer work. A heavenly light shines from this woman. I agree with Zara. Rachel has been sent to us for a purpose. It's time to make a change!"

Many of the elders around the circle nodded their heads in acquiescence. But the gnarled old woman I had seen beneath the tree when I arrived stepped forward to address the elders. "What makes you think you can you dispose of our traditions so easily? You defile the ancient ways by listening to this stranger!"

The elders next to her came and stood beside Zara and Hamor in a show of support. Those undecided stood looking back and forth between Hamor, Zara, and the old crone.

The old crone came toward me pointing her finger menacingly. "Who do you think you are coming here telling us to break our traditions? Take that blade and do what must be done!" she barked with glaring eyes.

I threw the sickle on the ground, saying, "I will not be be party to such a gruesome act! Human sacrifice is a mar upon your people!"

Before I could say another word the crone had snatched the blade up and slit the boy's throat. Then she stood there triumphantly glaring at me.

Aghast at the sight of the young body falling to the ground, I cried out, "Death will not bring you the prosperity you seek. Death breeds only death and more death. I offered you a new way, but you choose to be beholden to the bloodthirsty Astarte. She brings the Goddess tradition down, and necessitates the reign of Yahweh. Human sacrifice is an abomination! It's the mark of Cain upon your people. May the gods forgive you!"

25

ON THE WAY TO BETHLEHEM

STRANDS OF GOLDEN WHEAT WERE STILL CLINGING TO MY HAIR AND gown, when I returned home alone that night from the harvest rites. I took off my eyebead necklace and placed it beneath my camel litter, then went to bed. It was a fitful sleep, ravaged by anxious dreams in which I found myself caught between traditions with no place to stand. Israel was turning his back on me in my dreams. Zara and the wise women of Shechem were all enraged and beset with grief. The En Priestess was shaking her head looking at me in deep regret.

I awoke early the next morning afraid Dinah would be missed. Once dressed, I called Bilhah and made sure that Dinah's chores were done. Once her chores were completed, true to form no one, not even Leah, inquired about her. Three days passed and Dinah had still not returned home. I was continuing to negotiate her chores, when Israel departed for Bethel where he'd first seen the Angels of the Lord.

That same afternoon Prince Hamor came to pay his respects, and ask for Dinah's hand in marriage to his son Shechem. As Israel was away the older boys, Reuben, Simeon, and Levi greeted our guest. I heard Reuben call his mother with alarm in his voice, and ran to see what was going on. Hamor was celebrating Dinah's beauty and charms, as I drew near.

He interrupted his conversation at the sight of me. "Good day, Mistress Rachel! It's splendid to see you again. You must forgive us for the other night. The old ways are deeply rooted. It will take time, but I know my people have much to learn from you. I'm here to make the acquaintance of your family, and pay my respects. Of course, Dinah is still with us. The love birds have been inseparable."

Leah arrived just in time to hear Hamor's last remarks. She glanced at me with daggers in her eyes, then interrupted angrily, "How is it you know my sister, Prince Hamor?"

Hamor smiled at me bowing his head. "I had the pleasure of meeting Rachel at our harvest celebration the other day. You must be Mistress Leah, Dinah's mother?" he said smiling and offering his hand.

Leah nodded, and pulled her hand away, still perturbed.

"Rachel and your daughter, honored us by attending our Harvest rites. Rachel was our Wheat Mother, and Dinah our Wheat Maiden. They made a heavenly sight the two of them!"

Leah glared at me, saying spitefully, "I'm sure they did, Prince Hamor! And just where is my daughter now?"

The tone of Leah's voice alarmed Prince Hamor. His face went pale, as he stammered out, "But of course . . . please . . . forgive me . . . Mistress Leah! I was just telling your sons . . . Dinah is at home with my son, Shechem."

The look on Leah's face caused Prince Hamor to step back. Glancing back and forth between us, he continued haltingly, "You didn't know where Dinah was? . . . I beg your pardon, madam! . . . You must have been besides yourself with worry . . . I'm sorry! . . . So sorry! I would have come sooner, but I thought Rachel would have told you that Dinah was safe with us."

Leah's face looked strained and drawn, as she clutched Levi's arm for support. Had she not been glaring at me so intently, she might have fainted.

Seeing his mother so beside herself, Simeon began interrogating, "Do you mean to say that Dinah has been at your home with your son Shechem . . . and Rachel knew about it?"

Hamor nodded sheepishly looking over at me in confusion, as Simeon turned toward me with fury. "What have you done to your family, Rachel? Father will be outraged!"

Hamor interrupted, afraid things were getting out of hand. "Please, madam Leah! . . . Boys! There's no reason to be upset! My son's heart is quite set upon Dinah. I've come to ask for her hand in marriage. I assure you Dinah is very pleased. She's already consented to the match. Dinah will be a princess, and my son's first wife. She has the respect and love of our entire family. It will unite our tribes by blood, and make you part of our community. Please allow Shechem to marry Dinah. Name your price! There's nothing my son wouldn't give for the honor of marrying her!"

Leah was aghast. Her face was so impassive it looked as though it were made of stone. For once in her life she had nothing to say. Only her eyes were glaring. They darted back and forth between Prince Hamor and I in agitation, like birds before a storm.

Prince Hamor continued desperately trying to ingratiate himself. "Please! There's no reason for worry or contention. Ally yourselves with us by marriage. Give us your daughters and take ours for yourselves. Stay here with us! This land shall be open for you to live in . . . to move through . . . or to own . . . whatever you like. If my son can only win your favor, he'll give you whatever land you want. Demand a huge bride price from me! I'll give you anything you ask for. Only please, allow my son to marry Dinah."

Reuben, always the most sensible, interceded. "You must forgive us, Prince Hamor. Our father is not here and your news has come as quite a surprise. Give my brothers and I a chance to confer in private. Then we'll answer you."

Hamor nodded, bowing low. "Very well! I'll go speak with my son, Shechem. You can give us both your answer when we return."

Leah's boys went off to confer.

When Prince Hamor was out of range, Leah turned on me in fury. "How dare you take Dinah to some heathen harvest celebration? Israel and I made it quite clear how we felt about joining in the heathen rites of these people. But you didn't listen! You lead my daughter into those evil practices. I only wish Israel were home to see how you betrayed us. But never fear! He'll learn of it the moment he returns!"

I looked Leah in the eyes. "Hush, Leah! I'm ashamed of you. You're mother's daughter! How dare you call the Sacred Mating an evil rite! I'm not afraid of your threats! But I must say I find this anger of yours ridiculous. Dinah's gone for three whole days, and you didn't even notice. Now you feign distress! I'm sure you never gave Dinah a thought. The only thing that's foul is the way you treat your daughter! You don't care about her. If you did, you'd be glad for her. Dinah's never been so happy in her life. But you can't be pleased for her, because you're envious! You destroyed my happiness! Are you going to destroy her's as well?"

Leah's eyes narrowed, and her nostrils flared. She was so furious, she couldn't speak. All she could do was stand there stamping the ground like an angry bull. Finally she turned on her heels, going off to incite her boys. Feeling ashamed of the way Prince Hamor had been treated, I went to the gate to wait for his return. I wanted to apologize for the reception he'd received from my so-called family.

Prince Hamor didn't return with Shechem for quite some time. I only had a moment to apologize before Leah and her sons descended on us like a gathering storm.

Reuben, the eldest, spoke for his brothers. "We've had a chance to confer on our sister's marriage. As eldest I'll act as spokesman for our father, Israel, who is away. We're all in agreement. We cannot give our sister to an uncircumcised man in marriage. It is against our religion and would be a disgrace upon our God, Prince Hamor."

"We'll only agree to this marriage on the condition, that you and all your men are circumcised as is our custom. Then we will give you our daughters, and take yours for ourselves. We'll stay with you and become one great nation. If you do not to comply in this matter, we will be forced to take our sister and leave."

Hamor and Shechem looked at each other in silence pondering Reuben's words. Pleased that a solution had been found, Shechem was the first to speak. "Very well, Reuben! I accept your conditions, anything for the sake of marrying Dinah."

Shechem turned toward his father. "Will you also agree father?"

Hamor looked at his son with deep love and respect in his eyes. Sighing deeply, he turned to us nodding, and said, "I'm too old for this. But what can I do? My son is very much in love with Dinah. She's a special girl. Shechem is my only son. It's important to me that he be happy. I'll speak to my men. As Prince of this region I will see to it that every man is circumcised. I will go at once to speak to them. The rite shall be performed tomorrow at high noon before the sacred oak. The High Priest will do it, so that our Lord Baal may be a witness to this act. Please accept this as a sign of our good faith. Now let's shake hands and put all this behind us, so we can become one great people."

As soon as all the men had shaken hands, Hamor and Shechem departed to make preparations for the rites the following day.

I was left behind to be shunned by Leah and her sons, and to wonder at these amazing people who were willing to make such an enormous sacrifice for the sake of love.

Time passed slowly until Israel's return. Leah, and all her sons, even Reuben, refused to speak to me. They avoided my presence, fleeing at the sight of me. Zilpah was instructed not to set a place at table for me. Joseph and I ate alone together in my tent.

On the morning of Israel's return I awakened early, startled by Simeon and Levi shouting orders to one of the servants at the camel stables. I rose praying my ears were playing a trick on me. I could have sworn I heard Simeon calling the servants to get their swords.

What was all the commotion about? I went to the door of my tent. The sun was not yet peeking up over the horizon, and Simeon and Levi were climbing aboard their camels. Nathan was running across the yard as fast as he could, burdened by two enormous swords. His step was hurried by the impatient cries of Leah's sons. "Hurry up, Nathan! We don't have much time."

It was the crack of dawn. What was all the hurry about? Why did the boys need their swords? There was hardly a moment to think before they rode off brandishing their swords. The thought of those two hot headed young men flying about the countryside with their arms put dread fear in my soul. I dressed quickly and went to Leah's tent.

As Leah had been shunning me the past few days, I didn't bother to announce my arrival. I opened the flap and walked inside. Leah was lying in bed with a dark cloth over her eyes. But I knew she was awake. I could see her body jump as I entered. The next moment she was sitting upright. Groaning at the sight of me, she cried, "Oh, it's you, Rachel! You have some nerve coming in here after what you've done. Get out this instant! I can't bear the sight of you!"

This time I would stand my ground. "I'm not leaving until I get some answers, Leah! Where are Simeon and Levi off to, armed, and in such foul temper?"

Leah narrowed her eyes as she looked at me. A smug look on her face, she finally answered. "Where do you think they're going? They're going to Prince Hamor's to get Dinah, of course!"

My mouth dropped open in surprise. I repeated in disbelief. "To Prince Hamor's?"

"Don't be so naive! You didn't really think we'd allow Dinah to marry into these dreadful Canaanites, did you?" said Leah smugly.

I could feel the color draining from my face. Swallowing my pride, I questioned further. "If they went to get Dinah, why did they leave before first light? And why did they take their swords? These Canaanites may have their strange practices, Leah, but they don't come visiting with swords."

Leah was amused as she replied, "Are you incapable of thinking for yourself? I thought it should be clear by now. It was really a very clever plan. Dinah was disgraced before the entire town. So Simeon and Levi have gone to apply justice. The guilty must suffer."

Justice! As I saw it, it was more deception! Jacob! Laban! Now, Jacob's sons! Would it never end? A shiver ran down my back. In the next instant one of the gory scenes from the vision, the day of the harvest festival, flashed before my mind. My heart began to pound. My knees went weak. I had to leave the stifling confines of Leah's tent for fear I'd faint.

It was cold and bleak outside. The sky was stone grey. The scent of winter rain was in the air. What was I to do? Where was Israel, the great father of his people? No one would even speak to me. Simeon and Levi had probably reached the town by now. I grasped my pregnant belly. All I could do was return to my tent and pray for the people of Shechem.

In the midst of my prayer my vision suddenly opened. The streets of Shechem were quiet and desolate. The harvested crops were in the temple storehouse. The toil of sowing the spring wheat was over. Everything was still when Simeon and Levi entered town at first light, riding high upon their camels brandishing their swords. The men of Shechem were all in bed sleeping off the wound to their manhood. The two brothers headed straight for Prince Hamor's manor house. Levi was the first to push through the elaborately carved wooden gate. He entered the stately home by ramming in the door. Like a raging river overflowing its banks the two young men rushed through every room, disrupting everything searching for their sister.

It wasn't long before Levi found Dinah asleep in bed wrapped in Shechem's loving arms. He grabbed her clumsily, wrenching her screaming and struggling from Shechem's warm embrace. Then he slapped her terror stricken face, shouting, "Quiet, you little slut! Do you want to wake the entire household?"

Dinah's eyes were wild with fear. She froze with terror as Levi slung her across his shoulder like a sack of grain. Shechem's blood splattered everywhere, as Simeon ran him through with his sword. "Take this, for defiling my sister!" he shouted full of wrath.

Without so much as a second glance at the dying Shechem, Simeon ran through Hamor's house slaying all the poor defenseless men lying asleep in their beds. The cries of the terrified women and children rose throughout the household, a horrific choir of death drowning Dinah's anguished screams. Even the piteous cries of the innocent children didn't deter Simeon. He gouged the male children through, going about his task like a grim angel of death. Levi followed Simeon's gruesome trail of blood, stuffing a huge sack full of booty from the house, Dinah still slung across his shoulder.

Once back out on the street Levi bound Dinah's hands and feet together like a prisoner. Throwing her across his camel's saddle, he bellowed threateningly, "Wait here for us! You've caused enough trouble! If there's one word out of you, I'll make sure you never utter another sound!"

Then Levi took his sword and another empty sack and went in search of Simeon. It was easy enough to find his brother. Shrieks rose from every house Simeon entered like a howling wind of death travelling through the peaceful slumbering town. The bloodbath raged on and on all morning until every male in every house was slain. Shechem's narrow streets reeked of blood and gore.

The sun was high in the sky when Simeon and Levi returned to their sister. Dinah was in a deathlike swoon. Locked inside a petrified silence, she hadn't dared to budge from where Levi left her in front of Hamor's house. The streets of Shechem were silent as a tomb. Though it was mid day not a living soul was on the streets. The narrow winding lanes were as deserted as they had been at first light. All the men were slain and the women and children who survived were hiding in their homes cringing in fear.

Levi and Simeon were drenched in blood and exhausted from their rampage. Their faces were hot and sweaty, and their eyes glazed over with bloodlust. Levi was seated upon a stolen donkey driving all the livestock they'd seized down the narrow quiet streets. Simeon was seated atop a wagon drawn by oxen piled high with heaps of plundered riches.

Dinah was lying motionless across the camel saddle where Levi had left her earlier that morning. Her pretty face was gripped by a deathlike pallor. She shook with fear the moment Simeon touched her. Though she hadn't uttered a single sound for hours, her anguished cries rang out as soon as she saw his blood stained face.

Simeon pulled her down from the camel, shouting, "Cries and whimpers! That's all the thanks we get for saving you!"

Then he threw her in the wagon atop the enormous pile of booty. Tying their camels to the wagon he looked over at Levi. "Do you believe this, brother? Listen to her crying! Isn't it just like a woman? We go to all the trouble of rescuing her from these heathen, and this is all the thanks we get!"

Simeon turned on Dinah savagely as he climbed aboard the wagon. Raising his arm, he shouted, "Stop it, Dinah! Stop it this instant! Or, I'll really give you something to cry about!"

Shaking and incoherent, Dinah's anguished cries continued.

Temper flaring, Simeon screamed, "What's the matter with you? We just saved you! Is this the thanks we get?"

Dinah's vacant eyes hadn't registered a single word he said. Her frenzied cries merely rose higher in response to the fury in his voice.

Exasperated, he shook her violently. "What's the matter with you? Have you lost your mind? This is all your fault! You and that cursed Rachel! Maybe next time you'll think before you go running off to disgrace yourself. Now be quiet! We're taking you home!"

True to her word Leah was lying in wait for Israel's return. She swooped down upon him like a vulture, shrieking loudly and tearing at her hair. Israel regarded her in exasperation, then demanded, "Calm yourself, woman! What's come over you?"

Beside herself, Leah responded, "I can't calm myself! Something terrible's happened, Israel!"

Israel looked at Leah like a scolding father. As Nathan approached to take his camel, he said reproachfully. "I'm gone only two days and something awful's happened!"

Nathan shrugged his shoulders. "I don't know anything about it, master." he said leading Israel's camel away.

Israel turned to Leah again. "Come now! Get ahold of yourself woman! Tell me what's happened!"

There was no getting out of this one. I had to confront the situation head on. I'd only just arrived, when Leah started up. "Look who's here! The impudence of some people! Of course, Rachel here is the cause of all the trouble. You wouldn't believe me when I told you that she stole father's household gods. But you'll have to believe this. Rachel took Dinah to the women of Shechem. She brought her to one of their lascivious Goddess festivals. Dinah was raped there by Shechem, son of Hamor, and prince of this region."

Israel turned and stared at me in disbelief. "Is this true, Rachel?"

I gazed at Israel calmly, then responded, "Dinah wasn't raped, Israel. She chose to partake in a Sacred Mating rite with prince Shechem. They fell in love, Israel! Dinah's in love! I've never seen her so happy!"

Israel didn't say a word. He just stood there glaring at me in silent rage, contempt pouring from his eyes. When he got control of himself, he said, "How could you do this to me, Rachel? Such heathen rites are in defiance of everything I believe in . . . everything I've ever taught you. Yet you take my only daughter, and give her to these loathsome people. Then you dare to speak of love! Dinah's only a child! What does she know of love? But you . . . you should have known better! How can I ever trust you again? Yahweh will never forgive you! Didn't you realize what a grave offense you were committing?"

Leah smiled with satisfaction, growing calmer the longer Israel screamed at me. Until she stood gloating with pleasure beside Israel. Pain choked my heart to see the two of them united in their self-righteous anger. Their joint self-righteousness was almost more than I could bear. I was wearing my eye bead necklace, and had to answer truthfully.

"Do you want to know why I did it, Israel?" I inquired, looking Israel in the eyes.

He shook his head, and I responded, "I took Dinah with me because I felt sorry for her. She's treated like a maidservant in this family and utterly neglected. No one even noticed she was missing for three days. How can I not feel sorry for her being brought up in a patriarchal household where women are shown no respect? We're treated like chattel . . . or children . . . or slaves, and given no choice but to do your bidding."

Israel stood there completely dumbfounded as I continued, "I did it because Dinah begged me. Yes! She begged me to take her to a place where she could see a woman, who was a priestess and treated with respect, and not like a servant. I took her, because I wanted her to find some self-respect."

"I know how important it is to have self-respect, because I've had to live in this patriarchal household revolving around you all these years without any pride, or respect. I'm not your chattel, Israel. I have my own destiny! I'm a Naditu Priestess, though you never acknowledged it! I was born to be in the Sisterhood of the Eye Goddess, and follow in my mother's footsteps. I had hoped for a Higher Marriage with you! One in which we could respect each other and grow together as we served the God and Goddess in our own ways."

"We had great plans in our youth, Israel. Or can't you remember? We were saving ourselves for each other so we could have what you called a marriage of spirit as well as flesh. We were going to discover a new way together. Our Higher Marriage was to be a Ladder to Heaven, and help promote the regaining of the spirit light body. But you allowed Laban and the Black Hand to cheat us out of all of that. You got mired in the earth sleeping with my so-called sister. Your blind lust and greed for progeny has changed our lives forever. How can I have any self-respect? I'm not even allowed to speak my own mind in this household. You don't treat me like a Priestess. You don't even treat me like an individual. I'm just one of your harem . . . one of your many wives. You can't appreciate me, or see me for who I am, because all you're interested in is blind obedience, and male progeny."

"You don't appreciate Dinah either. Though she's the best of all your children by Leah. You treat her like less of a person, because she's not a boy. You didn't give her a naming ceremony like you did your sons. To this day her birthdays aren't celebrated. You don't instruct her about your God. I bet you even fail to bless her when you die! How can you blame me for wanting Dinah to have a chance at something else?"

My passion spent. I stood there hoping Israel would relent having heard the truth. But it was no use! Israel gritted his teeth and recoiled from me, tense and motionless as a snake about to strike. His face was stern with judgement, when he said, "Who do you think you are speaking to me this way? I'm your husband . . . Yahweh's chosen . . . The father of a great people. How dare you address me like this?"

Gripping my full belly for strength, I spoke up loud enough for the babe inside my womb to hear. "I am a Naditu Priestess of the Eye Goddess Ninhursag! I have the right, and the duty to address the injustice before me!"

Leah could not contain herself another moment. "Slap her, Israel! Slap her!" she said, interrupting brashly. "That's what father had to do when she got so willful."

As Israel raised his hand to strike me, I looked him in the eye, saying with contempt, "You've always done what Leah wanted, Israel. But are you going to stoop so low as to strike a woman who's pregnant with your child?"

Israel's face reddened, and he dropped his hand. Sensing his extreme discomfort, Leah put her arm around him. "Don't listen to her, Israel. She's brazen! I don't know who she thinks she is."

I'd had enough. The words were out of my mouth before I could stop them. "You two deserve each other! Maybe you did know what you were doing in the dark of your wedding night!"

They were both looking at me in consternation, when I turned toward Leah. "I'm not brazen, Leah! You are! You betrayed the Goddess! You betrayed me! And you betrayed your Higher Self, because the evil eye of your envy was always fixed on me. You're brazen and pathetic for always horning in on me and wanting what was mine!"

Suddenly there came the sound of thundering hooves. Baffled by all the commotion, we turned to look at the cloud of dust rising on the horizon.

Distraught, Leah said, "Now Israel, don't be angry with the boys. It's not their fault. They only did what they thought was right. What else could they do? They couldn't allow our family's honor to be trampled in the dirt."

"What have they done?" asked Israel sharply. "You're not making any sense, Leah. What's going on?"

"It must be Simeon and Levi!" I said quickly. "They left here at day-break to bring Dinah back. They were armed with swords."

"Simeon and Levi were armed with swords!" repeated Israel shaking his head.

"If Rachel is through, perhaps I can finish my story now." said Leah angrily. "Prince Hamor was here two days ago to ask for Dinah's hand in marriage. He said he'd pay any price. The boys were very clever, Israel. You would have been proud of them. They must take after you, and their grandfather Laban. They played the most ingenious trick on Hamor and Shechem."

Still puzzled, Israel glared at Leah impatiently. "What kind of trick?"

"They told Hamor it was against our religion for Dinah to marry Shechem, unless he and all his men were circumcised. They agreed to it. All the men in town were circumcised the next day."

Israel's mouth dropped wide open. "They were circumcised? All the men of Shechem agreed to that?" he asked in disbelief.

Leah looked at Israel proudly, as she said, "Yes! They were all circumcised the very next day."

The cloud of dust was almost upon us now. It seemed to be taking Leah forever to get to the point of the story. So I interrupted, "That's just the half of it, Israel. Simeon and Levi never intended to keep their end of the bargain. They left at the crack of dawn this morning to retrieve Dinah. They took their swords with them. I'm afraid those two young hot heads have set upon all the poor defenseless men of Shechem."

Our conversation was interrupted by Simeon's and Levi's shouts. I couldn't see them clearly through the cloud of dust, but my flesh crawled at the arrogant tone of their voices. "Father! You're home. Wait til we tell you what we did. You're going to be so proud of us! We got Dinah! And just look at all the riches we've amassed."

Israel was so furious with me, he hadn't deigned to look at me as I spoke. Nonetheless, I could see by his pursed lips that my intimations had not fallen on deaf ears. We stood together in anxious silence as the dust cleared. When it settled I was aghast at the spectacle before us.

Levi was covered in blood and caked in dust. He sat upon an ass, herding an enormous group of cattle, sheep and donkeys, crying out impatiently for the servants to help him. "Nathan! Aaron! Samuel! Get out here! Put these animals in a corral. We have to inspect them before putting them in with our livestock."

Simeon dropped the reins on the oxen he'd been driving. He too was covered in blood and driving a wagon piled high with stolen riches. In the next moment I spotted Dinah lying limp and lifeless as a corpse atop the heap of treasure. I gasped out loud to see blood stains on her gown, and began heading quickly for the wagon.

Leah began screaming. "Keep away from my daughter, Rachel!"

No one else was going to see about her. Afraid for Dinah's life, I continued towards the wagon. I was almost there when a hand grasped me from behind. I struggled to free myself, but it was no use. I was heavy with child and most ungainly. And it was Israel's strong hand that had grabbed hold of my hair.

His eyes blazing with anger, he pulled me around to face him. "Didn't you hear what Leah said? This is your fault! You're forbidden to ever speak to Dinah again! Go to your tent and start packing! We have to leave here as soon as possible."

I was smarting with anger. Israel had spoken to me like an erring child in front of everyone.

Turning to leave, I caught sight of Leah's gloating face. She wasn't going to see about her daughter. She was too busy delighting in Israel's reprimand of me to have even checked on Dinah.

I started slowly for my tent. After going only a short distance I turned around to see if I could catch a glimpse of Dinah. She was still lying across the enormous pile of booty. No one was taking the time to see about her condition. Levi and the servants were attending to the stolen livestock. Leah was looking on protectively as Israel interrogated Simeon.

From where I stood I could just hear what Israel was shouting. "All this wanton killing! And to listen to you, you're proud of it! It's a disgrace! I won't have you bragging about killing an entire town of defenseless men. Just look at you, covered in blood from head to foot, and toting a wagon load of stolen goods. Is this what Brother Nimah taught you? I pray Yahweh will forgive us your offense."

"Now Israel, don't be so hard on the boys. It was all Rachel's fault! What else could they do?" implored Leah, interceding for her sons.

"They could have waited for me to return before taking it upon themselves to slay an entire town!" exclaimed Israel.

Levi came and stood before his father. Simeon got down from the wagon as Israel continued, "You've both done unbelievable harm putting me in bad odor with the people of this land, the Canaanites and Perizzites. We only have a few men. They could unite against us and destroy all of us."

With Levi now beside him, Simeon grew more bold, and retorted, "They're non-believers! Their lives are of little value! Yahweh's on our side! He'll understand! What were we to do? Allow our sister to be treated like a whore?"

"That's enough, Simeon!" barked Israel.

Then he turned and began inspecting the wagon piled high with stolen riches. When he returned, he went to Leah saying, "See about your daughter! There's no time to lose. We have to leave shortly. There may be reprisals.

I could hardly believe my eyes. Leah didn't go look after Dinah. She called Zilpah to see about her.

Israel continued with his sons. "Get those idols of foreign gods out of the wagon! Bring them to me! I'll bury them under the Oak of Moreh. Take off those ridiculous earrings! Wash yourselves, and change your clothing! We must leave for Bethel and build an altar of atonement. Hurry! Tell all your brothers and the servants that we're leaving! We don't have a moment to spare!"

They rushed about without giving another thought to Dinah. My heart felt like it would break, as I watched Zilpah untying Dinah. Not one of her brothers, not her father, or even Leah helped Zilpah pull Dinah down. They were all too busy to show any concern for her.

Zilpah called Nathan who had just returned from herding the livestock into the paddock. "Come quickly, Nathan! Dinah needs help. Bring me some cold water! Be quick! I can't lift her by myself."

Nathan came running with a water skin. Zilpah doused Dinah, as Simeon and Levi rummaged through the enormous pile of booty. I watched with bated breath until Dinah stirred. Zilpah gathered her in her arms helping her to sit up. Dinah began speaking incoherently. "Where am I? . . . Where's Shechem? . . . Shechem? . . . Who are you? . . . Where's Aunt Rachel! . . . Please get me Aunt Rachel!"

Dinah was pale as a shade from Arallu. But no one seemed to care, as she sat there mumbling in a daze, like some prize booty atop the mound of stolen goods. Even after being doused with water, it took Dinah some time to recognize Zilpah. When she did, she also saw Simeon and Levi ransacking through the booty in search of the idols. At the sight of their bloodstained faces, she began screaming.

Her blood curdling cries pierced my heart. I was filled with rage. It was inhuman that I couldn't go to her when she needed me. Dinah was pale and grief stricken. She had been torn away from the only happiness she'd ever known by brothers, who'd never shown the slightest interest in her before. What would become of Dinah? She'd been wrested away from a man who loved her, and a family who had opened their arms to her in loving recognition.

I was sure her brothers hadn't stopped to ask Dinah what she wanted. Knowing Simeon and Levi, they'd probably been too callous to even shield her from the gruesome murder scene. Then they dragged her home to a family, that had never shown any interest in her, with the same delicacy they'd shown the other spoils. A chill went through me and I shuddered. Looking at Dinah amongst the spoils, I had the awful sense I was seeing the future of patriarchal women. A future in which women would be treated like chattel, and hustled along with all the other plunder.

My heart ached inside my swollen breasts to think of these cruel patriarchal men with only Leah, and no Mother Goddess, to refine them. I was amazed at their ready violence, and their crude sense of proprietorship over their sister's virginity which could unleash such a gory rampage. We were only so recently on patriarchal soil, yet the bloodbath had begun. What would become of us as a people? I remembered the scathing visions I'd had the day of the harvest festival, and an enormous sadness washed over me.

I looked back at Dinah. Tragedy was etched on her pretty young face. My heart went out to her. The scars would run deep. She was the only person there I could relate to, yet I wasn't even allowed to speak to her. Patting my full belly, I was forced to think. What would the future be like for the daughter I was carrying? Dinah's marriage, like my own, had been defiled by greed, and a complete lack of understanding of the sacredness of love. Would love survive the Age of Iron without a Mother

Goddess to nurture and protect it? Or would it too become a battle-ground . . . a battle between the sexes?

How could these patriarchal men have respect for love when they didn't revere the Goddess? From their behavior it was obvious all they understood was power, conquest, and material acquisition. But how could it be otherwise? How could you know love when all you wor-shipped was a male Warrior God with no female partner to balance or temper him? Watching Simeon and Levi rummaging through the wagon with no thought for their sister's condition, tears came to my eyes. I felt fear for the generations of patriarchal women to come, who wouldn't have the inspiration or protection of the Goddess, the upholder of the sacredness of love, as well as life.

Zilpah finally got Dinah to her feet, and they began walking slowly towards Leah's tent. On their way Dinah's eyes inadvertently glanced in my direction. A faint haunted smile crossed her lips, and she immedi-ately began walking in my direction. Leah was standing guard outside her tent waiting for just such an occurrence. Immediately she came and grabbed her daughter by the arm, steering her away from me.

I couldn't hear what Leah was saying, but I didn't have to. From now on Dinah and I would be confined to exchanging anguished glances. What had happened to all the freedom and respect we'd experienced at the harvest celebration? The harvest rites seemed so long and far away, it was as though we'd celebrated them centuries ago. I was left with noth-ing but memories, and haunting questions. What would happen to the women of Shechem without their men? Would there ever be another love feast in honor of the God and Goddess?

There was no time to think. We had to push on to Bethel, so Israel could build an altar of atonement to his God. Atonement not for his son's wanton killing, or their deceit, but for his son's and daughter's pol-lution from conversing with foreign gods. We had to leave within the hour. No thought was given to my condition. Heavy with child, I was prodded along and given no more consideration than one of the preg-nant ewes. I wanted to cry out with each jarring movement that wrenched my body and the precious gift of life within.

Riding atop my camel the injustices of a lifetime had time to burn into my soul. Where was the reverence for life? My life? The child in my womb's life? Dinah's life? The men's lives who'd been slain? Or their families who'd been robbed of their fathers and brothers, their goods, their livestock, and even their cherished household gods? I wanted to scream out but tears choked me. All I could do was cry as I felt the crushing wave of the future come down on me. I cried. And I couldn't stop crying, because I couldn't forget the harrowing visions I'd seen of what was yet to come.

These, my children, are my tears. The lamentation your hallowed book speaks about. My tears have never stopped. They've kept on flowing throughout the centuries. Tears for the loss of the Goddess and Her traditions. Tears for the loss of the children who would know the God and Goddess's love. These were the children I longed for but could not have. Children who would know the equality of men and women, and understand the sacredness and interdependence of all life. Children, who would respect each other, and all of nature as the fruitful by-product of the God and Goddess's love.

I sat upon the terafim the entire way to Bethel, or I fear I might not have made the journey. I was still crying when Israel went to build his altar. When Joseph helped me down from my camel there was fear and worry in his eyes. "Are you alright, mother?" he inquired. "You're in such pain. You've been crying ever since we left Shechem. Why are you so sorrowful?"

My condition made me bold. Taking Joseph aside I spoke to him more frankly than I ever had before about his brothers. "We were forced to flee Shechem, because of the foul deeds of Simeon and Levi."

"What have they done, mother?" entreated Joseph with a troubled look.

I continued in a halting voice. "Dinah lay with Prince Hamor's son, Shechem, as part of a harvest rite. It was her choice to do so, but it angered her brothers. When Prince Hamor came to ask for her hand in marriage, Leah's sons plotted revenge. They tricked Prince Hamor and Shechem into thinking they would give him Dinah as a wife, if they were circumcised. They agreed, and all the men of Shechem were circumcised the following day. While the men still lay in their beds recovering, Simeon and Levi sneaked into town and murdered every last one of them."

My brothers are murderers? Mass murderers?" cried Joseph in disbelief.

"Yes! They slaughtered every last defenseless man of Shechem. As if that were not heinous enough, they stole all the town's livestock, their goods and treasures, even their household gods."

"I tell you this, Joseph, because I fear for you. Beware of Leah's sons! Israel cannot see them clearly because they stand within his own shadow. He makes allowances for them and forgives their every foul deed, because they're his sons."

Pain took me over just then and I couldn't continue. Joseph's expression was grim, but the light of truth was in his eyes. Though young, the wisdom of the Nefilim was in his veins. He would remember.

We soon left Bethel. We weren't safe even there in the house of God, as Israel was in fear of dread reprisal. I was weak and near exhaustion. I had started bleeding, and was fast losing strength from the strenuousness of our journey. The pain behind my heart was like a vast river of torment, carrying me I knew not where. Somewhere in the midst of my suffering, I felt a soft warm light surrounding me. I was being overshadowed by a sweet female radiance, that strengthened with every step my camel took.

When we approached Bethlehem I could go no farther. I had to stop. I sent Joseph to the head of the caravan to announce my time had come. Joseph knew all was not well with me. He had been riding close to me all day. When he returned from advising Israel of my condition, he refused to leave my side.

I got off my camel near a large outcropping of rock which stood like a pillar rising up to the Goddess of Heaven. I would pitch my birth tent nearby. After Joseph finished putting up my tent, I instructed him to dig a large hole in the middle of the tent. Then I took the terafim, and my eyebead necklace and placed them in the ground.

When I finished burying them I called Bilhah and had her lay my blankets atop the holy relics. Then Joseph and I placed some special stones I'd brought from Haran around my bed. Joseph stood by me as I anointed them with oil and prayed to consecrate the ground with my blood under the eyes of the God and Goddess. Only then could I lay down.

It was a long cool night that seemed to stretch endlessly into the following day. My body ached all over and I was racked with pain. A burning fever took hold of me as the pains of labor intensified. I felt as though I was imprisoned in a dream. The events of the long night all blurred together into one as I rode the cresting waves of pain. All I can remember is the bleating of my ewes as they clustered around the tent to comfort me. There's also a brief memory of Israel coming in to take Joseph off to bed. And Joseph wailing and struggling time and again to return to my side.

Only Bilhah stayed with me the whole long night. Her steady hands bathed my fevered brow with cool water in an attempt to douse the fire raging inside me. In the wee hours of the following morning I was still in agonizing labor. My womb was clenched, and refused to open. The pain became so unbearable, I was pushed into a full trance state. Then it no longer mattered that I was being blamed me for what happened at Shechem, or that Israel failed to look in on me from time to time. I could travel out of my body and move forward and backward in time—one link in the vast chain of the Naditu Sisterhood.

I was carried back to the ancient well in Haran to my initial meeting with Jacob. It was good to see Jacob's proud youthful spirit before it had been compromised by Laban. I witnessed the miraculous strength our love had inspired in him as he removed the mighty stone from the well. Then I was carried back to the spring celebration when I gazed into the waters of the well, and caught my first glimpse of him. My vision at the well extended even further back in time. I saw an elderly man with a kind face, named Eleazar, who had journeyed to Haran. He was praying for a fitting bride to meet him at the well for his master Isaac. A young woman, who called herself Rebekah, drew water from the well and approached Eleazar to give him drink. I saw Rebekah consent to marry Isaac, and leave Haran. Then I was taken to an unfamiliar land lush with palm trees, and groves of terebinth. There I saw a woman named Sarah. She had been visited by angels and was laughing in merriment at the thought that she would give birth to a son in her later years.

These were my Sisters, my spiritual family. I was proud to be one of them. The pain intensified suddenly. I was pulled back into my body just in time to see Bilhah wrench a squealing baby out of me. The tent flap opened at the sound of the baby's cries, as it had not opened before to mine. Israel walked in, a thin shaft of sunlight following him into the dark recesses of the tent. In the piercing stream of light I saw my infant was a boy.

Another son!! The realization struck me with the force of a deadly blow. This was not the daughter I dreamt would carry the Naditu lineage onward into the patriarchy. Anguish swelled within me. My body grew heavy. I spoke as from a great distance with the little strength I had left, struggling to pronounce the baby's name. "Benoni! This is Benoni, son of my sorrow, son of my ill luck."

But even on this birthing bed as I poured my blood out in the Goddess's sacrament of life giving, Israel would not respect my choice. Taking the baby in his arms he renamed him, saying proudly, "This is MY son. The son Yahweh has given me. He shall be called Benjamin, not Benoni. He is the son of my right hand, the son of my good luck."

Did my suffering mean nothing to Israel? Were my pronouncements of so little consequence? Renaming our son, Benjamin, was the last crushing blow. And I was forced to remember Israel's grim pronouncement, that whoever had stolen the terafim from Laban must die. Was this child truly Israel's right hand? Was he executing the force of Israel's word?

Just then Joseph burst into the tent. Fighting his way past Israel he immediately sensed the gravity of my situation, and only looked cursorily at his brother. Throwing himself down on my bed he grasped hold of me, as if the very strength of his love could keep me with him. "Mother! . . . I love you, mother! . . . Please be well! . . . Stay with me! . . . I need you! . . . Don't leave me! . . . . Please don't leave me!"

I was too weak to even respond. Yet in the moment our eyes met the imminence of my death was revealed to me. I knew I was looking for the last time at the one most dear to me. The one who made the pain of my whole life worth living.

I took a moment to gather the little strength I had left. In a voice no louder than a whisper. "My body may leave you, but I shall never leave you, Joseph. You are a part of me, as I am a part of you. I will watch you from afar, and speak to you through your dreams. Never fear! You will not be alone. The Nefilim, the Star People from Kak.Si.Di. will watch over you and see to it that you receive all the strength and guidance you need to meet your destiny."

Joseph took my hand struggling to gather strength to receive what I had said. Tears poured from his eyes, but a bright white light shone all around him, as he said, "I don't want to let you go, mother."

Looking into his sorrowful eyes, there was so much I wanted to say to him. But I could not speak. To see Joseph in distress troubled me, but the brilliant light surrounding him showed me he would not be alone. Just gazing at his face I felt peace. Joseph was my comfort, and my strength, my precious link to my starry home and the God/Man from Kak.Si.Di., the Eye Star of the Goddess. Joseph had come down to me in accordance with the will of heaven in keeping with the wisdom and timing of the Starry Ones, not my own.

The Great Ages had shifted. Who was I to think I could shape the future? All was not lost however. Humankind's stellar ancestry would continue on. The lineage of the starry Nefilim, the Family of Light, would flow through Joseph. I'd had to wait many long years for Joseph to be born. But he would not forget the Goddess Ninhursag or the Starry Ones of Heaven. Joseph would be a savior for his people. He would carry on Abraham's gauntlet moving the Sumerian legacy away from the reptilian Anunnaki and onward to the stars.

She Who Watches had not abandoned me. Soon I would have to face Her truth in the great Hall of Judgment. Had I learned nothing from my sojourn here on Earth? I had been so willful and slow to understand. Only now with death staring me in the face did I realize I had overstepped my bounds, thinking I could will myself a daughter to carry on the Naditu Sisterhood. In my desire for a daughter, I had forgotten I was a mere link in a vast spiritual chain. I could not forge those links in accordance with my own will. It was presumptuous of me to think I knew the Goddess's purpose. All those years of barrenness, suffering, and humiliation had still not tempered my impulsive will.

Israel left my tent taking Benjamin with him. He departed without so much as a word to me, or noting my condition. My womb ached. My arms felt cold and heavy, and so empty without my infant son. Israel didn't care. He had fought the great fight against the dark angel Nanna/Sin. Yet Laban and the Black Hand had left their mark. The Lunar Cow had been put before the Solar Ewe. Inanna had usurped the place of Ninhursag, just as Leah had taken mine. The once proud Sisterhood had been crushed. Jacob and I had not succeeded in the Higher Marriage that would bless the land and all its people with peace and love, and serve as the necessary counter balance during the Age of Iron. Was this the end of the Naditu Sisterhood? Would centuries of patriarchal women grow up Motherless on account of me? Was the spiritual suppression of patriarchal women the bitter fruit of my transgressions?

Israel was furious with me. He was consumed in righteous indignation and would not be back. Only Joseph and Bilhah would stand by me to the end. Bilhah's face was worn with grief and the strain of the long night. She was filled with fear and cried ceaselessly. I wanted to reach out to comfort her, but I was weak and losing vast quantities of blood to the steadily growing pool around me. I prayed Bilhah would remember to burn my garments and bed linens, offering my blood to the Queen of Heaven as in the days of old.

Just to breathe was an enormous effort. My life blood draining out of me, I prayed the offering of my life would bring me closer to the Goddess and the purpose of the Starry Nefilim. As the life of my body waned my spirit was given wings, and I was free to travel into the future. I saw Joseph in the prime of life. He was in a foreign land beside an enormous statue that was part human and part lion, overseeing the handing out of enormous sacks of wheat and grain. My heart was filled with joy. Joseph had followed the Naditu Sisterhood down to Magan, the land that still lived in harmony with the star teachings from Kak.Si.Di., home of the Lion People.

Then I felt the same sweet presence I sensed overshadowing me on my way here to Bethlehem. It coagulated into a vision of a serious young woman deep in prayer with a starry light surrounding her. As I watched she was visited by one of the shining Nefilim. This great being of light addressed her as Mary, and announced she was chosen to be the Mother of God. Through her would come the long awaited Messiah to usher in the Age of the Fishes. The redemption of humankind would flow through her.

I saw Mary again. She was heavy with child and travelling with a male companion, she called Joseph. They were on a long journey. White doves flew beside Mary moving with her wherever she went. A brilliant star shone in the sky guiding the two by day and night. It was amazing but as I watched they made their way here, to Bethlehem. In the starry light such visions are made of, I saw Mary ready to give birth. There was no place for Mary and Joseph anywhere in town. The brilliant light from above beckoned them onward leading them to a small stable in the countryside . . . here . . . beside the same rock pillar outcropping where I had buried the terafim. On this very spot, still strewn with the rocks from Haran, Mary gave birth to a Son of Light and Grace inside a humble stable with only a few shepherds to honor them.

Tears of joy filled my eyes. The Black Hand had not succeeded. The Naditu Sisterhood lived on. It might be forced underground, but it would not die out. With this realization all pain and sorrow left me. I was filled with peace and joy to be united with the spiritual Sister of my deepest soul. I gave thanks to the Eye Goddess for this final vision, that blessed my death, and gave new meaning to my life. I surrendered willingly thankful to be of service to the Naditu Sisterhood consecrating this ground, and opening the way for Mary and her Child of Light.

As my spirit left my body I was surrounded by a great white light and greeted by the Starry One. "Well done, Rachel! Burying the terafim at Bethlehem and consecrating the ground with your blood, you've opened a portal through to other dimensions. Your death has opened the way for Jesus the Christ, Son of the Most High, to come down to Earth in the next Great Age the Age of Pisces."

Rachel's Farewell

This dear children is my story, I gladly share with you. I am your patriarchal mother source. You are the Children of Aquarius, the children I longed for but could not have as the time was not yet ripe. My tears have been your tears, the suffering of the individuated Feminine in men and women within the patriarchy. Jacob's and my failure at the Higher Marriage was a missed opportunity. But this is the dawning of a New Age. You are being awakened and invited to move forward into the next Great Age—the Age of Aquarius.

Yours will be a glorious future if you heed the lessons of the past. Aquarius can be a true Golden Age of peace and universal Brotherhood and Sisterhood. Aquarius is the Age of Liberation, Equality, and Empowerment for all humankind, a time in which the Feminine can achieve greater acceptance in men and women. The Higher Marriage is the sacrament of Aquarius. Men and women can now join hands and take a vast leap in consciousness together. The Masculine and Feminine in each individual is to be harmonized so you become more fully integrated, and can access the light body.

These are not the only gifts of Aquarius. The Waterbearers of Aquarius are the shining Nefilim, the great Angels of Heaven, who travel the skies to this very day. They have been watching lo these many centuries waiting for the Children of Aquarius to gather and remember their kinship with the stars. You are on the threshold of a great change in human consciousness. Those of you who are sensitive can already feel the acceleration. When enough hearts and minds are open a great shift in human consciousness will occur.

The Waterbearers are pouring forth the great Light of Heaven. The Earth and your entire solar system shall be transformed as you move into the Photon Belt, a shower of golden light sent from the Prime Creator when your solar system enters the constellation of Aquarius. The starry light of the Photon Belt will release the secret DNA code Enki and Ninhursag inserted in the genetic material of earthlings millennia ago. You, children of Aquarius, are destined to return to your original twelve strand DNA coding and be awakened into full consciousness. Your Ancient Spirit Eyes and Ears shall open. Your intuitive capacities will flourish and once more you'll be linked with the Starry Ones.

The threshold of universal Brotherhood and Sisterhood is here. In Aquarius the great Ladder to Heaven is being offered to all humankind.

Glossary of Terms

ANCIENT EYES AND EARS The gifts of clairvoyance and clairaudience which belong to all those who still have a connection to the ancient spirit body through their ancestry with the Starry Ones. The mark of the Naditu Priestess, and the favor of the Eye Goddess Ninhursag.

ANU The head of Nibiru and all the Anunnaki in heaven and on Earth. He lived on Nibiru, the twelfth planet in our solar system, but came to Earth to visit and oversee the Nibiruan mining of gold. He, like all the beings from Nibiru, was part reptile which is why He was said to live for thousands of years.

ANUNNAKI space travellers, the Ancient Ones from Nibiru (the twelfth planet in our solar system) who came to colonize Earth and mine gold ca. 450,000BC. They were intelligent reptilian beings who possessed great technological advances and weaponry, and helped found the early Sumerian civilization. They could live for thousands of years but their hearts were cold, and they had little compassion or regard for human life.

ATHTAR The planet Venus, the Star of Love, and sister planet of Earth. A liberated planet within our solar system. Its inhabitants are highly evolved light beings who transferred life to Earth in ancient ancient times.

BROTHERHOOD OF THE BLACK HAND an unscrupulous male secret society under the control of the Moon God Sin, bent on keeping all power in the hands of men. They were the unseen hand behind all events, and the sworn enemy of Ninhursag and the Naditu Sisterhood. Known in other times and other places as the Brotherhood of the Snake, the Brotherhood of the Dragon, or the secret government behind governments, they were the controllers of the known worlds' economy.

CHERUBIM a class of protective guardian angels, the Lion People from Kak.Si.Di.

EHULHUL TEMPLE The temple dedicated to Nanna/Sin in Haran, and headquarters for the Brotherhood of the Black Hand. The exact replica of the Sin temple in Ur, which was destroyed.

ENKI also known as **EA** which means house of water, was the Sumerian God of Wisdom and Magic. He was the chief scientist of the Anunnaki and much renowned for his great engineering projects, and his creation of humankind along with his sister Ninhursag. Enki was from KaK.Si.Di., the star system of Sirius. He came to Earth with Ninhursag to help humankind in their spiritual evolution. He ruled the Apsu, the land down under, (Egypt and Africa) for the ancient Sumerians. He was humankind's great benefactor, coming to their aid against the cold hearted Nibiruans.

ENLIL Lord of the Airspace. First son of Anu born on Nibiru. The Supreme Lord of Sumer, and head of all the Anunnaki on Earth, He presided over the Assembly of all the Anunnaki at his headquarters in Nippur. He was known for his eternal feud with Enki and for his callous indifference to humankind.

EN PRIESTESS High Priestess of She Who Watches, the Eye Goddess Ninhursag. The famed oracle Priestess who alone could approach the Stone that Whispers, the communication link with Kak.Si.Di., at the Eye Temple at Brak.

EYE TEMPLE The Temple dedicated to the Eye Goddess Ninhursag at Brak in the Khabur valley of northern Mesopotamia/Syria (named after Sirius). The ancient shrine of She Who Watches, and headquarters of the Naditu Sisterhood.

HIGHER MARRIAGE A marriage relationship which is integrated on the spiritual, psychological, intellectual, emotional, and sexual levels. An equal partnership where both parties life purposes are aligned, and they help each other evolve to fulfill their highest destiny.

INANNA/ISHTAR/ASTARTE The daughter of Nanna/Sin and a ferocious warrior, whose craving for power could not be tempered. Rejected by the divine kings of Sumer such as Gilgamesh, she took up with Sargon of Akkad, who had none of the blue blood of the Star people in his veins. With him as her battleaxe she devastated the land of Sumer and took over Ninhursag's place.

KAK.SI.DI. The Eye of Heaven, the sun behind our sun. The ancient Sumerian term for the star system Sirius, the brightest star in heaven and home to Ninhursag and Enki. The Eye Star is the great star of women and the Goddess. In distant times it gave life to gods and men. It is the great seat of wisdom within the universe. Star Beings from Kak.Si.Di. brought knowledge of crystals, the stars, seeds and production methods of many of the precious grains to Earth in ancient times to uplift humankind and stimulate spiritual evolution here. Kak.Si.Di. guides the Naditu Sisterhood and the great White Brotherhood.

KIRIBU Winged animal guardian statues. Winged lion stone statues reminiscent of the Lion People from Kak.Si.Di. guarded the important entrances to the Eye Temple in Brak.

LIGHT BODY The ancient spirit body known to the Egyptians as the ka.

LUGAL The term used for the rulers of ancient Sumer.

MAGAN The ancient term for Egypt, headquarters of the Sirian Star Wisdom.

NADITU PRIESTESS One of the ancient Sisterhood of Seerers of the Eye Goddess Ninhursag. To be a Naditu Priestess your lineage had to derive from the Star Beings from Kak.Si.Di. Naditu woman were often barren. Their destiny was to mate with Star Beings from Kak.Si.Di., and conceive the God/Kings and great men of old.

NANNA the Sumerian term for the Moon God Sin in his full moon aspect.

NEFILIM The Elohim, the God/Men. A Hebrew term used to describe all those who from Heaven came to Earth in ancient times to seed the ancient civilizations. The Nefilim came from many different star systems, as well as from Nibiru, the twelfth planet in our solar system. Some came to share their prodigious gifts with humankind. Others came to exploit the Earth, like the Anunnaki. Ancient myths from many diverse cultures describe their adventures and refer to them as gods.

NIBIRU The Planet of Millions of Years, the twelfth and hidden planet in our solar system out beyond Pluto, that travels in an elliptical orbit of 3,600 years. Nibiru was home to the Anunnaki, who were part reptile and part human. For more information on Nibiru see Zecharia Sitchin's amazing scholarly series the *EARTH CHRONICLES*, Avon Books, N.Y.

NINHURSAG The Eye Goddess, She Who Watches from her throne up in Kak.Si.Di. Ninhursag came to Earth from Kak.Si.Di. in ancient times along with her wise brother Enki to uplift humankind. She was revered throughout all of Mesopotamia as the Great Mother Goddess, because she gave birth to Adam, the Anunnaki's first primitive worker. She instituted the Naditu Sisterhood, the order of Chosen Women, so that Star Beings could mate with selected Daughters of Earth to accelerate human evolution. She was the protector of humankind against Nanna/Sin, and the patron of the ancient God/Kings, who were nourished by the starry light of her star Kak.Si.Di. In Egypt she was known as the Goddess Hathor.

NINURTA Son of Enlil and Ninhursag. The Champion of Heaven who regained the Tablets of Destiny and the other objects of power when they were stolen by Sin from his father Enlil.

SIN The Moon God in his aspect of crescent moon. One of the worst of the Anunnaki, Sin was known as the Great Deceiver for having usurped the Moon power from the Goddess, and daring to betray his own father Enlil. He stole the objects of power from Enlil at Nippur hoping to gain supreme control of Earth. Ninurta, Ninhursag's son by Enlil, recovered the stolen objects and returned them to his father. Sin and his legion of fallen angels were wounded and vanquished. Their wounds required them to nourish themselves on human or animal blood. They were exiled to Earth, where they engendered chaos and discord, living off the anguish and violence of humankind. Sin was the secret controller of the Brotherhood of the Black Hand, and sworn enemy of Ninhursag and the positive light beings from Kak.Si.Di.

SUGUTU The class of women in ancient Sumer known as the fertile Birth Mothers.

TERAFIM Rachel's mother's precious oracles. One of the most powerful tools of the Naditu Order used to communicate with the Starry Ones on Kak.Si.Di. Only Ninhursag's most select initiates at the Eye Temple were trained to use them.

YAHWEH The patriarchal Father God of Abraham, Isaac, Jacob.

Julie Bresciani, Ph.D. is a professional astrologer who was trained and certified as a Jungian analyst at the C.G. Jung Institute in New York City. She has taught Astrology, Jungian Psychology, Feminine Psychology and other related subjects at the C.G. Jung Institute in NYC, Marymount Manhattan College, and Temenos Institute for Psychotherapy in Westport, Ct. Over the past fifteen years she has led group rituals on HEALING THE FEMININE privately and at the New York Open Center, Wainwright House, Rye, N.Y., and Temenos Institute. She has a Nature Preserve to protect Big Horn Sheep in Arizona, and currently lives on a ranch in Wyoming with her husband and son, where she conducts an extensive nationwide practice over the phone, while she writes her books.

TO ORDER BOOKS OR VIDEO CASSETTES PLEASE WRITE OR CALL:

ASTRAEA CIARA PUBLISHING CO.
PO BOX 118
DEVILS TOWER, WY. 82714
307 467-5246

AVAILABLE FROM ASTRAEA CIARA PUBLISHING CO.

BOOKS

RACHEL'S DESTINY AS WRITTEN IN THE STARS by Julie Bresciani Ph.D.
    an epic journey in Judeo-Christian karmic release $19.98
    with priority shipping and handling $25.00

Quantities of 10 books $150.00 with priority shipping and handling $175.00

Quantities of 20 books $200.00 with priority shipping and handling $240.00

VIDEO CASSETTES

INTRODUCTION TO ASTROLOGY by Julie Bresciani Ph.D.
    Eight 1 1/2 hr classes with shipping and handling $206.00

INTERMEDIATE ASTROLOGY by Julie Bresciani Ph.D.
    Eight 1 1/2 hr classes with shipping and handling $206.00

JUNGIAN CONCEPTS IN THE NATAL HOROSCOPE
    by Julie Bresciani Ph.D.
    Eight 1 1/2 hr classes with shipping and handling $206.00

FOR INFORMATION REGARDING ASTROLOGICAL READINGS WITH JULIE BRESCIANI PH.D. OVER THE PHONE, PLEASE CALL 307 467-5246.

If you have a favorite local bookstore you think might be interested in carrying RACHEL'S DESTINY AS WRITTEN IN THE STARS, please send the name, address, phone number, and the name of a contact person, to ASTRAEA CIARA PUBLISHING CO. at the above address.

Name: _____

Address _____

City _____

State _____ Zip Code _____

Tel:_____ Fax:_____

Order _____

_____

_____

_____

_____

_____

Amount Enclosed _____

Make check or money order (for faster processing) payable to: **ASTRAEA CIARA PUBLISHING CO.**